REWIND - The Price of Fate

Everhide Rockstar Romance Series – Book 5
by
Tania Joyce

EVERHIDE
ROCKSTAR ROMANCE

REWIND– The Price of Fate by Tania Joyce
Published by Gatwick Enterprises
First Edition: 2021 | Second Edition 2026
Brisbane, Australia.

REWIND – The Price of Fate : 2nd Edition
Everhide Rockstar Romance Series – Book 5
EPUB format: ISBN: 978-1-923653-10-8
Paperback: ISBN: 978-1-923653-11-5

Cover design by DesignRans and Gatwick Enterprises
Edited by CreatingInk

Tania Joyce: www.taniajoyce.com

Keywords and subjects
Rockstar romance, new adult romance, contemporary romance, enemies-to-lovers romance, surrogacy romance, accidental pregnancy romance, rockstar wedding, celebrity romance, love after loss, heart-wrenching romance, band romance, musician romance.

For believers in fate.

Chapter 1

HUNTER

On the outskirts of the Bronx, I trudged across the cemetery's rain-soaked lawn. Each step grew heavier, harder, slower. As I stuffed my hands into the pockets of my leather jacket, the emptiness in my heart threatened to implode and crack my ribs. The constant throb in my head thudded in my ears. On autopilot, I passed one headstone, then another. One plaque, then another. When I reached the top of the gentle sloping hill, my heart ached so much I stopped underneath an evergreen to catch my breath. Tears lurked like thieves at the back of my eyes, ready to steal my composure. Today was an anniversary, but not a celebration. One year ago, I'd lost my son.

I sucked in a ragged breath. The scent of freshly mowed grass and damp earth pummeled my senses. With stinging eyes, I scanned row after row of graves. Row after row of lost lives. Row after row of heartbreak.

There. In the distance. *Kara.*

On her knees. Arms wrapped around her waist. Crouched in front of our son's memorial stone.

Crying.

Shit.

Losing Ryan had torn my soul and sliced it to pieces with a

blunt machete. The wound hadn't healed. I wasn't sure it ever would.

My girlfriend's distress added to the constricting pain in my chest. She'd stormed out of our penthouse in Tribeca without me. I'd been delayed in my home studio with my Everhide bandmates, laying down a track. We'd been on a roll. The song had finally come together. But we'd run over time by an hour. Kara shouldn't have gotten pissed off. She should've waited. Not even music would've kept me from coming here today. Remembering our son together was too important.

It didn't matter how much money I had, who I was, or how many advancements medical science had achieved—nothing had saved our son. Born at twenty-four weeks, Ryan had been too weak to survive. That was what the doctors had said.

But it was bullshit.

I clenched my teeth so hard my jaw ached. Doctors claiming to be experts had failed our child. Had failed *me* . . . again. They'd said my best friend's sister would survive leukemia . . . She hadn't. Doctors had said my arm would make a full recovery after my accident . . . It hadn't. I splayed my fingers by my side, and a dull ache throbbed beneath the scar on my forearm. They'd said my son was in good hands . . . They'd lied. I wanted to scream, yell, punch a wall, and make the hurt go away. How could I ever put my faith in doctors again? Not sure I ever could.

I glanced over my shoulder. Giles and Mick—our bodyguards— had remained by our cars to give Kara and me some privacy. Not that I had much of that these days. The paparazzi had probably followed me here, ready to snap us in distress. But today, I couldn't care less.

Taking a deep breath, I ambled down the hill to the third row. I tugged at the neckline of my sweatshirt and rubbed at the new niggle in my throat. I shouldn't have mucked around with Kyle and Gemma on vocals earlier. *Fool.*

As I approached Kara, her sobs drilled fresh holes into my heart. How would we get through this?

"Hey." My voice barely cracked above a whisper. I didn't want to startle her. Squatting beside her, I stroked the back of her head, her long golden-brown hair slipping like silk through my fingertips.

Tears zigzagged down her cheeks. Her gaze never left the engraved stone.

Ryan Collins.
03/24/19. 18:07—03/26/19. 05:17
Make every second count.

I pulled out a palm-sized ceramic memorial heart from my top jacket pocket and stared at the silver metal plate engraved with a teddy bear wearing sunglasses, playing a guitar. I ran my finger over the words *"Rockin' it in heaven"* scribed at the bottom, then placed it next to Kara's flowers. I kissed my fingertips and pressed them against my son's headstone. "Hope the angels are taking good care of you, little man."

Kara clutched her hands to her chest, keeled forward, and cried harder. "Hunt, I miss him so much."

I crawled onto the picnic blanket beside her, sat on my haunches and drew her into my arms. As she clung to my jacket, the sting in my eyes turned to acid. I held her closer, tighter. Swaying gently, I let my grief consume me.

"I miss him too, Pearl." I rested my cheek against the top of her head. "Every fucking day."

"He got taken from me. From us."

My chest shuddered.

"I know." Tears escaped me as I kissed the top of her head. Haunting images flickered behind my eyelids. Ryan. In the incubator. So tiny, the size of my hand. Covered in tubes and wires. Machines breathing for him. *Why did modern medicine fail? Why?*

"He was so beautiful," she sniffled. "He had your hands. Your long fingers."

"He had your nose."

"I remember what it felt like to hold him." She pressed her

cheek harder into my chest. "To touch him. How he smelled."

"Me too." That milky newborn scent would be embedded in my memory for life.

She sobbed against my sweatshirt. Her tears soaked through to my skin. "We only had him for a day and a half."

My heart didn't want to beat. It hurt too much. "Not long enough."

The breeze rustled through the nearby trees, and a few dead leaves swept across the lawn. I drew Kara closer to ward off the chill.

"I'm so scared," she sniffled.

"Of what?" I rubbed my hand over her back in slow circles, wanting to soothe her pain.

"That I'll forget those things."

I caught her shoulders and turned her to face me. I brushed a tear from her cheek with my thumb. "No. You won't. He's in your heart, your soul. You won't ever forget. But time will make this easier. I promise." I hoped it was one promise I could keep.

Shuffling around to sit beside her, I curled my arm around hers and clutched her hand. She rested her head on my shoulder. The scent of her floral perfume calmed my mind. Her warm touch enveloped me and eased my unsettled heart.

She pulled her cell phone from her purse and opened the photos we'd taken of Ryan in the hospital. As she slowly skimmed through the images, we laughed, cried, and reminisced about the good times and difficulties we'd gone through before we'd lost him. But fresh worries sparked to life. Kara had looked at these photos too often . . . daily, weekly. I wasn't sure that was healthy. No matter what I'd done, the fun we'd had, the places I'd taken her to, or the love I'd made to her, nothing had made the bursts of happiness last. I wanted that to change. I wanted to fill the void Ryan had left. Be all she ever needed.

Damn. I'd never thought I'd say that about a girl. But it was the truth.

I kissed her temple, lingering there a moment. "Kar, we've had one hell of a year. We lost our baby. We came close to losing Gem.

We've had many ups and downs. But that's all behind us. We have exciting times ahead. You have your fashion. I have my music." I entwined our fingers and kissed the back of her hand. "We have each other. Let's focus on what lies ahead, not the past."

She sniffed, and tears pooled on the rims of her eyes. "I love being your stylist. I love traveling. I love you. But—"

"Uh-oh." I feigned a chuckle and nudged my elbow against her arm, trying on one hand to stop the fear knocking at my heart and on the other, trying to lighten the mood. "This is bad, isn't it?"

Gazillions of thoughts bombarded my mind. I'd been so preoccupied with album preparation lately, we hadn't spent much time together. Did she want to quit her job? Go back to fashion design? Start her own label? I was all for it. I'd support her if she did. She was a brilliant designer. I wanted her to do something she loved. Or *shit* . . . Did she want to break up with me? Was she that pissed at me? Or . . . *oh crap* . . . spin that around. Did she want to get married? My heart slammed against my ribs. A cold sweat broke out on the back of my neck. Just because our best friends— Kyle and Gemma, and Lexi and Hayden—had recently tied the knot, I wasn't ready to put a ring on it. We'd only been together for nine months. Kara was my first serious girlfriend. Yeah, we'd taken things fast and moved in together after three months of dating, but I wasn't ready for marriage. Not sure I ever would be.

My finger shook as I brushed the tip of her nose. "You always get this little wrinkle right here when you get serious." Drawing my shoulders back, I braced myself for her blow.

She lifted her chin and met my gaze. Pain swirled in the depths of her dark blue eyes. My heart lurched at the intensity. Her chin quivered. A tear fell and caught on her cheek. Lunging forward, she collapsed against my shoulder and wailed over her sobs. "I want to have another baby."

The dull ache inside my head turned into a splitting jackhammer. *A baby? What the fuck?* I didn't see that one coming. I wasn't afraid of being a father anymore; but not yet. Not so soon after losing Ryan. "I know you do. But we can't. Not now."

She drummed her fist against my chest and clutched at my

shirt. "Yes now. I don't want to wait any longer."

I squeezed my eyes shut. Nausea pooled in my gut like I'd drunk too much tequila. Ryan's death had created new fears—ones I didn't know if I had the strength to face. Having to put my faith in the hands of doctors to manufacture our baby after I'd experienced so many previous medical failures was hard to fathom. Nothing about it would be natural—her frozen eggs, my sperm, a surrogate. How could I rely on doctors to create life? What if it didn't work? I couldn't endure more heartbreaking loss. I was sure Kara couldn't either.

I caught the tip of her chin with my fingertip and tilted her head back. I searched her face, looking for an answer to *why now*? Was this her grief talking? But no . . . the clarity in her eyes made it clear she was dead serious. *Crap.* I lowered my gaze. My shoulders sank. "Babe, we can't. The next two years are in motion. Albums, singles, promo, tour. The timing isn't right."

"It'll never be right." Tears slipped down the side of her nose. Each one struck my heartstrings like a hammer. "What happens after this album and tour? You'll do another one. Then another. I know the drill."

Yep. My life had been on repeat for eight years. *Record. Promo. Tour. Record. Promo. Tour.* It wasn't about to change. I didn't want it to. I loved my life. Music was it. "We're too busy." I'd had to recalibrate my brain after losing Ryan and refocus on what was important . . . Kara and my band. The pressure to release another number-one album had come from all sides—our record company, the fans, and my own expectations. Do more. Do better. Do something bigger. "Pearl, I'm sorry."

Kara was the best thing that had happened to me in a very long time. I didn't want to lose her. But the possibility of repeating what we went through with Ryan scared the living shit out of me. I cupped the side of her face and wiped away her tears. "I'm not saying no forever—just not now. Let's enjoy the next couple of years before we look at our options."

"Options?" She closed her eyes and tensed her jaw. Her tone tightened. "I don't have options. I can't have a baby. I have to use a surrogate. That *is* my only option. And I want to start now. It's a long process."

I dragged my hand down my face and swiped it across my mouth. Frazzled by her outburst, my head spun, overloaded with my demanding music obligations. My heart still ached for Ryan. "This is not the time to contemplate having a baby. I'm about to go away." I'd be upstate for the next two months with Kyle and Gemma writing songs in preparation to hit the recording studio in late May. "The plans for our next album and the tour are nearly finalized."

She clutched my arm; her fingers dug into my flesh. She opened her mouth as if ready to argue, but she fell against my chest and sobbed. Wrapping my arm around her, I held her close and let her cry. As I swallowed, my throat hurt even more. *Not good.* Too much emotion. Too much crying.

I kissed the top of her head. "Pearl, we need to go home. It's cold and almost dark." Late March still had chilly nights. "My throat's aching. I can't afford to get sick. You don't need to catch a cold either."

She stared at Ryan's memorial stone. After a few moments, she straightened, sniffed, and nodded. "Yeah. Okay." She dug a tissue out of her purse, wiped her eyes, and blew her nose. "But it hurts to say goodbye." She placed her hand on the headstone, shuffled forward, and kissed the plaque. "I love you. I miss you. So much. Every day."

Damn, that speared my heart. I hated seeing her so broken. With one last glance at the gravestone, I prayed. *Ryan, we love you. Take care, buddy.* Would the hole in my heart ever heal?

I blinked the dampness from my eyes, clambered to my feet, and helped Kara stand. Arm in arm, we headed back through the cemetery to our cars and patiently-waiting bodyguards.

I jutted my chin toward Giles, who'd driven Kara here in a town car. "Thanks, man. You can head off. I'll drive Kara home." I turned to Mick. "Are you right to follow?"

"Sure thing." Mick pulled on his motorcycle gloves, zipped up his leather jacket, and headed toward his bike parked behind my car.

After Gemma's kidnapping, I refused to go anywhere without security. I never wanted a crazed fan to come after me, or worse, hurt Kara.

I pressed the key remote to unlock my Ford GT supercar and opened the passenger door. Before Kara got in, I pulled her into my embrace. Nuzzling against her neck, I absorbed her sweet rosy scent, relishing the warmth of her arms around me. "We'll get through this. Together."

"I know." Her voice held no conviction. She smiled a sad smile and ducked into the car seat.

I closed the door and ran around to the driver's side. I jumped in and started the engine. The car roared to life. I'd wanted Kara to come away with me upstate, just so I could make sure she was okay every day. My band and I had already changed our plans. We were no longer heading to LA, opting to stay closer to home. Kara could join us, relax, read, and rejuvenate. But no matter how hard I'd tried to persuade her, nothing had worked.

We headed off, with Mick trailing behind. During the drive home, Kara had barely said a word. She'd stared out the window with fresh tears rolling down her cheeks. No doubt caused by me saying no to a baby.

But now wasn't a good time. *Was it? No. No, it wasn't.*

We were still healing. The only way to get better and stronger was to live our lives to the fullest. We had to surround ourselves with friends and family, and cherish each other's love and support.

My focus was set.

I had to write a new album. And make Kara forget about this *having-a-baby* business.

I'd throw her a surprise birthday party in two weeks and shower her with gifts. I'd come back to the city as often as I could during my stint away. I'd take her out to dinner, shows, and events, and make love to her at every chance I got.

But no matter how much I loved Kara and wanted to do everything I could for her, my priority was clear. For the next two years, music had to come first.

Chapter 2

KARA

I shrugged out of my woolen coat, tossed it over the back of the living room sofa, and slipped off my boots. I wiped the dampness from my eyelashes with a flick of my fingertips. *No more crying.* Gliding across the hardwood floor, I headed toward the grand piano. The city lights streaming through the full-length windows cast soft hues of blue and gold over the furniture. I loved the cool, calming effect. I needed that after a long day. Leaning my hip against the Steinway, I took a deep breath and gathered my scattered thoughts. The cemetery hadn't been the place to blurt out I wanted a baby. Far from my finest move.

But I'd made up my mind.

I wanted a child.

Hunter's reaction? . . . Not the outcome I'd hoped for. But not unexpected. He'd never handled earth-shattering news well and liked to avoid confrontation at all costs. He was a master at changing the subject, creating distractions, and circumventing topics. But this one wouldn't disappear.

Splaying my hand over the unease swirling in my belly, I closed my eyes. He just needed time to calm down and think things through. That was all. *I hope.*

I wanted to be a young mom. From my research, finding a

surrogate to having a baby took at least eighteen months. If we didn't start now, it wouldn't happen for a couple of years. I wanted to come home from the tour to a baby, not wait until after to begin.

But?

What if he never came onboard? Never wanted to have a child with me? Did we have a future together? My heart clung to my ribs so it wouldn't fall to the floor. I loved Hunter so hard, but if he didn't want a child, was having a baby more important than being with the man I loved?

. . . Yes.

I grabbed onto the edge of the piano to stop my knees from buckling. I prayed I'd never have to make the choice. Having a baby would give me the family I'd longed for. It'd give me someone to care for, someone to love for all eternity. It'd give Hunter the love, the adoration, and the purpose he craved. Having a baby would fill the void from losing Ryan.

He'd said 'not now' to a baby. Not never.

How long could I give him before I needed a decision? *A week? A month?* That'd work. *Absolutely.* I'd back off in the short-term. After I'd met with a couple of surrogacy agencies, I'd bring up the conversation again. I didn't want to pressure Hunter, but I wanted to bring the *let's-have-a-baby* timeframe forward to now.

That was if the first embryo worked.

It had to . . . my odds weren't good.

I only had eight frozen eggs.

The shutting of kitchen cupboard doors and clinking of glassware dragged me from my spinning thoughts. I packed them away for another day.

"You want ice?" Hunter asked as he cracked open a fresh bottle of Jack Daniel's in the kitchen.

"Yes, please." I grabbed the remote off the sofa, flicked on the sound system, and turned on my playlist. The second Alicia Keys' angelic voice filled the room, I stretched my head from side to side. The tension in my shoulders dissipated. Each slow chord, each smooth melody, each soulful note that resonated through the speakers wrapped around me. It penetrated my skin, meandered through my veins, and recharged every cell.

Just what I'd needed.

Hunter joined me by the piano. In the dim lighting, his azure eyes shimmered bright, but too much sadness loomed beneath the surface. It punctured the center of my chest. The day had been hard for both of us. Now I wanted to put it to rest.

"You okay?" I swept a loose strand of his long, dark-brown hair off his brow and ran my fingers through the soft waves that fell to his shoulders.

"Yeah." He handed me a drink and raised his glass. "Here's to Ryan. May the angels watch over him always."

"To our baby boy. Until we meet again." I clinked my tumbler against his and took a tiny sip.

Hunter downed half his JD, then placed it on a coaster on top of the closed piano. He edged toward me, threaded his fingers underneath my hair, and massaged the back of my neck. "Are you feeling better now? It's been a rough day."

That was an understatement. I probably looked like a mess. My skin was no doubt blotchy from my earlier tears. My eyes would be red. My makeup, non-existent. Lifting my chin, I stitched on a brave smile. "Yeah. It's hard to let go. But I want the hurt to stop. I want to move on and remember Ryan in a good way. He brought us together. He made us stronger. We have such a great life together."

Hunter had music. I had my work with Everhide. As their stylist, I sourced and coordinated their outfits for every performance, appearance, and event. I loved attending fashion shows and working with designers across the globe, and influencing trends and latest must-have items. Some days I missed designing. I still tinkered, creating the random dress for myself or my girlfriends when needed. But no amount of money or fabulous career would ever fill the loss of our child. Only another baby would.

"Yeah, we have it good." He grabbed his drink again. "To us. To living life to the fullest." He downed the rest of his JD in one gulp. "Fuck, that's good." But then he winced, clutched his throat, and swallowed hard again. "But the burn is new."

"Hunt?" I flattened my hand against his chest. Concern lilted my tone. "Something's not right? You should go to the doctor." In the five and a half years I'd known him, he'd never been sick. He'd never had a cold, the flu, a stomach bug, or a fever. Nothing.

"Nah. I'm fine."

Who was he kidding? "You leave tomorrow." I'd barely see him over the next two months while he was away with Kyle and Gemma, writing their new album. "You should get a checkup before you go."

"Nah. I'll promise to take it easy for a couple of days." He took my glass and placed it on top of the piano next to his. Sliding his hands around my waist, he stepped forward, erasing the gap between us. With my shoes off, I was only a couple of inches shy of his six-foot-two height. He rested his forehead against mine. "Just being here with you makes me feel better." He drew me closer, so close I could feel his heartbeat against my chest. "You're the only medicine I need."

"I'm not sure I can cure anything."

"I can think of one thing." His eyes glinted as he tilted his hips, pressing his crotch against mine. I giggled as heat coiled through my core. I hadn't expected that—not after such an emotional day. He had a profound effect on my body, and he knew it. Was that good? *Hell yeah.* He dipped his chin and touched his lips to mine. So warm. So tender. With one flick of his tongue, he deepened our kiss. Slow. Gentle. Delicious. My mind blurred, and the world disappeared. His intoxicating citrusy Dior Sauvage cologne filled my head. I kissed him back, savoring each taste and touch.

Grinning, he pulled back and dragged his thumb across my lower lip. "Hmm . . . I feel better already."

The husky rumble in his voice weakened my knees. My pulse, my heartbeat, my breath quickened like I was backstage before a fashion show. The temperature between us rose. But guilt invaded my brain and slithered across my skin. I clutched his shoulders and dug my nails into his flesh. I shouldn't feel this want for him on the anniversary of losing our son. It was Ryan's day . . . But I wanted to put the hurt behind me. "Definitely better."

I tipped my head to the side to give him access to my neck. He kissed up the length of my throat and across my jaw until he met my mouth. Tingles skipped up my spine. My therapist had told me I should take my relationship with Hunter slow after a bad breakup and losing Ryan. But with Hunter, there was no such thing as slow. That was just the way I liked it. I threaded my fingers through his thick hair. "I always want to be with you. Be close to you. And always, always want to make love to you."

That was what I wanted. To feel him. Love him. Touch him. Savor my connection to Ryan.

He smiled over our kisses. "I'm always down for that." His hands circled my hips, then he hoisted me onto the piano. Edging between my legs, he gazed up at me. Hunger darkened his eyes. "You . . . sitting on my piano . . . is *very* sexy."

I smoothed my hand over his hair and tucked it behind his ears. "You are sick, aren't you?"

"Yep. We established that years ago." The want in his eyes blazed brighter as he unbuttoned my dress pants. He wriggled them down my legs and pulled them off my feet. With a flick of his wrist, he dropped them on the floor. "You want me to shut the shades?"

"No." I sat upright and shook my head. This was our home. Our sanctuary. With its tinted windows, no one could see into our penthouse—not without a telescopic lens. *Ugh.* I didn't want to think about that. I'd had enough run-ins with the paparazzi to last a lifetime.

I circled my fingers over his shoulders and linked them behind his neck. "I think you've shattered most of my inhibitions."

"You can't have any being with me."

"I've learned that. Like the time at the Belize airport, and at the Global Music Awards in London, and oh, in the restroom at Hayden and Lexi's wedding."

"That was freaking hot. You looked stunning in that bridesmaid's dress. I had to have you."

"You have me." I drew him closer and kissed him. I was his, here and now, but could I hold his interest forever? He'd made every bad boy known to man look like an amateur. My ex, Conrad, had lost regard for me and left me for another woman. Would Hunter do the same? He adored me, treated me like a queen, but I wasn't the skimpy-dressing, flesh-baring type of girl he used to hook up with before we'd dated. My insecurities about keeping Hunter's eyes, and his hands, from wandering constantly hovered beneath the surface of my skin. His recent withdrawn moods, when he claimed to be focused on his music, didn't ease my worry. Was he growing tired of me? Was that why he didn't want to have a baby with me?

No. Don't go there. Stop with the wild tangents.

We loved each other. We belonged together.

I hooked my finger into the top of his jeans and yanked his hips against mine. "Are you sure you want to do it here? On your piano? Isn't it your pride and joy? I wouldn't want to scratch the surface."

"If we do, it'll be worth it." He eased my panties off and dropped them next to my dress pants. "Every time I sit here and play, I'll picture you naked."

Smiling, I wrinkled my nose. "Sounds kinda porn-ish. But I like that. Now take this off." I caught the bottom of his sweatshirt, pulled it over his head, and tossed it onto the floor. Raking my gaze over his ripped abs, smooth chest, and the tattoo swirls covering his shoulder, my pulse quickened. *Oh yeah, he's mine.* "I love you. You know that?"

"Yeah, I do." He slipped off my knit top and unhooked my bra. They joined the other clothes. As he pulled me forward, I wrapped my legs around his waist. I brushed my hands over his soft stubble, tilted his head back and reconnected our lips. Every warm flick of his tongue against mine stoked the fire in my belly. Every soft stroke of his fingertips on my skin left goosebumps in their wake.

A wicked grin curled across his mouth. "Let me show you how much I love you . . . lie back."

Chapter 3

KARA

As "Fallin'" crooned through the speakers, I lay down. The piano's glossy black surface cooled my blazing flesh. Hunter trailed fiery kisses from one breast to the other, down my stomach, and across my old cesarean scar. Then lower. Lower. Lower. *Mmm.* His hot breath teased my sensitive skin in gentle waves. He flicked his tongue, dragging it through my slit, taunting me with each swipe. Anticipation and fevered need burned inside me. He knew exactly what I needed to forget my heartache, my stresses, even if it was only for a little while.

I wriggled, and a desperate moan tumbled from my lips. "Hunt . . . please."

With a rush of warm air, his mouth claimed me. *Oh yes.* My eyes fluttered shut as his searing tongue worked its magic. Licking. Kissing. Sucking. I gripped onto the side of the piano as my hips pulsed. He fucked me with his fingers, slow and steady. Twisting and turning. I floated on the piano's surface like it were a cloud, rising higher and higher. All my troubled thoughts disappeared. Lost in his touch, I murmured and moaned. The need for release coiled tighter and tighter inside me. My breaths shortened. My heart hammered. My body screamed. *Yes . . . there.* He swirled his tongue over my clit. With a hard suck and languid lick, he took me over the edge. "Holy. Shit." Panting, I quaked and shuddered and pulsed. Sparks of electricity shot up my spine and tingled my toes. Every nerve in my body hummed as he continued his onslaught. I rode the current of bliss, pulsing against his mouth until I couldn't take it any more. I tapped him on the shoulder and collapsed. My thighs shook as I released them from around his waist. "You're so good at that."

He grabbed my hands, hauled me upright, and lifted me off the piano. Satisfaction shimmered in his eyes and glistened on his lips. "Years of practice."

"I'm glad I reap the benefits." But I didn't want to think about his past. Not now. Not ever again. "But I want more."

I entwined our fingers and guided him over to the fluffy rug in front of the flat-screen TV. We sank onto the floor. As he lay back, I took off his jeans and boxer briefs. The scorching heat from his body enveloped me as I touched, tasted, kissed and caressed every inch of his naked flesh. Everything about him—each sculpted muscle, each piece of ink, each hard plane—was a work of art, a true masterpiece, something to be admired. I could love him all day long.

But his throaty groans deepened, growing more intense, more needy, more desperate.

He rolled on top of me, and our gazes locked. Hooking his hand beneath my thigh, he drew my leg up toward my hip and slowly eased inside me. He filled me as he thrust in deep. *So good.* Skin on skin, my heart beat in time with his. Our slow, sensual pace turned into rich, ravenous pleasure. Rocking hips. Roaming hands. Entwined legs. Luscious kisses. Liquid touches. Languid penetration. He drove away my pain, my heartache, our loss. With a hard thrust, he closed his eyes, moaned, and quaked. As he spilled into me, his cock throbbed. My pussy pulsed around him. Lost in each other, we kissed, touched, and savored the moment.

Warmth flooded my chest. If he loved me as much as I loved him, surely he'd want a family.

I had to hope. *Pray.*

Catching his breath, he braced his arms on either side of my head. "I love making love to you." He smiled a sexy smile before it disappeared and a pinch formed between his eyebrows. "But I didn't expect that today."

"No. Me either. But it was beautiful. It was a Ryan moment." I cupped his cheek. My heartbeat flickered like a candle in the breeze. Whenever Hunter played Ryan's song, or we recollected something about him or my pregnancy, we called it a *Ryan moment*. The memories we'd always treasure. This day, this snapshot in time, would be added to the list.

"Yeah. It was." He handed me his boxer briefs to clean up, then he pulled a throw off the nearby sofa and draped it over our bodies. Stretched out on the rug, locked in his arms, I rested my head against his shoulder.

I cuddled in close and breathed him in. "I'm gonna miss you while you're away. We've barely spent a night apart since we moved in together."

He caught my hand and kissed the inside of my wrist. "Come with us."

"I can't. I have work."

He rolled onto his side and flipped me down onto my back. As he hovered over me, a smoldering sauciness shimmered in his eyes. "I know you have a *very* good relationship with your boss." With his fingertip, he drew a line from the tip of my nose, over my chin, down my throat, then caught the throw covering my chest and dragged it lower and lower until he exposed my breasts. He circled my nipples. They hardened into peaks. The corner of his mouth curled in a playful smile. "He won't mind if you clear your calendar. In fact, he insists."

He licked the tip of my boob. I flinched beneath the flick of his tongue and at the soft blow of cool air. Goosebumps charged across my skin. I giggled, tugged on his hair, and pulled his head away. "Sorry, *boss*. I can't. I have a ton of meetings and events to go to, and Flint is flying in from LA to discuss being his stylist."

He furrowed his brow. "Flint? I thought you were joking at Christmas about taking on other clients. Aren't you happy working for us anymore?"

"I am. But Flint's band is doing well. They're about to tour again. He wants me to sexy-up his bad-boy rock-star image." Not that he needed much help. If the headlines were anything to go by, he was on track to surpass Hunter's reputation. I straightened the throw over my chest. "I love my job. But working with Flint will be fun." Lowering my voice, I threw in a hint of tease. "Are you jealous I'll be spending time with him and not you?"

"Me? Nope." His tone remained smooth as satin. "I don't get jealous."

Not even a little bit? "Are you sure?"

"Yep. Not ever."

Pity I couldn't say the same thing.

A devilish grin slid across his perfect lips. He lowered his head and nuzzled into the small of my neck. Then, he nipped, licked and sucked the soft flesh until it hurt. *Ow!* "But just so you know . . . and he knows . . . you're mine. Marked accordingly."

I rubbed the damp love bite. Kinda liked him marking me as his. "You have nothing to worry about. It's business."

He narrowed his eyes, drilling into me with his electric gaze. "I've seen your schedule. You can come back to meet him. Cancel everything else."

Yes, I could do that, but I didn't want to interfere with Hunter's work. I ran my fingers over his shaved cheek. "No. You don't need me there distracting you." I wriggled my hips against his groin to show him exactly what I meant.

A low growl rumbled deep in his throat. "But you're the sort of distraction I love. I need to take breaks."

"I know. But you need to be focused. And I have—" I lowered my gaze and fidgeted with the tassels on the throw. *Shit.*

Hunter was put on this planet to entertain, to sing, to write songs. What he shared with Gemma and Kyle was phenomenal. He lived his dream every day . . . and I had to follow mine. While he was away, I had plans of my own.

"Have what?" he asked.

My career wasn't my endgame. Being a mom was.

I had to make it happen.

My heart rattled against my ribs like buttons in a tin can. Why couldn't having a baby be easy? I didn't want him to react like he did earlier. Not after making love. But I wouldn't lie to him.

I sucked in a breath to steady myself, to stop myself from shaking. "I've booked meetings with two surrogacy agencies to find out more information. Hunt, I love you, and I want a family and want to start the process." I'd googled. I'd read every website. I was prepped. This was what I needed to do.

A roar rumbled in the depths of his throat. "Kar. We just talked about this." He leaped to his feet, swiped his jeans off the floor and yanked them on. "We can't have a baby. It's not the right time."

I sat upright, clutching the throw to my chest. "A baby won't happen overnight." I stood and wrapped the blanket around myself like a bath towel. "The laws have changed. We can do this here in New York. It could take months to find a surrogate. Then months for her to prep, have IVF, have our baby. We can plan the due date."

He dragged his fingers down his face, leaving white streaks on his cheeks in their wake. "Fuck. Not now."

"Yes, now." I *had* to rely on someone else to have my baby. My body had failed to carry Ryan to term. Would someone else's do the same? It terrified me. I had to put my eggs into someone else's basket . . . literally . . . to bring my child into the world. My pulse pounded in my temples like gonging church bells. "I want children. Don't you?"

Shards of ice flashed in his eyes, so brittle and fierce my skin prickled with frostbite. "How can you say that? After everything we went through with Ryan?"

My heart bent and buckled. He hadn't wanted Ryan at first, but he'd changed his mind. He'd fallen in love with our baby. He'd wanted to be a father. I took a step toward him, but his body turned stiff as starch.

"Hunt. Breathe. We can do this together." I splayed my hand over my heart. "Become a family."

"We are a family." He waved at the large photo on the far shelving crowded with music awards, at the picture of us with our four best friends in Belize. "You, Kyle, Gem, Hayds, and Lexi are more of a family to me than the one that brought me into this world."

"I know." I dug my nails into my palm until it hurt. I understood his apprehension. He'd never had a close relationship with his parents. I hadn't with mine either. But nothing had deterred me from wanting a family. After years of trying to have a baby with my ex, Conrad, and failing month after month thanks to my severe endometriosis, I'd had eggs harvested for IVF. Eight eggs had been frozen successfully. After losing Ryan and having a hysterectomy, surrogacy was the only option. I wanted to use my eggs. "But I want a baby. With you."

"We haven't been together long. Until we're more certain about us, our future, let's not rush into anything."

"I am certain." I kept my voice calm yet firm and buckled my determination up tight. I refused to let go of my dream. I stepped toward him and placed my hand over his heart. "We are still new. Life together is amazing. We don't have to get married." I'd signed so many legal documents and agreements with Hunter we were basically married anyway—Everhide's non-disclosures, confidentiality agreements, and our living arrangement documents to protect our individual assets had been put in place. Waiting for a marriage proposal that may or may never happen wasted time. "If we learned anything from losing Ryan, it's that life can be short and unpredictable. We don't know what our future holds." I still had trust issues, but time would conquer them. "I hope we're together forever. But regardless of what happens, it doesn't change that right now, I want nothing more than to have a baby with you. I love you. Please . . . just think about it."

"Fuck." He stormed over to the piano and slapped his hands on top of the lid. It sounded like it stung. "It's not the day to talk about this." The pain in his voice tore my heart in two. "Today is about Ryan. Not about having another child." He charged past me. "This conversation is over. I need to go pack."

He took off down the hallway. His heavy footsteps padded on the hardwood floors. My heart thudded in time.

I drifted over to the piano stool and sank onto it. Dizziness swam through my head. *Well . . . that didn't go to plan. Not that I had one.* Closing my eyes, I took a deep breath to clear my mind. Hunter needed time to process what I'd said. He needed to do a Taylor Swift and calm down. I didn't need his help to select an agency or to find a surrogate. I could do that on my own. But after that . . . I needed him. I wanted him to want this. Fighting back my tears, I stared at the city lights. I never wanted to have to choose between him and having a child. With every inch of my soul, I wanted both.

He had to come around. We could do this. This was right.

I'd trickle information to him. Remind him how exciting it would be to have a child and what an amazing father he'd be. I'd make him feel part of every decision. I'd make having a baby work with our busy schedule.

I clutched the throw against my chest and fought the ache in my heart.

There was no doubt in my mind.

It was the perfect time to start the surrogacy process.

It was the perfect time to have a baby.

I just prayed it would be with Hunter.

Chapter 4

HUNTER

Hidden away in a private mansion upstate New York near Woodstock, I sat in front of a mic in the fully decked out music studio. Ready to cut a demo with Kyle and Gemma, I took a deep breath to clear my head. But thoughts of Kara and babies bombarded my mind.

We can't have a baby? No way. Not now. Not . . . Ugh!

I hadn't handled our conversations about babies well. I'd freaked out and stormed off. I hadn't wanted to discuss the subject further. Now, three days later, the ongoing tension lingering between us was like a fuse about to blow. Our phone calls had been short. I didn't want to talk about babies. But Kara didn't have to say anything. Her silence was just as powerful. No matter how hard I tried, my brain wouldn't put the topic to rest.

Was I too harsh? Was I too quick to say no? Could we make it work?

No, we can't. We have the tour. What was she thinking? A baby? Oh man . . . I'm so freaking fucked up.

Gemma, tinkering on the grand piano a few feet away, speared me with her emerald gaze. "Hunt, you with us?"

I adjusted the mic and straightened the pop shield. "Yep. All good." *Far from it.*

"I need one more minute." Kyle hovered over the control panel. He puffed at his long, dirty-blond hair falling across his eyes, and typed on the keyboard, prepping to record the first take of vocals. "This computer is so fucking slow."

I scanned the room decked out with drums, guitars, keyboards, cords, cables, and microphones. Two pizza boxes lay empty on the floor by the door—last night's ten o'clock dinner. Our notepads and pages of lyrics lay in piles on the coffee table next to half a dozen empty cups. The three of us had barely taken a break since we'd arrived. This song had taken hold of us. We'd played around with it all day yesterday, locking down the right lyrics, melody, chord progressions, and beat. Now we were ready to scratch the track.

After taking several deep breaths, I ran through some warm-up scales—a few lip trills and hums. For days, I hadn't sung so I could rest my throat as much as possible. The niggle in my throat had almost gone.

But what about Kara? A baby? Shit!

As I closed my eyes, nausea pooled in my gut. I'd felt less sick on a plane being thrown around in rough turbulence.

I'm not ready to have a baby? Am I?

I'd wanted Ryan. But after losing him, did I even want children? Was I only leading Kara on? This was why I'd avoided relationships in the past; they caused nothing but problems. I'd do anything for Kara, but having a child by choice was too much of a huge leap. Not one I was prepared to take at this stage of my career.

But what if it is?

Fuck!

My mind was more hot and cold than Katy Perry's.

Kyle made some keystrokes, then pointed at me. My eyes remained glued to the monitor in front of him. "Hunt, you ready?"

"You bet." I brushed my crazed-baby thoughts aside. Excitement took over and hurtled through my veins. First cuts of new tracks were always raw, but the thrill of laying down new material was as addictive as oxycodone.

Headphones on. Lyric sheet in hand. Mic in position. I picked up my travel mug off the floor and took a big swig of hot Throat Coat Tea. I swirled it around in my mouth and swallowed the licoricey lemony brew. It was too sweet for my liking, but it did wonders for my vocal cords. I'd sing steadily, not push my voice too hard. I hooked my headphones off one ear and gave Gemma and Kyle the thumbs up. "Let's lay this fucker down."

Gemma played, goofing around with the tempo on the keys. Fast. Slow. Hard. Soft. Then settled on moderato. "Go for it."

The zing in her tone was contagious. The electric charge in the air jumping between the three of us struck me right in the center of my chest. When a song came together—the lyrics, the melody, the bridge—it was magic. It had me edging the stool closer to the mic.

"Let's go." Kyle peered at the screen covered in the music production software's graphs, channels, mixer controls, and sound wave bars. Flicking switches and pressing buttons on the control panel, his eyes lit up like Manhattan's skyline at night. He clicked his fingers. "Hunt. Gem. From the top. Three. Two. One. Go."

I wriggled my headphones into position. Gemma's heavy, vivacious tune filled my ears. I flicked and straightened my piece of paper covered in blue scribbles, crossed-out lines and rewritten lyrics. As I cleared my throat, I tapped my other hand against my thigh in time with Gemma's beat, and sang:

> *Someone like you should've come with a warning sign*
> *Should've seen you comin' but I was blinded by your light*
> *I couldn't believe it.*

I frowned and clutched my throat. A chill slithered through my veins. My voice was too raspy. I caught sight of Gemma. Furrows formed between her eyebrows. She'd no doubt heard the same thing.

But I kept singing.

> *Someone like you should've set off my alarms*
> *But lost in your eyes, I was captured by your charm*

I couldn't believe it

Determined to get this demo done, I filled my lungs, expanded my diaphragm, and relaxed my shoulders, ready to hit the high note.

Never thou—I'd fi—someone li—you

My voice cut and cracked over the words.

L—vin' you i—all I wa—na do
You are m—guiding lig—
Wan—to hold you eve—nig—

My heart rattled like a rusty gate. What was happening? The lyrics came out broken, half with no sound at all. *What the . . .?*

Kyle hit the stop button. Worry flooded his dark-brown eyes. "Dude. What the hell was that?"

I ripped off my headphones and shrugged—anything to hide the slice of fear that had coiled around my neck and cinched like a noose. My voice shouldn't be that hoarse.

Gemma smirked, jerking her chin at me. "You finally hitting puberty at twenty-six?"

"You wish." I smirked half-heartedly and took another sip of tea. I had a two-octave, four-note range; I could sing the damn song. "I mustn't have warmed up enough. Gem, take it down a key. Let's go again."

"Wait." Kyle waggled his finger back and forth between Gemma and me. "Swap. Hunt, you play. Gem, you do vocals. Hunt, you don't want to fuck your voice."

Too right. My voice was my life. Without it, I'd be nothing. A nobody. I never wanted to be like the teenager I was back in high school ever again. "It's fine. Let's do another take."

But the moment I hit the chorus, my voice broke again.

"Fuck." My pulse pounded inside my head like a cymbal being hit over and over and over. I didn't need problems with my voice on top of my problems with Kara. I ripped off my headphones, leaped from the stool and punched the shit out of the microphone, knocking it onto the hardwood floor. *Smash.* The pop filter and stand split apart. The mic rolled and skidded toward Gemma.

She jumped to her feet. "Hunt. Stop. It's okay."

I rubbed my eyes and then scratched my fingernails down the front of my neck. "I can't hit the note. That's ridiculous. It's not even high. What the fuck?"

"Are you sick?" Gemma lowered her butt back onto the stool. "Getting a cold or something?"

"No." I shook my head. "I'm fine." Other than Kara and her baby talk screwing with my head. "Just . . . give me five. I need a break."

I grabbed my travel mug of tea, stormed out of the room and headed out onto the deck of the immaculate eight-bedroom home that overlooked the Ashokan Reservoir. I sat on the top step, closed my eyes and drew in big, deep breaths of fresh mountain air. *There's nothing wrong with my lung capacity. Just my fucking voice.* Taking a sip of tea, I let the warm liquid trickle down my throat to ease the niggle. It didn't help. *Shit.* As I stared at a distant sailboat gliding over the shimmering silver waters, my leg jiggled. Kara was right. I should've gone to the doctor. *But I don't feel sick.*

Sam and Mick, our security guards, sat talking at the picnic table underneath a nearby tree. Sam's tablet was propped against his water bottle, no doubt lit with the feed from the property's security cameras. It wasn't just overzealous fans finding us that was an issue; it was the assholes who wanted to steal our music and leak our tracks before they hit the market. We didn't want to come across either while we were here.

I grabbed my cell phone from my jacket and checked for messages. Ten emails from Bec, our personal assistant. Five from Sophie, our manager. But nothing from Kara. Just a new post to her Instagram account of her sifting through racks of clothes at the fashion house of Ivory Mink—some new designer she was in talks with to supply us with clothing. I zoomed in on Kara's smile. *Damn.* I missed her. What had happened to me? Where was the old me who loved being single? My women? My *fuck 'em and leave 'em* ways?

That *me* was gone . . . I didn't miss those days at all.

I loved Kara. But for the foreseeable future, I needed to focus on music. This album was too important. It'd be our sixth one—the second since leaving the hit-factory clutches of SureHaven-Grant Records. Each track would be more personal and deeper than anything we'd done before. This music would show the world who we were and how far we'd come.

Fire stirred in my belly. I couldn't wait to tour again. The handful of shows and one-off concerts we'd done over the past few months hadn't given me the same wicked dose of energy I got from performing every day on the road. I craved adoration from the fans. The hype fueled my soul.

Our next tour would be even better. Kara would be with me.

So much that had changed in me was because of her. The songs I'd penned couldn't hide that fact. But what about the future? I wasn't a big planner or goal-setter. I'd had Gemma and Kyle to help drive our music career, and a management team to guide our success. I just wanted to make records, perform in front of massive crowds, and live in the moment. But plan a family? *Ugh!*

I wanted to scream. But I fucking couldn't. I needed to protect my voice.

Footsteps on the deck pulled me from my thoughts. Kyle plonked down beside me and offered me a beer. "You want this?"

I waved the bottle aside. I'd love a cold brew, but the bitterness would rip my throat to shreds. "No thanks. I'll stick to this shit for now." I screwed up my nose at my tea and downed another mouthful.

"What's going on?" Kyle took a swig of his beer and glanced across the glassy lake. "I'm not talking about your voice; something else is eating you. You're distracted. So spill."

Kyle had been my best friend since elementary school. For twenty-one years we'd lived and breathed music and had formed an unbreakable bond. Gemma had connected with us in an uncanny way when we'd started high school. The three of us were so close, nothing went unnoticed. There was no point in lying.

"It's Kara."

"I gathered as much. She's been off since Hayden and Lexi's wedding." Kyle stretched his legs and crossed his ankles. "Is she pressuring you to get married?"

Thank God, no. "No . . . she wants to have a baby. Find a surrogate."

Kyle coughed and choked on a mouthful of beer. He wiped his lips on the sleeve of his sweatshirt. "Fuck. Are you serious?"

"Yep."

"Shit. A child? Wow. Having kids is the furthest thing from Gem's and my mind. The thought of dealing with shitty diapers, vomit, and crying, snotty-nosed babies doesn't do it for us. So I'm not sure what to say?" He winced and scratched the back of his undercut. "Do you want kids? I thought you guys weren't exactly over Ryan."

My heartstrings pulled and tweaked deep inside my chest. "I'm not. She's not. But man, having another baby?" A wave of overwhelming weight pressed down on my shoulders. "The idea of spending months at doctors, meeting surrogates, and undergoing IVF procedures does my head in. I don't want to think about it."

"Looks like you already are." A broad smile charged across Kyle's face, then he downed another mouthful of beer. "You could propose. Planning a wedding would keep her occupied for months."

I punched him in the bicep. "Fuck off. I'm not ready for that. She doesn't want to get married." *Wait? Why not?* My heart did a double take. Kara had wanted to marry Conrad from the moment they'd started dating. Why not me? Wasn't I marriage material? I was hot, rich, famous, and fun. I loved her and treated her right. So what if I liked to party hard, was occasionally an egotistical, arrogant asshole, and had lost count of how many girls I'd slept with? Since falling for her, there'd been no one else. She was it. We'd worked through most of our issues and continued to deflect her family's constant disapproval. Would our relationship last? Who knew? But I had no intention of going anywhere. I was in this for the long haul.

But why did she want a kid now?

I rubbed my closed eyes. "Everything's so fucked up."

Kyle rested his elbows on his knees, the beer bottle dangling from his fingertips. I eyed the other bottle resting beside his hip. Drinking it grew more and more tempting. Then I swallowed. The dull ache had returned, irking me just as much as someone singing flat. *Yep. No beer.*

Kyle turned his head toward me. "When Kara got pregnant, you changed. You went from hell no, to hell yeah. You wanted to be dad. Is this any different, knowing that it'll take time to find a surrogate?"

Whose side was he on? What happened to brotherhood for life? But I'd asked myself that same question a million times since Kara mentioned wanting a child. "Yeah, it is. This will be our decision, not an accident. It'll be weird having someone else carry the baby. And I'm not sure I have the strength to handle it if it doesn't work."

Kyle clutched my shoulder. "Yeah, you do. You made it through losing Ryan. Now you have each other. And no matter what happens between you and Kar, whatever you decide, Gem and I are here for you."

"I know." We were each other's ride or die. In this life and the next. But sitting here in the quiet, as I contemplated having a baby, a strange warmth embedded in my bones. I could picture Kara smiling, holding our baby in her arms. The three of us . . . together. Was that what I wanted? "*If* I had a baby, it'd change everything. We have the album, promo and the tour all planned. I don't want to alter our schedule or miss out on anything."

"You better fucking not. We're doing this shit forever. But you were prepared to make changes for Ryan." He half-heartedly shrugged his shoulder. "You were terrified then, too, but you didn't walk away."

"Kara and I weren't together. We'd agreed to co-parent. I'd just see my kid when I could. But this time it'd be different." I rolled my travel mug between my hands. "That's what has me fucking scared. If we do this, this is the shit. Commitment. Family. Life together. If I *don't* have a baby with Kar, I could lose her. I don't want to do that."

"Then you have your answer."

I stared at the rim of my travel mug. "This whole love thing sucks."

"Yep," Kyle smirked. "But it's damn good, too. And we write awesome songs about it." He drained his beer and picked up the spare. "Hunt, just don't rush into making a decision. Be sure it's what you want. But do me a favor? Please keep baby talk away from Gem. I don't want her getting any fucked-up ideas."

"Gem?" I chuckled. "I don't think you have to worry about that. When Mother Nature handed out the maternity gene, she was drinking JD at the bar with us."

"Too right. And I want to keep it that way." His tone softened. "I want to savor every second with her. Just be us, forever."

I glanced at Kyle. The dark shadows circling his eyes had deepened. "You still not sleeping?"

"Nope." He shook his head and gazed into the distance. "Not well anyway. I just lie awake watching her, man. Just to make sure she's there. If I sleep, it's not for long. Nightmares are a bitch."

Gemma's kidnapping had affected all of us, especially Kyle. I loved Gemma fiercely, like a sister. Coming close to losing her had been another wake-up call, reminding me how short and precious every moment was. I rolled my travel mug between my hands. I wanted to treasure every day I had with Kara. But damn . . . I wished Ryan was part of it. I'd wanted to be a dad. I'd wanted to see my son take his first steps. Teach him to play the guitar and the piano. Take him around the world. But it'd all been snatched away.

Damn, I wanted Ryan.

Would another child fill the void inside my chest? Was having a baby worth the risk? Could I push my fears aside and rely on doctors and science and medicine to have a child with Kara?

Maybe.

I stood and dusted off my hands on my jeans. "Come on. Let's get back to it."

"No." Kyle grabbed the beer bottles in one hand and rose to

his feet. "You need to head back to the city and go to the doctor. Get your throat checked. We don't need you to lose your voice this close to hitting the recording studio."

"I won't fuck with my voice. You guys can do vocals for now. If it hasn't improved by the end of next week when we go home for Kara's surprise birthday, I'll see the doctor. I'm sure it's just worry and stress. Nothing serious."

On top of the long days working on songs, I'd organized a surprise party for Kara next Friday, the day before her birthday . . . with a lot of help from Bec, our assistant. Friends, cake, catering, and a venue had all been booked. I'd think of something special to do on her actual birthday. What did I buy for my girlfriend who had everything? Jewelry? A purse? Lingerie? *Hmm.* They were easy options. Or . . . I closed my eyes and swallowed the dry lump in my throat. Could I give her what she really wanted?

Kyle slapped me on the back. "Fine. But go make an appointment to see the doctor anyway. You can cancel it if it's not needed. I'll be inside with Gem, laying down that track. But knock before you enter. You know . . . just in case we're doing something you don't want to see."

"Seen it all before." It wouldn't be the first time I'd walked in on them going at it, and I was sure it wouldn't be the last. Those two were made for each other. I felt the same way about Kara. I wanted to live in the moment, not worry about the future or rush into forever. *Fuck.* But the gaping hole Ryan had left in my heart burned hot. No amount of music or lyrics I had written had expressed the true depth of my loss.

No new baby would ever replace my son.

No new baby would make up for my initial mistakes with Kara.

But a new baby would give me the chance to do things right.

Well . . . Holy. Crap.

Kyle headed inside, waving over his shoulder. "Love you, man."

"Love you, too." I chuckled and diverted toward the kitchen to make another cup of tea. The doubts about my throat lingered in the forefront of my mind. I'd best make an appointment. I searched my cell phone and dialed our otolaryngologist's number.

At three-thirty next Friday, before Kara's party, I'd find out what was wrong with my throat.

I hoped it was nothing.

But I wasn't naïve. I suspected what the problem was. I'd avoided admitting it for days.

If correct, it could change the course of this album.

Affect my singing.

Risk my career.

And the very thought of that scared the living shit out of me.

Even more than having a baby.

Chapter 5

HUNTER

I hated sitting still. It drove me nuts. With my gaze set on Dr. Vanessa Petrofski's framed medical certification on the far wall, I fidgeted with my platinum signet ring as she ordered me to open my mouth and say, '*Ahh*'.

"Ahh."

She held down my tongue with a wooden depressor and peered at her monitor.

The live footage of my pink, slimy flesh and white vocal cords coming from the endoscope camera shoved up my nose and threaded down the back of my throat filled the screen. *Gross.* I didn't want to look, but just like watching the gore and mayhem in horror movies, the allure roped me in.

"Say '*Ahh*' again." She wriggled the scope. Left, then right. Up, then down. "This time, scale your voice upwards."

Too easy. I puffed air through my nose, trying not to laugh as the probe tickled the back of my mouth. The few drops of anesthetic spray stopped me from gagging, but each wriggle and tug of the tube itched. My fingers twitched, wanting to rip the contraption out.

I relaxed my shoulders and took a deep breath. "Ahh. Ahh. Ahh. A—A—"

Shit.

Vanessa pulled the scope out of my nose, placed it on a metal tray, and handed me a tissue. Concern flickered in her gray eyes. "What have you been doing to yourself?"

I rubbed and wiped my tingly nostrils. "Nothing. Why?"

"Hunter. You have vocal nodules."

I what? My heart stumbled against my ribs. My vision blurred. My ears rang like wailing sirens. I'd wanted my suspicions to be wrong, but they weren't. *Vocal nodules? Fuck!* Every singer's worst nightmare. I squeezed my eyes shut, but nothing blocked the diagnosis from drilling inside my head. Maybe I'd misheard the doctor. "You're shitting me, right?"

Vanessa shook her head. "I'd never joke about something this serious."

"Are you sure?" Each breath I took ripped my lungs. Vanessa had traveled with my band during our second world tour. She'd been our crew doctor before she'd become an otolaryngologist and had rarely cracked a smile. No matter how hard I'd goofed around, teased her, or gotten her drunk, she wasn't the laughing kind. But maybe she'd changed.

Her mouth drew into a thin smile. Her voice remained calm and clinical. "Sorry, Hunter, but I'm sure."

No. No. No. NO!

"Have you pushed your voice when you sing? Overexerted yourself? Partied too hard?"

"No." I wiped my clammy palms back and forth on my jeans. "We're working on our new album. I thought I had a bit of vocal strain, but the hoarseness never went away."

"See here." She turned to her monitor and pointed to six tiny bumps that looked like blisters on the image of my vocal cords. "These lumps are all nodules." She tapped her fingernail against the largest mound. "This one is quite bad."

"But . . . but I've always looked after my voice. I've had professional training since I was six. I've done nothing crazy. There was one day at home when Kyle, Gem, and I sang like idiots. Would that have caused the damage?"

She swiveled on her chair to face me. "These nodules may not necessarily be caused by singing. Any screaming, loud talking, or yahooing around may have caused them."

"Shit!" The after-party at the Global Awards in London, Hayden's bachelor party in Brooklyn, and his wedding at MoMA skipped through my mind. There'd been excessive drinking, hollering and yelling. Typical partying, really. "So now what?"

"You say you've had a hoarse voice for a couple of weeks, whereas I'd say, by the look of the nodules, they've been there for a couple of months. I advise you to have surgery to have them removed."

My heart thundered hard and fast. "Surgery?" *No fucking way.*

"Yes. I can book you into the Massachusetts General Hospital in Boston, where I operate every second Thursday. We're renowned for our vocal corrective procedures. The sooner you have them removed, the better. You'll need as much time as possible to heal before you sing again and hit a grueling schedule."

Sweat trickled down my spine, dampening the small of my back. Heat snaked beneath the surface of my skin like I'd broken out in a fever. Was I reacting to the anesthetic spray? No . . . it was the thought of surgery.

I stretched my neck from side to side. "I can't have an operation?" I *never* wanted to set foot inside a hospital ever again. Not after what I'd been through. Brushing my thumb along the inside of my forearm, I traced my silver scar. It stretched from my wrist to an inch below my elbow, branching like jellyfish tentacles. My accident was still vivid in my mind, like it had happened yesterday, not seven years ago. In London, the wrap party after our first world tour had been wild. But crashing through a glass door still haunted me. I'd been drunk and high as a kite and sliced my arm on the broken shards. I remembered the blood, the dangling flesh, the visible bone. The hospital. The surgery. The general anesthetic. Waking up in excruciating agony. Being violently ill and vomiting. I'd felt like dying. The operation had left me disfigured and with ongoing issues. A low-burning ache flared in every tendon in my forearm when I played the guitar too much.

"There must be other options. What about vocal therapy?" Surely that was all I needed.

"Therapy may improve your vocal function. Correct breathing techniques strengthen and improve cord flexibility. But Hunter, my honest advice is to have the nodules removed. While there are risks with the procedure—scarring, hemorrhaging, possible paralysis—you have more chance of getting a chipped tooth than of having temporary or permanent damage done to your vocal cords."

Risks? With each one the doctor listed, my heart raced faster than Usain Bolt shooting over the finish line. I couldn't think about the risks. They were too high. "I'm not worried about my fucking teeth. They can be fixed. They're all veneers anyway." I wasn't born with this million-dollar smile. "But any damage to my vocal cords could ruin my career."

"I understand." Vanessa softened her voice and folded her hands in her lap. "But if you don't have them removed, they may become calloused, rupture, and cause more problems. Then there'll be no other option."

No-no-no-no. Nausea congealed like glue in my gut. My pulse throbbed inside my temples. Letting out a slow, shaky breath, I kept my tone firm and level. "Doc, I'll try therapy first. I'll do anything to avoid surgery." I'd place my bet on natural remedies and pray I was a lucky man.

"All right." Vanessa's shoulders slumped. "Try therapy. But do it religiously. I'll email my report to your therapist. Do you still use Annelise?" I nodded. "Make sure she focuses on semi-occluded vocal tract exercises and relaxation techniques."

"Got it."

"Come back and see me before you record. If they're not healed, you won't be hitting the studio."

Oh yes, I will. The nodules will be gone. They have to be. After a few therapy sessions, some more rest, they'd disappear for sure. "I'll be fine. Thanks for seeing me on such short notice." I stood and shook Vanessa's hand. "I mean it, Doc. I'll do anything to avoid the knife."

"Laser, actually."

My fingers flinched and flexed. I wanted to wipe the sly smile off her face. I didn't care if it was a knife or a laser. I didn't want to go near either of them.

But as I walked out of the medical center and collapsed on the rear seat of my waiting town car, a wave of fresh worry washed over me. Reality hit. I rubbed my index fingers against my closed eyes and fought back the sting. But it was pointless. Tears welled, threatening to fall.

I had nodules.

My voice was damaged.

Fuck!

***

Twenty minutes later, I entered Gemma and Kyle's building and headed to their floor. I punched in my access code to their two-story condo and walked inside without knocking. My whole body was numb, on autopilot. I didn't have long before I had to get to the venue for Kara's surprise birthday party, but telling my best friends about my vocal cords was a priority. This affected them too.

I searched downstairs, in the office, and in the music room, but they weren't there. I stopped at the bottom of the stairs and called out. "Kyle? Gem?" *Crap.* Panic clipped me on the back of the head. *Don't yell! Idiot. Think of your voice.* This total vocal rest thing would kill me.

"Yeah?" Kyle's voice drifted down from their bedroom. "We'll be down in a sec."

I sank onto the linen sofa and let my head fall back. The image of the sore blisters popping and oozing on my vocal folds, flickered behind my eyelids. *Ugh! What a nightmare!*

High heels clip-clopped on the wooden staircase. "Hey, I thought we were meeting at the bar," Gemma called out from halfway down the steps. Kyle trailed behind her. "Is Kar still at the salon?"

I couldn't lift my head—it weighed as much as a pipe organ and resonated with a mind-splitting drone like one too. "Yep." My first birthday treat for her was to be pampered . . . facial, mani, and pedi. She loved them.

Gemma, dressed in a glittery forest-green party dress, took a seat next to Kyle on the adjacent sofa. "So? What did Vanessa say?"

Every pore in my body constricted as I gripped the arm of the sofa, sat upright, and dug my fingernails into the fabric. As our gazes met, the color drained from Gemma's face, and Kyle's smile morphed into a panic-ridden frown.

I sucked in a deep breath and struggled to form words. "I have vocal nodules."

"Oh, no." Gemma's eyes pooled with tears. Her hands shot over her mouth.

"Shit. How bad?" Kyle raked his fingers through his hair, leaving tousled track marks in their wake. "Do you need surgery?"

"Hopefully not." The ache in my chest tightened around my heart as I filled them in on needing vocal rest and therapy. I had to avoid alcohol. Closing my eyes, I clenched my jaw. Vocal nodules would not get the better of me. I'd beat this. I was strong. Dedicated. Determined. Therapy would cure me. But no matter how much I hammered resolve into my brain, fear coiled up my spine like poisonous venom. "How will we finish the album?"

Gemma rushed over and sat on the sofa beside me. She wrapped her arms around my shoulders and kissed the top of my head. She sniffled and wiped away a tear. "We'll work it out. We always do."

I rested my head against hers. "What if my voice isn't better by the time we hit the studio?" I hated the wobble and rasp in my voice.

"That's weeks away. You'll be better by then." Kyle reassured me, but the concern in his tone betrayed him.

Doubt swirled in my stomach like oil on an unsettled ocean. I didn't need this additional stress. The mix of Kara wanting a baby, my vocal issues, and the countdown to recording, compounded inside my head. *Thud. Thud. Thud.*

Gemma hugged me tighter. "We have access to the best doctors. You'll be fixed before you know it."

"What if I never get my range back? Singing is who I am." I was the whole package—not just the wrapping. I had an incredible voice, was good looking and a great entertainer. Losing one of those traits would kill me. *Oh shit.* Worry skipped through my veins. My fans might unfollow me in droves. I thrived on their adoration. I couldn't live without it. Yep, my ego didn't want any blows.

Kyle leaned forward, clutching and wringing his hands together. Worry swam through his dark eyes. "We know, bud. But Miley Cyrus, Sam Smith, Adele, and Keith Urban have had vocal surgery. Look at them now. They're fine."

A chill cut through my veins. "Yeah. But knowing my luck, I'd end up like Julie Andrews. Doctors fucked her voice. I don't want to end up on the messed-up list. I don't want an operation." Needles. Hospitals. Machines. *No, thanks.*

Kyle pinned me with his gaze. "Hunt, your health comes first. You do what you have to do to fix your voice."

"I will." I wanted to avoid surgeons as much as hoes with herpes. "But right now . . ." I glanced at my watch. "I've got to get to the bar for Kara's party. I'll call Sophie and give her the update." Our manager would have contingency plans in place by morning, but I didn't want to have to put any of them into action. "And please don't mention this to Kara. I don't want to ruin her party. She'll want me to have the surgery. We'll end up arguing. I don't want that. Not tonight. I'll tell her tomorrow."

"You sure?" Gemma stood, smoothing her hand over the hip line of her dress. "She'll know something's wrong."

"Nah." I stared out the huge, oversized windows that had uninterrupted views toward Lower Manhattan. Could I put on a façade for Kara? Pretend nothing was wrong? I was a performer, an actor, an entertainer. *Hell yes.* I wouldn't ruin her night. "She'll be so excited and swept up by seeing her friends. Just smile. Have fun. Drink champagne . . . except . . . I can't fucking do that. *Ugh.* I hate this already. But we know how to entertain, so let's make this a night she'll remember."

Gemma's concern morphed into energized speculative curiosity. She raised an inquisitive eyebrow. The hair on my arm prickled. "Are you going to propose?"

"What? No." *No chance.*

"Have you made a decision about the baby?" She continued her quizzing as she returned to Kyle's side.

I puffed air through my nose. I'd roped my friends into several conversations about Kara and babies over the past two weeks. We'd discussed every for and against, and I'd yet to come to a solid conclusion. But they were better than any therapist. "I'm not rushing into anything, Gem. There are a few things I need to sort out. Things with Kara. Okay?"

If Kara and I were to have any kind of future, baby or not, there were parts of my past she needed to be aware of. Things that may have her running for the hills. Reasons why she might want to leave.

That was a conversation for tomorrow.

I jumped to my feet. "But right now, it's time to party. All you two have to do is make sure Kara arrives at the bar on time. Everything else is set." I smoothed my hands down the front of my floral Givenchy button-down shirt and tugged on the ends of the cuffs. After visiting the doctor today, the last thing I felt like doing was celebrating. I couldn't drink, and my mind was stuck on my issues. But for tonight, I had to push them aside . . . for Kara.

"We'll be there. Let me show you out." Kyle leaped to his feet and walked me to the door. But when he spun around, fear had returned to his eyes. "Whatever your decision is about a baby, Gem and I are cool with it. But we're more worried about your voice. Tonight, we'll be watching you like a hawk to make sure you take care of your throat."

Not going crazy at a party would be a first, but I'd survive. "I'll behave. I promise." I smirked, but my apprehension held me hostage. Every time I swallowed, the lump in my throat was there. Just like the scar on my arm, the nodules never disappeared. Not what I needed.

"Good. Love you, man." Kyle opened the door. "Let's go party . . . with some hot herbal tea."

"Fuck you."

"See you soon, dude." Kyle slapped me on the back and sent me on my way.

"Love ya." I waved over my shoulder and headed toward the elevator.

As I walked down the laneway that separated my building from Kyle and Gemma's, worry festered inside my head.

Now I've got two things to keep from Kara tonight. I had to avoid talking about my voice problems and baby decisions.

Crap! I hoped I could pull it off. I was usually good at being guarded, distracting people with fun and jokes, being spontaneous, and not caring about consequences. But when something was on my mind, Kara was just like Kyle and Gemma. She was perceptive and saw through my bullshit.

If I keep my distance, play the consummate host, and ensure her champagne glass is always full, she shouldn't get suspicious.

Avoiding the topic of babies? *Too easy.* Avoid talking too much? *Fucking nightmare.*

But I was terrified of permanently damaging my voice. I'd duct tape my mouth shut if it meant the nodules would heal.

I'd do whatever it takes—therapy, rest, no alcohol—to fix my throat.

Anything to avoid surgery.

But right now, I had to switch into party mode.

Tonight was all about Kara.

Time for her birthday celebrations.

Tomorrow I'd know our fate.

Chapter 6

KARA

On the rooftop bar overlooking the Hudson River, I took a long, large sip of my fifth champagne. Hunter had been amazing, surprising me with a birthday party with thirty of our friends. But he'd barely been by my side all night. *What was with that?* He should be celebrating with me, not talking to everyone *but* me. Was he avoiding me to stay clear of further baby talk? *Well...* I held my chin high and drew my shoulders back. He had nothing to worry about. I'd promised not to mention it again until I'd met with the surrogacy agencies at the end of next week. His lack of attention hurt, but my tough exterior wouldn't fray like thin organza.

I had my girlfriends. Champagne. I was set.

Tilting my head back, I downed the remains in my flute. Each tiny champagne bubble popped and tickled my nose. As the gas heaters toasted my shoulders, and loud music thumped through the venue's speakers, I swayed on my studded Valentino stilettos. I waved my empty glass at Gemma. "More, please?"

Hunter swept over from the bar with a fresh bottle of Krug and popped it open. "Here you go, birthday girl." He poured, topping up my glass.

Slinking up to him, I tugged on the front of his shirt. Was he looking after me? Or trying to get me drunk? I wasn't sure which.

"Thank you. Stay with me."

He kissed my cheek. "I'll come back. Soon. I'll just say hello to some more of our guests."

"Leave that." Gemma pointed at the bottle in his hand. She grabbed it and sent him on his way with a flick of her wrist.

My gaze lingered on Hunter's back as he disappeared through the crowd. Something was off. He was usually all over me, kissing me, hugging me, seductively touching me, always ogling my boobs. There was none of that tonight. No PDAs or dirty whispering in my ear that left my panties wet and my body craving him. My heart shrank to the size of a button. Wanting a baby *had* caused a crack in our relationship. I'd hoped he'd warm up to the idea, and our love would burn brighter, not be snuffed out like a campfire doused with water. But I'd prepared myself for the consequences. Now that the chain reaction had started, I had to find the strength to face the finale.

Tomorrow . . . Enjoy tonight . . . Deal with Hunter tomorrow.

I stuffed my concerns into my purse and snapped it shut like it was Pandora's box. I'd open it later. Much, *much* later.

"Yo, Kar." Lexi, my other bestie, standing beside me, clicked her fingers. "Stop gawking at your man. Here . . ." She grabbed a cupcake off the table weighed down with food and drink and stuffed it into my mouth. "Happy birthday, bitch."

Perfect distraction, Lex. I moaned, and my eyelids fluttered closed as I savored the sweet treat—chocolate frosting, vanilla cake. A total sugar overload. Just what I needed. "Oh, yum." I touched my fingertips to my lips and wiped the corners of my mouth. "That is soooo good." I loved sweets but usually avoided them. I didn't need another gossip site taking a swing at me, saying I was fat. I'd grown skin as thick as an old leather boot, but I'd prefer not to be tomorrow's headline.

My sister, Naomi, jostled past a group of friends I used to work with at Conrad's Fashion House, and joined us by the food table.

While I took after our dad in looks—super tall, straight as a pole, head of thick hair—Naomi, at two years older, took after our mom—average height, angelic in movement, and had a perfect slender figure. Growing up, we'd been complete opposites. Naomi loved her books, math, golf, and tennis—everything our parents loved. I liked ice hockey, creative art, and ballet—everything my parents wished was a passing phase. Naomi thrived in our family's stockbroking organization. I had defied my parents' Wall Street dreams for me and moved into fashion. I lived and breathed it. Despite our vast differences, I loved my sister very much.

Slipping her arm around my waist, Naomi rested her head against my shoulder. Her bobbed, fine golden hair tickled the top of my arm. Naomi raised her half-full flute. "To my baby sis. Happy birthday for tomorrow."

"Woohoo!" I hooked my arm around Naomi's neck, drew her close, and pressed our cheeks together. "This is so awesome. I have all my favorite girls here to celebrate."

Lexi smiled a playful, saucy smile. "So, do you know what Hunt's bought you?" She grabbed a chocolate-coated profiterole and stuffed it into her mouth.

I homed in on Hunter like he was a flashing neon sign. He leaned against the bar at the far end of the terrace, talking to Hayden and the guys in his backup band. As I scanned his dark jeans, button-down shirt, and his hair tied back in a man-bun, my temperature jumped. Heat crept up my neck like it always did when he was near. But then, my heart wobbled and ached. *God, I love him. Please don't let us be over.* "No, Lex. I have no clue."

He lifted his travel mug to his lips. My hot high took a nosedive into frigid waters. I fidgeted with my pearl necklace. Was he drinking more herbal tea? Not whiskey or beer? *Hunter? Not drinking?* Was he saving his voice for recording? But Gemma and Kyle were drinking their weight in alcohol. His sore throat should be better by now. If he were ill, surely he would've told me.

I drowned the unease swirling in my stomach with a swig of champagne. Sewing on a big smile for the girls, I drew my shoulders back. "Hunt's thrown me this incredible party." Trying to pump excitement into my voice, I waved at the DJ pumping out the tunes, the twinkle lights wrapped around poles and in strands overhead, and at the table covered in food and drink. "I don't need anything else for my birthday." *Although something small would be nice.*

But right then, more champagne would be good. I held out my glass to Gemma. "Fill her up, please?"

"My pleasure." Gemma topped up our flutes, ignoring the bubbly overflow, then placed the near-empty bottle on the table. "We're here to party, so stop glaring at Hunt."

I took a quick sip of my drink and flicked the froth from my fingertips. "Something's off. Maybe you can enlighten me. You've been away with him. What's happened?"

Gemma winced, then ripped her gaze away from me and chugged down her champagne like it was cool water.

A shiver ran up my spine. *Oh, shit. Something had happened.* "Gem? He's not drinking. Is his throat still bothering him?"

"Shit, Kar." The humor dissolved from her face. Too much champagne swirled in her eyes. "Please cut Hunt some slack. He's had a rough couple of weeks. An even rougher day. He's putting on a brave face for you. We all are."

My fingers tensed around my flute. *Brave face?* "What? Why?"

Gemma's eyes widened, and her hand shot over her mouth. "Oh crap. I'm not supposed to say anything. Damn champagne."

"Say anything about what?" I glanced at Lexi and Naomi. Their faces were blank. They had no idea what was going on either.

Gemma cursed under her breath and slumped her shoulders. "He's really upset. Not too much rattles Hunt, but this has. He's been diagnosed with vocal nodules."

"What?" My breath shot from my lungs. "He told you but not me?" That hurt. It stabbed my chest like a blunt arrow. Why couldn't he tell me this news? He always rushed to Kyle and Gemma first—not me. Some days I felt like the third leg . . . in this case, the fourth. I never wanted to come between the bond he shared with them, but it would be nice to be on par.

Grimacing, Gemma hugged her flute against her chest and swayed on her feet. "He didn't want to ruin your party."

"But I'm his girlfriend." *No, wait. I'm his fucking partner.* "He should've told me."

Concern hit my head like a shot of tequila. I had to make sure he was okay. Be there for him. Take care of him. But when I took a step in his direction, Gemma caught my arm.

"Wait. He will tell you. Tomorrow. He only came to Kyle and me because this affects us in a big way. We might have to delay recording the album, even the tour." Gemma wrinkled her nose. "I'm sorry. He's gonna kill me for letting it slip."

Lexi shook the shock from her face. "Does he need surgery?"

"Hopefully not." Gemma hooked the shoestring strap of her dress back onto her shoulder. "But he has to rest and have vocal therapy. Stress isn't good for him." She winced and softened her voice. "I'm sorry, Kar, but the baby talk hasn't helped. You've really freaked him out."

Fire crawled up my neck. I wanted to charge over to Hunter and demand he tell me everything, but the truth slammed into my chest. I had shocked him. Telling him I wanted a baby on the anniversary of losing Ryan wasn't ideal. But I had to be honest with him. "I know I did. But that's no reason for him to avoid me and not trust me with important news."

"Kar, I love you. And he does too." Gemma rubbed my arm. "But your timing sucks. You know our plans for the next two years."

Gemma was nothing but music, music, music. So was Kyle. They were perfect together. It's what they lived for. But I'd sensed a change in Hunter. He wouldn't be with me if he didn't have room in his life for other interests. He'd been prepared to be a father before. I had to hold on to the thin filament of hope he still wanted to be one. I jerked my chin back, unwavering and defiant. "Yeah, I do. And we could fit a baby into that schedule. Life isn't all about music, Gem. I want a baby. A family. With him."

"Whoa." Lexi held up her hand. "Back the fuck up. I come home from my honeymoon and LA to this? I am missing way too many pieces of the pie. Fill me in. Kar, you want a baby?"

Waves of frustration and hurt curled through my veins in fevered currents. Explosions of love, want and unquestionable desire for the man standing across from me flooded my heart in hot bursts. Nothing was straightforward when it came to Hunter.

It never had been. We were an extreme case of opposites-attract, but we worked. Tilting my head to the side, I nodded at Lexi. "Yes. I do."

"Oh wow, Kar." Bewilderment shot through Naomi's tone. "My life is soooo freaking boring compared to yours."

My shoulders sank an inch. "You wish. Two weeks ago, I told Hunt I was ready to find a surrogate. He flipped out." I knocked back a mouthful of my drink, letting the sweet liquid diffuse the hurt bubbling in the pit of my gut.

"Holy shit." Lexi's eyes widened to the size of big buckles. "Are you sure you're ready? After Ryan?"

Why did everyone keep questioning me? I was ready. I scooped my hair back over my shoulder. "Yes. I am. I'm meeting with two agencies next Friday."

Gemma guzzled her champagne as if her life depended on it, then coughed and cleared her throat. "I love you and Hunt, but please don't ask me to be your surrogate. Babies are not on my agenda. Not ever."

"Or mine." Lexi shook her long, crazy curls, flicking them against her cheeks. "Hayds and I have a lot of lovemaking to do. We have to make up for seven years of just being roommates."

I gave them a warm smile and splayed my hand across my chest. I had the best girlfriends. They were so strong, so confident. I loved them so much. "Girls, don't stress. You can't be a surrogate. You haven't had your own children. You're not candidates."

"Oh. Thank. Fuck." Gemma grabbed the bottle of Krug, upended it, and poured the last few drops into her mouth.

Naomi draped her arm around my shoulders and hugged me close. "Finding a surrogate will be exciting."

I staggered on my feet and leaned back against the table to steady myself. "Yes. Maybe. But everything about surrogacy frightens me. I'm terrified I have to find someone I don't know to have my baby. What if they lie about being healthy, physically and mentally? What if they find out who we are and won't give up the baby? I know the laws now protect us, but I'm concerned if they found out it's Hunt's child things wouldn't go smoothly." I rounded my shoulders and half-hugged myself. "But I know in my heart I want a baby. All this stress will be worth it when I hold my child in my arms."

"That's so true." Naomi sighed. "I loved being pregnant. But damn, having kids is a handful. I love my career and my daughter, but I barely get to see her. Do you want our father prepping your child for Wall Street like he does with Dakota?"

"God no." I rolled my eyes. "I'll be lucky if he wants anything to do with my child. Daddy hates Hunter."

"Um . . ." Gemma butted in. "You're talking like Hunt's onboard with this."

Naomi's mouth curled into a bemused smile. "If he isn't, she could always use a donor."

The prickly vibes that shot off Gemma jolted my head backward. She glared at Naomi. "Why would you say that? Hunt loves Kar. He'd do anything for her, but having a baby is a massive decision. A life sentence. Losing Ryan totally fucked him up. He's still getting over what happened."

I hooked a loose strand of hair behind my ear. Gemma would defend Hunter with her last breath. She got along well with Naomi, but no one could say anything against Hunter. Gemma would pulverize them to the ground.

I lowered my chin. The ache in my heart threatened to split it open. Hunter loved me, but was it enough? Did he love me as much as he loved Gemma and Kyle? Obviously not. "Gem's right. He's not on board yet. I'll worry about what to do when I find a surrogate."

"You're all fucking crazy," Lexi hollered and clutched her side. "Enough baby talk. My ovaries hurt just thinking about it. I need more champagne."

"So do I." I knocked back the last mouthful in my flute. "Let's head to the bar." I pointed in the wrong direction and laughed. "Oops . . . the bar's that way." I swung my finger in the right direction. *Shit.* I'd lost count of how many drinks I'd had.

Lexi linked arms with Naomi. "We'll grab the drinks. Gem, you take Kara to mingle."

"Deal." Gemma took my hand and led me across the terrace toward Bec, Sophie, and their partners. But after a few steps, my vision blurred. A cold sweat broke out on my brow. My stomach rocked like a boat on a swirling sea. "Gem." I froze. "I don't feel so good."

"You going to be sick?"

"No. I just need fresh air."

"Um . . . we're in fresh air. We're on a fucking rooftop."

I staggered over to the edge of the terrace and flapped my hands in front of my face. As I stood a few yards away from the gathered guests, the music blared like we were in the middle of a nightclub. "I don't think that cupcake is sitting well in my stomach."

Gemma laughed low and rubbed my back. "I think it's more likely the two bottles of champagne you've guzzled."

"Ugh! Maybe. Just give me a minute." I rested my arms on top of the brickwork and put my head down. The world spun. *Shit.*

A large hand swept up my back, underneath my hair and massaged the base of my neck. His touch felt cool against my burning flesh.

"Kar?" Hunter's voice hovered above me. "You okay?"

"No." I stood upright and spun to face him. Everything that had happened this evening exploded like a bomb inside my brain. "Why aren't you with me? Why didn't you tell me about your vocal nodules?"

He flashed evil eyes at Gemma.

Gemma grimaced. "Sorry." She flicked her hand toward me. "But she went off about babies. I broke out in a rash. It just slipped out."

I closed my eyes. I didn't want to upset my girlfriends with baby talk. But I needed someone to talk to. Hunter didn't want to listen to me either. Maybe my sister was my best option for downloading my dramas onto in the future.

Hunter sighed and slipped his arm around my waist. *Oh . . . that is better.* The floor seemed less liquid with him holding me up. "It's okay, Gem. Thanks. I got her."

"You want me to stay, Kar? Or are you okay with Hunt?"

I leaned against the wall. Commotion weaved like a loom inside my head, but I needed to set things straight with Hunter. "Give me a few minutes, please?"

"Sure. I'll be right over here if you need me." She backed away. A big grin drew across her face. "Don't do anything I wouldn't do." After blowing us a kiss, she twirled on her heels and rushed to Kyle's side.

I turned to Hunter. I stabbed my finger against his chest so hard I nearly snapped off one of my newly manicured nails. "Talk. Why are you ignoring me?"

"I'm not. I've kept *some* distance, but trust me, I can't ignore you." He grabbed my hand, held it against his heart, and kissed me on the cheek. "I'm sorry I didn't tell you about the doctor. I didn't want to upset you. I wanted tonight to be all about you, not me."

Shit. I curled and uncurled my fingers on my other hand. How could I be mad at him for wanting to make my night special? "That's thoughtful of you, but it hurt too. You should've told me. What affects you affects me, and vice versa."

He snaked his palms around my waist, gliding over the red beading and lace of my dress. "Oh . . . you affect me all right." His gaze fell to my cleavage and then jumped back to my face. His eyes smoldered and shimmered. "Have I told you how fucking hot you look in this dress?"

"No, you haven't. But thank you." I softened my tone, but nothing stopped irritation from skipping through my veins. We were more than lovers. He had to open up to me more and be more honest. I grabbed onto the collar of his button-down shirt and shook him. "Stop diverting off topic. You can trust me. Tell me anything."

He lowered his chin and nodded slowly. "I'm trying, Kar. Gem and Kyle have been all I've had for so long. Some habits are hard to change."

My head spun like a Coney Island carousel. "I know. But I'm not fragile. Just talk to me."

"Okay."

"I want to know how you feel."

"About my throat?" He winced. "I'm petrified."

The fear in his eyes was real, but he was still being guarded, not his usual self. No singing. No dancing. No hands all over me.

"I'll help you through it." I tugged on his collar again.

"I know you will."

Alcohol took hold of me, and all my unanswered questions rolled off my tongue. "What about a baby?"

He shook his head. "Not for discussion tonight."

"I want to crawl inside your mind and know everything about you."

He pursed his lips, as if trying not to laugh. "That's just weird."

"I want to be your everything."

"You're up there."

Was he just saying things I wanted to hear? His every comment was short and abrupt. Or damn it, was I just too drunk? "Hunt, I want to know what you're thinking."

His eyes glinted. "No, you don't."

"Yes, I do."

"Okay." He leaned forward and whispered in my ear, "I wanna take off your panties and fuck you up against that wall."

I flicked my hand against his chest and blushed. "You're right. I didn't need to know that." I wouldn't let his flirtations distract me. But my pulse jumped a notch of its own accord. I caught my bottom lip between my teeth, looked back over my shoulder at the building's brick wall, then spun around to meet his gaze. I wrinkled my nose. "The wall? Really? You have a thing for walls, don't you?"

"Yep. And cars, and beds, and chairs, and tables, and floors, and dressing rooms. Do you want me to go on?"

"You're crazy. But that's what I love about you. I think . . ." I swayed, stumbled on my heels, and fell into his chest. "I think . . ." *Shit.* My mind went blank. I couldn't remember what I had wanted to say. Then, his citrusy cologne filled my head and invaded my senses. The fragrance was too sickly, too sweet, too seductive, too, too much. My stomach churned like I'd drunk a gallon of gluggy sugar syrup. I broke out in a cold sweat.

Hunter chuckled and tightened his hold on me. "I think you're adorable. I think you've had enough champagne. And I think it's time I took you home."

I lifted my chin, nearly losing my balance backward. "But it's my party."

"It's late. Gem and Kyle can stay with everyone. Let's say goodnight." He took my hand and drew me toward our friends.

Curling my arm around his, I leaned toward his ear and lowered my voice. "Can we do it up against the wall at home?"

"If you're still standing by then . . . absolutely."

"You're on."

But by the time we'd said our farewells, and Hunter and Mick had walked me home, I could barely keep my eyes open and my legs moving. Once we were inside our building's lobby, Mick let us be.

As the elevator opened to our penthouse, my head spun like a bobbin winder. All night I'd been up and down with my emotions—happy he'd thrown me a party, upset he'd avoided me, gutted he hadn't told me his news, and devastated that he'd had no change in heart about having a baby. No matter how hard I'd tried, I couldn't dislodge the sense of distance growing between us. I didn't like the dread. I'd been on this crazy ride of a day for long enough. Time to hit stop.

Hunter half-carried me to our bedroom and sat me on the bed. "You big party animal, Kar."

Half-asleep, I forced my eyes open. I wrapped my arms around his neck and tried to kiss him, but he grabbed my hands and placed them by my side. He eased off my shoes and my dress, and helped me into my pajamas, then dashed into the bathroom and returned with a hot facecloth for me to wipe off my makeup. "There. All done. Now hop into bed."

I crawled up to the pillows and flopped onto them as I lay down.

He drew the soft sheet and quilt over me and tucked me in. "There's water on the nightstand. Some Advil. Get some sleep, Pearl. You're gonna have a hell of a hangover tomorrow."

"I'll be fine. I don't get hangovers."

"Yeah . . . we'll see about that." He kissed me on the forehead. "See you in the morning, birthday girl." He turned off the light and headed out of the room.

My heart squeezed against my ribs. *What? No lovemaking? No up-against-the-wall sex?* I closed my stinging eyes, clutched the quilt to my chest, and curled onto my side. The scent of him lingered—on the sheets, on the pillow, on me. Why didn't he stay? Every reason from no babies to a breakup drifted through my head. I was too drunk to know which one was trending. I hated the unknown. One way or the other, I had to find out what was going on in his mind.

Tomorrow . . . I'd have it out with him tomorrow. Once and for all.

Chapter 7

KARA

The hangover from hell split my head in two before I pried my eyes open. My head throbbed, my mouth tasted like dry lentils, and my stomach roiled with queasiness. I'd tossed and turned all night. My restless sleep had been filled with breakup nightmares. My chest ached, and dread weighed down my bones. *They'd just been bad dreams, right?*

Piano music drifted down the hallway. I clutched the pillow over my ears. Why did Hunter have to be so loud? I dragged myself out of bed, plucked a clump of mascara from my eyelashes, and staggered toward the music. *Why did I drink so much last night? Oh . . . that's right. Hunter had avoided me.*

I stopped at the end of the hall to listen to him play. He sat with his back to me; he didn't know I was there. As I glanced around the living room, my heart sank like a submarine to the bottom of the sea. There were no flowers, no balloons, no birthday presents waiting. After the surprise party he'd thrown me last night, I shouldn't expect fancy gifts. But at least one flower would've been nice.

Or was this a sign? Not everything between us was rosy.

It hadn't been for weeks.

Since I mentioned a baby, everything had turned into short

phone calls, quick texts, and elusive conversations. It hadn't helped that he'd been away.

But no matter what the day held, this year's birthday had to be better than last year. We'd just lost Ryan. Nothing would ever come close to being that horrid. Not even if Hunter called it quits.

My heartbeat snagged like a zipper on fabric. I couldn't go on in this gray zone. I'd wanted to wait until after meeting with the surrogate agencies to talk to him about having a baby again. But not knowing where his thoughts were killed me. If he didn't want a child, there was no point in delaying the inevitable. By the end of the day, I had to know if he was in or out.

I swayed on my feet. Did I have the strength to do this?
Yes.

Once my head stopped spinning.

I wrapped my arms around myself and leaned against the wall. Each muscle on Hunter's back rippled beneath his shirt as he played. His toned arms flexed as his fingers glided over the keys. Would this be one of the last times I heard him play like this?

His soft, slow tune, deep chords, and the moderato melody enveloped me. It was a beautiful piece of music, but sadness lingered between each note. What was he writing about? Me? Ryan? What had inspired this hypnotic, haunting piece? He'd stop occasionally, jot down something in his journal on top of the piano, then stick the pen behind his ear or grip it between his teeth, and continue to play. But there was no singing.

Last night plowed into me like a runaway Rolls-Royce. *That's right. Vocal nodules.* I closed my eyes. Another challenge we had to face. Hopefully together.

I drifted toward him and slid my arms around his shoulders. He jumped, jerking sideways along the stool. "Shit. You scared the crap out of me."

"Sorry." I quirked a sorry-not-sorry smile and kissed him on the head. "Morning."

"I was in the zone. Don't do that." He placed his hand on his chest. "My heart is still racing." He turned back to the keys and played a few chords, then glanced up at me. "Oh, happy birthday.

How's the head?"

Nothing like making me feel special on my big day. *Not.* "Fuzzy."

"Can I finish this, and then I'll grab you breakfast?"

My jaw tensed. So did my hands. "How long will you be? Ten minutes or an hour?" I kept my tone soft, my agitation at bay. He got so wrapped up in music he often lost track of time, like he'd done on the anniversary of Ryan's death. Was he about to do the same on my birthday?

Sighing, I rubbed my tired eyes. Being honest, I wouldn't mind the delay this morning. I needed time for my headache to disappear.

He chuckled softly and rubbed my arm. "Fifteen. Tops."

"Fine." *We'll see.* "May I?" I pointed to the stool.

"Sure."

He shuffled over so I could sit beside him. I rested my head on his shoulder. "I liked what you were playing."

"Yeah? Thanks. I've been up half the night working on it."

Wow. I really must've been drunk. I hadn't heard anything. "Is it just the music, or lyrics too?"

He bobbed his head, his wavy hair brushing his collar. "Tons of words."

"Can you sing it for me?"

"Umm . . ." He cleared his throat and grimaced. "Just softly. I can't strain my voice."

"Just say them then."

"Okay." Wriggling on the stool, he positioned his foot over the pedals. His long, slender fingers floated over the ivory keys, soft and fluid. He played and . . . spoke the words.

> *We've been down this troubled road before*
> *Staring at crossroads, not knowing which way to go*
> *Who's gonna be the one to roll the dice?*
> *Take the first step and stop the fight?*
> *We've been loving and hurting for so long*
> *I don't know where we went so wrong*
> *Nothing with you is black or white*

But why does being with you feel so right?

The melancholy tune and deep words hit me low in the gut. Were these lyrics about us?

We've been over these mountains before
But why does each climb hurt to the core?
Who's gonna be the one to drop the rope?
Who's gonna be the first to let go?
We've been loving and hurting for so long
Didn't know you were the one who made me strong
Nothing with you is black or white
But why does being with you feel so right?

Don't want to hurt you, don't want to lose you
I love you so much, but I'm unsure what to do
Is this the end of the line or the start of something new?
All I know is I can't breathe when I'm not around you

But...
We've been down this troubled road before
Around in circles we go once more
Who'll draw the line in the sand?
Be the first one to drop the other's hand?
We've been loving and hurting so long
Don't know if and where I belong
Nothing with you is black or white
But why does being with you feel so right?

I wiped a tear from my eye. Even with Hunter saying the words instead of singing them, the song packed a brutal punch to my ribs. "That's so sad." I drew in a pain-filled breath and made sure my heart was in check. "Is it about us?"

He stared at his fingers tinkering on the keys. "Yes, and no. It's about many things—past relationships, hurting people you love, not knowing when to let go, being afraid. Confused. Frustrated."

My heart constricted like I was being stuffed into a bandage dress two sizes too small. He was so calm and casual about the heart-wrenching song he'd written while my whole body imploded. I didn't want to cause him any hurt. "Do I frustrate you?"

"Sometimes." He nodded in time with the slow chords. "But so does not finding the right words, lyrics, and notes to express the thoughts pummeling my head. Not singing frustrates me. Having to do all this shit to rest my voice frustrates me."

"Oh." But on a positive note, the song wasn't *all* about me. Or maybe it was. *Shit.* I couldn't let this doubt linger. I had to get this over and done with. I placed my hand over his. My fingers trembled. "Hunt, we need to talk. About us."

He swiveled to face me and clutched my hand in his. His gorgeous azure eyes swirled like unsettled waters. "I know we do. But please, I need to take you somewhere and show you something first. Let me grab your breakfast, and then we'll head off."

"Where do you want to take me?"

"Do you trust me?" He stood and held out his hand to help me stand.

"Yes." I did. Ninety percent of the time.

"Then you'll have to wait and see."

Okay. I could give him a couple of hours.

I followed him over to the kitchen and sat on a stool. "What do I wear?"

"Something casual. Jeans. Shirt. Bring a cap."

"Oh . . . all right." My stomach dropped. I'd hoped he'd take me out somewhere fancy for lunch, then to the ballet or the theater after dinner. Hunter loved going out and being on show for special occasions. Didn't my birthday count? Obviously not.

He dashed around the kitchen, made me a cup of tea, and placed an almond croissant he'd bought from my favorite patisserie onto a plate. But as I ate the delicious treat and sipped my drink, he never stood still. He drummed his fingers on the countertop, eyed the wall clock, and fidgeted with his hair.

Some birthday!

At least the food and tea had dulled my headache. I licked the last few crumbs from my fingertips. "Thank you. I'll go take a shower." I headed toward the hallway but paused at the entrance and glanced over my shoulder. "You want to join me?"

His eyes glinted but didn't shimmer with their usual *hell-yes* sparkle. He smiled and shook his head. "Maybe later."

Maybe? Ouch. This wasn't good. Hunter turning down sex was like a raging alcoholic refusing a drink . . . It never happened.

Okay . . . I got this . . . Prepare for the worst.

No matter how hard I tried to give myself a pep talk, my heart ripped at the seams with each step I took toward the bedroom.

In a daze, I showered and dressed. Whatever Hunter had planned, I wanted to see it through. For him. He deserved that. He wasn't the one who'd ruffled our happy life together.

I had.

And I had to prepare to live with the consequences.

Chapter 8

KARA

As Hunter drove my Mercedes through the tunnel toward New Jersey and headed south, his fingers tapped the steering wheel. His eyes never left the road. Every minute that passed, my stomach swirled with a combination of intrigue and sheer dread. I had no clue what he had planned or what lay ahead. This had to be the strangest birthday ever.

He peered in the rearview mirror. "Mick's following us too."

"That's fine. I'm used to it." I'd be concerned if Hunter's bodyguard wasn't there.

After Gemma's kidnapping, we'd learned the hard way never to slacken off on security. Our buildings were monitored, our cars were tracked, and we were shadowed wherever we went. I'd grown accustomed to someone always covering us. It was our normal.

After taking Route 95, Hunter turned at New Brunswick and drove toward Montgomery, his hometown.

Why was he bringing me out here?

The houses thinned, and the roads widened. An hour and a half after leaving Manhattan, Hunter turned onto a curved, tree-lined street and pulled up in front of a property with a high solid fence. A rundown low-set house stood toward the back of the gentle-sloping block. Other old ranch-style homes with large open yards stretched along the narrow road. This area was nowhere near as flash as the other places and homes we'd passed on the way here.

He switched off the engine and stared out the windshield. My pulse quickened. "Hunt, what is it?"

I had no idea where I was. I'd never been to this part of New Jersey before.

"Let's hop out."

"Fine." I opened the door. On my tiptoes, I stepped onto the small stones and rocks to avoid the mud and long grass. I met him in front of my car. I flicked my hand at something that flew in front of my face. *Ew! Was that a bug?*

Hunter chuckled. He slid onto the hood and patted the spot beside him for me to sit. I glanced down the road. Mick had pulled up on his motorcycle a hundred yards away. *Cool.* I still might need to hitch a ride home with him.

I hoisted myself up next to Hunter. The engine was hot beneath my ass. "Why did you bring me out here in the middle of nowhere?"

With his feet resting on the front bumper, his legs jiggled. He fidgeted with his signet ring. "Kar, for the past two weeks, I haven't stopped thinking about what you said at the cemetery. You're so sure about us. About what you want. Whereas I like to live in the moment, ride by the seat of my pants, and not think beyond the next album and tour. You're so smart, and ambitious, talented and full of class . . . except your mouth. I've turned you into a gutter rat."

Where was this conversation going?

I fastened on a smile and nudged his arm. "You have not. I've always sworn." Was he trying to let me down gently? There was no need. *Just rip the band-aid off, Hunt. Just do it. No need to save my feelings.*

Grinning, he stared toward the ground in front of him. "Okay. I believe that. But here's the thing." He wriggled on the hood, shuffled back a few inches and turned to face me. "We haven't been together long. Eighteen months ago, you despised me. I feel that for you to be certain about us, you need to know everything about me. So today . . . for your birthday . . . I want to give you my past. I want to show you where I came from and what my childhood was like." *Oh wow!* A wave of overwhelming warmth flooded my chest—he trusted me with this. The vulnerability in his eyes snagged my heart. I could tell that this was difficult for him. "If you don't know those things, you can't be sure of our future."

"Yes, I can." I placed my hand on his thigh. "I know all I need to know."

"No. You know the surface since I became famous—about the girls, the fans, the music, the money. But you and I come from very different worlds. I need to do this."

"Why?" Was he afraid I wouldn't love him because of where he came from? I wished I could erase his doubts. Having his child to show how much I loved him was at the top of my list.

"Please?" Deep furrows etched into his brow. "I know you've met my parents and Jenny, but my childhood wasn't easy. I came from nothing. Had nothing. Was nothing. I need to show you this part of me."

"Okay." My voice was as meek as a mouse.

He jutted his chin toward the low-set house. The small ranch-style home with its brown roof and beige shiplap had seen better days. Overgrown hedges ran along the front on either side of the faded red front door. "This is where I grew up. My old house."

My breath hitched. My hand shot over my heart. This place was so far removed from my Upper East Side upbringing, or the house he'd bought for his parents in Chicago, or from the multi-million-dollar penthouse we lived in now.

He pointed toward the left end of the house. "My room was in there. It was just big enough to fit a single bed and a small closet in it. I used to sneak out of the window at night, go down the street to Kyle's, around to Gem's, or hang out with friends down by the creek. We rode our bikes everywhere."

"You had a yard? I'm so jealous."

"I hardly ever played outside. I've always been into music."

"I'm still jealous you had grass outside your front door." I'd grown up in a condo on the twentieth floor on the Upper East Side. My playground was Central Park. The play areas were always overrun with kids, fighting and squabbling over taking turns on the slides and swings. My nanny hated taking my sister and me there to play while our parents worked.

"Unfortunately, the fence was necessary to keep Jenny safe. She could wander off. One day she got out, and we couldn't find her for hours. She'd gotten lost walking toward town. She scared us half to death."

"That would." My volume took a dive. I'd met his autistic sister. She was brilliantly smart and Hunter's biggest fan. He was so protective of her, loved and adored her. His heart of gold and his compassion were two of the many things I loved about him. The fact he liked to hide it, not so much.

"Hop in." He patted me on the leg. "The tour has just begun."

He drove a couple of hundred yards down the curved road, and stopped. He pointed at a small, shabby two-story home. Beige and brown seemed to be the common color scheme in the area.

"Whoa, this place hasn't changed at all." He leaned toward me and peered out the window. "This was Kyle's house. We had our gear set up in the garage. His mom taught music in the front room. His bedroom was at the top left. I hung out here more than at my place."

I could picture him, Kyle, and Gemma, three gangly teens, jamming on their guitars inside the car space. But my heart bled. Kyle no longer had any immediate family. He'd lost his parents in a car accident and his sister to leukemia. Hunter and Gemma were close to Kyle's family. The loss had hit them just as hard.

Two short blocks away, Hunter pulled up outside another home, a small gray cottage with a tiny yard, surrounded by a chain-wire fence. "This was Gem's house."

My eyes stung, not from judgment or pity, but from pride in how successful they'd become. Gemma had always said she'd grown up in a house not much bigger than a shoebox; she was right. Seeing where my friends had come from made me love them even more. They'd worked hard to make something of themselves. They'd followed their dreams and had turned their passion into mind-blowing success.

"We never had money. We went to the local high school and never had fancy clothes, cars, or anything."

"But look at you now. You've achieved so much. Every day you inspire millions of people to follow their dreams. They live and breathe your music. You touch people's souls. Hunt, this made you who you are."

"I was lucky. But I'm not sure that this world, the one I grew up in, is one you'd ever care for or want to be associated with."

Why wouldn't I? I wasn't a naïve uptown girl anymore. He'd opened my eyes. "It's part of you, so yes, it is." I couldn't read him. He gazed at our surroundings, not at me. Something was still troubling him. I couldn't wait to get to the bottom of it.

"We'd better keep moving." He straightened and put the car into gear. "There's more to show."

He drove past his old high school, the tavern where Gemma's mom had worked, the police station where Kyle's dad had been stationed, then he pulled into a large parking lot outside a burger joint.

"I can't believe how open it is out here." I jumped out of the car. "No high-rises, no car-filled streets, no taxis. It's so green and gorgeous. I feel like I'm in the country."

"Yeah, but it's no country club like you're used to."

"What?" I splayed my hand across my chest and fluttered my eyelashes. "You mean there's no valet parking and hot towels on arrival?"

"Definitely not."

I giggled as he took my hand and led me toward the shop. "Be prepared to have your mind blown. These are the best burgers on the East Coast. This is where I used to work after school two days a week."

He opened the glass door. The bell buzzed, and he led me inside. The smell of greasy food hit me. My stomach rumbled, reminding me of my dull hangover. Yes, I needed food. But my brain grew more confused as the day went on. When was my world with him supposed to come crashing down? While we were here?

"Hunter? Is that you?" A large woman with a hairnet over her dark curls shuffled around the counter and wiped her hands on her apron. "Oh, my God. It *is*." She gave him a crushing bear hug, then cupped his cheeks. "Look at you. My, oh my, you've grown so handsome."

Hunter threw an *I'm-sorry-about-the-interruption* grin to a gray-haired man sitting at a nearby table who didn't seem to know what all the fuss was about, then winked at me. "I only turned out okay thanks to braces, no more pimples, a million-dollar makeover, and growing my hair long."

I laughed. I remembered seeing a photo of him at his mom's house in Chicago. When he was young, he had short, curly hair. "You turned out okay, I guess."

Stepping out of the woman's vise-like hold, Hunter hooked his arm around the lady's shoulders. "Kar, this is Rosa. She is the reason I can't cook. She fed me too well."

"Oh, don't be silly." Rosa swatted her hand through the air and blushed. "You were the best cashier we ever had." Rosa turned to the kitchen. "Marco, Fredrick, come see who's here."

While Hunter caught up with his old work colleagues, I scanned the photos on the wall. A picture of Hunter, Kyle, and Gemma hugging Rosa graced a small frame; their signatures covered the bottom of the photograph.

Rosa walked up to my side. "I always knew the three of them would become famous. They're just magic together, aren't they?"

"They sure are." Was that what today was about? Resetting his foundations?

"He used to be so quiet and shy, kept his head down and did his job. But boy oh boy, when he played or sang, he became the sun."

"Yeah, I know."

"Let me make you some burgers. I won't be long."

Hunter pointed to a table for us to wait at. He took a seat, leaned forward, and rested his elbows on the surface. "I saved every dime I made here. I bought my first electric guitar from a pawnshop in New Brunswick. My parents got so mad because I did it without their approval. But I wanted one so badly, and they couldn't afford it. They thought one old second-hand acoustic was enough. At Christmas, our tree never had many presents under it. My presents were often music lessons or books of sheet music. I rarely got toys. Jenny would just break them."

"But that made you appreciate what you were given." I clutched his hand. "Hunt, I know my life was the extreme opposite. My sister and I were spoiled. We had toys that I'm sure we never played with or even opened. Our parents thought that buying us everything would make us happy when all we wanted was for them to play with us, or take us to the park, or go to an ice hockey game. But they did nothing but work and socialize. Nae and I may have had a different upbringing, but it doesn't mean it was happier or better."

"I've met your dad." He smirked. "Give me the nanny any day."

I still didn't know what his game plan was, but I loved learning about his past and that he was opening up to me more than he ever had before.

"Okay." Rosa waddled over, waving a large brown paper bag at us. "Burgers are ready. With extra pickles for you, Hunter." She ruffled his hair. "I remembered."

"You're a legend, Rosa. Thank you." He stood and took the bag. After many hugs and kisses and promises to return, we headed back to the car, takeaway burgers in hand.

Another short drive led us to a park. After grabbing his backpack and my picnic blanket out of the trunk, we settled down in the shade of a tree by a small, trickling creek.

I took a mouthful of the burger and groaned. "Oh wow. This is delicious." Ketchup and grease trickled down my fingers. The explosion of meat, melted cheese, and salad erupted in my mouth.

"Told you they're the best," he said, nibbling on a fry. His broad smile amplified the glint in his eyes.

"This is way better than going to a fancy restaurant in the city." I tucked a flyaway hair behind my ear and tilted my head to the side to attack the burger from a better angle.

"You sure? Seeing where I grew up, learning about my past, hasn't made you want to run screaming back to New York?"

"No." I shook my head and wiped sauce from my chin with my napkin. "It's made me love you more. I know this was hard for you. We may come from different worlds, but we're in the same one now, and we're doing what we love. Together."

His brow furrowed as he stared toward the blanket. "Do you think we're going too fast?"

The air prickled around me. *Oh-o. Here it comes. The blow.* I swallowed the dry lump in my throat. "What do you mean?"

"Us? Moving in together?" He put down his burger and took a swig of water.

"No. Why? Are you having second thoughts? About us?" Did he want me to move out? *Oh God. Please say no.*

"I won't lie to you." He recapped his bottle and tossed it onto the blanket beside his burger. "I have a constant battle going on inside my head. My heart says jump now, fly high. Logic says slow down, take a step back. You're all I've thought about, talked about, and written songs about since being away."

My blood ran cold. I put my burger down, wiped my fingers on a napkin and placed my hand over my stomach to calm the skittish butterflies. "So, what are you saying?"

He shuffled a couple of inches closer, took my hand in his, and entwined our fingers. I smiled a sad smile at the little shake I detected in his touch. "Kar, you continually drive me crazy. In good ways and bad. You have me bashing my head against the wall one minute, wanting to fuck you against it the next. You've done that ever since you got pregnant with Ryan. But I like that you challenge me and don't fall at my feet. One thing I can't deny is how much you've gotten under my skin. You've woken something in my soul, something that has never gone away, not even since we lost our baby, and that is . . . I want kids."

My heartbeat tripped over itself, then sprinted to the top of a mountain at record speed. Had I heard him correctly?

He grabbed his backpack, dug around inside it, and pulled out a red square box the size of my palm. "So, here. Happy birthday."

My breath hitched, excited and nervous. What could it possibly be? I wasn't sure what direction this conversation was taking anymore. This wasn't a proposal; it wasn't a ring box. I took the gift. My fingers fumbled as I untied the gold ribbon and opened the lid. Nestled inside on a bed of soft white satin was a sterling-silver baby's pacifier.

My hand shot over my mouth. Tears pooled in my eyes and tumbled down my cheeks. "Oh. My. God." My whole body trembled. Goosebumps exploded across my skin. "Is this . . . is this what I think it is?"

He took my free hand. "Kar, I love you. I don't know what our future holds, but I'm in. Let's be fucking crazy and have a baby."

I shrieked at the top of my lungs and shot forward. I flung my arms around his neck and kissed him. Kissed his lips, his cheeks, his forehead. "Are you serious?"

"Yeah. I'm not sure I'm ready. I'm not sure I ever will be. So, like before, let's jump in at the deep end. We'll sink or swim together."

I straddled his lap. "We'll swim. I'll make sure of it." My heart soared into the clouds and exploded like fireworks on New Year's Eve. Nothing could ever bring me down. "This is the perfect birthday present." I kissed his lips long and hard. "I was so worried. I thought you wanted to break up with me."

"What?" He jerked his chin back. "What gave you that idea?"

I wiped the tears from my eyes with my fingertips. "You freaked out about having a baby. We haven't talked much since you've been away. You kept your distance at the party last night. I thought I'd broken us." Thank God my nightmares had been wrong.

"Oh shit, Pearl." He cupped my face. "I'm so sorry you thought that. My head really has been on the album . . . and you and babies . . . and my throat. Last night, I didn't want you to worry. I didn't want to let this slip. You're a huge part of my life, and I know I struggle with balance. I'm not sure if I'll ever achieve it, but I promise to keep trying."

I ran my thumb across the curve of his gorgeous lips, then rested my forehead against his. "I love you. I can't believe it. We're gonna have a baby."

His eyes glistened as he caressed the back of my head. "Yeah, we are. I'm terrified. You know that? Doctors. And procedures. And the risks."

"Me too." I combed my fingers through his hair. "But everything will work out. You'll see."

"I hope so." His voice shook with doubt. "And when we do this, we need to make sure the baby is due after the tour."

"Absolutely. It's a long process, but it will be worth it. You focus on mending your throat, writing your album, and the tour. You let me worry about the baby."

"Okay. But we're in this together, Kar. I mean it."

"You had me at *baby*." I pushed him back onto the grass and kissed him. The excitement and fear in his eyes reflected my own apprehensive feelings. We didn't want to lose another child. But his commitment to having a family—and willingness to face the challenges ahead—was the best birthday present ever.

Wow! A baby.

The day had taken the most unexpected turn.

My heart couldn't pump the blood around my body fast enough. My mind raced like wildfire. He'd agreed to have a child. He wanted a baby. There was no time to waste.

I had to find a surrogate.

I didn't want to give him any opportunity to change his mind.

I wanted a baby more than anything.

The wheels were in motion.

Now I had Hunter on board, nothing could go wrong.

Chapter 9

HUNTER

Of course, Kara wanted to tell her parents the news.

I'd tried to talk her out of visiting them but had failed. Why couldn't she just call? Text?

Lunch at Walter and Carol's condo was never fun. Being civil to them and keeping my hands off Kara was always a challenge. Today would be extra hard, especially after celebrating her birthday yesterday . . . and all last night . . . and this morning. Heat still coursed through my body as we walked up to the entrance of her parents' building. Her cheeks still blazed red after we'd made out like teenagers in the town car on the way here. I couldn't bring her down off her *we're-gonna-have-a-baby* high. I didn't want to. But her parents surely would.

I wanted to break the baby news to her folks and head home as soon as possible so we could continue where we'd left off . . . on the floor, in our walk-in closet, as hot as hyenas in heat.

Just inside the building's lobby, I drew her to the side and kissed her. Not some lame brush of my lips against her sweet mouth, but a kiss that was hard, deep, and carnal. One to let her know I wasn't going anywhere.

"You ready for your parents?" I wiped a smudge of her lipstick off the corner of her mouth with my thumb.

"Yes. No. *Shit.*" She placed her hand over her stomach. "They won't like the news, will they?"

"Nope. Don't care."

The way her face had lit up when I'd told her I wanted a baby had been breathtaking, but the sex that had followed had totally blown my mind. Our marathon session had been one of the hottest nights I'd ever had. And I'd had a lot of fucking sex. Every cell in my body still hummed. I'd lost track of how many times I'd made her come, or I'd buried myself inside her. Yesterday, at the park, I'd felt her up as she straddled my lap. Her climax and tears of happiness had been the sweetest thing to witness. The blowjob she'd given me in the car on the way home had nearly caused me to crash twice. We'd barely made it inside our penthouse before I'd fucked her up against the hallway wall . . . *Finally, wall sex. Yeah, baby.* We'd done it on the sofa, on the kitchen counter, in the shower, on the bed and on the floor. Just thinking about it gave me a semi. Better kill *that* before I see her dad.

But a baby was what Kara and I wanted.

I didn't want the buzz to die.

"You look amazing," I said as we headed toward the elevator. Her cheeks still held a rosy glow. I intended to make sure it stayed there.

"Thank you." She blushed even more and pressed the call button. "But we have to behave."

I spun her to face me and crushed my body against hers as I pinned her against the tiled wall. "Never."

I kissed the small of her neck and held her close. God, I loved this woman.

The elevator doors opened, and she dashed inside, giggling.

On her parents' floor, she rang the doorbell. Their housekeeper, Martina, let us in and took our coats and Kara's purse. "Good afternoon, Ms. Knight, Mr. Collins." For a tiny, slender Mexican woman, her voice was loud and strong. She reminded me of Gemma—petite and powerful. "Everyone is gathering in the living room. Please come through."

I'd only been to Kara's parents' place a few times. Their home, with its gray-tiled floors, black and white artwork, and charcoal suede furniture, resembled a modern art museum rather than a multi-million-dollar condo on the Upper East Side.

"Hi." Naomi jumped up from the wingback armchair with her wine in hand and hugged Kara. "Happy birthday for yesterday. Did you have a good day?"

"It was a-ma-zing." Kara touched her throat. The bonus present I'd bought her—a gold necklace with blue sapphires and smooth pearls half an inch apart—matched her navy retro dress perfectly. "Hunt gave me this."

And a ton of orgasms. I winked at Kara, then gave Naomi a kiss hello on the cheek.

"Hi, Hunter. Kara's necklace is gorgeous. You did good." Naomi nodded, then sipped her white wine.

"Happy birthday, Kar." Anthony, Naomi's husband, strolled into the room. In his red Ralph Lauren polo shirt, chinos, and loafers, he screamed *country club pinup model.* He held his red wine to the side, kissed Kara on the cheek, then turned to me. "Hunter, nice to see you." His handshake was firm and strong, yet his skin was super soft, like he'd never done a hard day's work in his life. He came from old money, so that was probably true. "Did you do anything special for Kara's birthday?"

"You could say that." My stomach flipped and fluttered as I slid my hand around her waist. "But we'd better wait for Carol and Walter."

"Oh, there's news?" Naomi's eyebrows shot skyward as she glanced at Kara's hand. "There's no ring, is there?"

"No." Kara held up her fingers and wriggled them. "Something better than that. We'll tell you over lunch."

"You need a drink?" Anthony pointed toward the kitchen. "It's the only way to survive a meal with Walter."

I chuckled; I liked Anthony more and more. "Sure. Kar will have champagne, but I'll have water. I'm on vocal rest."

"Jeez. I love wine too much to contemplate not drinking." Anthony downed the rest of his drink. "That must be hard, right?"

"You have no idea. But my voice is too important."

"That is dedication, man." Anthony turned toward the kitchen. "Stay here. I'll get Martina to grab the drinks."

"Thanks." I nodded as he left.

A pompous tone shattered the air. "Kara." Walter entered the room from the office with his arms held wide. Dressed in a black suit and tie, he looked ready for a formal dinner, not a casual lunch.

"Daddy." Kara pivoted on her toes and slipped into his embrace.

"Happy birthday, sweetheart." Walter kissed her, one cheek, then the other, then dipped his chin at me. "Afternoon."

Still no handshake. Still no warm greeting.

I formed something that I hoped resembled a civil smile and nodded. "Good afternoon, Walter. Nice to see you." *Not.*

But my heart hurt for Kara. She'd had a strained relationship with her father for most of her life, but she still loved him. Underneath her tough exterior, she was all about family. She wanted her father's respect, approval and wanted him to be proud of her. But no matter how successful she was, nothing had pleased Walter.

Carol, Kara's mom, decked out in a Dior cocktail dress, swayed into the room from the hallway. "Hello, dear." She air-kissed Kara. *Mwah. Mwah.* She wouldn't want to do anything that risked spilling her very full glass of scotch on the rocks onto the plush carpet. "Happy birthday."

But I liked to stir. I swooped in and gave Carol a big hug. She stiffened and giggled awkwardly. This family weren't huggers, and I had to change that. "Carol, you look younger and more beautiful every time I see you. Kara certainly gets her stunning looks from you."

"Why, thank you." She blushed and tugged her dangling earring. "Smooth, aren't you?"

"It's a gift." I might never win Walter over, but Carol was slowly warming to me.

Walter looked down the bridge of his nose and sniffed. "Lunch is served in the formal dining room. Shall we?" He turned, headed across the living room, past the kitchen and opened the huge double doors.

The dining room had an uninterrupted view over Central Park. I held out the chair for Kara to sit opposite Naomi. Opting for a seat as far away from Walter as possible, I sat next to Kara, across from Anthony at the black wooden table. Walter and Carol took the chairs at either end.

"This looks delicious." Kara eyed her dish.

The first course of smoked salmon and salad had already been placed. Set on fine white china, surrounded by shiny silver cutlery and crystal glassware, lunch looked more like fine dining than a casual family get-together. Once Martina had served us drinks, she scuttled out of the room.

I downed several mouthfuls of my iced water and let the cool liquid contain my eagerness to get this lunch over and done with.

Kara wriggled on her chair, placed her trembling hand on my thigh, then clutched my knee. I covered her hand with mine. How would she bring up the subject of babies? Through casual conversation, or would she just come out with the news?

"How was yesterday, dear?" Carol unfolded her napkin and placed it across her lap. "Did you do anything special, or were you too hungover after your surprise party the night before?"

I didn't miss the dig in Carol's voice. Kara's parents thought partying was all my friends and I ever did.

"Actually, we had a wonderful day." Kara glanced at me and smiled. Fear, nerves, and excitement skipped through her eyes. "We have some exciting news."

The blood drained from Walter's face. "News?" Horror blazed in the whites of his eyes, but within a blink it disappeared. He smirked and responded with his cutting lack of humor. "Does it involve you coming to work in the family business?"

My lungs deflated, and I shook my head. Walter would never give up. He'd always wanted Kara to work on Wall Street. I could never picture her doing that. Walter was worse than my father. My dad may have never liked me pursuing music, but not once did he say I couldn't do it.

"No, Daddy." She clutched my knee so hard I was sure my kneecap would crack. She drew back her shoulders and seemed to dismiss Walter's remark by drawing on a radiant smile. "Hunter and I have decided to have a baby."

Walter slapped his hand on the table; every plate and piece of cutlery jumped half an inch. "Like hell you are."

The fury and disappointment in Walter's eyes speared the center of my chest. "Walter, I don't think you have any say in the matter. This is our decision, and we're ready to find a surrogate."

"Oh, Daddy. Don't be an ass. This is so exciting." Naomi clapped, then pressed her hands against her chest. "Wow, Kar. On Friday, you were so worried about what Hunter would do. This is so amazing. Congratulations."

"Thank you." Kara's excitement tingled my skin, but her tone held some reserve. "But there is no need to get too excited until we've found a surrogate."

Carol downed another large mouthful of her scotch. "Kara, have you thought this through?" She caught her gold necklace with her free hand and twisted the chain around her fingertips until they turned white. "What about . . . Hunter's family history? Your lifestyle? Your health?"

Carol's low blow was a sucker-punch to my guts, riling every one of my nerves. "My family history? Do you mean the risk of our child being autistic?" These people were so sheltered, so naïve, it made my blood boil. "Just because my sister is, doesn't mean our child will be. And if it is, I'm in a better position than most to know how to deal with it." I'd dealt with the fear of carrying defective genes when Kara was pregnant with Ryan. We knew the risks and were prepared to take them.

"And what's wrong with our lifestyle?" Kara jumped in. "We have a great life."

Carol waved her glass toward me more than Kara. "The travel, the partying, the touring. That's not the environment to raise a child in."

"Oh, please." Kara flopped back in her chair. "Thousands of musicians have kids, Mom. We won't be the first."

"You're not married." Carol drained the rest of her scotch, placed the glass on the table, and then picked up the waiting red wine.

"We don't need to get married." Kara shot back without hesitating. "Get with the times, Mom. Hunter's lawyers had us sign so many legal documents when we moved in together, a marriage certificate won't change anything. We want a family."

True, but my heart wobbled and warped. *Did I want it all? Love . . . family . . . and marriage? Wow. Marriage?* The curtains were still drawn as to whether I wanted to venture down that path in the future. Kara and I never did things in order. Not sure we ever would. But if she was happy the way things were, so was I.

Naomi and Anthony sat still, not touching their appetizers, but their eyes darted back and forth between Kara and her parents as they argued like it was a table tennis match. I was ready to defend Kara, but she had everything under control . . . somewhat.

Walter wiped his hand over his face, rubbed his trimmed beard, and spoke through clenched teeth. "I won't allow this."

"Allow it?" Tears welled in Kara's eyes. "We don't need your permission. We're adults. This is our decision. It's what we want."

"Kara." Angry red veins crept up Walter's neck and branched across his throat. "I'm sorry you lost a baby and your ability to bear children, but this . . . what you want to do . . . is unnatural."

I hooked my arm behind Kara, rested it on the back of the chair, and rubbed her shoulder. It took every ounce of my strength to stay calm as I injected a touch of cockiness into my tone. "Believe me, Walter, I would love to make a baby the natural way with your daughter. We've certainly had a ton of practice."

Mortification flared in Walter's bulging eyes.

Cool!

I smoothed my hand over the back of Kara's hair and softened my tone. "We are worried about the processes and procedures. But surrogacy is the only way we can have a biological child."

"Kara, please." Walter ignored me. "Wait a few more years. Then, if you still want a child, you can adopt."

"Adopt?" Kara closed her eyes and took a slow, steady breath. "Of course, it's something we'd consider. Absolutely. But we want to try surrogacy first." Then, she threw a frosty glare at Walter.

"I can't believe you, who are all about family bloodlines and traditions, are so against this idea."

Carol grabbed the wine bottle from the center of the table and topped up her glass. She certainly loved her drink. "Kara, it's not the only reason. We're concerned about you. You struggled after losing Ryan, not just physically."

She straightened and wiped a tear from her cheek. "I'm fine, Mom. I'm in therapy. My doctor says I'm ready. Surrogacy will work. It has to."

The desperation in Kara's tone didn't ease my concerns about the process. But we would pursue every avenue until we had a child. "We're prepared to do whatever it takes."

"Naomi? Anthony?" Walter picked up his fork, stabbed a piece of salmon, and waved it at them. "Can you make these two see sense?"

Anthony took a swig of his wine and wiped the corner of his mouth with his fingertips. "Walter, when have you told a Knight woman what to do? Never, right? Kara's always wanted a child. And although I don't know Hunter very well, he seems like a decent guy who cares about Kara." Anthony threw us an encouraging smile. "If you want a kid, I say go for it. Nae and I are young parents. We love Dakota. Wouldn't be without her." He raised his wine glass. "I say congrats and good luck."

"Anthony, you're not helping," Walter grumbled. "You're as bad as they are."

"Maybe I'm worse." A sly grin slid across Anthony's face. "I married Nae when you didn't approve of me. And we've had a child. I'm not planning on going anywhere either. Love is love."

I could almost see the steam coming out of Walter's ears, like a kettle about to blow.

Huh. I'd thought Anthony was Walter's wet dream of a son-in-law. If Anthony, who was a Harvard graduate, came from an elite New York family, and worked on Wall Street, hadn't been good enough for Naomi, I'd never be good enough for Kara. I'd crawled out of the gutters of Montgomery, New Jersey, and had a reputation for being wilder and more reckless than a randy, drugged-up college boy at a Coachella after-party—but that was my past.

If Walter couldn't see how much I loved and cared for Kara, it wasn't my problem.

Narrow-minded people weren't worth my time or energy.

But peace and civility would be nice, for Kara's sake.

Naomi clutched Kara's hand across the table. "I'm excited for you. I wish you luck in finding a surrogate. If I can help in any way, let me know."

"Thanks, Nae. At least some members of this family are happy for us." She folded her hands in her lap and stared toward her untouched food. "Mom, Dad, I'm sorry you don't approve, but I'm used to that. I shouldn't have expected anything less. Why did I think you'd be happy?" She lifted her chin and pasted on a brave smile that filled my chest with warmth. "Hunt and I love each other, and we're having a baby. You can either be supportive or have nothing to do with your grandchild when it is born."

"Kara," Walter snapped.

"No." Kara ripped the napkin off her lap and tossed it on the table. "Sorry. I've lost my appetite. Hunt, let's go home."

"Sure, babe." I stood and drew her chair back.

"Kara, sit down," Walter fumed.

"No." Hardness and hurt set in her eyes. "You try to take away or put a stop to everything I love or want to do. I won't let you play any part in this. This is my life. Let me live it." She drew her shoulders back and sucked in a shaky breath. "Don't get up. We'll see ourselves out."

I placed my hand on the small of her back, guided her toward the front door, and collected our belongings. As our driver took us home, Kara sobbed against my shoulder.

"Well... that went better than expected." I rubbed her arm and kissed the top of her head. "He didn't throw me out the window."

"True." She sat upright and brushed her fingertips across her cheeks. "But I thought they'd be excited about having another grandchild. But no. They have the most insane, unrealistic expectations. Nothing I do, and no one I'm with, will ever be good enough for them." She sniffled. "I don't care what they think. I've followed my dreams for a long time—I will fight to my last breath to keep chasing them."

If she didn't care what her parents thought, why did she get so upset every time they spoke, or we visited? Why did she keep trying to win their favor? Was she holding out for a miracle? Walter was so set in his ways, I didn't think anything would break down his barriers.

I entwined our fingers and kissed the inside of her wrist. "And I will do all I can to help those dreams come true. I'm sorry lunch turned out to be shit."

"No, it's about to be perfect." She leaned into me, hooked my hair behind my ear, and brushed her fingertips over my stubble. "Let's order some takeout Thai food, have a bottle of wine, and do more of what we did last night."

"Now that, I can do."

Telling Kara's parents our baby news hadn't gone well, but I hadn't told my parents either. That was sure to be another dose of disappointment. We'd had enough drama for one day; my folks could wait until tomorrow . . . or next week . . . or the baby arrived.

Chapter 10

HUNTER

After dinner, I draped a throw over Kara. She'd fallen asleep on the sofa while watching a movie. We'd had a big weekend. I was leaving tomorrow, back upstate, to write the album, so I had to get organized. I headed into my office to pack my laptop. As I entered the room, my cell phone rang. *Shit. Mom.*

I shut the office door so I wouldn't wake Kara and put the cell phone to my ear. "Hey, Mom."

"No, silly, it's Jenny."

"Jenny Bear!" My tone lightened, but my chest sank. I missed my sister. I didn't get to Chicago often enough to see her. "How are you?"

"I'm awesome. I called to wish Kara a happy birthday. I'm sorry I didn't call yesterday, but I had to work. She's turned twenty-six, right? That makes you one hundred and six days older than her. She's an Aries. You're a Capricorn. I'm a Sagittarius. I know all the star signs."

"That's super cool." I spoke softly as I ambled around the office. "But sorry, Kara's asleep."

"Oh no. I worked late at the nursery again. I potted one hundred and twenty lettuce seedlings today. It's springtime. Time to garden."

"Yeah, it is." I didn't even own a plant, not a real one, anyway. I wasn't home often enough to water them; they'd just die. "Are any flowers blooming yet?"

I stopped at Kara's desk. A portfolio folder overflowing with sheets of paper leaning against the side caught my eye. I'd never seen it before.

Jenny rattled off flower names; I *yepped* and *yeahed* as she spoke. I squatted down and opened the folder on the floor. My breath hitched at Kara's designs. Page after page of dresses, suits, and couture gowns—all exquisite, elegant, and amazing. *Oh wow.*

Jenny's voice elevated with excitement. "Oh, Hunter, the cherry blossom trees are my favorite. They're so pretty."

"They are, aren't they?" I sifted through more pages. I paused at the tab at the end, written in Kara's cursive handwriting . . . *my wedding gown.* My fingers trembled as I turned the page. There, in long lines, lacy swirls, and cream colors, was a stunning dress.

"Are there any trees flowering around home?" I had to keep talking to Jenny . . . But damn . . . this design. Was this what Kara had wanted to wear if she'd married Conrad? I scanned the page and read the date. The air rushed from my lungs. She'd drawn this two months ago? But . . . but she'd said she didn't want to get married. What was going on? Hadn't she been honest with me? Did she want to get married?

Fuck!

"Hunter? Are you there?"

"Yeah, sorry, Jen." I rubbed my hand over my face. "I'm just tired."

"When are you coming to visit?"

"I'll make sure we visit during promo, okay?" That wasn't until the end of the year, but it would be my only chance.

"I'd love that." There was a scuffle on Jenny's end. "Mom . . . No . . . I'm talking . . . Mom wants to talk to you."

I grinned. Jenny hated giving up the phone. She loved to talk. "Yeah, okay."

Mom's gentle voice drifted through the phone. "Hello sweetheart, how are you?"

"Fine."

"You haven't called in weeks. Is everything okay?"

"Yes. No. Yes. I'm sorry." I stretched my neck from side to side. "Kyle, Gem, and I are working on our new album. We've locked ourselves in this house up near Woodstock to get it done. Then we hit the studio in late May to record . . . hopefully."

"Hopefully?" Mom didn't miss a thing. "Why wouldn't you record?"

"I have vocal nodules." That painful fact slammed into my chest like a derailed freight train. I sat on the floor and stared at Kara's design. She'd look amazing in this dress. As I ran my fingers over the drawing, I told Mom about my doctor's appointment.

"I'm sure you'll be fine." Worry hovered in her voice. "Just do what the doctor says, do the therapy, and you'll get better."

"Thanks, Mom." *Crap.* I may as well bombard her with all the news. "There's one more thing. Kara will probably kill me for telling you, but since you're on the phone . . . we're gonna have a baby. Do the whole surrogacy thing."

Silence.

Not a sound.

Not even a peep, a breath, a whisper.

I closed my eyes and rubbed my brow. "Mom? You hear me?"

The sigh that came down the speaker was as big as a tsunami. "So soon after losing Ryan? Are you sure you're ready? You're so young. You're planning another tour. Why don't you wait a few years?"

Why did everyone think we were too young? Not ready?

"Surrogacy is a long process, at least eighteen months."

"I like Kara. She's a lovely girl. But she's always wanted a baby. She was going to have Ryan with or without you. Is she pressuring you into this?"

Kara always pressured me, but not in a bad way. She made me think about others when I used to be so self-centered. She got me to be more open, even though that was still a struggle. "No. We've made this decision together. It's what we want."

"Are you going to get married?"

"No. She doesn't want to." Staring at her wedding dress design made me question that. Made me question my view on the tradition. I'd been raised to believe that one day I'd meet a nice girl, fall in love, settle down, marry, and have a family. Those things had never been on my radar until I hooked up with Kara, where a one-night stand had altered the course of my life. Everything about our relationship had been backward. It had been fast. Intense. Tumultuous. Would it ever slow down? I hoped not. "We love each other. We're happy. Can't we leave it at that?"

"I just don't want to see you get hurt."

"I don't intend to, Mom." I'd had enough hurt to last a lifetime. I learned from my past mistakes. My future with Kara would be based on our decisions and choices, no one else's. "I've gotta go. It's late. I'm tired. I have to head off early tomorrow. I'll talk soon, okay?"

"Okay. Love you."

"Yeah. Love you too. Bye."

I took one last glance at Kara's design before I put the folder back beside the desk. My mind raced. The past few days had been full of ultimate highs and hard blows. The lack of excitement from our parents about having a baby had left unease in my stomach. Walter had made me question whether I'd ever be good enough for Kara. *Fuck that shit. I love her.* Kara had implied she'd never wanted to get married. *But that dress?* Had I missed something?

No. We wanted a baby.

To hell with everyone who didn't see that we were good for each other or didn't support us. Our friends loved Kara and me. We believed in each other. We'd survive anything together.

The sooner I finished writing the album and returned home, the better. But right now, I had to pack and get ready to leave in the morning. Songs were churning in my head. I couldn't wait to put pen to paper.

Chapter 11

HUNTER

Back upstate to work on the album, I walked from the garage into the house and dumped my duffel bag at the bottom of the stairs. "Kyle? Gem? I'm back."

Shit! My throat. Don't yell.

I headed into the open-plan living room that overlooked the reservoir shimmering in the distance. Gemma sat at the dining table with her hands wrapped around a steaming cup of coffee.

"We're doing it." I held my hands out wide, unable to wipe the smile off my face. "Kar and I are gonna have a baby." I placed my keys and cell phone on the table, pulled out a chair, and sat opposite her. After the hellish lunch yesterday with Kara's parents and the underwhelming phone call with my mom, spending last night with Kara had cleared my mind. It had reaffirmed that having a baby was the right decision for us. Excitement churned through my veins and drummed in my heart. I wanted to channel all this energy into writing new songs. Nothing could dampen my high.

Except maybe Gemma.

Oh no . . . not my rock.

I didn't need her to be upset about the news.

She rested her elbows on the table and rubbed the sleep from her eyes, or maybe it wasn't sleep but shock.

I kicked her foot under the table. "You awake? Did you hear me?" It was near midday, but it looked like she'd just woken up.

Gemma threaded her fingers through her long brown hair and ruffled the silky strands. "Yeah, I did. I'm happy for you. Doesn't mean I don't think you're fucking crazy."

"Come on, Gem." I leaned forward and placed my hands flat on the table. "After talking to you and Kyle about this over the past two weeks, and you with your freakish intuition, you had to know."

Her eyes twinkled. "Yeah, the minute you mentioned babies, I kinda knew which way you'd go." She wrinkled her nose. "I just wanted to be wrong."

"Why?"

She reached over and clutched my hand. "My reason is purely selfish. After everything that had happened to the three of us this year, I wanted some normalcy in our lives. I wanted to live and breathe music again. Take some time to regroup, recharge, and reconnect."

"We will. That's why we're here." I covered her hand with mine. "Gem, I promise you, even when the baby arrives . . . this . . . with you, me, and Kyle . . . will never change. I swear on my life. Music is who we are. Nobody will ever come between us. We're family. Always will be."

She stared at our hands. A small smile curled across her lips. "Are you gonna marry her?"

The whole thought of marriage messed with my head . I ran my thumb over Gemma's wedding and engagement rings. A tug pulled at my belly button. Did I want to bind myself to Kara in that way? The answer was still unclear. "I don't know. She said she doesn't want to get married."

"Kara?" Gemma jerked her chin back. "Are we talking about the same girl?"

"I know. It's weird. I don't think I fit her model of pin-up marriage material. I'm not sure if she completely trusts me, and it upsets her that her dad despises me." I filled Gemma in on our lunch yesterday.

She smirked and leaned back in her chair. "Walter hates

everyone. He thinks we're arrogant, alcoholic, drug-addicted musicians who fuck around and don't deserve our fame and fortune. He thinks that because we won a YouTube contest and were signed with SureHaven, we don't have any real talent, and we won't have any longevity in this business."

So that was what Walter thought. If he cared to open his eyes, he'd see that was not the case. I'd never regret the path we'd taken. SureHaven Records had made us stars. We'd sacrificed our creativity for that. But now, free of contracts, we had control. We wrote and played every song and made every decision about our music. Our last album had outsold anything we'd done with SureHaven. We weren't going anywhere but up.

"And the trust thing with Kar?" She took a sip of her coffee. "That will come. Remember, Conrad broke her heart, and she's worried you won't keep your dick out of other women. I know you've changed. She needs to believe it too. Give her time. Don't ever be ashamed or apologize for your past. We had hell fun and will continue to do so. It's just with one partner now instead of a different one every night."

She was right. I'd never regret the wild times we'd had. But now my heart belonged to Kara. How would our future pan out? I had no idea. Having a baby was a step in the right direction, though. "Thanks, Gem. You're the best."

Her eyes glistened as she gave me a wink. "I know."

But as I closed my eyes, images of Kara's designs flicked through my mind. A wave of uncertainty washed over me. I stared at my fingers and drew squiggles on the table's glass surface. "Gem, how did you know?" My stomach knotted and quivered. "Know that you wanted to marry Kyle?"

She hugged her coffee cup against her chest and rounded her shoulders. Loved-up warmth shimmered in her eyes. Her tough exterior always melted when she talked about Kyle. I loved that my two best friends had fallen in love. "Once we got together, I knew I wanted to spend the rest of my life with him. But yeah, I remember there was a moment. It was one day at rehearsal for our last tour, singing 'Traveled.' He clutched my hand, gazed into my eyes, and bam, it hit me. *Me?* I'd never wanted to get married, but in that split second, underneath the stage lights, everything changed. I wanted to bind myself to him in every way. I wanted to wear his ring. Be his forever. It was that simple."

I scratched my stubble. There'd been no *bam* moment for me. "I haven't experienced anything like that with Kar."

"Maybe you won't. I know you love her. You don't have to get married. You're committed to each other, and you're gonna have a baby. That's exciting." She smiled over the rim of her cup. "I still think you're nuts. In a good way . . . but nuts."

I chuckled and nodded. "Totally."

"What's going on?" Kyle hollered as he lumbered into the living room and headed toward us. "What did I miss?"

"Hunt's lost his mind." Gemma giggled as she jutted her chin toward Kyle. "Did you see it lying around on the floor somewhere?"

"Nope." He kissed her on the head and sat beside her. "Hunt, what've you done now?"

"Decided to have a kid."

"Holy shit." Kyle reached across the table and fist-pumped my hand. "Dude, that's amazing. You've finally sorted out your crap. Bet Kara's ecstatic."

"Yeah, she is." Taking Kara to my hometown and showing her the life I'd had before my fame had sealed the deal. "And man . . . the sex. Holy fuck." I wiped my hand down one side of my face, then the other. My body temperature still hadn't returned to normal. "We seriously went at it all Saturday night and Sunday morning. My dick is so worn out I won't need to jerk off for at least two days."

Every time I licked my lips and swallowed, I could still taste Kara on my tongue. And fuck . . . still feel a dull niggle in my throat. *Damn nodules.*

Kyle chuckled and shook his head. "If you go that long without jerking off, I'll give you a fucking medal."

I threw him a goofy grin. Kyle was right. I probably wouldn't last. "Yeah . . . don't rush out and buy one. The only good thing about having to go back to the city on Wednesday for vocal therapy is I'll swing by home and see Kar. Slip in a quickie."

Ridges deepened on Gemma's brow as she fidgeted with her necklace, sliding the music-note pendant back and forth along the gold chain. "How often do you think you'll need therapy?"

"I'm not sure." I shrugged. "I hope Annelise will just give me some exercises to do, and I'll be done with it. I'll let you know after my appointment."

"Hunt, you do whatever therapy is necessary. No question." Gemma placed her palms on the table. "But if you have to head back for more sessions, when you're here, we'll have to be extra diligent with writing so we can meet our deadlines."

"Absolutely." An invisible wire tightened around my neck. If my nodules didn't heal, I wouldn't even make it to the recording studio. *Fuck.* "If you're worried about time, we could go home. Lock ourselves away at my place and work there."

"Nah, man." Kyle cracked his neck from side to side. "There are too many distractions. You know that. Bec and Sophie would be on the doorstep all the time. Friends would want to catch up and go out. This is the best way we work. Locked away with no interruptions."

My cell phone buzzed. A message from Kara lit the screen.

KARA: MISS YOU ALREADY.

I smiled and texted her back.

ME: SAME. LUV U.

I tossed my cell phone down. "You're right. No interruptions." My cell beeped again. Another message from Kara.

KARA: C U WEDNESDAY FOR LUNCH. 1PM.
I'LL BE NAKED, WAITING FOR YOU.

Anticipation twitched in my dick. I grabbed my phone and replied.

ME: I'M ALREADY HARD. C U IN 2 DAYS.

I put my phone down, and another smile tugged at the corner of my mouth. But when I looked up, a chill ran up my spine.

A muscle in Kyle's jaw ticked.

Gemma's green eyes fired arrows at me, pinning me to the chair. "Hunter?"

Shit. Gemma never called me by my full name. "What?"

"No interferences, right?"

"None." I held up my hands. "I promise." I hated that I'd been preoccupied with baby decisions and Kara's birthday over the past two weeks. Hated that I hadn't been fully focused. But now, that was behind me. I wanted to be consumed by music and churn out some incredible new tunes.

"Good." Her short tone drew me into line.

I didn't want being with Kara to cause problems, or for her to cause a strain between me, Kyle, and Gemma, or for her friendship with Gemma to be tested. This was why I'd wanted Kara here— so we could all hang out, write, and chill, and I could have her in my bed every night. For the first time in my life, envy of Kyle's and Gemma's relationship crawled through my veins. They were together 24/7. Kara and I weren't. *Balance. It's all about balance. I'd find it.*

But right now, it was time to work.

I pushed back my chair and stood. "You two need to get loaded with caffeine." I headed into the kitchen, turned on the coffee machine, and switched on the electric kettle for my tea. "I came up with some wicked lyrics on the way up here. I wanna see if we can spin them into something cool."

"Excellent. Let's go." As Gemma rose to her feet, the chair legs scraped against the glossy tiles. "Anything to stop talking about you and babies."

"But . . ." I stood two inches taller, placed my hand over my chest, and failed to contain my smile. "I love talking about me." Maybe I should rein it in. I'd ear-bashed them enough with my dramas over the past couple of weeks. As the coffee brewed, filling two cups, I folded my arms and rested my hip against the counter. "Gem, are you scared that if I keep talking about babies, you might want one?"

"Fuck no. Not on your life." She came over, grabbed her coffee, and took off toward the studio.

The moment Gemma disappeared down the hallway, I turned to Kyle. "What's gotten into Gem?" She'd been fine moments ago.

"Don't know." Kyle headed for the fridge and grabbed a stack of pancakes the chef had left. "But I'm sure we'll find out."

I spooned two tablespoons of my loose-leaf Throat Coat Tea into the teapot infuser and filled it with boiling water. Gemma had certainly dented my buzz. Why was it that the second I'd resolved one issue, another one sprang to life? The last thing I needed was for Gemma to be upset. Did it have something to do with Kara? My nodules? The baby? All the above? Gemma was my strength, my backbone, my grounding. Whatever was bothering her, music would get to the bottom of it.

Bring it on.

But the air didn't clear all afternoon. Nor the next day.

Every time Kara had called or texted, Gemma had glared at me, played harder, or had stormed out of the studio.

What was with that?

On Wednesday morning, I sat next to Gemma on the sofa in the music room, electric guitars propped on our laps. Kyle was still asleep. The song we'd left unfinished last night had kept me awake in bed until sometime around two.

I flexed my fingers, hovering them over the strings. "Come on, Gem. Something about this chorus isn't right." The tone, the tempo, maybe the whole melody was wrong. Gemma had an unrivaled talent and could twist songs around. I needed her to work her magic.

"It's fine."

No. We never settled for *fine.* Each song had to be phenomenal. Anything less was unacceptable.

I glanced at my phone on the coffee table. *No messages.*

Gemma played the chords fast, stiff, and jagged. It prickled the hair on my arms. Her usual warmth and vibrant energy had taken a plunge to the bottom of the reservoir.

Closing my eyes, I locked my jaw. *This is ridiculous.* I was over her mood.

I was over resting my voice.

I just wanted to sing—to vocalize what I could hear inside my head instead of her trying to interpret the raw notes I played. "No, Gem. Not like that. Do you think it should be higher, and not so fast?" That wasn't right either, but I had to suggest something. "Start here." I strummed the chords—A, E, D. I mouthed the words softly, attempting to relay the melody.

> *Su—mer days —nd star filled n—ghts.*
> *L—ng slow w—lks and br—ght c—ty l—ghts.*
> *Hold—ng your h—nd, steal—ng a s—deways glance.*
> *Tell me h—nestly.*
> *Is this the st—rt of s—mething?*
> *S—mething good. S—mething mad.*
> *S—mething wild. S—mething m—gic.*

It tore my heart apart every time I sang, and my voice cracked.

"Sorry." Her blunt tone badgered my head. "I'm not feeling the vibe yet. Play it again."

I slammed my hand against the strings. The twang reverberated through the amp. "What is your problem? We always talk. We never hold anything back. So spill. You've been pissed at me ever since I told you I wanted to have a kid. I thought you were okay with it."

Her shoulders deflated as she lowered her chin and shook her head.

"Gem?" A shudder rumbled like low thunder through my chest. What was wrong with my Gem? I clutched and rubbed her knee. "You can tell me anything. You know that. No boundaries. No bullshit." We'd been through too much together. Our bond was unbreakable. Nothing she said would ever dent our friendship. "Whatever it is, out with it. Because seeing you like this is killing me."

It seemed like a lifetime passed instead of seconds before she spoke. "It has nothing to do with you having a baby. I'm happy for you and Kar. I know you're excited. But you're not focused."

Focused? I was, wasn't I?

I glanced at my phone on the coffee table again. Still no messages from Kara. I had to leave in ten minutes for therapy.

"See?" She waved her hand toward my cell. "Even now, you're checking your phone. You're here, but your mind is elsewhere." She rested her arm on top of her guitar. "You need to block the outside world. Let the music take over you. You should know what's wrong with this song."

I stared at the sheet of music she'd written, re-read my lyrics, and replayed the tune inside my head. Frustration coursed through my fingertips. "I can't see it. Hear it. It needs your touch."

Gemma played the song. "Yes, but you can usually pick the problem. You're not connecting with the lyrics because you're distracted by Kara's constant calls and texts. We'll just get into a groove, and she'll call. You'll talk for thirty minutes instead of five." She strummed downward, then covered the strings with her hand, cutting off the sound. "I want us to create the best songs we've ever written. We do that when we let the music rule us. You're not allowing that to happen."

The thin edge in her voice punched me low in the gut. *Fuck.* Had I been that bad? I had taken most of Kara's calls. It wasn't my fault I suffered from FOMO. "I'm sorry. I'll tone it down. I'll talk to her."

"Thank you." Her serene tone held a fierce undercurrent. "Kyle feels the same way. We're here to write. Call Kar at the end of the day or when we have breaks. But no interruptions while we're in here."

My phone buzzed on the coffee table. *Fuck. Kara.*

Gemma glared at my cell. Emerald daggers blazed in her eyes like she wanted to stab it.

My fingers twitched to answer the call, but I let it go to voicemail. I held out my hand and patted the air. "Gem, chill. She's calling to find out what time I'll be home."

"Uh-huh." She zipped her fingers down the guitar frets. The screech sliced through the air and pinched the taut tendons in my neck.

"I hate having to go back to the city for therapy and hate that we're losing an afternoon of work. But until my voice is better, I need a bit of slack."

"The therapy isn't the problem."

Shit.

I had been distracted. *Idiot!* But no more. "You and Kyle have me one hundred percent. This album means so much to us. Call me when Kyle gets his ass out of bed and I'll work on this song with you as I drive. Or take the afternoon off, and we'll work on it tonight when I get back. I'll do whatever it takes—you know that." I rubbed her back and gave her a gentle nudge. "I'm sorry. I didn't realize my calls bothered you."

The faintest smile touched her lips as she play-punched my arm. "What do you think no interruptions meant?"

I hooked my hand around her head, drew her close, and kissed the top of it. "You should've told me sooner, not let it fester. Don't do that. I don't want you pissed at me. Not ever. I'll talk to Kar. She'll be cool." *Probably not. Fuck!*

There was nothing like pressure from Kyle and Gemma to be more focused. Nothing like being worried about my vocal nodules and having therapy. Nothing like my girlfriend wanting every second of my attention. Everybody wanted a fucking piece of me, but there wasn't enough of me to go around. "I've gotta go." I stood and placed my guitar on the rack. "We'll finish this song later."

"Will do." She flopped back onto the sofa and continued to play. "Kyle and I'll be here."

My chest cinched. The pounding in my head grew stronger. I hated having to leave. What if they came up with awesome lyrics, an amazing riff, or a sick beat without me? I didn't want to miss out on any part of this album's creation. *Fuck!* I had FOMO. *Big time.*

I picked up my journal and cell phone and stormed out of the studio. I needed to get out of the house before I blew a circuit. I'd let the roar of my supercar's engine rev through my veins as I raced back to the city. I'd rework that song in my head until I found the right melody. I'd stop home, take Kara to bed and make hard, hot love to her until she screamed my name.

Damn I need a good fuck. Some good ol' stress relief.

But Gemma had been right. I had to zero in on our music, not Kara. I had to stop thinking with my dick. *That'll be a first.* I wouldn't let Gemma and Kyle down. Not ever.

When I got back tonight, I'd be refreshed. Reset. Recharged.

I grabbed my keys, my backpack, and a bottle of water. I headed to the garage. I jumped in my car, planted my foot, and sped toward the city.

I had to fix the song, have sex, and do therapy.

I couldn't wait for this afternoon to be over. Then I could get back here and do what I was meant to do. Write music. With Kyle and Gemma. With no more interruptions.

Chapter 12

HUNTER

Fucking traffic. The drive back to the city was a nightmare. The traffic had made me late. With no time to spare, I'd driven straight to vocal therapy. I hadn't swung by home to see Kara. Now, she was pissed at me. So was my dick. I'd racked up a list. Gemma and Kyle were frustrated by my lack of concentration. Mick had yelled at me for driving too fast on the freeway.

I was on a roll. How many more people would I infuriate today?

Or worse . . . who would irk the fuck out of me?

Annelise, my vocal therapist, was doing a fine job.

"Hunter." Sitting opposite me at her desk, she scanned the emailed report and images of my vocal cords she'd received from Vanessa, my otolaryngologist. With her hair in a tight bun, thin-framed glasses and pencil skirt, Annelise had that whole sexy businesswoman thing going on but had the personality of a ruthless drill sergeant. I'd learned that the hard way working with her preparing for our last tour. If I'd goofed around, she'd make me do twice as many vocal exercises as Gemma and Kyle combined. "Your nodules are bad. I'm not sure if therapy will correct them. Not within the timeframes you want, or ever."

That wasn't what I wanted to hear.

Digging my fingers into my thighs, I took a deep breath. "It has to, Lise. I need to give this my best shot."

"If you had surgery, you'd heal in several weeks." She pushed her glasses higher on the bridge of her nose. "You don't want to damage your voice further."

"I won't. I assure you." Determination set like concrete in my bones. I'd had enough of people telling me what I should and shouldn't do, or what was and wasn't possible. *Gemma. Kyle. Kara. Vanessa. Now Annelise*? "I'll do the therapy." I'd book that in. "I won't drink." The odd whiskey wouldn't hurt. "I won't overexert myself." Except sex—I couldn't go without that. Maybe just not like the marathon session I'd had last weekend. *Sorry, Kar.* "I've got this."

"For your sake, I hope so." She sighed, smoothed her hands down her skirt, and stood. "If you're going to be stubborn, I promise to do my best to get those cords back into shape, and I hope the nodules will heal." Pointing to the padded yoga mat on the floor by the piano, her sympathetic smile turned into a wicked grin. The niceties were over. It was time for torture. "Let's begin with some warm-up exercises."

I rolled my eyes, fell to my knees, and crawled onto the mat. I could do these drills without thinking. Lying on my back, knees bent, I ran through her relaxation techniques and easy onsets. With my mouth partially closed, I made *Nng*, *Zzz* and *Vvv* sounds. Then, sitting upright, I did straw phonation. Controlling my breath, I blew voiced and voiceless sounds into a glass of water. The hardest things to do were not to laugh or pull weird faces at Annelise as I did them . . . or stop my mind from wandering.

A tune played inside my head. I'd come up with a wicked beat during my drive here. It was perfect for the song I'd been working on with Gemma this morning. I'd recorded it, hummed it into my voice memo, and couldn't wait to get back to the studio to write the music. That's where I wanted to be, immersed in songwriting. But instead, I was stuck here, running through mind-numbing vocal exercises.

"Hunter?" Annelise kicked her pump against my Nike. "Are

you with me? Or daydreaming?"

"I'm here." *Unfortunately.*

She waved toward the bare wall a few feet from the piano. "For the next exercise, come over here, stand with your back flat against the wall, and squat to engage your core. Now that your voice is warmed up, let's see where it falters when you sing."

Diaphragm breathing exercises. I half-grinned as I followed her across the room. I'd prefer to do other things up against the wall. Something that involved Kara, being naked, and her long legs wrapped around my waist. If she didn't have to head out to the Hamptons for a boutique opening, I'd be high-tailing it home to make up for lost time earlier today.

But the moment my spine hit the wall, and I sank into position, nerves wrapped around my throat like icy-cold fingers and squeezed. Would my voice hold? Even after warming up? *Crap.* I wouldn't let doubt win. "Lise, you know I can do this."

"We'll see." Annelise stood by the piano. Her long French-manicured nails tapped against the keys. "When I play a note, hum for ten seconds, soft, slow, and consistent. Ready?"

I sucked in my stomach and filled my lungs to capacity. As she played F3, I sang. "Hmmmmmmmmmmmmm." *Phew. Too easy.*

"Up we go. Next one." Annelise hit A3.

"Hmmmmmmmmmmmm."

By the time Annelise hit Middle C, boredom dripped from every pore in my body. This was ridiculous. Pointless. Why couldn't she give me something difficult? These exercises were for beginners.

She clipped the top of my head with her fingertips. "Concentrate."

"Hey," I snapped, then grinned. Good thing we were friends.

She hit E4.

I mumbled under my breath, inhaled and hummed. "Ar—mmm—mmm—m—"

Shit. My heart stumbled and collapsed onto the floor like a house of cards.

"There it is." Annelise clicked her fingers and pointed at me.

I winced like she'd slapped me in the face. Even after vocal rest and warming up properly, I still couldn't scale my voice. *Fuck!*

"And what's with this?" She stepped toward me and stabbed her finger against my shoulders. "Are you lazy? You're all shoulders when you breathe. They shouldn't move." Then she flicked the back of her hand against my diaphragm. "Is this on vacation? It better not be. Use it. And you hard-onset that hum."

"I did not." *Oh shit, did I?* My mind had been on other things . . . Kara, songs, getting out of there.

"Oh. Yes. You. Did." She'd been our voice coach for years. She didn't miss a thing. "You're not breathing properly. You're carrying way too much tension in your neck. You've picked up some bad habits since I saw you before your last tour."

"No. I just wasn't concentrating." Bad habits? *Never.* I'd always been adamant about singing correctly.

"The hum never lies." There was too much nonchalance in her tone. "Let's run through this again. This time, to lessen the strain on your voice, hold the hum for five seconds instead of ten. Ready?"

Crap. "Yes." I wriggled my back against the wall, engaged my stomach muscles, ready to hum. But my cell phone rang in the back pocket of my jeans.

Kara.

What could she want? Just when I'd refocused, Kara scattered my thoughts like marbles dropped on a floor.

"Just give me a sec." I needed a break from Annelise's ego-crushing, fear-strangling therapy anyway. I walked over to the window on the opposite side of the room and answered Kara's call. "Hey. What's up?"

"How was therapy?"

"I'm still here."

"Oh, shit. Sorry. I thought you'd be finished by now."

"No. I'm still being tortured." I winked at Annelise and gave her a thin smile.

"Oh no . . . anyway. I'll be quick." Kara didn't miss a beat. "Can you come with me to the surrogacy agency meetings on Friday? The sooner we decide on which one to use, the sooner we can sign the paperwork, book in for our counseling sessions, and work out what type of person we want for a surrogate. You also have to have a medical—well, a sperm test—to make sure your swimmers are swimming. Do you want me to make the appointment for you?"

A dull throb erupted in my temples. Did she not take a breath? "Whoa. Kar. What the fuck?" I closed and rubbed my eyes. *So. Not. Urgent.* "Slow down. Why the hell do I have to have a test? I think from knocking you up the first time we know there is nothing wrong with my swimmers."

"It's just procedure. So we don't waste my eggs."

Her voice was so light and airy, so happy, as if she had no cares in the world. But for me, every second I wasn't writing music, not resting my voice, not with her, not singing, not with Kyle and Gemma, was lodging compounding tension deeper into the back of my neck. It knotted in my stomach and twisted tighter and tighter between my shoulder blades. "Fuck." I wiped my hand down my face. "I'm not being tested now. No freaking way."

"But I want to make sure we're set to go."

"We will be."

She groaned, then sighed. "Fine."

Oh, she so wasn't. But she'd have to live with it. I wasn't jizzing into a cup until absolutely necessary.

"Also . . ." Her tone dialed up to rapid-fire work mode. "Ivory Mink wants to dress you. This is so exciting. She's huge. I've got a fitting lined up for the three of you when you come home."

My head fell back, and I stared at the ceiling. *Was she serious? Telling me this now? In the middle of an appointment? To tell me things that could wait or that she could just put into my calendar?* I bit down on my molars and sucked in a jagged breath. My wire thinned, close to snapping. "That's great. But. I'm. At. Therapy. I have to go."

"Oh. Okay." She spoke at one hundred miles an hour. "I'm just so excited about work and having a baby."

"I know you are. I am too." Not right now, I wasn't. "Love you. Bye." I ended the call and stuffed my cell phone back into my pocket. *Fuck!* Were all girlfriends this demanding? This interrupting? *Whoa.* Kara did call and text a lot. But I was a fool for always answering. Well, not anymore. *No. Freaking. Way.* I had to get my shit together. I'd talk to Kara and tell her to tone it down. After this session.

That wasn't a conversation I looked forward to. I'd prefer to ignore problems and hoped they'd go away.

I headed over to Annelise. "I'm so sorry about that."

Annelise's hazel eyes blazed as bright as the fluorescents overhead. "That's okay. But it was hard not to overhear. Are you and Kara going to have a baby?"

Crap. Me and my big mouth. A muscle in my jaw ticked like a time bomb. I didn't need this information to leak to the media. I didn't want to be hounded in interviews, cover up the truth, or upset Kara. We'd gone through enough harassment after losing Ryan. "No. Yes. Fuck."

"Hunter, don't stress." She peered up at me, her smile small but sweet. "Patient confidentiality, remember?"

I rubbed my hand over the tip of my chin. I'd known her for years. I could trust Annelise. "Yeah, we're looking into surrogacy." Just the thought of having a baby, committing to it, still felt surreal. In a good way, though.

"I wish the two of you the very best."

"Thanks." I leaned back against the wall and squatted into position. "But I don't want to think about babies until my voice is better. Let's do this exercise again."

After twenty minutes of humming and making weird chanting sounds, and running through several breathing techniques, I straightened and shook the ache from my legs.

Annelise dipped her head. "You did well today, Hunter. But there's a lot of work to do. Going forward, you'll need at least two sessions a week. Rest as much as possible. If you must sing, focus temporarily on more head voice than mixed and chest. It's less strain on your vocal cords." She frowned and waved her finger at me. "But no belting and avoid hard onsets."

"But—"

"No buts. Fixing your voice will take time and patience.

During your sessions, we'll work on your breathing management, articulation, trills, and resonance. We'll also work on relaxation and visualization techniques too."

Oh, I'd been visualizing all right, but too often I'd pictured Kara naked, not focused on my singing. *Idiot.*

I picked up my backpack off the floor and hooked it over my shoulder. "Lise, we're in the middle of writing an album and record next month. I can't afford to take off half a day, twice a week, to come back to the city. Can we Zoom our sessions or, even better, will you come to me? We're staying at this house up near Woodstock. I'll pay for your time, your travel, any expenses, and even feed you. We have a chef at our beck and call."

"I can't do that." She folded her arms and leaned her hip against her desk. "I have other clients."

"Don't care." Hardness set in my jaw. I wouldn't take no for an answer. "Reschedule them."

"No."

"How many patients do you see in a day?"

She lifted her chin a fraction of an inch. "Six or seven. Why?"

"I'll double your daily rate. I'll hire a driver for you. Just come. Please?" I play-punched her arm and threw her my best irresistible smile, packed with charm.

She inhaled sharply and smoothed her hands over her skirt again. "Fine. But there is no need to double my rate. We'll do one session via Zoom, and you can book a driver for the other. I'll do this because I care about you and won't mind escaping the city once a week. Plus, your cords will be an interesting challenge. I'll have my assistant let you know what days I'll be there. Please email me the address."

"Done." I gave her a huge hug. "Thank you. You're the best."

"Okay. Get going." She pushed out of my embrace and walked me to the door. "Make sure to practice your soft onsets and hums every day. Take it slow. Be patient."

"I'll do my best." But I was about as patient as a thoroughbred in a barrier before a big race. I hated having to hold on to my reins, stay in control, and walk instead of gallop. "See you soon, Lise."

I stormed out of the doctor's office, jumped in my car, and headed north. I punched my fist against the steering wheel. I'd hoped Annelise would've given me some exercises to do for a couple of weeks and that would've been it. Her confirming my nodules weren't good sent jolting shockwaves through my heart.

Maybe I could learn to live with the nodules.

Was that even possible?

Some singers went for years before being diagnosed with nodules. I had to find a way to sing with them. Modify my techniques so I wouldn't damage my voice further.

Fuck.

As I sped up the highway, my head ached from a day of overload.

But it wasn't over yet. I had one more issue to deal with. *Kara.*

I cracked my neck from side to side and dialed her number.

Her voice filled the car's Bluetooth connection. "Hi, babe. I'm almost at Southampton. Giles has cursed the whole way. What is with the traffic today? Where are you?"

"I'm on the freeway, about to cross the George Washington Bridge." I planted my foot on the gas. The horsepower in my car kicked in, and I overtook an Uber Eats delivery guy on a mint-green Vespa. *Ugh.* Those scooters shouldn't be allowed on the road. *Too slow.* "Therapy sucked. I need two sessions a week."

"Oh. That isn't good. But yay. We can catch up when you come back for them."

"No. I won't be coming home for my appointments." I winced. "Annelise will come to me."

"Oh." I could picture her racking her brain. "So, does that mean I won't see you until the awards show in three weeks?"

"Yeah. Unless you come visit."

"You know I can't." Disappointment hovered in her voice. "I have something on every day. And you need to focus."

"Yes, I do. And . . . about that." I wrung my hands on the steering wheel, checked my rear-view mirror, and merged onto the bridge. "We need to tone down the number of times we call and text each day." I hated this. She'd loathe it even more. Her messages helped take my mind off my worries. She wouldn't like the lack of attention. "Gem and Kyle had a go at me. We rented this studio to avoid distractions. So, we'll have to talk first thing in the morning or late at night when I'm finished."

"So, I can't call you?"

"Not during writing time. The hours we work vary each day, so it's best I call you when I'm free."

"But there are so many things we have to discuss. We need to sort out having a baby, and work, and shows, and—"

"And we will. When I'm home." I wouldn't let her guilt-trip me into feeling bad for dedicating time to my work. This was part of my job. I rarely had to stand up for what I wanted, but when I did, nothing swayed me. I'd only be away for a few more weeks. "Okay?"

Silence. It drilled into my skull and made my head ache.

"Fine." Her sharp tone cut like ice.

Shit! Every time she'd said things were *'fine'*, I knew otherwise.

"Hunt, I can't change the surrogacy agency meetings. They took too long to secure. You should be there."

I clenched my teeth and tugged on my seatbelt. I wanted to be involved, but the timeframes didn't align. With a deep breath, I set titanium in my resolve. "I'm sure you'll manage without me. We can talk about the details afterward. But you're the one who has to be happy with the surrogacy agency. I'll go with whoever you want. I'm sorry I can't make it. The album comes first for now. I promise to call. It just might be at weird times."

"Whatever," she sighed. "I have to go. Talk to you later."

"Sure. Love you. Bye."

I ended the call.

Fuck. She wasn't happy. But I'd had to draw the line.

This was supposed to be one of the best times in my life. It was almost summer. I was about to record a new album. I had a great girlfriend and was planning to have a baby. But instead of being excited, I had to do therapy, rest my voice, manage my time better, stay off my phone and stop my FOMO. I didn't like these new rules and restrictions. Rules and I weren't friends. *Damn it!*

I thumped my fist against the steering wheel again. Hitting the highway, heading for Woodstock, I clenched my jaw and put my foot down harder. I drove faster and faster. There was too much shit to sort out. Too much to do. Too much stress. How was my voice supposed to heal when every tendon in my neck was tighter than the space between a virgin's legs?

Arrrrgh!

So much for fucking relaxing.

I needed music. I needed a good jam. I needed it now.

Chapter 13

KARA

I begged the hotel elevator to go faster. I had half an hour to dress Gemma and the guys for the red carpet. I'd spent most of the day running around Manhattan, visiting private showrooms, sourcing a backup dress for Gemma. The one I'd ordered from Italy for her to wear to the Women in Entertainment Awards tonight hadn't arrived. But just as I was about to leave home, the courier had turned up with the dress in hand.

Nothing like cutting it close.

With the garment bags draped over one arm, I fanned my face with the other. I could do this. I could dress everyone for the red carpet in time. If Dolce and Gabbana had made the dress perfectly to Gemma's measurements, all would go to plan. I had the backup option if needed.

But once everyone was in their outfits . . . Hunter was mine.

I hadn't seen him for three weeks. Not since my birthday weekend.

Something good had come out of our time apart, though. I'd spent more time with my sister. We'd caught up for drinks, lunch, and she'd gone with me to meet the surrogacy agencies. After reviewing legal documentation and services, talking with lawyers, and going back and forth with Hunter via email and phone calls,

I'd decided on which one to use.

In a few hours, Hunter and I would be another step closer to having a baby.

Tomorrow, we'll sign the paperwork.

The zing in my veins couldn't be contained.

No amount of music, or work, or *limit-your-number-of-phone-calls-per-day* rules would keep Hunter and me apart. I wanted his hands on me all night. And I hoped the dress I'd selected to wear would ensure that happened. The butterflies in my stomach didn't just flutter, they swirled in overdrive. I normally would've snapped up this dress that was similar in style to J.Lo's Versace gown for Gemma to wear. But I'd wanted to up my sexy game and impress Hunter. And show the media I wasn't a boring, conservative uptown girl anymore. I placed my hand on my stomach to settle my jittery nerves.

Shit. I hope I can pull this dress off.

As the Marriott Hotel's elevator took me up to Everhide's suite, I placed my hand across one breast and then the other, wriggling them to make sure the Hollywood Tape was intact. I didn't want my boobs to fall out of the dress's plunging neckline. Smoothing my hand over the front of the silky peacock-blue skirt, I caught hold of the floor-length flowing fabric and tugged the front closed so the daring split up the center didn't show off my panties. This was the most audacious dress I'd ever worn. Despite being a touch apprehensive, I felt sexy and powerful, just like a sensual siren.

Owning it.

The doors opened, and I grabbed the handle on my cabin-sized bag full of stylist essentials—spare stilettos for Gemma, ties for the guys, needles and threads, scissors, socks, underwear, pins, and more trinkets than a haberdashery store—and dashed toward their suite. I swiped my access card and swept into the room.

Gemma sat at the desk in a robe while Carla, Everhide's make-up artist, applied finishing touches to her hair and makeup. Sophie paced the floor with her cell phone to her ear. Relief washed over her face as I crossed the suite.

"I'm here." I dumped the gowns on the sofa and unzipped the

main bag. I held up the short, one-shoulder, corseted black lace dress toward Gemma.

"Oh wow." She rushed forward and ran her hands over the fabric. "This is amazing. Quick. Get me into it. We're late." She ripped off her robe and stepped into the dress.

As I did up the zip, I scanned the suite. I hadn't had time to draw breath. "Where are Lexi and the guys?"

"Already dressed and gone." Gemma wriggled the outfit into place over her hips. She adjusted her boobs into the fitted top and mushed them together to form some cleavage . . . but failed. "They headed down to the foyer for pre-function drinks."

"Oh. Okay." *Damn it*. I'd wanted to see Hunter and make sure he was okay. "How's Hunt's voice holding up?"

"It's not any better." Worry skimmed beneath the surface of Gemma's voice as she slipped her toes into a pair of black glittery pumps. "We've changed the song for tonight. He's singing half of what he normally does."

My chest ached. He hadn't talked a lot about his nodules since his diagnosis. Maybe he didn't want me to worry, but I did. Tonight, I planned to make him forget all about his vocal cords when I got the chance.

Taking a step back, I assessed Gemma's dress. She looked like a goddess in anything, and this design was no exception. It hugged her petite, slender figure and showed off her gorgeous legs and toned arms. I walked around her checking the dress. "Does it fit okay? Any issues? Problems?"

"It's a bit loose around the top." She clutched her boobs and wriggled the corset.

"Wait." I dug into my bag of tricks and pulled out a pair of silicone bra fillers. "Stick these in." I handed them to her, and she stuffed them into the top. "Perfect. Let's go."

"Wait up, girl." Gemma caught my hand and eyed me up and down with a bedazzled glint in her gaze. She waved her hand toward my dress. "What is this? This is sexy as fuck. Like *hello-baby* wow!"

Carla nodded her approval as she packed up her makeup

kit. Sophie licked her fingertip, then touched the air, and made a sizzling sound. "Hot."

"Really?" I flicked the skirt and did a twirl. "It's not too much?"

"Ah . . . no. You look fucking fabulous." Gemma grabbed her clutch off the desk and gave me a cheeky wink. "Hunt won't keep his hands off you."

"That's the plan." I swiped my evening bag off the sofa and followed Gemma to the door.

But just before she opened it, she spun around. "Kar, can we keep the plans cool until later? We have to walk the red carpet, perform, then sit through the awards dinner. After that, I don't care what you do."

I drew a quick breath and pulled back my shoulders. More rules. I wouldn't play by any tonight.

I hadn't realized how much I called or texted Hunter until I'd been told to stop. But now our previously fun and flirty conversations throughout the day had turned into quick, to-the-point, sometimes tense, *I'm-too-tired-to-talk* conversations each night about the album's progress, my work, and our surrogacy agency options. Time apart had been hard. I couldn't wait until he came home in a couple of weeks so life could return to normal. "Gem, we both know Hunt won't miss the chance to be in front of a camera or perform. But I won't make any promises about how he'll look. He might be a little ruffled."

Gemma giggled and smacked her clutch against my arm. "Sassy. I like it. But work first . . . then play."

I tightened my hold on my evening bag and dug my fingernails into the beaded fabric. My blood set to simmer. I'd lost count of the number of times I'd had to cover for Gemma and Kyle, fix their attire, hair, and makeup because they couldn't keep their hands off each other. I was meticulous in time management. I'd fooled around with Hunter many times before shows, events, or appearances, and not once had he been late. I wasn't about to change that. "Since when have you ever played by the rules?"

Gemma fluttered her eyelashes and shrugged a sexy shoulder. "Never. Let's go have some fun."

"Here's hoping."

In the elevator, I rested my head back against the mirrored wall. Ever since my friends began work on their new album, time with Hunter had become a sensitive issue, even more so since he'd disappeared upstate to write. Parts of our lives would always require us to be apart—he'd be musicking with Kyle and Gemma; I'd be sourcing fashion from across the globe; and some of our social circles would never cross. That wouldn't change. But were our differences too great for *us* to work long-term?

No, don't go there.

My love for him squashed the thought like a bug and flicked it out the window. A smile curled across my lips, and warmth enveloped my heart. Our future *was* together. I looked forward to the day when we had a child, and I'd have a piece of Hunter that no one else had.

And we'll take a step closer to that tomorrow.

Stepping into the foyer on the sixth floor, I scanned the busy crowd. There was no sign of Hunter or our friends.

"Let's see if they're at the bar." Gemma pointed at the drinks service area across the other side of the room.

"Lead the way." I checked that my dress was in place. There were no apparent malfunctions. Everything was taped in.

Trailing behind Gemma and Sophie, I put one sparkling stiletto in front of the other, and strode through the room full of rock, television, and movie stars, VIPs, and industry executives. Music droned through the speakers, barely audible over everyone's loud chatter. Men with drinks in hand, and dressed in expensive tailored suits laughed in groups. Women waving glasses of champagne and decked out in designer gowns and elaborate couture clustered together. More fragrance and exotic scents than the perfume counters at Bloomingdale's filled the air.

As I reached the center of the room, an invisible force pulled me to a halt. Electric tingles shivered up my spine. I smiled and spun around. Hunter, rocking a black Tom Ford suit and tie, strode toward me like I was the hottest ticket in town. My heartbeat quickened to a foxtrot. Silver shards of fire blazed in his azure eyes as his gaze swept up my legs, over my stomach, across my breasts, and settled on my face.

His arm slid around my waist. His spicy cologne filled my head as he pressed his palm into the small of my back and pulled me hard against his chest. "Oh. My. God." He growled low and hot into my ear. "You look fucking incredible. Don't move, because I got a boner the second I saw you."

Shit. He wasn't joking.

"You've given every man in this room a hard-on."

"I have not." Heat rose up my neck and flushed my cheeks.

"Oh yeah? Look."

Holding me tight, he turned me around. People stared. I'd been so intent on finding Hunter, I hadn't noticed. Some glances were Hannibal Lecter-levels of creepy. Some were green with envy. Too many blazed with *what-the-fuck-is-she-wearing* judgment. Prickles crawled beneath my skin. I didn't know whether to steal Hunter's dinner jacket and cover up or strut around the room like I was on a catwalk and strike a pose.

Hunter grabbed my hand and drew me over to a clearing at the far side of the foyer. He glared at the group of men standing nearby.

"Hunt, what's wrong?"

He jerked his head toward the crowded room. "Every man here is eye-fucking you."

"No, they're not." Yeah. They kinda were. *Weird. Creepy.* I'd had a lot of attention thrown my way since I'd become Hunter's girlfriend, but I'd never experienced a lot of lustful, desire-filled looks like this before. It made me uncomfortable. But I wouldn't let Hunter see they affected me. I'd worn a provocative dress for Hunter, fuck everyone else. I raised an eyebrow. "I thought you didn't get jealous?"

"I'm not jealous. I'm making sure you're okay because everyone is gawking at you."

Sweet of him to have noticed and cared. But the rod in my back stiffened. I jutted out my chest just to show him how fantastic my D-cup tits looked in this gown. "So, what? You don't want me to wear sexy dresses? You really don't like anyone else looking at me?"

His gaze fell to my cleavage. Hunger flashed in his eyes, but he ripped them back to meet my gaze. "You can wear whatever you want. But this isn't you."

My simmering blood approached boiling point. *He does what he wants. Wears what he wants. Why can't I?* "Why isn't this me?"

"Because you're classy and elegant." His voice was a harsh whisper. "At home, you can dress up in anything sexy and as skimpy as you like. Trust me, I love it when you do. But that's for my eyes only, not half of New York."

Who was he to tell me what to wear? Fire skipped through my veins like a line of gunpowder set alight. "I thought you'd like it. I've missed you and wanted to ensure you wouldn't keep your hands off me."

He straightened his tie as if he were sweltering underneath his collar. "My hands would be on you regardless of what you wore. But if that dress makes you feel fabulous, great."

His clipped voice fueled my anger. Nothing about this reunion had gone according to plan. I lifted my chin. "It does. I feel confident and beautiful." Well . . . I had felt that way, but now with half the room looking at me like I was the appetizer, I wasn't so sure anymore.

He stepped in close, placed his hands on my hips, and lowered his voice. "And I'm all for that. But just so you know, you don't have to wear things like this if you don't want to. I love you for you. I feel amazing whenever I'm by your side, like I'm the luckiest man alive. Every day, I'm mind-blown that you want to be with someone like me. That I'm the one you want to be with."

My insides wanted to melt, but I drew in a deep breath, remaining defiant. "I'm sick of the press saying I'm plain and boring. Tonight, I want them to go *wow.*"

"Fuck what they say." He flicked his hand toward the roped-off press area full of reporters and cameras by the entrance to the main function room. "There'll always be assholes who write trash about us. Learn to ignore them."

My heart lurched against my ribs. I'd tried. Especially after Ryan's death and after I'd first hooked up with Hunter. *Damn it.* Had I been a fool to wear this dress?

No.

I'd seen the way he looked at women at other functions wearing similar attire. I wanted him to look at me like that when we were out, not just when we were at home. "Hunt, for once I wanted to be your hot, sexy girlfriend. Is there something wrong with that?"

"No . . . yes . . . no. Shit. I just want you to be you." He closed his eyes and tensed his jaw. Edging closer, he erased the gap between us. His warmth surrounded me as he cupped my face. "Pearl, I'm sorry. I don't want to fight. I've missed you like fucking crazy. My balls are aching." The heat from his touch seeped into my skin and doused my fiery attitude, igniting me with want. He hooked a loose strand of my hair behind my ear and softened his tone. "No matter what you wear, you're fucking sexy. Beautiful. Smart. Talented. Gorgeous. And *mine.*"

I placed my hand on his chest and fidgeted with a button on his dress shirt. "Hunt, the way you're looking at me right now made wearing this dress worth it."

He brushed his lips against mine and teased my mouth with a flick of his tongue. His eyes smoldered as he gave me a devilish smile. "It's not because of the dress. I haven't seen you for weeks. I'm horny as hell and missed you too damn much."

I threaded my hand beneath his dinner jacket, then clutched his fine ass. "How much?"

He kissed up the side of my neck and pressed his crotch against me. "This much."

Oh, God. He's hard. My throat turned dry. An ache erupted between my thighs. "We have to walk the red carpet in twenty minutes."

"I only need five." He grabbed my hand and dragged me across the room.

Yay.

But halfway through the foyer, someone caught my arm and

pulled me to a halt.

Shit. Who could possibly want to talk to me?

I turned to make quick excuses, but my eyes widened when I saw my favorite former client. "Elise? Hi. How are you?" I pinned on a sweet smile as I pried my hand out of Hunter's vise-like hold. I hugged Elise. I hadn't seen her since I'd left Conrad's Fashion House.

"I'm fabulous, as always, dear." Elise flicked her hand. The diamond bling on her wrist jingled and jangled. Elise peered at Hunter. "And is this your handsome beau?"

"Yes." I smiled, ignoring Hunter tugging on the back of my dress. I placed my hand on his arm. "Hunter, this is Elise. I used to design for her at Conrad's."

Hunter transformed into rock-star mode. His eyes sparkled. His smile dazzled with all its panty-dropping power. He took Elise's hand, drew it to his mouth, and kissed the back of it. "Nice to meet you."

"Oh." Elise blushed and fluttered her eyelashes. "So, you're the one who stole my designer?"

"Afraid so." He hooked his arms around my waist and dug his fingers into my hip, reminding me that time was of the essence. "I'm very lucky to have found such an amazing woman."

Elise took a dainty sip of her champagne. "Kara, I miss you at Conrad's. Where are you working now? I'd come to you for my dresses without question."

"Thank you, but I don't design anymore." The need to do so had been put on the back burner. The drawings and sketches I'd played around with over the past several months would remain tucked away in the home office. I loved my work and styling Everhide and a few friends. It was different, exciting, and challenging. I had no room in my schedule to take on anymore projects.

"She should design. She's *very* talented." Hunter softly and slowly scraped his fingernails up my bare back, threaded his fingers underneath my long hair, and kneaded the nape of my neck. His touch sent goosebumps spiraling across my flesh. I needed to have him. Pressing my legs together didn't quell the agony. He leaned in to kiss my cheek, then whispered in my ear, "But right now, I want you to be dirty. Dirty as fuck. Because, oh my God, I want you . . . now."

My knees weakened. *Oh, shit.* When Hunter talked like that, I turned into a hot mess. I swayed on my feet. My head spun like I was drunk, but I hadn't touched a drop. I had to get out of there, or I'd ravish Hunter in the middle of the floor.

Hunter's hand slipped to my waist. His fingers dug into my hip like metal claws. Commanding. Controlling. Claiming. The heat radiating off him ignited the air around us. Soon, I'd self-combust. Hunter dipped his chin at Elise. "Will you please excuse us? We have business to attend to."

"Yes, go." She waved us off. "Enjoy the evening."

Taking my hand, he charged toward the exit. We'd made a few yards before Ty, an R&B artist, hollered at Hunter.

Crap.

"Bro, it's good to see you." He stepped forward to greet Hunter.

Hunter's grip tightened on my hand so much, I thought he'd break my fingers. At least I wasn't the only one frazzled by the interruptions. "Yep. Sure is." Hunter slapped him on the back but barely broke his stride. "Bud, we'll catch up soon. Gotta go."

A low giggle escaped me. Hunter was on a mission. I loved it.

Before I had time to draw breath, he dragged me down the hallway full of meeting rooms. He tried door after door.

All locked.

Damn.

But the last one wasn't.

Chapter 14

KARA

Hunter pulled me inside a small meeting room and locked the door. All the venetian blinds were already shut. He caught me in his arms and walked me backward until my butt connected with the oval boardroom table.

"God, I've missed you." He kissed me, hot and hard. With a flick of his tongue, it became totally X-rated. Hot breath. Fiery tongues. Delicious taste. His hands were in my hair. On my boobs. Clutching my ass.

I whispered over our kisses and ripped off his dinner jacket. "We have ten minutes."

"I need less than two."

Shivers coiled up my spine. As he kissed my neck, he clutched handfuls of my skirt, ruffling the fabric up around my waist. The split skirt fell in soft folds on either side of my hips on the table.

He grinned against my lips. "I think I'm loving this dress more and more."

"Me too." Grabbing his belt buckle, I yanked it undone. My long fingernails fumbled with his fly, unzipped his suit pants, and released his rock-hard cock from his boxer briefs. *Oh yes.* Taking hold of him, I rubbed his dick. Smooth velvet over solid steel. "I think I like this more."

A low growl rumbled deep in his throat. "Fuck, I've missed your touch." He thrust against my hand. Once. Twice. Then, he took a step back. But it wasn't to stop. With nimble fingers, he yanked off my skimpy panties, raked his fingertips up my bare thighs, then slid them between my legs. My heartbeat jumped. My insides clenched in anticipation. *Yes. Touch me.*

A wicked grin inched across his gorgeous lips. He licked his thumb, pressed it against my clit and rubbed it in slow circles. *Oh wow.* The cool dampness against my blazing flesh shot shards of fire and ice into my core. My blood rushed to my head. As he drove a finger deep inside me, my body shuddered against him. *Yes.*

He moaned, deep and hungry. "I love it when you're wet for me."

I popped open his shirt buttons and glided my fingertips over his smooth chest, needing to feel every inch of his gorgeous body. "I don't need the foreplay." I hooked my leg around his hips and pulled him forward. "I want you inside me. Now."

"I won't say no to that." Grinning, he teased his cock against my opening. With a tilt of his hips, he entered me, gentle but firm . . . and right in deep. "That's. So. Good."

The moment our bodies connected and moved, heat charged through my veins. "God, I've needed you." My voice came out a breathless pant. Threading my fingers through his loose hair, I clutched the back of his head and drew his lips to mine. Three weeks of tension disappeared. "If you're going to fuck me like this, maybe you should go away more often."

"No. Being away from you is killing me." He thrust languid and slow, then hard and hot. "You have me until tomorrow night. We're gonna do this at every chance we get. We're gonna do it backstage. At home. Before signing up for a baby. And after."

My heart swelled to the size of the sun and blazed with summery warmth. He knew just what to say at just the right moment. "I'd love that."

With a deep moan, he pounded into me. Goosebumps skipped across my skin. As I brushed my hands over his thighs, his butt, and his back, every muscle in his body tensed, straining to fuck me quicker. Harder. Faster. The pressure on my clit spiraled me higher and higher. *More. There. Yes. YES!*

My orgasm ripped through me. Curling my toes, I savored the shudders striking every one of my nerve endings, our hot breaths entwining and the electric charges coursing through my veins. He thrust hard and deep and filled me with his release.

"God, I needed that." He wrapped his arms around me and held me close. I smiled as he convulsed against me. My pussy pulsed around his throbbing cock. I never wanted this feeling to end. He pressed his forehead against mine. "That was so fucking hot."

"Totally. And I'd love to stay here with you." I caressed his clean-shaven cheek, then gave it a tap. "But we have press duties. We have to go. Gem and Kyle will wonder where we are."

"They'll know." He grinned as he withdrew and tucked his dick back into his boxer briefs. He zipped up his suit pants and rushed to the sideboard to fetch the box of tissues sitting by a tray of water glasses. He handed it to me and stole another kiss. "Kyle had to hold me back when I first saw you, so I didn't make a scene running across the room."

"So the dress worked," I said, wiping myself clean.

"Too well." He picked up my panties and handed them to me. "Next time you wear something like that, make sure we're somewhere where I can fuck you first."

"Noted." I slipped on my underwear and realigned my skirt.

He glanced at his watch, then re-buttoned his shirt and re-tied his tie. "But we better hurry. Time to get on with the show. Hope Gem wins. She deserves it."

Reality slammed into my chest. Tonight was a celebration to honor women in the entertainment industry. I needed to get out of here and support my best friend. Gemma was one of the strongest, most influential and talented women in the music business. She inspired millions of people every day and rocked up a storm singing and playing alongside Hunter and Kyle. I treasured our friendship. We'd had our ups and downs, didn't always see eye to eye, but we'd be besties for life.

"No one is more deserving than Gem." Before I got too

emotional, I opened my clutch and grabbed my lipstick. I reapplied a fresh coat of red gloss to my lips and combed my fingers through my hair. There was no mirror, so I hoped I looked half decent.

"You deserve an award too. They should have a Best Supporting Partner Award." He shrugged on his jacket and straightened his shirt collar. "You need a special award for putting up with me."

I dropped my lipstick back into my clutch and snapped it shut. "No, I need therapy for that."

He smiled and kissed my temple. "You might be a lost cause."

"Never." I slapped him on the butt, turned on my heels, and led him out the door back to the pre-function area.

We found our friends drinking at the bar.

Kyle looked over the rim of his JD and chuckled. "Damn. That was quick."

"Don't need long." Hunter's grin was as wide as Mick Jagger's.

Gemma sidled up to me and nudged her arm against my elbow. "You even look like you've just fucked."

I pressed my palm to my fevered forehead. "We got carried away."

"You smell of sex too." Lexi wrinkled her nose, then raised her camera to take a photo of us.

Hunter wrapped his arms around my shoulders. His eyes glinted with satisfaction. "Worth it."

Abso-freaking-lutely.

Kate, Everhide's publicist, came through the crowd with her press pass dangling around her neck. With her tablet propped on her arm, she stopped in front of us. "You ready? As you walk into the ballroom, stop in front of the media wall for your photos. You know the drill." She scanned and scrolled through the document on her tablet. "Gemma, you have two interviews with *Entertainment Tonight* and *InStyle* before you take a seat. You're all at table two. Gem, your award category will be the third presentation after the main meal."

Hunter straightened his jacket. "It's about time this show started. I'm starving. I've worked up an appetite."

Kate glanced at him, sighed and sank her shoulders. "Goddamn it," she moaned and flicked her hand at him. "Couldn't you keep it in your pants for one night? You're about to be photographed, and you look like you've fucked in a field."

"Not a field. A meeting room down the hall."

Kate spun to me. "And you're just as bad as he is?"

"Well . . ." I shrugged. "He's been away too long."

She shook her head and glared at Hunter. A twisted smile curled across her lips as a hint of humor flickered in her eyes. "You don't pay me enough to put up with this shit."

"Yes, we do." He winked at her.

I took Hunter's arm, and we followed our friends into the ballroom. The attention was all on Gemma for the Women in Entertainment Awards, and not on Hunter and me for a change. Cameras flashed. Photographers hollered. Gemma posed. Kyle smiled, totally smitten with his wife.

When it was Hunter's turn to be photographed with me, we stepped in front of the media wall. The reporters and photographers' leering, hungry eyes sent a chill up my spine. *Shit. My dress.* I didn't want to satisfy any of their appetites. But I'd worn the dress to show the world I was Hunter's sexy girlfriend. I may as well put on a show.

I stuffed my nerves into my dress like they were a padded bra and lifted my chin. Smoothing my trembling hands over my skirt, I made sure my girly bits weren't exposed. I summoned my most dazzling smile. As I held onto Hunter's arm, I twirled, posed and showed off my long legs.

With each shot, I laughed. This dress was ridiculous—it was so not me. I'd never wear something like this again. My confidence came from being true to myself, not from being someone I wasn't. I'd stick to my classic designs, my diamonds, and pearls. I shouldn't have needed Hunter to point that out.

But the way he'd looked at me and ravished me played in the back of my mind. Was he telling the truth about what he liked me to wear? Were raunchy, risqué dresses what he wanted to see me in?

I sucked in a deep breath and closed my eyes. I had to believe he'd been honest.

Tonight's crazy quickie had been because we hadn't seen each other for weeks, not because of my dress.

He loved me for me.

Tomorrow, we'd sign with a surrogacy agency. We'd become a family.

That was sexy as hell.

But the sooner he finished writing the album and came home, the better.

The sooner we had a baby, even better.

Chapter 15

HUNTER

At the surrogacy agency and IVF clinic in Murray Hill, I sat next to Kara in the private waiting room, tucked down a corridor of the old building that had been converted into funky office suites. The sides of our heads pressed together as we scanned through the social posts on my cell phone while we waited for our appointment. My leg jiggled, and I wasn't sure if it was from excitement or anxiety. Today was the day. Six weeks after Kara had mentioned wanting a baby, we'd sign the paperwork.

Everything had happened so fast.

But new concerns had sprouted in the back of my mind.

During our phone calls while I'd been away, Kara had fretted over every minor detail—the legal agreements, timeframes, and procedures. Was it overzealous anticipation to start a family, the worry over someone carrying our child, or the doubts about whether IVF would work? They were all valid issues. I just didn't want her to stress.

Last night, I'd certainly taken her mind off her worries…before the award show, after it, and when we'd arrived home. That dress she'd worn? So fucking hot. So unexpected. I loved that she'd been daring, that we'd had a good laugh about it, but I hadn't liked other people staring at her. For the first time, jealousy had crawled under my skin. Kara was mine—no one else's.

"Oh. Wait." She pointed at a gossip-site article that had appeared in my newsfeed. It displayed a picture of us at last night's ceremony. "What's that say?"

I read the headline aloud. "Hunter Collins turns uptown royalty into trash." *What the fuck?* "Nope, I'm not reading that one. It's by Gerard Fucking Rivers from *Entertainment On-Show*. I'm not interested."

I went to flick past it, but she caught my hand. "I am. What did he write?"

"It won't be nice, whatever it is. You've gotta stop reading that crap." I didn't like her getting upset by the awful things the press wrote about us.

"I'd rather know what I have to deal with than be caught off-guard if someone asks me about it."

"I'll get Kate to give you more media training on how to deflect or respond to assholes like him."

She tickled me in the ribs; it was the only spot that made me jump. "Just let me read the article, or I'll find it on my phone."

"You'll be sorry." I tapped the link, and we read the article together.

Hunter Collins Turns Uptown Royalty Into Trash
Last night, at the Women in Entertainment Awards held in the Marriott Hotel, brought out New York's finest ladies from the television, music, theater, and film industries. While Gemma Lonsdale, lead singer and guitarist in rock band Everhide, walked away with Most Popular Female Music Artist, it was her fellow bandmate Hunter Collins and his girlfriend, Kara Knight, who stole the show. Wearing a DeMuir Designs gown that barely covered her private areas, Miss Knight clearly had Mr. Collins's undivided attention, and half the gathering's interest, as well.

"Told you, you looked hot." I scrolled down the screen. The

article continued:

*Has this bad boy rockstar ruined one of New York's classiest
ladies?*

Wait? What?

*We hope this is a one-off fashion faux pas on Miss Knight's front.
As Everhide's stylist, it's possible she was trying a bold new
move, but she clearly missed the mark and looked uncomfortable in the dress that left little to the imagination.*

"Missed the mark?" The anguish in her tone pressed hard
against my chest. This was why she shouldn't read gossip. "Was
that what everyone thought?"
"No, babe. Not at all."
The article continued:

*This was followed by a substandard performance by Mr. Collins
when he joined his bandmates on stage to sing their hit song,
"Traveled".*

"Substandard?" I fumed. "What the fuck?"

*Clearly distracted and lacking concentration, Hunter struggled
to hold a note and let Kyle and Gemma carry most of their song.
Fingers crossed this isn't a sign that Hunter's relationship with
Miss Knight is the demise of one of New York's most respected
daughters . . . or the demise of one of America's greatest young
rock bands.*

Ouch! I swiped off the screen and clutched my cell phone so tight I thought it'd snap in two. I normally didn't read gossip and never cared what anyone thought. But this was yet another hit at Kara *and* at my singing ability. That dug a knife into my soul and hacked at it with blunt blows. Would they ever see Kara for her amazing talent and her kindhearted soul, not just as the spoiled uptown princess I'd corrupted? Would they ever see how much I loved her? The media were as bad as Kara's dad. They had their blinders on. The truth never mattered.

But my singing? I closed my eyes and clenched my teeth. Being ripped apart for a poor performance was new. I'd given it my all, working within the constraints of not risking further damage to my vocal cords. My voice had cracked once, which I'd covered by dancing around, shredding on my guitar and playing it up to the audience. Had I been that awful? *Surely not.* Gemma and Kyle would've said something otherwise.

Kara's eyes swam with mixed emotions. Her eyebrows rose, then pinched together, then drew into thin hard lines. "The article's not that bad. We've had worse." She pasted on a flimsy smile, but her gaze was full of hurt.

I rubbed her arm. "Kar, you looked amazing last night. Don't let someone like Gerard get to you."

"I won't." Her voice came out soft and timid. "I went for a sexy siren but came out a Hollywood hooker."

"I would've slept with you either way." I hooked my arm around her shoulders and drew her close. "But give me you in a twinset and pearls any day, like today . . . mmm . . . total turn-on." I purred into her ear and loved that my compliments made her cheeks blush. "Do you want me to sue Gerard?"

She nudged her elbow against my arm. "No. I'm tough." She didn't sound convincing. "And you sang great. I didn't notice anything wrong, but I'm tone-deaf and don't have a musical bone in my body. To me, you nailed it." She swiveled to face me. "Since when do you care what people say, especially Gerard?"

Gerard had been out to slander me and my bandmates since we'd first signed with SureHaven Records years ago. He was an asshole who created scandal out of nothing and delivered speculation not truth. But sometimes he skimmed way too close to reality. "Since you became important to me."

Her gaze softened, and she smiled. "You're so sweet." She curled her arm around mine and leaned against me. "Let the gossipmongers say what they want. We know the truth."

But sometimes the truth hurts. *Fucking Gerard!* I had to fix my voice. I'd never be accused of being *"substandard"* again. And I hadn't corrupted Kara . . . maybe a little . . . She was the one who'd changed me for the better.

A petite lady with short auburn hair entered the room. Dressed in a baby-blue blouse with the Manhattan Fertility Group logo on the left lapel, she had a round face and kind smile, all motherly and sweet.

Kara jumped to her feet, and I followed.

"Hello. Nice to see you again, Miss Knight." She shook Kara's hand, then mine. "Mr. Collins, I'm Patricia Lee, your surrogacy specialist. Come on through."

In the office down the short corridor, I took a seat beside Kara. The black and white canvas on the wall behind the agent's chair depicted a happy couple holding a baby in their arms. My heartbeat jumped. That would be us soon. So freaky, but in a good way.

"Today should be a quick meeting. From the quantity of phone calls and emails between our lawyers, I hope we've addressed all your concerns."

"It took some effort, but yes." Kara's hand trembled on my thigh. The warmth of her touch didn't ease the momentous impact of what we were about to do.

"That's an understatement, Kar." I sighed, leaning back in my chair. I'd never multitasked like I'd had to do over the past few weeks. I'd switched from replying to emails and calls about surrogacy in the morning, to attending therapy twice a week over lunchtime breaks, to writing music every other hour of the day. Somewhere between all those things, I'd found a few hours to sleep.

"Mr. Collins." Patricia clasped her hands together and rested them on top of a manila folder on her desk. "You had issues regarding privacy. Is there anything outstanding you need to address?"

"No. I'm happy we can remain anonymous during the process, much to Kara's disappointment. She wants to scream *'we're having a baby'* from every rooftop." Kara's grip tightened on my thigh. This had been an area we'd argued over. She wanted to be on the surrogate's doorstep every day, but it just wasn't possible in our high-profile situation. "We want to ensure the surrogate remains safe."

I didn't want the lady to be hounded by the media or to have legal dramas if the surrogate found out we were the intended parents. Luckily, the laws protected us from such potential complications.

"But I want to ensure I'm part of the process." Kara leaned forward; frustration lodged deep in her tone. "I'd like to have updates and see our baby grow."

Patricia nodded. "And you will. You'll be involved in the selection of your surrogate. Once they are pregnant, you will receive regular reports, updates, copies of the scans, and photographs. If at any point you change your mind about the level of contact you wish to have, we will address this request with the surrogate. But she may not want to know the intended parents. It sometimes helps them remain less emotionally attached."

I rubbed my thumb over the back of Kara's hand. "Kar, we talked about this. It's for our child's safety."

"I know." She sniffed and nodded. "It's okay."

She wasn't, but I couldn't relinquish this request.

One of my biggest fears floated to the forefront of my mind. Nausea swayed through my stomach. My head ached as I scratched my stubble. "And Patricia, you assure me that once I jizz into a cup, my little fellas won't be used as donor sperm? I don't need some chick rocking up on my doorstep claiming to have my baby in nine months' time and find out it fucking is." Past false accusations had burned me badly. I wanted no gray areas or mishaps. No room for error. "It's only to be used with Kara's eggs. No staff member is gonna steal it, hold it hostage, or do God only knows what with it?"

Patricia's eyes glinted as she pressed her lips together. Was she trying not to laugh?

This had kept me awake at night more than once. What went on here in this building—all the IVF treatments and laboratory processes—made me feel faint. I loved that these procedures could give people the families they wanted. I just hated the hospital-vibe surrounding the clinic.

Patricia placed her palms flat on the desk. "I promise you, Hunter, our fertility clinic practices are ethical and safe. You're not the first celebrity we've dealt with. Your identity and your *little fellas* will be protected at all times."

"And the embryos will be screened for any known health issues?"

"Yes."

Her reassurance didn't totally erase my doubts, but it turned them down from a boil to a simmer.

"Anything else?" she asked.

"Yes." Kara wriggled on her chair. Excitement quivered in her voice. "Do you have a surrogate in mind? How long will it take?" Kara dug into her tote and pulled out a folder of printouts. "I have all our profile information here for you to speed up the process, so you can match us with a suitable candidate."

"Kara." Patricia's tone never wavered from being compassionate and understanding. "The paperwork today is step one out of many. I know you want a child and are excited to commence this journey. But patience is required. We'll guide you through each stage. We hope to find a suitable surrogate quickly. On average, it takes about four to six months."

Kara's impatient vibe snagged my chest. She wanted a family more than anything. I couldn't wait to have one with her either. "Kar would love to walk out of here with a baby today."

"If it were only that easy, Mr. Collins." Patricia sighed.

I blew a puff of air through my nose. "Nothing about this is easy, but we want a baby."

"Then if you're both ready, and have no more concerns, here are the final documents, approved by the lawyers, for you to sign." Patricia opened the manila folder in front of her and handed me two fat documents held together by a small bulldog clip. "The appendix at the back details all fees, milestones for payments, and review dates. Your changes are in the enclosed amendment, and your non-disclosure and confidentiality agreements are also included."

I took the document and placed it on the desk before me. My hand shook as I scanned the back pages to make sure our last changes were in place, then I closed it. My heart pounded and thundered, raced and rolled as I stared at the front page:

SURROGACY AGENCY AGREEMENT
BETWEEN

MANHATTAN FERTILITY GROUP
(HEREBY REFERRED TO AS THE AGENT)

AND

MR. HUNTER COLLINS AND MISS KARA KNIGHT
(HEREBY REFERRED TO AS THE INTENDED PARENTS)

Shit! There it was in black and white.

I wiped my clammy hands on my jeans. I was ready to sign my life away . . . no . . . to set my future. I picked up the blue pen off the desk and glanced at Kara. I threw her a sexy grin. "You sure about this? You want to have a baby with me? This is your last chance to back out."

Was she prepared to deal with more gossip, more slander, and a crazy life with me? And bring a child into the world?

She hooked one arm around my shoulder and caught my chin in her other hand. She leaned in and brushed her lips against mine, so tender and soft, complete with a nervous quake. "No backing out. I want to have your baby, Hunt."

"I want your baby too, Pearl. Let's do this." My hands trembled as I printed my name and scribbled my signature on the dotted lines.

Tears welled in Kara's eyes as she repeated the process.

Yeah. This is huge. So freaking amazing.

Patricia took the documents and signed them too. She handed us back one for our records. We'd just placed our future in someone's hands. The baby wheel had begun to spin.

Holy. Crap.

Shit had just gotten real.

Very, *very* real.

Chapter 16

KARA

I dropped my tote inside the door of my sister's Upper East Side condo and held my arms wide.

Dakota, Naomi's four-year-old daughter, rushed into my embrace. "Auntie Kara."

After a long and exhausting day at work, Dakota's cheery smile lifted my spirits. "Hey, monkey. Missed you."

I kissed the top of Dakota's head, then reached inside my bag and grabbed the gift I'd brought for her.

Dakota snatched the box from my hands. Her round blue eyes sparkled at the sight of the Barbie-sized doll with long brown hair and green eyes, dressed in leather pants and a jacket, holding an electric guitar in one hand and a rhinestone microphone in the other. "Oh my God," she squealed and jumped on the spot. "It's Gemma. I've never seen this in the shops."

"You're the first to have one." The latest release of Everhide merchandise wouldn't hit the stores until next month. At least this doll resembled Gemma; the ones made of Kyle and Hunter looked nothing like them.

"Thank you, Auntie Kara." She hugged the box against her chest. "I love it."

My heart skipped in time with Dakota's excitement. I couldn't wait to have a child and see their little face glow every time they opened a present. But my dream had an excruciating timeframe. It had only been nine days since we'd signed with the agency. Everything was in motion. But they hadn't found us a surrogate yet. Patience wasn't one of my virtues.

The waiting had kept me awake at night. Every email or call I'd received, I'd hoped it'd be from the agency. Work hadn't kept me preoccupied enough. The anticipation had eaten me alive.

But a night off with my sister might lower my anxiety . . . for a few hours anyway.

I brushed the tip of Dakota's nose with my fingertip. "You're very welcome. You take good care of Gemma. Can I see your mom?"

"Yeah, she's in the office."

"Mmm." I bent forward to meet Dakota's height. "She shouldn't be working on a Friday night. Shall we go get her out of there?"

"Yeah."

I grabbed my tote and hooked it over my shoulder. Dakota wrapped her tiny fingers around my hand and dragged me down the hallway. The whole place smelled of delicious roast chicken. *Oh, yum.* My stomach grumbled. I hadn't had a decent meal in days. I'd been too busy at work. Too tired to care. Too worried about a baby.

Dakota jumped into the middle of the office doorway and yelled at the top of her voice. "Mommy, Auntie Kara's here."

Naomi paced behind her desk, earbuds in her ears, talking to someone on the phone. She silenced her daughter with a slice of her hand across her throat, then pointed her finger at the hallway for her to leave.

"Sorry, Mommy." Dakota lowered her chin, crushed the doll-box against her chest, and scurried toward the living room.

I followed her and dumped my tote onto the tan leather modular sofa. "Why don't I play with you until your mom's finished? We can open your new doll."

Dakota's eyes lit up like a Christmas tree, but then they went out like someone had pulled the plug. "Thank you, Auntie Kara. But it's not playtime. I have to take a bath. Nanny Erika is waiting for me. Mommy will get mad if I'm not in my jammies before Daddy gets home." Dakota put on her brave face. "Maybe after dinner we can open Gemma."

What child would wait to open a present? *Oh . . . my sister's.* Naomi always enforced regimented rules in this house. She was too harsh, like our father. I never wanted to parent like that. I was much more of a free spirit.

"After dinner. Deal." I nodded.

"Yay." Dakota squealed, then skipped down the hallway toward her bedroom.

I turned toward the office and waved at Naomi to grab her attention. I threw her a *what-the-hell-is-taking-you-so-long* glare.

Naomi held up her hand and splayed her fingers. *Five minutes.*

I cupped my hand and mimed *want-a-drink.*

Naomi nodded eagerly, giving me the thumbs up, but she never missed a beat in pacing the floor and talking on the phone.

I helped myself to a bottle of rosé in the wine fridge and poured two glasses. I curled up on the sofa and looked out the window across the dark sprawl of Central Park and over to the tall buildings on the Upper West Side. I didn't miss living in this part of the city. The view was amazing, but it was too close to my parents. They lived three streets north of here. I preferred being half of Manhattan away.

Five minutes later, Naomi came out of the office. She swiped her glass off the kitchen countertop and joined me in the living room. "Hey, Kar. When I sent a text, I didn't think you'd come. You must be bored without your friends around."

That was true. I was crazy busy with work. But with Gem and the guys away, Lexi in LA working on Everhide's documentary, and Hayden in Boston catching up with his old band, my social life had stalled. I'd been tempted to drive north and spend the weekend with Hunter, but I didn't want to distract him—not when he was close to finishing writing.

"You said you wanted to see me." I curled my feet underneath me and swiveled the stem of my glass between my fingertips. "So? What's up?"

"Um . . ." Naomi tugged on her dangling ruby earring and slid deeper into the sofa. She glanced toward the huge wall clock, the office, then waved toward the kitchen. "Did you want something to eat? I could grab some cheese and crackers."

I narrowed my gaze. Something was up. Naomi dealt with millions of dollars every day, trading stocks, bonds, and options like it was easier than breathing. She'd never gotten stressed or flustered. But she was now. Had something gone wrong at work? I prayed not. "I'll wait for dinner. I'm not hungry." I was, but food could wait.

Naomi downed half her glass of wine, then dabbed the corner of her mouth with her fingertips.

"Nae? Are you okay?"

"Yes . . . yes . . . everything's fine."

Oh. It. So. Wasn't. "Where's Anthony?" He was more of a workaholic than Naomi. Was she waiting for him to come home before she told me what was wrong?

"He's still at the office." Naomi leaped from the sofa and headed to the fridge to grab the wine. She topped up our glasses, placed the bottle on the coffee table, and sank down beside me. "It's my night with Dakota. He'll be home around eight."

I puffed at a loose strand of my hair that had fallen across my forehead. I could relate to the long workdays and operating on a different schedule to my partner.

Naomi twisted toward me and tapped her fingernails against her glass. "How's Hunter? How's the writing going?"

"Excellent. They'll be away for another week. Then, they'll record. The songs are amazing. He calls me every night and often sings to me or plays whatever they've been working on. It's so cool." Our conversations were less strained since we'd signed with the surrogacy agency. So much better indeed.

"It must be tough having your very own rockstar serenade you every night."

I fluttered my eyelashes. "It's tough, but someone has to do it."

"How's his throat?"

I tilted my head to the side. What was Naomi's game plan?

She rarely asked about Hunter. "He thinks they're okay. Gem isn't so sure. He's been taking it easy, doing therapy, and has to see the specialist when he comes home."

Naomi stared into her wine glass. "And . . . any news from the agency?"

"No." I slumped against the sofa, the leather squelching behind me.

Naomi had been so supportive. She'd helped me weigh the pros and cons of each agency methodically and meticulously. She'd helped me with the legal jargon and questions my lawyer had raised about the agreements. Naomi had approached the process like negotiating a business deal. Cool, calm and collected. Quick and decisive. I hadn't spent this much time with my sister in years. It'd been nice to reconnect.

She didn't look up. "And Hunter's excited?"

"Yes. He signed the dotted line." That had been one of the most amazing moments of my life. That had embedded him deeper in my heart. We'd be parents. Together. This time, by choice. Because we loved each other. "But waiting to find a surrogate is killing me. Even if we found one tomorrow, we have to go through further processes and agreements before IVF starts."

Time pressed like a lead weight against my chest. The process took way too long.

Naomi wriggled on the seat and took a quick sip of her wine. "Say you found someone today or tomorrow, how will you work around Hunter being on tour next year? You're going to be with Everhide, right?"

"Yes. It's my job to dress them. When we find a surrogate, we have to make sure the baby is due after the tour."

"What if it's not? Or can't be?"

"What?" My head spun. "What are you talking about?"

Naomi put down her wine on the coffee table and turned to me. She took my free hand in hers. Her skin was so pale and soft. Her fingers, long and slender. But her whole hand trembled. My heart shuddered; something was wrong. Was she sick? Getting divorced? Oh no . . . *pregnant?*

No. She'd been drinking.

Naomi rubbed my hand. "What you went through, losing Ryan and having a hysterectomy, broke my heart. I know how desperate you were to have a child. I love that you've trusted me and wanted my help in selecting a surrogacy agency. I feel we've grown close again."

"Thank you. I feel the same way." I sat upright. Confusion rattled my brain. I didn't know where this conversation was going. "You've been my rock since Hunt hasn't been around."

"So . . ." She fidgeted again. "Do you honestly love him and want a child with him?"

"Yes. He's amazing. He's intense. And crazy. And acts like a child half the time. He has a heart of gold and wants a family, too. In our world of music and fashion, we're happy. But I want a baby more than oxygen. It's the missing piece of my soul. I need to do this."

"You're weird."

"I know." I smiled and took a sip of my wine, then rested the glass on my knee.

"And you still don't want to get married?"

"No." *Maybe?* Every time I'd thought about marrying Hunter over the past few weeks, my guarded heart had threatened to crack. He'd edged toward not just being the one, but the perfect one. But until I truly believed he'd be faithful, I'd remain a tad cautious. If we could survive the tour, we'd survive anything. I was no longer opposed to the idea of marrying him—just not yet. "One day it'd be nice, but it's not necessary. I'll love him forever. No matter what."

"Okay then." Naomi nodded and squeezed my hand. "I wanted to wait until you two were home together, but I'm no good at sitting on decisions once I've made them. So, here's the thing." Concentration furrowed her brow. "All this surrogacy talk set my mind in motion. I hate seeing you stress about using an agency. So, I've done some further research. I've talked to Anthony. I went to the doctor and had some tests done."

Wait? What? My heartbeat struck my ribs harder and harder.

I sat straighter, daring not to breathe.

"I'm fit. I'm healthy. I've had a child. I loved being pregnant. *I'm* a candidate. So let me do this for you. Let *me* be your surrogate."

"W-what?" My chin trembled. Tears pooled in my eyes. "What did you say?"

"I don't like the thought of having any part of Hunter inside of me—not even a sperm-infused embryo. But this is for you. For the two of you. I want to have your baby."

The glass slipped from my fingertips and smashed on the timber floor. Fragments of crystal skipped across the floorboards. Wine splattered in all directions. I threw my arms around Naomi's neck. "Holy shit. *Holy. Holy. Shit.* Do you mean this?"

"Yes. But . . ." She pulled back and held her thumb and index finger an inch apart. "There's one tiny hiccup. We need to do it sooner rather than later. We might be moving to London next summer to open a new office. So, if we can pull the time frame forward, let's make a baby. You need to impregnate me now so it's due *before* the tour."

"Ahhhh!" I screamed so loud they would've heard me in Queens. "Oh my God." I held out my hands. "I'm trembling all over. I never even considered you'd do something like this because of your job, and you didn't want any more children."

"Kar, I only have to grow a baby and spit it out. It's yours after that." My sister had brass balls bigger than the Wall Street Bull. "We'll use the agency, sign a legal agreement, and make sure everything is a legitimate business transaction."

"You . . . you . . . are fucking amazing."

"I know." Naomi stayed cool and collected. "Hunter better realize that too."

"Oh, he will. He will. I'll get him to agree on timing. Don't you worry about that."

Oh shit. I had to tell him the news. I reached for my tote, found my cell phone and went to call him. But I stopped before I dialed his number.

I had a better idea.

My heartbeat pounded and thundered inside my head. I

lunged forward and hugged Naomi. "Can I take a raincheck on dinner? This news is so huge. I have to go see him."

"Okay. Calm down. Stop bouncing. That's fine. Go . . . before you break more things in my house." Naomi waved her finger toward the broken wine glass. "I'll clean this. Call me once you've told him. Then, we'll come up with a plan."

"I love you. So much." I could hardly see through my tears as I grabbed my tote and ran toward the door. "Bye. Talk soon."

I wasn't on cloud nine . . . I was on cloud one hundred and nine. I'd have a baby sooner than planned. This was unbelievable. Nothing stood in my way.

But my gut ripped my head out of the clouds, and I crashed onto the ground like my wings had failed. Convincing Hunter wouldn't be an easy task.

Especially not if having a baby clashed with his music.

Having a baby due before the tour would be crazy.

Taking a newborn around the world would be even more insane.

But if it meant having a child, I was up for the challenge.

Should I break the news to him casually over a drink? Burst through the door and blurt it out? Tell him while making love?

Shit. I had no idea. Having a child had taken a new direction I'd never expected. My mind raced with a zillion ways to tell Hunter as Giles drove me home. Within an hour, I'd showered and packed a bag for the weekend.

I jumped in my Mercedes and headed for the mountains.

I couldn't get to Hunter fast enough.

As for how to tell him we'd found a surrogate?

I guessed I'd just have to wing it.

Chapter 17

HUNTER

I lay on the floor of the studio with my rhythm guitar propped across my hips. I clutched my stomach; it ached from laughing so hard. "Gem, your mind is in the gutter."

Sitting cross-legged on the floor next to me, Gemma slapped my thigh. "It's right there with yours, babe."

God, it felt good to laugh. That real, deep, belly-aching laugh. It felt like ages since I'd had one. Music had been the key to de-stressing. No turmoil about having a baby loomed over my head. *Decision made.* No studio deadlines daunted me. *Songs were written, ready to record.* The only snag ahead was my voice.

I closed my eyes and swallowed hard. I hoped my throat had healed. New techniques from therapy had helped. I could sing. But my appointment with the specialist next week would give the final verdict on recording.

Kyle flopped back on the sofa, wiping the tears of laughter from his eyes with the ball of his palm. "Gem, you make every song sound X-rated."

She played the fast beat on her electric guitar, her fingers tinkering with the strings at a pace. "We aren't PG-13 anymore."

"We've never been PG-13." I quirked a grin. "We've sexed up every angsty song we've ever sung. Parents put chastity belts on their teenage daughters before they came to our shows."

"That's because you used to fuck them." Kyle sniggered.

"So did you." I slapped his shin.

"True." He shrugged and plucked his bass.

But wait . . . Oh shit. What if I had a baby girl? When she grew up, would I keep her away from the boys who were out for nothing but sex? *Hell no!* I'd be telling her to '*tap that*' and move on. Have fun. Live life. My daughter . . . or son . . . would fuck like a rockstar too.

"We had a ton of fun." Gemma bobbed her head as an impish grin curled across her lips. "And look what happened. We all fell for people right on our doorstep. Don't you love that?"

"Yeah. It's cool." I stretched out my legs and stared at the ceiling.

Slipping my fingers along the neck of my guitar, I strummed in time with Gemma and Kyle. The fun song we'd worked on about hooking up had us in stitches. Maybe after weeks away from home, long days of writing, and our brains working overtime, we were beyond tired and had gone off on a weird tangent. That wouldn't be a first.

I hummed a few notes, then sang.

> *My mama don't like you*
> *She thinks I'm crazy for being with someone like you*
> *But I ain't listening*
> *Because being with you is what I'm meant to do*
> *You're all I think about*
> *Every hour, every night, and every day*
> *I got it bad for you*
> *Yeah, you're tattooed on my brain*
> *Can't wait until I see you*
> *Preferably naked, with you on top*
> *Let's get down and dirty*
> *Is it wrong I never want to stop?*
>
> *Hell no. I don't think so*
> *Yeah, I don't think so*

I pictured singing this song in front of an audience. I'd glide across the stage, roll my hips, and make all the girls scream. *Nice.* Gemma took over.

My daddy don't like you
He thinks I ain't thinking straight when I'm with you
But I ain't listening
Because I've got a fever just for you
When we're together
Making love is all I wanna do
Do you want to do it fast, hot and dirty?
I'll try anything when I'm with you
You've got me on my knees feeling holy
God knows I'll give anything a shot
Just tell me that you want me
Is it wrong I never want to stop?

Hell no. I don't think so
Yeah, I don't think so

"Holy shit." Kyle fell back on the sofa, rolling in laughter. "We're gonna have to stop, because for some strange reason, this song is making me horny."

"Oh, yeah?" Gemma's eyes glinted. She placed her guitar on the floor and crawled over to the sofa. She ran her hands up his thighs and kissed him. "Should we take a break?"

I snorted and shook my head. "Nope. No breaks. You can fuck later. We have work to do."

We'd only had dinner an hour ago. I wanted to nail down this track. I wasn't sure it'd make it onto the album, but it had been fun to write. Since coming away, we'd written twenty-five songs. By the time we finished next week, we'd have more than thirty to record at the studio . . . providing my vocal cords had healed. I flicked my guitar pick at Gemma and hit her on the back of the head. "Who's not focused now, Gem?"

"Ow." She rubbed her scalp. "Fine. But maybe leave this one

for later. Let's work on something else."

There was a knock on the door, and in walked Kara.

Holy shit!

I shoved my guitar aside and shot to my feet. I rushed over, wrapped my arms around her and kissed her neck, her lips, her cheeks. My heart raced as fast as my mind swirled. Holding her close, I inhaled the scent of her floral perfume. God, she smelled so good. Like roses. "Hi. But what are you doing here?"

"Kar?" Gemma's voice drifted closer as she stepped toward us. "This is a surprise. It's good to see you."

"It sounds like you were having fun." Her embrace lingered around my shoulders.

I stepped back, and my heartbeat stumbled. Her eyes were bloodshot. Her cheeks blotched. How had I not noticed those things? *Oh . . .* I'd been too excited to see her.

"I hope I'm not interrupting." She cast an I'm-sorry glance at Kyle and Gemma. "But I had to see Hunt and tell him the news."

"What news?" Gemma's voice spiked.

A shiver slithered up my spine. "What's happened? Is everything okay?"

Her eyes welled with tears. "Yes. Hunt, we have a surrogate."

"What?" My heart hit my skull and rattled around inside my head.

Kara's eyes glistened as her chin trembled. "Nae wants to have our baby."

"Naomi? What the fuck?" Words came out, but I couldn't comprehend what she'd said. My knees buckled, and I stumbled back a step. *Her sister? Holy. Shit!*

Kara nodded and sniffled and wiped her teary eyes. "She's talked to Anthony. Has been to the doctor. She wants to use the agency so that there are no gray areas. We sign contracts. We pay her. We do everything by the book."

"Holy crap." My pulse soared as I caught Kara in my arms, picked her up, and swung her around. "This is insane. Incredible, but insane." This was one less thing to stress about. I placed Kara on her feet and kissed her lips. But there was tension in her mouth.

Maybe I'd celebrated too soon.

She placed her hand on my stomach and tugged at the bottom of my T-shirt. "Can I have a quick word about something else? Just over there?" She waved her finger toward the piano keyboards on the far side of the studio.

"Do you need to be alone?" Gemma jerked her head toward the door. "You want us to leave?"

"No." Kara jumped in. "Just give me a minute."

"We won't be long." I winked at Gemma. I took Kara's hand and drew her over to the other side of the room. I spun to face her and cupped her cheek. "I can't believe Nae wants to be our surrogate. That's amazing."

"It is." She trembled beneath my touch. Excitement danced in her eyes. But then, cute crinkles formed on the bridge of her nose, and she drew my hand away. "But there's one tiny little catch. She's moving overseas next summer, so we have to do this now. As soon as possible."

The color drained from my face. "Now? How now?"

She drew in a deep breath and stuffed her hands into the back pockets of her white skinny jeans. "Like . . . right away. We have to have the baby before the tour."

"Oh, shit." I sank onto the nearby piano stool. My heart beat crazy fast. Too much chaos hurtled through my brain. The long months ahead would be full of promos, rehearsals, travel and shows. How could we have a baby before the tour?

Kara took a seat beside me. I shuffled a fraction sideways so we could fit. "Hunt, my sister has offered to do the most incredible thing for us. If she can have the first procedure within the next month or two, the baby will be due in early April. That's perfect. The tour kicks off in July. If she can't have it until later, I'll come home and hire someone to fill in for me."

My heart crashed into my ribs. How could she contemplate not including me? "No. I'm not missing out on our child being born."

We shouldn't be talking about baby due dates for months. If we did this now, I'd lose twelve months off my two-year *live-it-up-before-a-baby* plan. Why did Kara always have to bend the rules?

Was having a child now a change I could accommodate?

Kara rounded her shoulders and pursed her lips, acting like this wasn't a big deal. "When are you announcing the tour?"

"December." I rubbed the back of my neck. "With the release of the second single."

"Once we know when Nae can have the procedure, we'll know the due date. Can't Sophie and Olsen work their magic and adjust the tour dates? Can't we have the flexibility to be home for the birth of our baby and have a few weeks off until we can travel?"

Frustration curled through my hands as I clutched my knees. "Tour dates aren't like a dentist appointment that you can change at the drop of a hat. We can't just turn up at a venue, or shuffle around an entire leg of a tour and go, '*oh, sorry we can't make those dates—how about these?*' Venues are booked out for months . . . if not years . . . in advance. There's a ton of logistics and travel to coordinate."

"I understand that." Kara lowered her chin. Her voice was barely audible. "I know how much touring means to you. It's just a worst-case scenario."

I glanced at Kyle and Gemma lazing on the sofa, waiting for our return. They wanted to tour as much as I did. I closed my eyes and tried to stop my head from throbbing. I lived for touring. I didn't want to change any dates—not even for a baby. I wanted to be on stage.

But . . . if we timed it right?

Shit.

I rubbed my hand over my face. Once. Twice. Three times. "Kar, do you seriously want to bring a baby on the tour?"

Kara knocked her knee against mine and hooked her hair behind her ear. "I wouldn't be with you if I didn't see myself traipsing around the globe with our child."

"But a newborn?"

If anyone could be a mom and coordinate the tour wardrobe, it would be Kara. But she'd never been on a full tour. It was a total adrenaline rush, an exhilarating high . . . and completely exhausting, utterly hectic, and highly draining.

"Fuck." The hammering inside my head grew louder and louder. "Kar, this is a massive change. I wanted to come home to a baby, not take one on the road."

She ran her hand up and down my thigh. Her touch was soothing, but I needed more of a deep-tissue massage in my shoulders to work out the knots. "We'll make it work. We always do. But you're Everhide. The world bends over for you. I'm not asking you to change the whole tour, just maybe the start date so we can have a baby."

There might not even be a tour if I couldn't sing. *Fuck!*

I closed my eyes and took a deep breath. I hooked my arm around her shoulders and kissed her temple. Her hope and elation wrapped around my heart and filtered through my veins. I loved seeing her happy. "You keep hitting the fast-forward button, don't you?"

"I don't mean to. But life is short. We've got to live life to the fullest. Isn't that Gem's motto?"

"Yeah, it is." I slipped my arm off her shoulders and took her hand in mine, resting it against my leg. "But we had a plan. This is such a huge change."

"But it's a perfect one." Excitement skipped through her voice. "We can see Nae all the time."

If we did this now while we were at home, we could witness our baby's growth and be there for the birth. *Oh, man.* I so wanted that. So did Kara. Naomi as our surrogate erased the issues of having to remain anonymous. There'd be no need for emailed reports and updates—we'd see every stage with our own eyes. *Brilliant.*

We'd have a baby sooner rather than later. That'd be incredible.

But taking a newborn on the tour would be crazy. Sleep, travel, and routine would be thrown into turmoil. My blood pressure spiked just thinking about it. Was stress now a permanent fixture in my life? It seemed that way.

"Kar, I don't want to change the tour. Too much planning is already underway. It's too hard to reschedule. But . . ." My heart broke out in a cold sweat. I couldn't believe I was about to say this. I was insane, wasn't I? "*If* we can have the baby before kickoff . . . I'm in." Her eyes brightened. Her smile shone like a night sky full of stars. But before she said a word, I held up my finger. "If not, we stick to the original plan and do this after the tour. If Naomi moves to England, we'll fly her home for the procedure if she still wants to be our surrogate. If not, we'll find someone else."

"But—"

"No buts, Kar." I shook my head. "Hopefully, we'll have no issues. But if we do, if an embryo fails, we'll have to wait. I'm sorry. I know how much you want a baby, and so do I. We have to be logical and sensible about this. We have to work around the tour." *Damn*. I'd never thought I'd be the rational one.

She stared at our clasped hands, pursed her lips, then nodded. "Okay." But when her gaze met mine, fear as dark as the reservoir's waters rippled through her eyes. "I don't want any of our babies to fail."

"Neither do I." I had to find the strength to cope if they didn't make it. "But we have to be prepared." *Was I?* Could I survive more loss and heartache? With recording, my voice, the tour, and babies to worry about, did I have enough reserved to do this? Could I be everything to everybody? Would my voice hold? Would the fans come to our shows? Would Kara and I get through this? *Yes* . . . No matter what happened, I had to be there for her. But who'd be there for me?

Kyle and Gemma . . . always.

Fuck. Having a baby now changed everything. *Again.*

"Let's go tell the others." I stood and helped Kara to her feet.

As we walked across the room, Gemma winced and smiled an I'm-sorry smile. "We should've left, but we heard some—well, most—of the conversation. The acoustics in this studio are really good."

Shit. I'd forgotten about that.

"Oh." Kara lowered her gaze. "And?"

Kyle scratched the side of his cheek. "So much for waiting until after the tour, hey?"

I hooked my finger into the rear belt loop on Kar's jeans and tugged her hip against my side. "We'll make it work . . . *if* it works."

"I think you're both batshit crazy wanting a kid." Gemma's eyes glinted as she smirked. But her playful tone quickly morphed into serious business-mode. "We know how much this means to you, but we don't want to delay the tour's start date."

"And for the bus legs . . ." Kyle's voice swung with honesty and humor. "We'll have to rent another coach. We're not being kept awake by a crying baby. Sleep is too precious on tour. You've seen me—I'm like a grizzly bear with a hive stuck up my ass if I don't get enough rest."

He wasn't lying.

There'd be many details to work out *if* Kara and I had a baby.

A wave of elation and agony tore at my heart. Not traveling on the same bus as Kyle and Gemma would be hard. We'd done that on every tour. We hung out, wrote songs, and had fun. We'd stay up all night talking when we should've been resting. Some traditions couldn't be abandoned, not completely anyway. "I'm sure I'll spend the odd night with you when we're in the creative mood."

"Maybe." Kara cuddled into me and rubbed my stomach. "If I let you off baby feeds and diaper changes."

"We'll take turns." I kissed the tip of her nose. "And we'll have at least ninety-five crew with us. I'm sure some of them would love babysitting duties. We might add it into their contracts."

Gemma picked up her guitar and strummed a chord. "Well, congrats on finding a surrogate. But can we have no more life-altering changes that may affect the tour?" Her lips drew into a thin smile. She was clearly over more baby talk, but at least she supported our decision.

"I'm down with that." I chuckled. But the reality of my voice problems slammed into me like a sledgehammer. "Let's focus on having a tour to go on first."

"Hell yeah." Kyle grabbed his bass and swung the strap over his head. "I wanna finish that song we were working on. You staying, Hunt, or heading off for the night?"

"Um . . ." *Damn.* I wanted to stay . . . and wanted to be with Kara.

Kara jumped in, placing her hand on my arm. "Hunt, stay. I'm tired after an emotional evening and the long drive. I don't want to interfere with your work. But if it's okay, I'll stick around for the weekend. A break will be nice."

"I'd like that." I smoothed my hand over the back of her hair. The long, soft strands slid beneath my fingertips. "I'll stay down here for just a bit longer. We were right in the middle of a song when you rocked up."

"I'll leave you to it." She leaned in and whispered in my ear, "But just so you know . . . I'll be naked in bed, waiting for you."

"Mmm. Incentive. I like it." I gave her a quick kiss. "Let me show you to our room."

"I can manage. Just point me in the right direction." She tapped me on the butt. "Stay. Work. Have fun. I'm not going anywhere."

God, she was incredible. Her understanding made me love her even more.

I walked her out of the studio, and at the bottom of the steps, I pointed toward the bedroom. As she disappeared up the stairs, my mind spun like a record player. There was something about Kara. Every time I was with her, I just wanted to leap further. Fly higher. Go faster. There was never any sign of slowing down.

Now that we had a surrogate, and the timeframes had changed, it was even more imperative than ever to savor the months ahead with our friends before the baby came. *Damn.* I'd wanted one more tour before things changed. But after losing Ryan, I'd learned life was too short and precious. I couldn't wait to have a kid. Until then, I wouldn't hold back. I'd live every moment—live it hard and fast.

I just hoped I wouldn't burn out in the process.

Chapter 18

KARA

I woke, the bed beside me empty, cold, and unruffled. I rubbed my eyes and my face, then glanced at the digital clock. 2:07 a.m. Hunter hadn't come to bed. Was he still in the studio working with Kyle and Gemma? Did he ever sleep normal hours?

Nope. Not as long as I'd been with him.

I rolled onto my back, stretched my arms wide, and a smile charged across my face. He'd agreed to have a baby sooner than planned. He wanted a child just as much as I did. That filled me with tingling vibrations from my head down to my toes.

But my stomach cinched and sank into the mattress. I'd hoped Hunter would've joined me by now. He hadn't finished work early to be with me, not even after spending a week and a half apart. Despite being dead tired after a long day and drive here, it would've been nice to have a quickie. But I knew the rules. Writing time was writing time. No interruptions.

What if he'd fallen asleep in the studio? Maybe I should check on him. Make sure he was okay. Screw no distractions. I hadn't come all this way to sleep alone.

No longer tired, I swung my legs off the bed. I put on my lace-trimmed slip and panties, then grabbed my black silky robe off the bedroom bench and shrugged it on. As I made my way downstairs, a muffled, sexy drumbeat mixed with a soft, sensuous electric loop drifted from the studio. I tiptoed toward the door and peered through the glass panel. There were no signs of Kyle and Gemma. They must've crashed for the night. Hunter sat at the end of the sofa with his guitar propped across his lap. With his pen jammed between his teeth and his hair loose around his shoulders, his fingers strummed the strings. He stared toward his laptop playing music on the coffee table. The concentration etched onto his face made my heart flutter and flip. I loved watching him work and was always blown away by his talent and ability to write songs. I knew what it was like to be so absorbed, so lost in the creative process that the world around you disappeared. The simmering embers in my heart threatened to ignite. I missed designing, but with a baby due and a tour in the not-too-distant future, I couldn't return to it. I had no capacity to take on interests that would demand more of my time.

But I had time for Hunter.

I opened the door and inched inside. He looked up. The tiredness in his eyes disappeared and a smile curled across his mouth. "Did I wake you?" he whispered.

Why was he whispering? Nobody else was around.

"No. But I thought you would've come to bed by now."

"Sorry. I lost track of time."

As always.

I drifted over to him, slid my hand across his shoulders, and kissed the top of his head. "Are you okay? About the baby and timeline changes?"

"Yeah." Furrow lines chiseled his brow as he nodded. Bringing the date forward was a huge adjustment, and it would take a few days for the news to sink in for both of us. "It's a good change. Crazy, but good."

I pointed at his laptop. "Are you working on the same song as before?"

"No. Something new."

"I like the sound of it." As I stepped in front of him, he swung his guitar out of the way, and I slid sideways onto his lap. "It sounds a bit like The Weeknd's 'Starboy.'"

He grimaced and paused the loop. "No, it doesn't."

"Yes, it does. It's all slow and sexy, but . . . different. Will you play it for me?"

"Okay. But sit here." He shuffled deeper into the sofa, spread his thighs wide, and tapped the seat between his knees.

I slipped onto the sofa and leaned back against his chest. He hooked my hair to one side and kissed my neck, his lips lingering beneath my earlobe. He inhaled deeply. I loved the way he breathed me in. It sent goosebumps skipping across my skin. He swept his nose along the curve of my ear. "I missed you."

"Same." I ran my fingers down his arms; the hair tickled my fingertips. "You gonna play me the song?"

"You wanna learn it?"

"I can't play."

"I'll show you."

He restarted the loop on the laptop and positioned his guitar over my lap, resting it against my tummy. "Hold here." He took my left hand and curled my fingers around the neck. Then he took my other hand and placed it over the body of the guitar. As he teased his lips against my ear, he curled his hands over mine. "This is how you caress a guitar. Hold it gently, but firm. She'll respond to your touch."

Smiling, I flinched as shivers shot down my arms. "*She* will?"

"Yeah." His breath rushed in warm waves down my neck. "Now strum the strings like this. Slowly. Evenly. Softly." He caught my earring between his teeth and tugged on it. My pulse quickened. I wasn't sure how much of a guitar lesson this would be.

"Press down like this." He placed my finger on one string on the top fret. "This is C. That's it. Now strum downwards in time with the drumbeat. Ready? One. Two. Three. Strum."

As my fingertips glided across the strings, he nipped and licked the soft flesh of my neck. Tiny tremors shot over my skin. Quivers rippled through my stomach.

He chuckled and rested his chin on my shoulder. "There. You've played a note."

"I think I'll leave the playing to you. Is your throat okay? Can you sing for me? I love the sound of your voice."

"Hmmm." He wriggled his hips. "I love the feel of you next to me."

"It's good to be here." My stomach fluttered as my hand fell onto his thigh. I glided my palm along the length of his jeans and squeezed his knee. "Play for me. Please?"

"Lean back so I can." He sat straighter, and I rested my head against his shoulder.

His fingers glided seamlessly over the strings. The seductive, raunchy beat looping through the laptop speakers and the sexy strum of his guitar charged the air. The connection with his body raised my body temperature, and the want for him blazed to life deep in my core.

He swept his lips along the line of my jaw. "I wanted to write a song that got people in the mood for dirty dancing, flirting . . . and fucking."

"Maybe we should see if it works?" *Oh yeah . . . it was working.*

"I like the way you think." He put his guitar down beside the sofa, then tapped my leg for me to stand. Once we were on our feet, he took my hand and drew me into the center of the room. He twirled me in a circle, then wrapped his arms around me, my back to his chest. The hypnotic music and heavy bass penetrated my bones, warmed my blood, and took over my heart rate. *Boom-da-da-boom. Boom-da-da-boom.* He caught my hips between his hands and swayed from side to side. I had no other option but to move along in time.

With his lips near my ear, he sang in a low, breathy voice.

> *Come over here, everything'll be just fine*
> *Put your hands on my body, move in time*
> *Dance with me girl, but know there's a line*
> *This is all very cool, very sweet, and sublime*
> *But let me tell you what's really on my mind*

My heartbeat quickened as I ran my hand down his strong

thigh and dug my fingers into his muscles. "And what would that be?"

"Shh." He ran his hands across my stomach in ticklish swirls, then worked his way upward to capture my breasts. As he massaged them, my nipples hardened into agonizing peaks. He moaned softly. "God, I've missed these."

His voice coiled through my veins and heated my blood. Every touch, every kiss, every move turned me on. My head fell back as I savored his touch. "Hunt?"

As we slow-danced to the music, he slid one hand over my hip, down my thigh, and caught the edge of my slip. He dragged it up a few inches and circled his fingers over my bare flesh. He smiled against my ear and sang.

> *I wanna taste your mouth, claim your lips, baby, make you mine*
> *I wanna bend you over, touch your skin, take you from behind*
> *I wanna make you wet, make you beg, and want me more*
> *Fuck you so hard, you feel it in your core*

Yep. Song worked.

I spun around and kissed him hard. Fire ignited in my chest as our tongues teased and tasted each other. The Throat Coat Tea he drank made him taste like a candy store—of licorice, peppermint, and lemon drops. I had a sweet tooth and wanted to eat the whole damn shop. Wrapping my arms around his waist, I tugged his body flush against mine. His hard-on pressed against my crotch, fueling the heat coiling through me.

His eyes darkened, smoldering with want. His nimble fingers untied the knot on my robe. Running his hands across my shoulders, he caught my robe, dragged it down my arms, and let it fall onto the floor. A smirk quivered across his lips. "Very sexy."

The seductive music enveloped us as we danced. Thigh to thigh. Hip to hip. Heart to heart. He raked his fingers up my back. My skin blazed beneath the cool fabric of my slip and his wicked touch. Drumming like a marching band, my heartbeat thudded against my ribs. I buried my fingers in his hair and kissed him. Held him. As our breaths entwined, I didn't know where I ended and he began.

Bending his knees, he rocked and circled his hips. My body did what he commanded and moved where he wanted it to go. *Damn.* He could dance. Hitting the next verse of his song, his voice came out all low, sexy and gravelly.

> *Don't play innocent with me, I see it in your eyes*
> *I wanna go down on you, get between your thighs*
> *Kiss and taste you on my tongue*
> *Making love to you is where I belong*
> *Don't play hard to get, stop wasting precious time*
> *Take off those panties, let me touch you deep inside*
> *I know you want me to, so let me make you . . . hot*

"I'm definitely hot." I grabbed the bottom of his T-shirt, yanked it over his head, and tossed it aside. Fanning my fingers across his toned pecs, I dug my nails into his fiery flesh. "I definitely want you to touch me."

"Good." He fell to his knees and swirled his fingers over my thighs, drove them up under the hemline of my slip, and across my silky panties. My core clenched with hungry anticipation. The desire in his eyes blazed like wildfire. "Pearl, come down here."

I sank onto my knees, and he was quick to discard my slip. My hair fell in long waves down my back, tickling my bare shoulders. My whole body hummed as his eyes raked over my nakedness.

"Lie down."

"If you insist." I stretched out on the soft rug.

As he crawled over me, he kissed his way up my legs, nipped my hips, licked my breasts, then claimed my mouth. He drove his hips against mine, pulsing in time with the music. The pressure of his hardness digging into my panties was a hot overload. His eyes shimmered as a cute smile curled across his lips. He continued to sing.

Nothing sweeter than you calling out my name
Fucking you always drives me insane
Let's get it on, get down on the floor
Let me give it to you more and more

He sat back on his haunches and eased off my panties, hooking them over my ankles and tossing them aside. He wriggled out of his jeans and boxer briefs. Edging between my legs, he brushed his hand across my stomach and gave me a saucy smile. "Gem is supposed to sing this part, but let me know what you think?" He dipped his head and kissed across my hip line.

Boy, come on, don't be shy. I promise you I won't bite

He grazed his teeth over the arch of my hip.
My eyes fluttered closed. *Yes. Bite me. Bite me.*

Why are you resisting me? You know you shouldn't fight
Give in to this feeling, 'cause you know it's right
I wanna take you home and get you in my bed
Rip off your jeans and, baby, give you . . .

Working his way between my legs, he ran his tongue up the length of my slit. My breath shot from my lungs. *Oh yeah.*

Rub you hard, rub you soft, get you on the brink
There's no innuendo, it's exactly what you think
I wanna fuck you, be with you until you lose your mind
Let me give it to you, baby, because you are mine

"Wow," I panted, threading my fingers through his hair. "Totally turned me on. Now fuck me."

"Oh no." His eyes smoldered as he looked up at me. "I'm going to make slow, torturous love to you. I've missed you. I want to let every inch of you know how much."

Closing my eyes, I surrendered to his mouth between my legs, his touch, his kisses . . . his tongue. But he didn't let me orgasm. Torture was an understatement. He held me on the edge, at the point of begging. My muscles screamed as he meandered his way back toward my lips. I tugged on his hair and wrapped my legs around him. "Hunt. Please."

"I love it when you beg me for it."

"Just . . ." I wriggled my hips and tried to move. I wanted him inside me. But he wouldn't budge.

He chuckled and eased off me. "Lie . . . sideways." He pointed for me to face away from him. As I rolled onto my hip, he edged in behind me. As he kissed my shoulder, he ran his hand over my thigh and drew my leg back over his. "This way, I get to slide into that hot, wet pussy of yours." He nudged his cock between my legs, found my opening, and thrust into me. *Oh yes.* "And I can touch you at the same time." His fingers glided over my abdomen and headed lower. He teased them through my slit then circled and teased my clit. *Wow.* "And that's so hot."

Glancing over my shoulder, I cupped his face and kissed him.

My blood surged through my veins. Our bodies rocked and pulsed together. And oh, his touch. Total. Melt. Material.

"You feel so fucking good," he growled into my ear. "Tight and wet, and when you push back against me, I love how you clench around me."

"Like this?" I nudged my hips backward and tensed my pussy.

"Fuck. Yeah." He buried his face in the hollow of my neck and thrust into me again and again and again. "Shit. It's been too long, Kar. Too long."

His breath rushed like a hot summer wind across my skin. My heart pounded harder and faster. "Don't stop," I panted, reaching back to cup his cheek. The only bad thing about this position was I couldn't touch him enough. But I wasn't complaining. I was too close to exploding. "There."

With his cock filling me, he continued to tease and stroke my clit. "I love it when you want my touch. My dick. Me to make you come." He didn't relent. He increased the pressure of his fingertips. My muscles screamed for release. He thrust deeper, harder, then his voice rasped in my ear. "You're so mine."

That was all it took to send me over the edge.

"Oh. Yeah." My breath panted. My orgasm barreled through my body. It tingled my toes and sent shivers up my spine. It hurtled through my veins at lightning speed. Every part of me pulsed and throbbed. *Oh. So. Good.*

As I quaked and shuddered, Hunter moaned, thrust into me hard and found his release. Smiling and chuckling softly, he kissed my neck, and held me close. Little jolts jerked his body as his cock throbbed inside me. "Damn, Pearl." He panted to catch his breath. "It's been too long. That was so good."

Spent, with sweat slicking our skin, he wrapped his arms around me and hugged me from behind.

I entwined our fingers and held his arm against my chest. The drumbeat still played on loop. My heartbeat still thudded in time with the electric rhythm. "I think I just found a new religion."

"Well, I am a rock god."

I slapped his arm. "You're so full of yourself."

"You're only drawing that conclusion now?"

"No. I had you figured out a while ago."

"I'm easy to please. Music and you are all I need." He sat upright, crawled over to the laptop, and stopped the music. "I'd say the song worked."

"Too well." I grabbed my panties and pulled them on. "You'd better not release that as a single. I don't want fans trying to fuck you during promo."

"They do that regardless of any song. But they know I'm with you." He kissed my cheek and stood. He found his boxer briefs and yanked them on.

"That doesn't stop them, though." I pulled my slip over my head and wriggled it into place. I'd witnessed him in action too many times before we were together. He'd given up his wild days for me. Some days that was still hard to comprehend. Would he remain faithful when surrounded by temptation? Caution still had a hold on my heart.

"No." He shrugged and helped me stand. "They can try to get

to me, but they'll be disappointed every single time. I'm yours."

I put on my robe and tied the sash. "You know I worry."

"Why?" He cupped the sides of my head and kissed my forehead.

"You've never had to say no before." His commitment hadn't been tested yet. The tour would push it to the limit.

"Trust me. Nothing and no one is gonna change the way I feel about you. I'm yours. I'll handle the fans. You focus on our baby and let me know the date when we can go knock up your sister."

My heart cartwheeled and backflipped. Every time I had a moment of doubt, he pulled me straight back into line. He said the right things, the most adorable things. He made me fall for him a little more each time. "I will."

"Come on." He swiped his jeans and T-shirt off the ground, then held out his hand for me to take. "Let's go to bed."

But as we headed upstairs, gray clouds kept pummeling my thoughts. There were so many aspects of Hunter's promotional schedule and the tour I didn't look forward to. The fans groping and screaming and trying to get to Hunter had always rattled me. But he loved the attention. He fed off it. Without the fans, Everhide wouldn't be the huge success they are today.

I loved being part of the ride. I just wished the majority of the fans didn't want to fuck my boyfriend. Given half a chance, they would. I guessed this was another challenge we'd yet to face in our relationship, one I wished we could avoid. If we were to have a forever kind of future, I'd have to trust him. On the last tour, my heart hadn't held together, and I'd walked out on him.

I prayed that wouldn't happen again.

Chapter 19

HUNTER

Carrying two cased guitars, I charged through the glass doors into the recording studio on Eighth Street. I'd worked up a sweat rushing from Vanessa's on Madison to Greenwich Village. Day one of recording had my pulse racing, but my brain spiraling after yet another throat examination. Vanessa's warning throbbed inside my head. *"If you strain your voice, you'll do more damage."*

No . . . I won't let that happen.

It was a risk, but nothing would stop me from recording.

Taking two stairs at a time, I headed for the control room, past the main recording studio. It was like I'd entered a time warp into the sixties. Round and rectangular Persian rugs dotted the floor. A mural of rainbows and stars filled the center wall. Mounted posters of albums and artists filled the gaps between the drapes, and warm lighting threw hues of orange and gold across the wooden floors and paneling.

At the end of the hallway, I pushed open the door, and cool air-conditioning hit my hot face. My band's management team—Kate, Sophie, Bec and Clayton, our creative director—sat around the oval table. Kyle and Gemma swiveled back and forth on the office chairs in front of the channel console. Hayden—our drummer and best buddy—lazed on the dark green sofa at the far end of the room. There were no signs of our production crew yet.

Phew! I'm not the only one running behind.

After propping my guitars against a speaker, I walked across the room and high-fived everyone. "Hi. Sorry I'm late." I reached Hayden last. "Hey, man. Good to see you." My chest swelled. I was stoked to have him work on this album. It'd be his first time as our new drummer. He was a legend and would add flair to our songs during the final recordings.

Pulling up a chair beside Gemma, I wiped my hands on my jeans. "Did I miss anything?"

"Nah. Kyle's just loaded the tracks into the system." She spun her chair toward me and rolled closer. "We've been waiting for you."

The nervous titter in her voice snagged my lungs. All eyes in the room pinned me to my seat. Prickles shot over my skin. It was as if everyone held their breath. The anxious vibe warping the air wasn't about playing or hearing our demos for the first time—it was for the update on my voice.

Kyle peered around Gemma and jutted his chin toward me. "So, what's the verdict?"

I rubbed the back of my neck, then my shoulder. It did nothing to relieve the tension. The decision to proceed with recording lay in my hands. I'd battled with the choice, lost sleep over it, and had a constant headache. But with the right techniques and precautions, the risk would be minimal. "The diagnosis isn't brilliant." I grabbed a bottle of water off the table, cracked it open, and took a sip. "Two nodules have gone. Three are smaller. One is the same. There's an improvement, but I'm not fully healed."

"What does that mean?" Sophie, our manager, swept the tails of her paisley headscarf and blonde locks back behind her shoulder. "Can you record?"

"Vanessa still thinks I should have surgery. *I* still said no. After much discussion and with Lise's help, yes, we have a green light." There was nothing like playing Russian roulette with more than one bullet in the cylinder. "Let's lay the softer tracks down first to give my throat more time to heal."

"Yes. All right." Sophie pumped her fist.

Clayton clapped. Kate's shoulders relaxed. But everyone else remained reserved.

"Are you sure about this?" Gemma tilted her head to the side. Her gaze drilled into me for the truth.

The concern in her tone knotted my stomach. She'd want the best for me. Gemma and Kyle wouldn't hesitate to cancel recording, promo, and the tour if I couldn't sing. They'd put their careers on hold for me. But I didn't want the ride we were on to falter. We'd worked too damn hard to get here. I didn't want to let anyone in this room down. "Yes. Absolutely." Projecting confidence into my response didn't stop my insides from shuddering, or doubt from tormenting my mind. If only the niggle in my throat would die, everything would be fine.

"Hunt." Kyle rested his elbows on his knees. "If at any time you question your voice . . . we stop. Don't overdo it. We have plans to accommodate your baby; we'll do the same for your vocal cords."

My heart fell onto its knees and prayed. "Let's hope neither is an issue." Since coming home a week ago, baby plans had taken flight. If everything went according to schedule, I'd have a child on the way within a couple of weeks. The album would be done within two months.

"Olsen and I are already on the baby thing." Bec didn't look up from typing notes into her tablet. "We have a backup plan. He worked his tour manager magic and secured alternate dates for the first month of the tour. Let's hope those dates aren't needed."

"Thanks," I said. "Now let's hope my voice doesn't fuck up. I'd hate to cancel everything."

"Then have the surgery, idiot." Bec glared at me like I was a moron.

I chuckled. Bec didn't take bullshit from anyone. I loved her to pieces. "Nope. I've got this." *Fuck. I hope so.*

"Okay then. Let's get to work." Sophie rubbed her hands together and jumped to her feet. "I'll go grab the production team from their office. I can't wait to hear the tracks."

The songs we'd written were totally kickass and had turned

out better than we'd expected. We'd created heart-wrenching ballads, dance-floor tracks, party tunes, friendship numbers, and love songs. The fans would love them. Every track had been penned from the heart. Now, we had to lay them down. I closed my eyes and clutched the cross on my necklace. Life was about to hit sonic speed. I had to keep up. As long as my voice held, everything would be fine.

***

Every time I'd stepped into the isolation booth to record vocals, I'd broken out in a cold sweat. When I'd sung, I'd held back my power. It'd driven a knife into my heart and twisted it around and around. I hated not giving my best.

By week two of recording, I'd gained confidence in my voice. By week three, I was determined to push harder. Today we had to put the final touches on our upbeat song, "All I Want." It needed backing vocals, some overlays, and some extra magic touches to the beat.

But no matter how hard I tried to focus, my mind was elsewhere. My nerves weren't just on edge about singing high notes, but also on meeting Kara and Naomi in two hours.

Today was Naomi's first embryo implant . . . and hopefully the last.

Five days ago, Kara and I had visited the IVF clinic. I'd jizzed into a cup. Since then, my little swimmers had partied hard with Kara's eggs in a petri dish and made little embryos. Scary . . . but awesome.

As I paced behind the eighty-channel console, I ran through vocal warm-up exercises. Kyle, Hayden, and Reynold, our production engineer, focused on Gemma. My ears were half-tuned in to the recording of her takes in the isolation booth. Her incredible voice filled the room. *Damn, she's good.* I should be paying more attention, providing feedback, making suggestions, but I glanced at my watch. Time was ticking. My body turned feverish. I hoped these overlays and adlibs wouldn't take long.

"This has to be a single." Hayden drummed his fingers against his leg in time with the beat.

I let the raw electric guitar riff zip through my veins and consume me. It was one of my favorite tracks. "Yep. The moment we wrote it, we knew it'd be a hit." There was nothing wrong with being a bit cocky.

At the end of the song, Reynold spoke into the intercom that fed into the isolation booth. "Great job, Gemma. That's a wrap."

Seconds later, she bounced into the control room, jumped past the guys and pointed both index fingers at me. "Your turn, goofball."

"Cool." *Shit.* I wiped my clammy palms on my jeans and took a deep breath. I grabbed my travel mug of Throat Coat Tea and headed for the booth. Recording backing vocals was usually fun. We'd sing whatever came to us, hit us in the gut or filled our heart. We'd record a ton of alternate 'yeahs', '*ahhs*', '*oh-babys*' and '*whoas*', along with chorus lines, sung high, low, fast, and slow. I usually fought Gemma and Kyle to hit the booth first. I loved belting out my adlibs, pushing my vocal range to the limit. But I rubbed my Adam's apple and cleared my throat. Now I had to approach these with restraint.

"Ready, Hunt?" Gemma spoke through the intercom.

I took a sip of my tea, positioned my headphones over my ears and gave her the thumbs up.

The hard line of the bass filtered into my ears. I closed my eyes and let the beat take over my body. Tapping my fingers against the headphones, I let the lyrics roll through my head.

> *Did someone stop the clock?*
> *Stop the world from turning?*
> *Coz the moment I saw you*
> *I lost my sense of direction*
> *My heart beat faster*
> *When I heard your laughter*
> *My breath grew quicker*
> *My mind spun crazier*

I saw my forever in you
Now there's nothing I can do
Because all I want is you
All I want is . . . you

I took a deep breath and scaled my voice.

Yeah. Yeah. Yea—h. Yeah. You

Shit. I'd try something else.

All I w—nt is yo—
Yo—
You

Fuck. My heart slammed against my ribs. Anything high killed my voice.

With grit and determination, I dug deep, using my diaphragm to control every breath, every sound, every note.

All I w—nt is y—
All — want is you
Yo—
You

Fuck!

Kyle's voice came through my headphones. "Hunt, like where you're going with this. Take your time. Don't force it. Drop it down a key."

But even singing lower, my voice cut out. Take after take, my voice wouldn't cooperate. My heart crumbled like a piece of paper and fell to the floor. I curled my hands into fists and dug my nails into my palms. Before I smashed the microphone to pieces, I had to get out of there. I sliced my hand across my throat to kill the recording. I ripped off my headphones and stormed into the control room. "I'm sorry." I clutched a handful of my hair and jammed my fist against my scalp. "I'm not sure if my voice just wants to piss me off or if it's because my head's elsewhere." My hands fell to my side. "I have to go."

"Oh wow." Kyle leaped to his feet. "Is it time?"

"Yeah." I grabbed my backpack off the sofa. "Today's the day."

"Go." Gemma rushed over and gave me a big hug. "Good luck."

"I'm freaking out." I kissed the top of her head and stepped out of her embrace. Visiting doctors was not my favorite pastime. At least I wasn't the one being pricked and prodded this time. I'd had enough of Vanessa examining my throat. "I hope this fucking works."

"So do we." Kyle slapped me on the back.

"All the best, man," Hayden hollered and waved from his stool by the console.

I let out a slow breath and looked around the room. I patted my jeans, searching for my cell phone. *Check.* Keys? *Dick! I'm not driving.* Wallet? *In my bag.* Had I forgotten something?

Why did I want to throw up?

Why did my ears ring?

Oh yeah . . . I was about to make a baby. *Epic.*

"Um . . . We're gonna take Nae home afterwards, so I'll see you tomorrow, okay?"

"Sure thing." Gemma play-punched my arm. "See you here at nine."

"Yep." I headed for the exit, halting before I reached the handle. I glance over my shoulder. "Love you guys."

"Stop procrastinating and get out of here." Kyle chuckled and waggled his finger toward the door. "Kara will be pissed if you're late. Go get your jizzed jelly into Nae. We'll finish this track and be ready to work on 'Surrender' tomorrow."

"Hell yeah. See ya." I yanked the door open and dashed out of the studio and into my waiting car.

Twenty minutes later, my driver pulled up outside the clinic in Murray Hill. I pulled my baseball cap low over my eyes and rushed inside the building with Mick tailing behind me.

Inside, instead of turning left to head into the surrogacy agency offices, I headed right along a bright, narrow corridor and into the IVF clinic's reception area. My heart raced as I pulled off my hat. *Holy shit. I'm here.*

The lady behind the desk gaped. Her eyes widened. Her star-struck gaze temporarily distracted me from my jitters.

I flashed her my award-winning smile. "Hi. I'm Hunter Collins." As if she didn't know who I was. "Is Kara Knight here?"

"Yes. I'm Jill." She smoothed her hand over her hair. Her cheeks flushed pink. "Miss Knight and Mrs. Astor are ready for you in the private waiting room down the hall. Follow me."

The moment I walked through the doors, Kara and Naomi jumped up from the gray sofa.

Kara flung her arms around my neck. "You're ten minutes late. Let me guess . . . recording went over time?"

I didn't miss her salty tone. Or that she trembled in my arms or was as white as a ghost. "You know me and music . . . Always." I flashed her a smile and stole a kiss. "But I'm here, aren't I?"

"Yes." Her shoulders relaxed, just a fraction. "Thank you."

I gave Naomi a warm hug. "Nae, you ready?"

"As ready as I'll ever be."

Did anything ruffle Naomi? Not a hair looked out of place. No fluster colored her cheeks. She seemed as calm as an island lagoon on a still summer's day. Lucky for her. I needed some of whatever she was on.

Hooking my arm around Kara's waist, I drew her to my side. "You okay?"

"Uh-huh." She bobbed her head. "Just nervous."

Yep. My knees shook too.

The door opened, and a nurse in blue scrubs walked in. "Hi, I'm Dianna. Dr. Arnold will see you now."

Kara clutched my arm. "Oh shit. This is it."

I stepped forward, but Kara didn't move. She stood frozen, staring at the door. I turned to her and brushed my thumb down her cheek. "Pearl? What's wrong?"

"I . . . I'm terrified."

"We've got this." Nae clutched Kara's hand. "Let's go."

"Okay." Kara nodded but couldn't mask her fear.

I followed the ladies into the doctor's office, wiping my hand over my three-day growth. I was just as terrified as Kara. Life was about to change forever. I took a deep breath and said a silent prayer.

Please. Fucking. Work.

Chapter 20

KARA

"Four embryos failed to form. The eggs failed during the insemination and culturing process."

"What?" My hand clutched at the stabbing pain shooting through my chest. My other hand seized Hunter's arm to stop myself from falling off the chair. My heart constricted to the size of a pinhead. Struggling to breathe, I glared at Dr. Arnold through the tears blurring my vision. Fifty percent of my chances of having a baby just went up in smoke. *Four chances. Gone. Just like that. No. No. No. No!*

"Four failed?" Naomi gasped. "That seems a lot."

Hunter's hand trembled as he entwined his fingers with mine. "How could you lose half of Kara's eggs? They were all right when they were frozen."

My breath ripped through my lungs. My whole body shuddered. "What . . . what went wrong?"

"Whether the eggs didn't survive while frozen, or they just didn't fertilize, we're unsure." As Dr. Arnold slowly shook her head, the beads in her shoulder-length black braids clinked together. Her tone remained level, yet sympathetic. "I'm sorry for the loss."

Hunter lowered his gaze. His jaw tensed. "You're sorry!" He spoke through tight lips. "You're supposed to be the best clinic in New York, and you've destroyed half our chances of having a child."

"We did our best, Mr. Collins." Empathy lingered in Dr. Arnold's voice, but then her eyes brightened. "What we have though, are four healthy embryos. Three have been frozen; one is ready for today."

"Four." *Yes.* I had to stay positive. Hold on to hope. Tears leaked from my eyes and caught on my cheeks. "Hunt, we have four potential babies."

He sucked in a slow breath and nodded. Drawing my hand to his mouth, he kissed the back of it. "Yeah. Better than none, right?"

"Naomi." Dr. Arnold sat tall in her oversized leather chair and gave her a small nod. "If you're set, we'll take you through to the treatment room for the procedure. Will Kara and Hunter be joining you?"

"I'm good to go." Naomi's voice remained even, but her eyes darted toward the door. Her feet jiggled. My sister wasn't as tough as she made out to be.

"Nae?" I swiveled to face her and clutched her hand. "This is your last chance to say no. I mean it. This is huge. Are you sure you don't want to change your mind?"

"Nope. I'm in."

My heart leaped and skipped. I couldn't see through my teary eyes. This was it. My dream of being a mom was about to take one massive leap toward fruition. But images of Ryan's lifeless body flashed through my mind. The horror wouldn't rest. I couldn't face that again. *Please work.*

Hunter rubbed my back. His eyes reflected my own fears. "Kar, are you ready for this?"

I exhaled slowly to calm my nerves. "Yes ... No ... Yes."

"Hunt, what about me?" Naomi half-grinned, stood and grabbed her purse. "I'm the one who's about to have some crap rammed up my vagina."

"You've got this, right?" Concern shot through his voice.

"Yeah, absolutely." Naomi nodded.

I rose to my feet and gave her a big hug. "Whatever happens,

I love you."

"I know you do." She clasped my forearms and gave them a gentle squeeze. "Let's get this baby in me. You can both come in. But Hunter?" She pointed at him. "You're to go nowhere near my hoo-hoo. Got it?"

Hunter stood and stuffed his hands into the back pockets of his jeans. He threw her a sly smirk. "I've seen more hoo-hoo than I care to remember. Don't need to add yours to the list."

"Yeah . . . good." Naomi took off after the doctor toward the room next door.

I giggled and wrapped my arm around Hunter's waist, and we followed Naomi.

In the treatment room, after changing into a medical gown, Naomi stretched out on the procedure bed. Hunter and I sat on chairs on opposite sides near her head.

The nurse covered Naomi with a sheet. "Just relax. The doctor will be with you in a moment."

I gripped Naomi's hand in one of mine and held Hunter's with the other, resting it on the pillow above Naomi's head. His palm was as clammy as mine. I glanced from Naomi to Hunter and back again. "I love you both. So very much."

Naomi wriggled on the bed. "Dakota needs a cousin. That's what I'm focusing on."

Hunter eyed the stirrups and medical equipment. "Every day I thank God I'm a man and never have to put up with any of this shit."

Naomi elbowed Hunter's arm. "You put up with my sister. That's torturous enough."

He quirked a grin. "I'll take Kar over this any day."

The doctor came in with a tray of tubes and implements and placed it on the swivel table. She sat in her chair and wheeled herself into position at the end of the bed. "Okay, Naomi. If you're ready, we'll begin."

Naomi nodded, and the nurse helped her place her feet into the supports.

I sucked in a deep breath. My heartbeat doubled its rate. This was it. My future baby was about to take hold. My abdomen, where my uterus used to be, fought the emptiness, the brokenness, the loss. I wished I was about to carry my child, not my sister. The doctor inserted the long, thin catheter containing one embryo into Naomi. My sister winced, grunted, and groaned. My insides tweaked and ached like I was experiencing the implant too.

Hunter tried to peek over the sheet, but Naomi slapped his arm. "Don't you dare."

He grinned, grabbed her hand and kissed the back of it. "I'm in you now, Nae. Too late to change your mind."

I wiped a tear from my cheek and smiled at Naomi. "Thank you."

"All done." The doctor placed the tube on the metal tray beside her and lowered her mask. "I need you to rest here for a few minutes. I'll come back shortly, and then you'll be right to go home and take it easy."

"Okay." Naomi closed her eyes and pressed her hands against her abdomen. The color drained from her face as she wriggled on the bed.

"Nae? Are you okay?" I stroked her forehead. Perspiration dampened her hairline. Her skin had taken on a grayish tinge. It was exactly how I had looked . . . and felt . . . when I'd lost Ryan. My stomach clenched and twisted into knots. *Please be okay.*

Naomi nodded slowly. "That wasn't pleasant. I'll be fine in a few minutes."

I kissed her brow. "You're amazing. We're gonna grow a baby."

"Nae, you cook him well." Hunter rubbed her shoulder.

"Him?" She raised an eyebrow. "What if it's a girl?"

"God help us." I rolled my eyes, but a big grin slid across my mouth. I'd love a daughter . . . a son . . . any gender would do as long as our child was healthy.

Naomi squeezed my hand. Her touch had turned cold and clammy.

"Nae? What's wrong?"

"Nothing. I'm okay. I've got this."

My heart wanted to skip around the room, but my gut wouldn't settle. It wouldn't until I held my baby in my arms. Forty weeks and counting until I was a mom.

After the doctor cleared Naomi to go home, I paced the waiting room while Naomi changed.

Hunter stepped in front of me and caught me by the arms. "Hey. It's done, Pearl." He scooped my hair behind my shoulders, his touch soothing and comforting. "Let's hope this works."

"It has to." My mind bolted in a new direction.

Oh wow!

Naomi.

Pregnant.

With our baby.

Holy shit!

I had to make sure she had everything she needed to grow a healthy child. Vitamins. Nutritional food. Supplements. I'd talk to Erika and make sure my sister ate well and avoided any soft cheeses and cured meats. Had no alcohol. No caffeine. No partially cooked eggs. I'd print out a checklist for Erika. I'd chat with Anthony to ensure Naomi didn't work long hours. I'd take her to mommy yoga, the expecting-mom's day spa, Lamaze classes, and make sure she had enough rest. There was so much to do. This was so exciting.

Naomi walked slowly out of the treatment room, clutching her purse against her stomach.

My breath hitched. "Nae?"

The color hadn't returned to her face. Hunter and I rushed to her side.

"I'm just a little lightheaded. Nothing serious. Dr. Arnold has cleared me to go."

Hunter hooked his arm around Naomi's waist and helped her walk out of the clinic and into our waiting car. She'd insisted she was capable, but Hunter wouldn't take no for an answer. I climbed in on one side of Naomi, and Hunter, the other.

As our driver took off, I pointed to the fresh water bottles stashed in the net on the rear of the driver's seat. "Do you need a drink?"

"Kara. I'm fine. Stop fussing." Naomi rested her head back. Her eyes fluttered closed. Her shoulders stooped.

So much for being Superwoman. Some things even knocked my sister flat.

"Do you need me to pick you up anything? More vitamins? Supplements?" I asked, keeping my voice soft.

"No." Naomi shook her head and kept her eyes closed. "I'm good."

"What about—"

"Kara. Stop." She rolled her head toward Hunter. "How do you put up with her?"

"I've been away for two months."

"Ugh . . . maybe I need to go somewhere for the next nine months so I can keep her at bay."

"I might join you." Hunter chuckled.

"You know I can hear you?" I smiled at them. I loved Naomi had the same witty banter with Hunter as I did. It always made us laugh.

We arrived back at Naomi's condo just after four p.m. Hunter helped Naomi into the building, half-carrying her into the elevator and up to her floor. She looked paler and paler by the second.

"I think I need to lie down," she said as she opened her door. "Just in the living room for now."

"I got you." Hunter helped her inside.

But the moment I walked in behind them, a chill shivered up my spine. I could smell the putrid cologne before the door closed. *Fuck.* This isn't what we needed right now.

"Hunt," I whispered loudly. "Daddy's here."

"Great," Hunter moaned. "What's the likelihood of him being in a good mood?"

"Zero." I followed him and Naomi down the hall. "Always zero."

Chapter 21

KARA

"I told him not to come today." Naomi eased down the hall, holding onto Hunter's arm. As we headed into the living room, Anthony rushed from the office and helped Naomi over to the sectional sofa. My parents sat at the far end of the U-shaped couch, glaring at us as they drank alcoholic beverages. We ignored them, making sure Naomi was taken care of first.

After she lay down, Anthony grabbed her a pillow and draped a throw over her waist.

"Hey honey." He kissed her on the lips, sat behind her head, and stroked her hair. "You need anything?"

"No." She wriggled her head on the pillow and yawned. "I'm just tired."

"Mommy." Dakota rushed from her bedroom dressed in a pink princess outfit. She placed her hand on Naomi's stomach, and her eyes widened. "Is my cousin in there?"

"Sure is."

"Wow." She straightened her tiara. "I can't wait to meet them."

Erika appeared in the hallway. "Dakota." She coaxed Dakota with a wave of her hand. "Come. Leave your mommy to rest."

"Okay." She kissed Naomi on the cheek. "Love you, Mommy. Bye."

My heart swelled as I curled my arm around Hunter's elbow. But then I glared at my father and mother. Dad rested a scotch on the rocks on his knee. His posture was as rigid as a broom.

I stood straighter. "What are you doing here?"

"I got the days muddled." His tense jaw ticked. "I thought the procedure was tomorrow. I came to talk sense into Naomi one last time."

My heart shattered into a million pieces and fell onto the floor. "Well, you're too late."

My mother jumped to her feet and smoothed her hand over her linen dress pants. "I need more wine." She waved her empty glass. "Anyone else want a glass?"

"Carol, I'll help." Hunter unwound his arm from around mine and followed her into the kitchen.

Numb, I sank onto the sofa next to Anthony, across from my father. "You wanted to talk Naomi out of being our surrogate? Why Daddy? You've known about this for weeks."

"Yes, I have." Walter swirled the ice around in his crystal glass. "And every day I've tried to change her mind."

"And every day, I've told you to butt out of it, Dad." Naomi raised her head an inch off the pillow but collapsed as if it weighed too much. She placed her hand on her abdomen and rubbed it in slow circles. I hoped she was okay. "This is Kara and Hunter's baby we're talking about."

Hunter and Carol returned with drinks. A fresh scotch for Dad. Bottles of water for Naomi and Hunter. Wine for Anthony, my mother, and me. No surprise, Mom's glass was twice as full as everyone else's.

I took a sip. The sauvignon blanc had a zesty bite, but it was refreshing after the long day. I'd need a whole bottle to put up with my father. But I turned to my sister. "Nae, why didn't you tell me Daddy didn't want you to do this?"

"No point." She sighed and shrugged. "He couldn't talk me out of it."

God, I loved her so much.

"You have responsibilities, Naomi." Walter leaned forward, his gaze icy and hard. "The company is expanding across the country and growing internationally, and now you'll need maternity leave to have the baby. It's poor timing."

"No, it's perfect timing. Especially if London comes off next year." Naomi's voice grew fainter and fainter. "After I give birth, we'll move."

Sitting on the sofa arm beside me, Hunter wrung his hands around his bottle of water as he glared at my father, no doubt wishing it was my dad's neck. "Why didn't you want Nae to be our surrogate?"

"She's had her family," he snapped.

"And she's hopefully giving us ours," Hunter placed his hand over his heart. "Naomi is the best surrogate we could hope for. What she is doing for us goes beyond words."

Every time Hunter stood up to my father, it stole my breath. He didn't take crap from anyone, not even my intimidating dad. Another thread snapped around my guarded heart as I fell even more in love with him.

Redness consumed my father's neck and blotched his cheeks. "She doesn't need to put her body through this strain again."

"Um . . . women have babies every day." Hunter smirked, then took a swig of his water. "It's kinda what they're biologically designed to do."

"After having some time to get used to the idea, I think what Naomi is doing is wonderful." Carol downed half her glass. "I'll have another grandchild to spoil rotten."

I raised a questioning eyebrow. My mother wasn't much better than my father, but at least she tried to be nice, and genuinely would love another grandchild. "Thank you, Mom. I look forward to it." I kept my end goal in sight. Life with Hunter and a baby. I didn't need anything else. A family of my own was all I'd ever wanted.

Walter scoffed and shook his head. "How can you look forward to having a child out of wedlock? I raised my daughters to believe in family and tradition. Not that I'm complaining that you're not married, because Hunter, you'll never have my blessing to marry my daughter."

Hurt pummeled my ribs. My heart couldn't take any more. My father wasn't just attacking Hunter, but me as well. I slammed my wine down onto the coffee table. "Daddy, stop. Please." I wiped a tear from my eye, then tugged on Hunter's shirt sleeve. "I'm sorry, Hunt. Let's go."

"In a sec." Hunter clutched my shoulder and glared at my father. "If one day I decide to marry your daughter, Walter, I won't be asking for your approval. We don't need it. Whatever your ongoing petty grievance with me is, get over it. I don't have time or the energy to waste. I *am* committed to Kara and our baby. She's the one who doesn't want to get married."

"So she does have some sense," Walter mumbled under his breath and sipped his scotch.

Wait. What? Did Hunter want to get married? *Oh, shit.* Every time he'd brought it up, I'd shut him down. Killing the dream of marriage helped me to focus on what I wanted most out of life. I wouldn't destroy my relationship with Hunter with too many expectations, like I'd done with Conrad. Having a baby was more than I'd ever expected. It was more than enough.

But the seal on my marriage fantasy cracked a fraction. The vision of being in a white dress, saying *I do* with Hunter, surrounded by millions of flowers and gorgeous crystal chandeliers, with champagne glasses overflowing, and dancing beneath twinkling lights twirled through my head like Cinderella and her prince at a ball.

No. I wouldn't believe in fairy tales. Not again.

"Dad, we don't need to get married to prove that we love each other." I ignored the flinch in Hunter's hand. "But one day . . . we might venture down that path. Naomi is hopefully pregnant with *our* baby. *Your* grandchild. Can't you for once be happy for me? For us?"

"How can I when this is just another one of your rebellious antics?" Walter downed a mouthful of scotch. "Only this one has lifelong consequences. You're throwing away your future, three generations of Knight family tradition and business, and our legacy, to run off and play house with a rockstar."

"Yeah, she is," Hunter seethed. "Can't you see how amazing Kara is? That she's following *her* passion and dreams? Not yours. *Our* home is one of love and support, true loyalty and commitment. It is one of fun and laughter. That's the home we want to provide for our child—not one of ridicule and control."

"I want what is best for my daughter." My father's lip twitched and curled into a sneer.

"Then open your eyes and see what that is." Hunter never raised his voice, but every word packed a punch. My dad's knuckles whitened as he clenched his scotch glass. His eyes bulged in their sockets. His nostrils flared.

"Hunt, it's okay." Shaking all over, I couldn't take any more of my father's disapproval. I had to get out of there. "Let's go."

"It's not okay." The fire in Hunter's tone crackled. "You don't deserve to be treated like this." He gave a stiff nod. "But yes, let's get out of here. I have an early start at the studio tomorrow. You know . . . because I'm a no-hoper rockstar . . . recording our sixth album . . . preparing for our fifth world tour."

I bit my lower lip to contain my smile. Hunter's salty sarcasm aimed at my father lightened my mood. "Absolutely. And I'm nothing but your personal shopper who dresses you."

"Hmm." His eyes twinkled. "I prefer it when you undress me."

Anthony and Naomi laughed softly. Steam erupted from Dad's ears. Mom was lost in her wine.

Hunter stood, stepped over to Naomi and kissed her on the forehead. "Nae, thank you. We'll see you soon." He shook Anthony's hand and waved farewell to Carol.

I repeated the process. "Love you, Nae. Take care. Let me know if you need anything."

"Will do. Love you. Don't worry about Daddy. He'll come around," she said, as if he wasn't in the room.

I wouldn't hold my breath. If anyone could smooth things over with our father, it would be Naomi. But I didn't want her to stress. It wasn't healthy for the baby. "Don't waste your time. We'll be okay. You keep our baby safe."

Hunter took my hand in his and we headed home.

As the driver headed south, I collapsed against Hunter's arm. Running into my father hadn't been pleasant. It never was. I didn't want that old-school narrow-mindedness around our child. I didn't want him stressing Naomi out. Hunter didn't deserve to be talked to like that. My father was the one who needed a lesson in good manners and respect.

But my heart cried. I'd wanted my parents' love and support. It'd never come. Hunter was the father of my child. We were about to become a family.

Family?

New deep grooves pinched my brow. Hunter's reaction to marriage was new. I'd obsessed about tying the knot with my ex, Conrad, and had driven him into another woman's arms. I didn't want to do that to Hunter. I loved him too much. He wanted to have a baby with me and was committed to that.

That was enough.

I'd never ask for another thing.

Why would he want to marry me and be part of *my* family when my father was so awful to him?

But I closed my eyes and for a few brief minutes before we arrived home, I let the dream of having everything ... Hunter ... a baby ... getting married ... swirl through my head. But the second the car stopped, I came back to reality.

I'd learned not to be greedy.

Not to expect too much.

Not all dreams were meant to come true.

Chapter 22

HUNTER

It took twelve days. Twelve days for Naomi to lose the embryo.

Sitting in the live recording room at the studio, strumming chords on my guitar, I stared at the lyric sheet resting on the music rack. I couldn't focus on the words. Couldn't see the surrounding studio. Couldn't feel the music in my heart. Leaving Kara at Naomi's this morning had left me feeling useless, helpless, hopeless. Fucking doctors. They'd failed. *Again.*

There'd been a possibility that the first implant wouldn't take, but no matter how much I'd tried to prepare myself, the blow still drove a nail through my heart. But with a long day of recording ahead, I had to put the loss behind me. Move on. Try again. For Kara.

The door swung open, and Kyle, Gemma, and Hayden strode into the room.

Kyle, dressed in his trademark ripped jeans, black T-shirt and leather jacket, clapped his hands. "Woohoo. I'm pumped. You ready to record, man?"

"Yeah. I guess so." The shrug of my shoulders was as lackluster as my tone. Normally, I'd be the one bounding around the studio, hyped to lay down another track. I missed the days of not worrying about anything other than music, but now Kara, babies, Naomi, and my voice clouded every thought.

"Hunt?" Gemma came over and rubbed my back. "What's up?"

I struck a low, slow chord on my guitar and let the reverberations sink into my chest. It helped to lessen the ache. "Naomi lost the embryo." I prayed Walter wouldn't weave his way into Naomi's head and convince her not to try again.

"Oh, no." Gemma combed her short nails through my hair. "How is she? How's Kar?"

"Kar's a mess. Nae's okay. It didn't even take."

She squatted and looked up at me with hooded eyes. "You want to go?" She rubbed my knee. "We can kill the day here without you."

"No. I'm fine." I covered her hand with mine. "We'll try again in six or so weeks. I need music to take my mind off what happened."

"Sorry it didn't work." Kyle grabbed his bass and sat on the stool beside me. "I guarantee we'll take your mind off babies. We're halfway, bud. Fifteen tracks done. Fifteen to go. Let's get Hayds behind those drums and lay down another song or two."

Hayden stretched his arms above his head and swayed from side to side. "I can't wait to show you what I came up with for the track 'Gravitate.' I worked on it last night. It's total dance floor material."

"Awesome." My friends' enthusiasm ignited my spirit. This song held so much magic. We'd written it the night after I'd signed the surrogacy papers with Kara. Kyle, Gemma and I had channeled the indescribable bond we had for each other and our partners. My draw toward Kara defied logic. When we were together, everything felt right. Not even her family dramas could discourage me from being with her. But her dad had upset her. She wasn't sleeping well, checked on Naomi every day, and drowned herself in work. Was it just her way of coping with stress, excitement, and anticipation or something else? *Ugh!* I didn't have time to delve into the problem. I had to focus on finishing the album.

I waved toward the drums. "Hayds, let's hear it."

"I freaking love this song so hard." Gemma grabbed her guitar and dragged a chair over to join me and Kyle. "This has to be a single. In fact, I think it should be the first."

"I'm with you." Kyle plucked his bass. "This song is the shit."

The vibe radiating off my three friends coursed its way into my bloodstream, giving me the boost I needed. After playing the track through several times, hearing Hayden's tweaks to the beat and the added pause before the chorus, I was back to my normal self, mucking around, laughing, and having fun. I needed this. "It's brilliant, Hayds. Where's Reynold? We need to lay this down."

"I'm here." Reynold's voice came over the speakers from the control room. "I've been listening. I've recorded some of the runs. You guys make my job so easy."

I ripped out a riff on my guitar. "That's the plan."

Over the following three weeks, I'd spent long days fitting in vocal therapy and staying at the studio until the early hours of the morning, working tirelessly and relentlessly to complete the album. Track after track had slowly morphed into final cuts. Final cuts had turned into the shortlist of songs that would make it onto the album. *Kiss This*, our sixth studio album, had come to life. It was our way of saying, '*kiss our asses*' and '*fuck you*' to every industry asshole who'd said we'd never make it.

After seven weeks in the recording studio, I fell into a group hug with my friends and Reynold in the control room and jumped around in a circle.

"We did it," Gemma shrieked. "It. Is. Done."

"This album is the best we've ever made," I hollered as elation, pride and love for my friends filled my chest. I'd meticulously looked after my voice, had attended vocal therapy religiously, and had gone to regular checkups. I'd made it through. My voice had held. I'd even re-recorded the tracks I'd originally struggled with. My nodules hadn't reduced in size, but I'd learned to manage them, sing with them, live with them.

"We need to celebrate," Kyle cheered as he picked up Gemma, swung her over his shoulder, and carried her toward the door. "We'll grab the crew and hit a bar."

"Hell yeah." I followed close behind. "Even I deserve a drink after this." I'd almost forgotten what whiskey tasted like after drinking so much tea. One or two drinks wouldn't hurt.

I texted Kara to join us, but she declined. It was late, and she was already in bed. Hmm . . . I'd join her soon. But it wasn't like her not to come out.

At a wine bar near the recording studio, I downed a few drinks. "Cheers to the best group of friends. To many number-one hits. May we live and breathe music forever."

"Here's to that," Kyle hooted as we all clinked glasses.

The only person missing was Kara. At one a.m., I made my excuses and headed home. After showering, I curled in beside her and kissed her neck. I breathed in the scent of her rosy, perfumed skin. *So good.* Half-asleep, she rolled toward me and pulled my lips to hers. *Hmm.* Making love to her was a much better way to celebrate the end of recording.

***

August was a blur of marketing meetings, photo shoots, creative briefs for film clips, promotional scheduling and rehearsals. After shooting the cover for the album, I lazed, stretched out on my sofa with Kara in my arms. She was sifting through Lexi's photos from the shoot.

She held up a printout of the album cover Lexi had designed. "Your asses look hot in leather."

I glanced at the image. Against a white background, we were dressed in black. Kyle and I stood on either side of Gemma, our arms crossed behind her back. Our hands were shoved into the back pockets of her leather pants. Hers were buried in one rear pocket of Kyle's pants; the other was in mine. "Everybody's ass looks hot in leather. But yes, mine looks fucking awesome."

She jerked her elbow back, hitting me in the stomach. "You're so vain."

"Yep. And you love it." I kissed her on the cheek. But as I ran my hand over her side and blouse, my breath snagged. Her ribs, bony and bumpy, had become more prominent over the past few weeks. Her sexy curves had shrunk. She'd lost too much weight.

She wasn't sleeping any better, worked insane hours, and drank more alcohol. With the day for Naomi's second implant growing nearer, she never relaxed. Even now, she fidgeted with her rings, wriggled her toes, and shuffled against my chest. Was she terrified of another failure as much as I was? I hoped not. "Babe, you're fading away. You need to eat more."

"No, I don't. I've been busy running around the city every day, working for the band." She trailed her nails across the hair on my arm, tickling my flesh. "Besides, I needed to lose a few pounds."

"No, you didn't . . . I miss your curves." I ran my hand over the arch of her hip, her short floaty skirt, and down her thigh. I loved her body next to mine. So close. So warm. So divine. "If you're too busy, do you need to hire help?"

"No. I like being busy."

"I like you. Especially this bit." I pressed my lips into the small of her neck. "And this bit." I grazed my teeth over her shoulder. "And this—"

Before I could slip my hand underneath her skirt, her cell phone rang on the coffee table. She shot upright and lunged forward to answer it. She swiped the screen and put it on loudspeaker. "Hi Nae. What's up?"

I groaned and rolled onto my back. Covering my eyes with my arm, I half-heartedly listened to the conversation. My dick, straining in my long running shorts, wasn't happy. So much for getting some action.

"I have to go to Houston in two weeks for a conference." Naomi's tone prickled my ears. "I forgot I'm keynoting. It was planned months ago. Plus, I have to catch up with some clients. I can't get out of this trip. I'm so sorry, but we'll have to skip a cycle."

Miss a cycle? My heart snapped like a slingshot. I hauled myself upright next to Kara and listened with full attention.

Kara closed her eyes and rubbed her brow. "But that means we'll have to wait until mid-October. That pushes the due date into the beginning of Everhide's tour."

"I know," Naomi sighed. "I'm sorry. It's either that or wait for months."

Fuck! I'd never wanted to change the tour's start date, but I didn't want to delay our next IVF procedure either. I was as impatient as Kara . . . *Wait.* No, I wasn't. But fate had other plans regarding our child.

"It's fine, Nae." Somehow, I kept my voice level. "But in October, we'll be away on promo." I grabbed my cell phone off the table and scanned Kate's preliminary promotional agenda. "We'll be in Australia."

"You don't have to come to the procedure," Naomi said. "It'll be no different from last time."

Kara's eyes welled with tears. "No. I'm not missing it. I'll come home."

"But, babe, I can't." I'd promised to be here for every moment of this baby. Was there time to change the promo schedule? *Shit.* I wanted to get back in front of the fans and perform. This was only an implant. Not the birth. I'd seen one—that was more than enough. "You wanna come back without me?"

"For our baby, yes." Kara nodded. "I don't want to delay it further."

The distress in Kara's tone played agonizing chords on my heartstrings. Closing my eyes, I took a breath to unravel the knot in my stomach. If Naomi didn't have an embryo implanted in October, we'd have to wait until sometime during the tour so the baby would be due at the end. I didn't want to wait that long. The final show of the tour seemed like a lifetime away. "Neither do I. Nae, October it is. Let's hope this one works."

Chapter 23

HUNTER

Fast cars. Late nights. Thirteen days in LA filming two video clips had been a rush. Now back home, my friends and I took one last chance to have a break before the launch of our new single . . . and before our lives were wrapped up for months on end doing the promo and the tour. Taking advantage of the mid-September summer heat, everyone headed out to Kyle's beach house in Amagansett for a mini vacation. Sunshine. Swimming. Rest.

After throwing a football around and having a dip in the ocean with Kyle and Hayden, I picked up my towel from the sand, dried my face, and headed up to the house where the girls lazed outside on the deck chairs. Gemma had her earbuds in, listening to music. Lexi read a book. Kara stared at her cell phone. It was as if she didn't see me. The need to cause a stir skipped in my stomach. I tiptoed behind her to scare her, but I caught sight of her screen and stopped. It was a picture of Ryan in her arms.

Shit. My heart sank through the boards of the deck and hit the sand with a thud. Why did she still look at those images? Nothing would bring him back. She should be excited and looking forward to Naomi's next procedure, not dwelling on our past.

Pretending not to see the photo, I jumped beside the chair and shook my wet hair over her, spraying droplets everywhere.

"Ahhhh," she shrieked and dropped her cell phone onto her lap. "You scared the crap out of me."

"Good." I threw her a beaming smile and swooped in to kiss her lips. Taking a seat beside her, I leaned over her legs, resting my arm on the other side of the chair. "Whatcha doing?"

"Nothing."

Oh . . . was that how she wanted to play this? Why couldn't she admit to looking at the photos? Was she afraid of what I'd say?

I didn't know what to do other than distract her. "I need a shower. You want to join me?" I cocked one eyebrow and held out my hand, hoping she'd take up my offer.

"Okay."

Yes!

She slipped her hand into mine. Color rose in her cheeks. "Only because you look extra hot, all wet, ripped, and I couldn't take my eyes off of you playing in the waves."

I ran my hand over my bare stomach, flexing my abs and rubbing the droplets of water into my skin. "You like what you see? Then my plan worked."

She giggled as I helped her to stand and led her toward the door.

"Yo!" Lexi clicked her fingers, halting us in our tracks. "But keep it down. You two kept us awake last night. Fuck quieter. It's a small house. We don't need to hear it."

"No chance. I love making Kar scream." I slapped her on the ass.

"I wasn't talking about Kara." Lexi peered over the rim of her sunglasses.

I just grinned and drew Kara into the house.

But after some sexy loving, I walked out of the bathroom, wiping my towel over my freshly shaven face only to find Kara curled up on our bed with the sheet drawn to her chest. The bottle of pills on the nightstand caught my eye.

I rushed around to her side of the bed and sat beside her. "Pearl, what's wrong? You sick?"

"No." She snuffled, wiped a tear from her cheek.

I jerked my chin toward the nightstand. "What are the meds for?"

She tilted her head toward the bottle. "It's just some Xanax."

"Why do you need that?" I leaned against her, hugging her hip. "Talk to me? Please?"

"My doctor thought they might help manage my anxiety." She sniffled and adjusted the pillow under her head. "Just being here, in this house, brings back too many memories. To when we stayed here after losing Ryan."

I circled my thumb over the dip in her lower back and stared at the mattress. I preferred not to think about all those months ago. "But you've been here since then."

She smiled a sad smile. "I know. It hurts every time."

I sat forward and brushed her hair off her forehead. "But think about all the good times we've had here. The parties, the vacations, the bonfires, and time with our friends. In a month's time, Nae will be growing our new baby and we'll have so much to look forward to."

Her chin quivered. "I'm so scared of it failing again."

"Me too." I took her hand in mine and squeezed it. "But whatever happens, we'll get through it together."

"Yeah. Maybe." Her voice, soft and distant, was barely audible.

An ache stabbed my chest. *Maybe?* Why wouldn't we make it? Of course we would. What could I do to reassure her I'd be here for her? What could I do to stop her from dwelling on the past? *Fuck!* This was exhausting!

Shit . . . stop . . .

"Kar, we've got this." I meant that from the bottom of my heart. Something about her just made me want to fight and never let her go. "Why don't you get some rest? I'll come get you for dinner."

"Okay."

I kissed her forehead, dressed, and slipped out of the room. I headed downstairs to the kitchen and poured a shot of Jack Daniel's. At least this would make me feel better.

Gemma came in from the deck and closed the sliding glass door behind her. "Where's Kar?"

"Having a rest." I knocked back my shot, then placed my empty glass on the countertop. "I'm worried about her, Gem. I saw her looking at the pictures of Ryan again."

She slipped onto a stool opposite me and pushed her sunglasses onto the top of her head. "I've seen her do that too. She's worried about Nae losing another baby. She'll be okay. Just give her some space."

I didn't want space. I wanted to be by her side. Help her. "I don't know how to deal with this, Gem."

"That's the joy of being in a relationship." Gemma folded her arms and rested her elbows on the counter. "Some days are easy; others are fucking hard."

I jerked my chin back. "When have you had a hard day with Kyle?" Okay, that wasn't fair; they'd had a lot of rough times. I'd seen their hearts shatter, their souls torn apart, their love tried and tested, but they'd made it through. They'd been ridiculously happy since their wedding last year. Was the heartache and pain worth it? I hoped so, because they gave me hope that one day, I'd be like that. With Kara. Would a baby be the solution?

"Okay." Gemma chuckled, playing along with my wisecrack. She understood me better than anyone else. "I've heard *some* people have good and bad days."

"You goose." I grabbed her a glass and poured us a drink.

"Should you be drinking this close to promo?" Gemma pointed to my glass.

"Just one . . . and a bit." I tipped the whiskey down my throat and swallowed it. God, that was good. "I needed to take the edge off."

"No more. We need your voice for promo."

"Yes, Mom."

At present, my voice seemed to be the least of my worries.

***

By the end of September, every radio station and entertainment TV show buzzed with excitement for the release of our new single. The past two weeks had been a whirlwind of rehearsals, interviews, and private hearings. I'd been caught in the hype, infected by the adrenaline coursing through my veins. Even Kara's mood had brightened . . . most of the time. But she'd lost a couple more pounds; circles darkened her eyes. I prayed it was nothing more serious than our crazy work schedule and worry over Naomi's next IVF treatment. Every time I asked her if there was something wrong, she'd brushed me off and said she was fine.

I'd done the same thing regarding my voice.

We were as bad as each other.

My last appointment with Vanessa wasn't positive. My nodules hadn't changed. The largest one was still a concern. But I'd done the therapy. I could sing. I could live with them. They'd disappear eventually.

All my hard work was about to pay off. Promotion for the release of our new single had ramped up into a frenzy.

We were everywhere.

As Kyle, Gemma and I drove home from a photoshoot through Midtown, I'd been delegated to the back seat of Kyle's Range Rover.

As we stopped at a set of lights, I shot forward and pointed out the windshield at a bus. "There it is."

The promotional shot for our single, of the black Ferrari I'd driven during the filming of the video for "Gravitate", our logo, and a close-up of Gemma's glittery lips, covered the entire vehicle.

"Argh!" We all shrieked like first-graders and stomped our feet.

Every time we saw advertising for our music, it was a huge thrill, just like it had been when we released our first song all those years ago. It had never gotten old. If anything, it had gotten even more exciting because now we were in control. We never took anything we had achieved for granted. We worked damn hard to live our dreams.

"That looks so cool." A buzz hummed through Gemma's voice.

"I loved that car." It'd been wicked to drive through LA late at night. "I think I'm gonna buy one."

Gemma swiveled and glared at me. "You can't fit a baby seat

in that."

Fuck. I hadn't thought of that.

As we passed the main intersection at Times Square, Kyle slowed down. The cover image of our single lit up a billboard, flashing and dominating the neon landscape.

My heart faltered. *Just wow!*

Kyle peered up at the LED sign. "I'll never get sick of seeing our ugly faces up there."

"Nope. Never." I agreed. The image of us at night, in LA, with highway lights swirling behind us, was racy and raunchy. I freaking loved it. "This album is going to blow everyone out of the water." I was so sure of that, even the marrow in my bones tingled. "It all starts in two days."

"I can't wait." Gemma clapped and stamped her feet.

Her energy was contagious—not that I needed it.

This album would kick ass.

***

On October 1st, our single "Gravitate" hit the airwaves. Within twenty-four hours, it had hit number-one in seventeen countries.

I rushed home from last-minute rehearsals and found Kara watching TV. I pulled her to her feet and swung her round. "This is amazing. We're number-one."

"That's incredible." She hugged me tight. "You deserve it."

"We fucking rock." I placed her feet on the floor and clutched her shoulders. "I can't wait to hit the road."

Tomorrow, the promotional tour kicked off here in New York. We'd head to LA, New Zealand, Australia, Paris, and the UK. The music and the fans were ready. The fire in my soul burned hot and bright. I wanted Kara to be by my side for every crazy moment of the four-week publicity campaign. I wanted the hype and fun to fill her soul. But she'd miss half of it to fly home for Naomi's next IVF treatment and her mom's birthday. So, I'd savor every second until then. "Are you ready, Pearl?"

She slid her hands around my waist and clutched my ass. "Yes.

But I might have to get Bec to book another room for me. I'm not sure if I'll fit in with your ego."

"I'll upgrade to a king suite and make sure I can squeeze you in." I grabbed her hand, twirled her around, and sang a line from the single.

I gravitate, I radiate, toward you.

I dipped her backward, but instead of laughing, she groaned. "Ugh, I'm sick of your song already." The dazzle in her eyes suggested otherwise.

"Get used to it, baby. We'll be singing it for the rest of our days. The fans love it."

She stood upright and straightened her shirt. "Hmm . . . the fans." She lowered her chin and slumped her shoulders. "I'm not looking forward to them screaming and chasing you everywhere we go."

"What? That's the best part." I pulled her close and brushed my lips against hers. "But I'll be in your bed every night."

"You better be." She clutched my chin and gave it a gentle shake. "Now stop playing around." She tapped my cheek lightly. "You should rest. Don't strain your voice."

Her playful yet serious tone rammed a rod down my spine. I drew my shoulders back, closed my eyes and clenched my jaw. Pressure mounted inside my head. *Thud. Thud. Thud.* After weeks of non-stop meetings and interviews and rehearsals, I was over worrying about her, and over everyone telling me what to do. Rest. Don't drink. Sing this way, not that. Go here. Do this. Say that. Wear this. It was enough to make me want to scream.

I'd had enough.

Kyle, Gemma and I had just hit number-one. We were on a high. We needed to celebrate. Big time.

I'd sworn to live it up before Kara and I had a baby. That was exactly what I'd planned to do on this tour. Party. Sing. Give the fans what they wanted.

I wouldn't hold back. Not anymore.

Not for Kara. Not for anyone.
Bring promo on. Loud, hard, and fast.
It was time to fucking party.

Chapter 24

KARA

Nine days into Everhide's promotional tour, I'd touched down in Sydney, Australia, with my friends. The schedule had been more insane than preparing for New York's Fashion Week. Coordinating three to four outfits per day for each of them, working with local designers, managing deliveries, and making last-minute alterations had me working overtime. Every time they'd changed their clothes, a rush of adrenaline surged through my veins. Each look had pushed my creativity, quick thinking and flair, but my friends often tested my patience. Some days it felt like it would be easier to run a marathon in six-inch platform stilettos than to dress three hyped-up rockstars before a publicity appearance.

Like now.

"Stand still or I'll stab you with the needle." I quickly sewed a button back onto Hunter's dress shirt. He always wore the top half undone, but of course, one of the lower buttons had fallen off.

They were running ten minutes late to hit the stage. Luckily, it was a surprise Friday night gig at a nightclub near Circular Quay. No one other than the venue's management team knew Everhide were about to perform. Still, I hated slipping behind schedule, even by a minute. I wanted this show to be over and done with so I could spend time with Hunter before I headed back to New York tomorrow for Naomi's second procedure.

Since the promotional tour had started, we'd barely had any downtime. Stealing kisses before shows and short, hot moments had been fun, but I wanted to spend hours with him, not a few quick minutes.

Hunter jiggled his legs as he ran through vocal warm-ups with Kyle and Gemma. His eyes were set on them as concentration knitted his brow. My stomach flopped like last season's micro-mini handbag. Chances of alone time were slim. Nights like this often turned into all-night parties. And Hunter never said no to a party.

I snipped the end of the thread and placed the needle and scissors back into my *never-leave-home-without-it* stylist emergency kit on the nearby table. As I re-buttoned his shirt, there were no sexy, sly comments from him. No *"Leave it, the fans love seeing my bare chest."* No *"Kar, why bother? The buttons will only fall off when you tear me out of my shirt later."* No *"I prefer you taking my clothes off rather than putting them on."* I got nothing. He was in the zone, focused on singing.

"Time," Sophie called from the doorway.

Kyle grabbed his transmitter and in-ear monitors and hooked them into place. He wriggled his belt. "Kar, this is too loose. There are no more holes in it."

"Hold on." I grabbed my leather holepunch from my kit. "Why didn't you tell me back at the hotel before we left?" I rushed over to him and punched another hole in the studded black leather. "How's that?"

"Perfect."

"Good save, Kar." With his foot propped up on a chair, Hunter retied the laces on his combat boots, double knotting them. "We don't want Kyle to scare off the girls with his tiny package if his pants fall down."

"We all know it ain't tiny." Chuckling, Kyle smirked as he flicked his dirty blond hair out of his eyes.

"Well, shit." Gemma waggled her finger toward Hunter's crotch. "Better not lose *your* jeans then, because we all know

Kyle's bigger than you."

"You fucking wish." Hunter's eyes twinkled as he placed his boot on the floor.

I giggled, but only for a second. Hunter had time to joke around with his friends, but not with me. Was he just nervous about the gig? That wasn't like him. Was he still worried about his voice? Absolutely. He hadn't mentioned anything to me, but I knew him well enough to know something wasn't right.

"Come on," Sophie groaned and waved them out of the dressing room. "You're late. Move it."

With drumsticks in hand, Hayden leaped from the sofa and joined them. For small gigs like this, Everhide's full backup band wasn't necessary. The four of them looked good together . . . and played even better.

I followed everyone to the side of the small stage. The DJ's heavy beat boomed through the speakers, vibrated through the floor and reverberated up my legs. I joined Lexi and Bec beside the heavy black curtain. I turned to give Hunter a good-luck kiss, but he had his eyes closed as he ran through more last-minute vocal warm-ups. Even I could hear that his voice had more rasp than it did a month ago. He wouldn't rest, and loved performing too much. I hoped he knew what he was doing.

Bryce, Everhide's stagehand, tapped Hunter on the arm, handed him his guitar, and gave him the thumbs up.

Hunter barely nodded.

Kyle, Gemma, and Hunter were in performance mode, focused and centered. Nothing entered that atmosphere until they came offstage.

Lexi darted around them, taking photos.

I slumped against the wall and made sure my heart was in check to face the aftermath of another show. Each day, more and more fans turned up at the hotels we stayed at, waited outside radio and TV stations for photos and autographs, or lined up for hours to see them perform at some promotional hotspot.

Hunter thrived on the hysteria and loved the adoration.

But it churned my gut every time girls touched him, hugged

him . . . kissed him. Jealousy was an ugly shade of green; and I hated that I wore it so well.

The worst thing was, Hunter had disregarded the fact that the overzealous fans bothered me. He'd ignored me and told me I had nothing to worry about. But I did.

Something about him was off tonight. Something more than his voice. It had my senses on high alert.

Bec nudged my arm. "You look like you could do with a drink."

"Please. Make it a double."

As I followed Bec to our cordoned-off table on the side of the club, the DJ announced the special appearance of Everhide. A wild, shrieking roar erupted from the over-packed nightclub crowd. It was so deafening I cupped my ears. As I weaved through the sea of people rushing toward the stage, my friends took to their mics. Hayden launched into a heavy bass drumbeat. Hunter strummed his guitar beside Gemma and Kyle. His eyes sparkled. His smile dazzled. The crowd had turned into a frenzy of waving arms, jumping bodies, and roof-raising screams.

I waved, trying to catch Hunter's eye, but he didn't glance in my direction—not once.

After ordering drinks, I sank onto a chair beside Sophie, Kate, and Bec.

"Kar, you look exhausted." Kate stirred her martini with the olive on a toothpick.

"I am." I swirled the ice around in my JD. I had Hunter to thank for my love of whiskey. I'd never thought I'd ever see the day where I preferred JD over champagne. But then, I'd also never thought I'd fall for a rockstar. "I underestimated how draining tours could be."

I'd never worked on a full promotional schedule with Everhide before. I'd only ever gone to shows here and there. But on this trip, I'd rushed with them from breakfast shows to talk shows to late-night shows—to radio stations to promo parties to live performances. From photo shoot to photo shoot. To interview after interview. They had back-to-back appearances, from six in the morning to midnight, nearly every day we were away. How would I survive a full tour? How would I do this with a baby? I wanted to be a hands-on mom and not employ a nanny, but the daily workload scared me.

"Do you need to hire an assistant?" Sophie sipped her rum.

"No." I didn't think I needed one. Not yet anyway.

"You don't have to be Superwoman." Concern swam through her eyes.

"Some days I wish I was. Dressing the three of them, and Hayden, and being with Hunter certainly keeps me on my toes."

"You're the crazy one who shacked up with him." Bec giggled over the rim of her vodka. "But you're the best thing that's ever happened to him. He's so much nicer and easier to deal with now that he's with you. And I don't miss throwing girls out of his hotel room or off buses or out of dressing rooms."

Nausea pooled low in my stomach. Everyone had a past. I just wished Hunter's didn't follow us everywhere. "Yeah . . . I don't need the reminder."

Sophie glanced at her watch, then at Everhide rocking on stage. "They're good tonight. The crowd is well behaved. They've got two songs left. They'll want to stay afterwards to have a drink and meet the fans."

Great. Even less chance of spending time with Hunter before I leave.

But Sophie was right.

After Everhide finished their set, they headed for the bar. Security surrounded them to keep the fans at bay. The pushing and shoving and never-ending swarm around my friends made my nerves shake. I worried about their safety. Especially Gemma, because she was so small.

I downed my third JD as they greeted the fans, but it quickly turned into them knocking back shots and drinking whiskey and beer with the partygoers. More hyped-up fans gathered around them. More photos were taken. The flow of girls levitating toward Hunter grew thicker and thicker. Closer and closer. There were too many kisses planted on Hunter's cheeks . . . the odd one hit his mouth. There was too much touching. Too much hugging. Too many flirty, suggestive looks. The fans were nowhere near as bad around Kyle and Gemma; there were a couple of feet between them. But with Hunter, there was barely any room for air.

I'd had enough. I pushed my chair back and took a step in his direction, but Bec caught my arm.

"You sure you want to enter the snake pit?"

"I've dealt with fans before."

"It's not the fans I'm worried about. Hunter will want to stay until everyone's said hello, had a photo, and he's signed whatever they want him to sign. Same with Kyle and Gemma. My advice? Let them be."

"Why?"

"They love their fans. This is like a drug to them. Don't interfere. It's taken me eight years to work out how they operate. Some nights they just need to let loose, have a few drinks, go a bit crazy. Like tonight. But this is part of their job."

I'd been to enough shows to know what they were like. "I understand that, but Kyle and Gemma aren't kissing and smothering every fan. Hunt needs to tone it down."

Bec puffed air through her nose. "Good luck with telling him to stop."

I flipped my hair over my shoulder and headed toward him. I edged my way through the sardine-packed crowd and threaded my hand around his waist.

"Hey." He hooked his arm around me and kissed my temple. "What's up, beautiful?"

"You remember I leave at four for the airport?"

"Yeah." He swallowed his JD and placed the glass on the bar counter beside him. "Give me ten more minutes."

I tugged on his arm and spoke into his ear. "Fine. But cool it with the girls, please? Tone it down. There's too much kissing. They're all over you."

"What?" He jerked his chin back. "No, they're not."

Gemma edged between us and held up her hand to ward off the fans. Security stepped in to block the crowd. She swayed on her feet and hooked one arm around my back, and the other around Hunter's waist. "Everything okay?"

I sighed. "Hunt's being too friendly with the fans."

"Am not." He shook his head.

"Yeah, you're a bit full on." Gemma wrinkled her nose. Her breath reeked of whiskey.

He shrugged and grinned. "I'm having fun."

"And I'm all for that." I hated the bite in my tone, but he'd gone too far. "Just do it without being overzealous with *every* girl."

"She's right." Gemma dug her elbow into his ribs. "I'd be pissed at Kyle if he was all over every chick." She blew a kiss to Kyle, who stood a few yards away at the bar having selfies with a couple of nightclubbers. He waved at her, then smiled for the camera. Gemma spun around and jabbed her finger into Hunter's chest. "Behave. You're not single anymore. You have my girl, Kar."

"You're on her side?" Disbelief elevated his tone.

"Yep." Gemma play-punched his arm. "Don't be a dick. I don't want to have to break your balls." She threw him a *I-love-you-but-cool-it-down* smile, clicked her heels together, turned, and returned to Kyle's side.

She didn't have to intervene, but I loved that she did.

"So, is that it, Kar?" Warning flashed in Hunter's eyes. "You wanna stay by my side and babysit me?"

"No. Not at all. But I will pull you into line when you go too far. What you're doing makes me uncomfortable."

"Then maybe you shouldn't come to gigs like this." A hard line set in his jaw. "I haven't done anything wrong. What do I have to do to get you to fucking trust me?"

My heartbeat stumbled back a step. "I do trust you." He'd pushed the boundaries tonight, though. He had to know there were limits. We were in a relationship. Where was the respect? I'd asked him nicely to tone it down. Why was he biting my head off?

He flicked his hand past my shoulder toward the waiting crowd. "I won't stop greeting the fans. I love it."

"I didn't ask you to. I can handle the hugs and photos, but not the kisses. The odd one on the cheek is tolerable, but not on the mouth. I don't think it's an unreasonable request." I glared at the fresh JD placed on the bar counter for him. "And why are you drinking? What about your voice?"

He swiped the glass off the bar and knocked it down. "It's fine. I'm only having a couple of drinks."

"You've had way more than a couple."

Shards of ice shot through his eyes as he brushed his fingertip down my nose. "I know what I'm doing."

"Do you? You get so caught up in all this attention, you lose sight of everything around you. You don't know when to stop."

"I wanted one night off." He held up one finger. "One night of not worrying about you, or you flying home, or about Naomi's procedure, or about my fucking voice. Is that too much to ask?"

"Yes. It is." Concern slammed into my chest. Hunter was usually cool and calm and didn't let anything bother him. How had I not noticed he'd been stressed lately? *Crap.* I'd been so consumed by my own problems, I'd been blind. Now I felt terrible and worried about him even more. "You don't have to worry about me and Nae, but you have to look after your voice. The doctor said no drinking."

"Fuck." He closed his eyes and rubbed his forehead. "Just stop *fucking* telling me what to do."

Flashes caught my eye. Onlookers snapped photos of us. Camera cases sparkled and shimmered, catching the disco lights. *Great . . .* I bet pictures of us arguing would hit TMZ by dawn. That wouldn't be a first. But I refused to back down. "Fine. If you want to stay here with the fans, so be it. But I have to go catch a plane."

I spun on my heels and headed back to our table. I tapped Giles, my bodyguard, on the shoulder. "Take me home, please?"

I grabbed my purse off the chair and headed past the bar for the exit. Just as I reached the top of the steps, Hunter caught my hand. "Kar. Wait. I'm sorry. You know I wish I could go with you to be with Nae."

I tugged my hand free. My heart ached. Every day since promo had started, he'd gotten more and more swept up by the fans. It was like I was an afterthought and having a child rarely entered his mind. Babies were always on my mind. Xanax was the only thing that stopped me from having anxiety attacks and worrying about Naomi's next procedure. Looking at the photos of Ryan kept my end goal in sight. "No. You want to be here with your band and your fans." I tilted my head toward our friends at the bar, but kept my eyes on Hunter. "Go. Have fun."

He shook his head. "I can't be in two places at once."

"I know that." All too well. I drew my shoulders back and smoothed my hand over my dress pants. "Go do your job. I'll see you in London."

"Fine. Love you." He gave me a quick, cold kiss on the cheek, then stormed off into the crowd.

I strode down the steps and out the door with Giles trailing behind me. Cameras flashed as I dashed from the nightclub and into the waiting car. *Fuck.*

My heart crashed against my ribs as I slumped into the back seat. I'd been stupid to fight with Hunter in sight of everyone, especially when he was drunk. But I worried about him. How could he resist all that temptation around him, day after day? How could I ever completely trust him?

What had my therapist said about our relationship?

Take it slow . . . *Nope*, we'd moved in together within three months.

Make a list of what I wouldn't tolerate in a relationship . . . *Ha*, as if I'd ever keep the female fans away.

Communicate . . . *Okay*, we could do better at that.

Understand he is not your ex . . . *LOL.* Hunter's reputation was worse. Conrad had left me for one woman; Hunter was God's gift *to* women.

Trust your instincts . . . *Shit*, we were more screwed up than any family on the TV show *Riverdale.*

I closed my eyes and took a deep breath. Twelve days away from Hunter would give me a break after the hectic months leading up to promo. The peace and quiet would do me wonders. I had to clear my mind, refocus.

I had to learn to deal with nights like this, otherwise, my relationship with Hunter wouldn't survive the tour.

Or was I kidding myself and just delaying the inevitable?

No . . . God, no.

We planned to have a baby.
We had to find a way to work.

Chapter 25

KARA

Thirty-six hours of travel from Sydney to New York seemed to take forever. Thanks to time zones, I'd left Australia with Giles on Saturday morning, and had arrived home on Saturday evening. As the plane pulled up to the gate at JFK, I switched on my cell phone. It instantly vibrated with messages. It didn't stop. *Crap! What's happened?*

I unlocked the screen. The first text was from Hunter.

> HUNTER: CALL ME ASAP. IT'S NOT WHAT YOU THINK.

What? I kept reading. More from Hunter.

> HUNTER: PEARL, WHERE R U?
> YOU SHOULD'VE LANDED BY NOW.
> PLEASE CALL ME.

My heart rate sped up to *let's-not-panic-yet* mode. I'd been delayed in LA, had sat on the runway for forty-five minutes before taking off, then circled JFK once before landing. I was only two hours late. I kept reading.

> HUNTER: PLEASE CALL. LET ME EXPLAIN.

> GEMMA: PLS CALL HUNT. HE'S LOSING HIS MIND.

HUNTER: I LOVE YOU. PLS CALL.
DON'T BELIEVE THE BULLSHIT.
I'M SORRY.

Shit! What had happened?

I scanned my emails. Google Alerts filled my screen with Everhide news . . . *Hunter* news. I clicked on the first link, and my heart stopped. Images of Hunter dancing with a girl, barely inches apart, at the club after I'd left, graced the top of the article. Then there was a picture of him walking into a hotel *with her*—it wasn't the one we'd stayed at. The next photo was of the two of them having coffee, tucked away in a corner booth at a café. Following that was a shot of them hugging, and the girl kissing Hunter on the cheek.

What the fuck?

I continued to scroll. There were more photos of me arguing with Hunter and leaving the club with Giles. *Shit!* The article headlines severed my heart.

Hunter Parties With A Mystery Girl In Sydney. Looking Hot!
Has Hunter Collins Got A New Girlfriend?
Kara Knight Walks Out On Hunter Collins. We Have The Exclusive Pictures.

My cell phone trembled in my hand as I struggled to read article after article. I tried to keep a clear head.

It's-not-what-it-seems. It's-not-what-it-seems. It's-not-what-it-seems.

But regardless of what I told myself, tears welled in my eyes. I had to get off this plane. I had to call Hunter. And find out what the fuck was going on.

Dashing off the aircraft, I found a quiet corner at the end of the passenger boarding bridge and called him . . . No answer. I texted . . . No reply.

It's nine a.m. in Sydney. Where is he?

But as I headed for the baggage claim area, a whole new level of drama unfolded. The paparazzi swarmed around the carousel.

Fuck.

"Giles." I couldn't hide the tremble in my voice. "We have a problem."

"I see that." He edged in front of me. "Let's make our way over to the security desk. I'll get more help to get you out of here. I'll call the driver. We might head out a different exit."

"We should have used VIP access." I'd never needed it before. I could usually travel without too much hassle. But this was a feeding frenzy, and I was the kill.

I didn't make it to the bottom of the escalator. The paparazzi spotted me and charged toward me with their blinding flashes. I put on my Prada sunglasses and tucked in behind Giles's broad shoulders.

"Miss Knight. Miss Knight. Did you and Hunter Collins break up?" the photographers yelled and hollered. "What did you argue about? Who's the girl Hunter spent the night with?"

He better not have.

The hounding didn't stop. With every step, I struggled through the throng of cameras and reporters. There were about thirty of them pressing closer and closer. My whole body trembled. My knees struggled to hold me upright. Giles wrapped his arm around my shoulders and shuffled me forward. In the madness, someone pushed us sideways. Another person knocked into me from behind.

"Argh!" I shrieked. I lost my balance and fell hard onto the cold concrete floor. Tears streamed down my face as I clutched my hand against my chest. "Ow! My wrist."

"Back off." Giles's booming voice hollered above. He hooked his hand underneath my arm and helped me to my feet. "Are you okay?"

"No," I sniffed and shook my head. "My wrist."

Airport security charged through the reporters and formed a circle around us. "Let's get you to the car," the head guard guided me forward. "Do you have luggage?"

"Yes."

"I'll get it," Giles jutted his chin toward the exit. "After we get you out of here."

"Okay."

Once I was in the car, I caught my breath. As security kept the reporters away from the vehicle, I burst into tears. I held my aching hand, and my heart trembled as much as my body. What had Hunter done to cause this much shit?

Ten minutes later, Giles returned with our luggage and tossed it into the trunk. He hopped in beside me, and the driver took off.

"Giles, we need to go to the hospital. My wrist is really hurting." I held it out to see the damage, but pain shot up my arm. A lump swelled underneath the skin. *Is it broken?*

Giles tucked a blanket over my lap. "I'm sorry you got hurt, miss."

"It's not your fault. There were too many reporters." There should've been none.

I tried to call Hunter again. Still no answer. I scanned the promo schedule. *Melbourne. Morning radio show.* Great! He'd be busy for another three hours.

After two hours in the emergency department, I walked out of the treatment room with a brace on my wrist. Luckily, it wasn't broken, just sprained.

Heading home, I steeled myself as the driver turned into the laneway that led to my building. The road was blocked with paparazzi. The driver hit the brakes to avoid hitting some idiot standing in the middle of the road with his long-range lens hanging over his shoulder. The second the other photographers saw the car, they ran toward us.

"Shit." Giles rubbed the thick two-day growth of stubble on his chin. "You want to go through this or head elsewhere?"

After the long hours of travel and time at the hospital, I just wanted to take a shower and go to sleep in my bed. "Through." No one would keep me out of my home. "We can go into the garage if that's easier."

"Probably not. Whoever's on the front door will help me get

you inside."

My pulse quickened as I nodded. *This can't be worse than the airport, right?* "Okay. Let's go."

The driver inched to a halt in front of my building. Giles opened the door, jumped out and helped me out of the car. The cameras went wild. *Click. Click. Click. Flash. Flash. Flash.* But luckily, the path to my door was nowhere near as bad as JFK.

Once inside, I let out the breath I'd been holding. "Thank you, Giles. You earned your keep today."

"Sure did, miss." He stood with his back to the front door, blocking me from the cameras angled in my direction. "Are you going to be okay by yourself? I'll stay here until I can arrange for extra security."

"Thank you. I'll be fine, but yes, security would be good." It'd make me feel safer. "Nae's appointment is on Monday afternoon. I'll see you then." That gave me a day to recover.

"Yes, miss. Have a good weekend."

"You too, Giles."

After he grabbed my luggage, I headed into the elevator and up to the penthouse. As I walked through the living room, my heeled boots clicked on the hardwood floors and echoed off the walls. The place seemed cold and empty without Hunter in it. I sank onto the sofa, clutched a pillow to my chest and burst into tears. "Why is this happening?"

It was near eleven in the evening, New York time, when my cell phone rang. Hunter's name lit the screen. I grabbed it off the nightstand and swiped to answer the call. "Hey."

"Oh, thank God." His breathy voice rushed through the speaker. "Are you okay?"

"No," I sniffled, afraid of what he had to say. "The paparazzi are everywhere. I got hurt. I sprained my wrist. Reporters are surrounding the building. I left you two days ago, and all hell has broken loose."

"Fuck. I'm so sorry."

"So? Who is she?"

"Camilla? She's an old friend, acquaintance . . . Fuck . . . She was in one of our video clips a few years ago. She was in Sydney on a modeling assignment."

"Ah-ha." Anger slipped into my voice. "And she just happened to show up at the club the second I was gone?"

"I didn't know she'd be there. She turned up with friends. Kyle and Gem can verify every detail. So can everyone else, including our security team. Fuck, I'll get the security footage if I have to. We gave Camilla a lift back to her hotel. We had coffee. We left. The fucking sites have cut Kyle and Gem out of every shot. They were right beside me or a few feet away, having photos with fans. There were tons of people around. I swear."

His voice just rang in my ears. "Did you sleep with her?"

"What? No." Exasperation shot through his tone. "Not the other night . . . but years ago, I did. Just once."

"I just thought . . . after our fight . . . and you'd been drinking . . ." I sat up against the headboard and drew my knees to my chest.

"Kar. Nothing happened."

"But she's gorgeous." Victoria's Secret stunning.

"Who? Camilla? She's okay. Too skinny for my liking."

"Don't lie. She's beautiful and has fantastic boobs." Images of Camilla's perfect tan, breathtaking smile, and deep brown eyes flickered through my mind. She was total swimsuit model material.

"No, your boobs are the best. Kar, please believe me." Tiredness swung through his voice. "I haven't slept. All I've done is worry about you and stress over how you'd react. I hate I can't catch up with an old friend without sending the world into a meltdown."

I understood his frustration. Life in the public eye wasn't easy.

"You do like attention though."

"Yes, but not this clickbait bullshit."

"Is that all it is?" I took a deep breath to steady my racing mind. I didn't want to fight or say something I'd regret.

"Yes." He said with a stress-filled rush. "Kar, the other night, I was a complete jerk. You have every right to be pissed at me. I should've been more mindful of your feelings. I shouldn't have let anyone kiss me. I'm so fucking sorry. Being drunk was no excuse. By the time I came to my senses and wanted to run after you to apologize, you were on the plane. Pearl, I never meant to hurt you. I'm sorry I got caught up in the hype. I fucked up. It won't happen again. Because I'm yours. Nobody else's."

His desperate plea tapped on my heart. His anguish slammed into me from halfway around the world. I'd been around long enough to know not to believe the gossip. It didn't mean it didn't hurt. This wasn't the first time we'd been the target of ruthless lies. He'd been snapped by the paparazzi last Christmas when we were in Chicago—the gossip sites reported he'd been out shopping with a mysterious girl . . . No, it'd been his fucking cousin. I'd been photographed a few months back at dinner, supposedly with a new man . . . No, I'd had lunch with our friend, my client, Flint.

I knew better than to jump to the wrong conclusion. The other night wasn't our normal. If we were going to survive, we had to work through the shitfests together.

"I do believe you." I closed my eyes and wiped a tear from my cheek. "It's just hard sometimes. I hate fighting." We rarely did; that's what hadn't helped the situation.

"Me too."

"And I'm sorry I brought up my issues in the club." My insecurities had gotten the better of me. "It was bad timing."

"Kar, you never have to apologize for telling me how you feel or for pulling me into line for being a dick."

Wow. My heart swelled. He had changed. We both had. Every storm we faced brought us closer together. From miles away, he claimed another piece of my heart. "Okay." I sniffled and nodded. "But you shouldn't keep things from me either. I hate that you're stressing about everything."

"Life is just crazy at the moment. And I miss you." He dialed down the volume of his voice. "Kar, I swear I will always be honest. I won't lie to you. If something had happened, I'd tell you. I've seen what lies and cheating do to people. I've hurt people I've loved in the past. I don't ever want to go through something like that ever again. I won't do that to you. Not ever. I love you so fucking much and don't want to fuck us up. I want you and only you. Got it?"

A small smile tugged at the corner of my mouth. He could be so sweet. I loved that. "Yes."

"Talk to me about something to take my mind off this crap. Have you spoken to Nae? Is she ready for Monday?"

"I haven't called her yet."

"I should've gone home with you. Gem and Kyle could've done a week's promo without me. I'm so fucking stupid."

"Yeah, you are," I whispered, wishing he was here.

"So, you go with Nae to the clinic and get her knocked up good, okay? I want a baby with you."

The heartfelt sincerity in his voice coiled around my heart, and the tension eased from my shoulders. God, I loved him. But clouds of doubt still lingered over my head. Would the gossip ever disappear? Or would it be a never-ending vicious circle we'd never break? No, probably not. But I wouldn't let the gossipmongers ruin what I had with Hunter. I was doing a fine job of that myself by being jealous of every girl who looked in his direction.

That had to stop. And stop now.

I had to trust him. I did trust him. "Hunt, I want a baby with you too. More than anything."

"Just know I'm thinking about you all the time. I'm sorry for all the crazy, but I've gotta go." He said softly then sighed as if exhausted. "We have promo all afternoon and tonight. We fly to Paris tomorrow morning. I'll call before we leave. You get some sleep, okay?"

"I will. You take care. Love you. Bye." I tossed my cell phone onto the bed and shuffled down to snuggle under the quilt. Running my hand over his side of the mattress, I skimmed across the imprint where he'd slept.

My head raced, replaying everything that had happened.

Until the other night at the club, promo had been fun. We'd laughed. We'd had a great time and looked forward to our baby. I'd let work stress and worry over Naomi's pending procedure get to me. I had to focus on the good things about Hunter—not the bad. I closed my eyes and hugged his pillow to my chest. Regardless of all our ups and downs . . . our fight . . . I believed he'd told me the truth. I trusted him. But if he ever betrayed me, I don't think I had the strength to survive another broken heart.

He was embedded deep in my soul.

I hoped I hadn't made a mistake in taking a leap of faith. On Hunter. On us. On our future together.

***

I woke at four a.m. after a few hours' sleep. *Damn jetlag.* Wide awake, I jumped out of bed and made a cup of tea. As I sipped my brew, I scanned my social media. My feed was full of articles and posts about the *"Camilla photos."* I flew past every one.
But Kate had sent me a link to a TikTok video. A video from Camilla. I clicked on it.

Don't believe the photos. I'm not with Hunter.
We're old friends and were catching up.
He's very much in love with Kara. He's totally smitten and devot-
ed to her.
Kyle and Gemma were with us. They've been cut out of the shots.
Sorry everybody, but Hunter is off the market.
Kara, own that, girlfriend.
I hope Hunter sues the pants off the reporter.
#FuckPaparazzi #FakeNews #GossipSux #ItsAllBullshit

The fans had replied with thousands of comments. *"Why do they make up such lies?" "Why do the paparazzi hurt the innocent?" "I knew it was fake." "Kara and Hunter forever." "I hope the reporter gets fired."*

I could only wish.

***

Early Monday afternoon, I headed to Naomi's place. The paparazzi outside my building had thinned to a few stragglers. But as my driver pulled away from the curb, Giles looked over his shoulder.

"I think we have someone following us on a motorbike."

Shit. "Going to my sister's is real world-shattering news." But if they followed us to the clinic, then baby gossip might explode. Naomi had wanted to keep the surrogacy private. I guessed I'd better warn her to be prepared.

After a quick stop at the drugstore, we headed uptown to Naomi's.

Erika answered the door. The sweet smell of freshly baked cookies drifted from the kitchen. My stomach grumbled. I hadn't eaten much since arriving home. My pantry was bare except for dry pasta.

"Hi Erika. Is Nae ready?"

"Yes, miss. She's in the office."

"Working?" A pinch formed between my eyebrows. "She's supposed to be resting." Heading down the hallway, I hollered, "Nae. I'm here."

"Hi." Her face lit with a bright smile as she came out of her office. Dressed in linen pants and a pale pink Chanel jacket, she looked set for a business meeting, not an IVF implant. "How was the travel?"

"Long." I handed her the bag from the drugstore. "I got you these. Don't get excited. It's just more vitamins."

"You don't have to buy them."

"I don't mind. Anything to do with our baby, I said I'd pay."

"Yeah, the medical expenses, the clinic, and the agency fees. But you don't have to buy me food and vitamins."

"I want to make sure you're taking care of yourself."

"I am. So back off."

"I'm sorry." I placed my hand on my jittery stomach. "I'm just nervous about today."

"Well, I'm good. But . . ." She raised one questioning eyebrow. "Is everything okay? Are we still all systems go?"

I lifted my chin, not liking Naomi's tone. "Yes. Why wouldn't we be?"

Worry flickered across her eyes. "I saw the gossip about Hunter and that girl, Camilla What's-Her-Face."

Oh . . . that! "It was all bullshit." I swiped my hand through the air. "Camilla's an old friend. Nothing happened." I truly believed Hunter. And Gemma would have eaten him alive if he'd done anything to hurt me. She was like my own mini-German Shepherd.

"So, you two are okay?"

"Yes." I rested my butt cheek on the kitchen stool beside me. "It's always weird for a couple of days when shit like this happens. But we're cool. Sydney just got out of control. We had a fight, too. That didn't help. Hunt's always so full on. He's go-go-go. Most of the time when we're together, it's magic. But when the fans are out, it's a different story. I got jealous of the girls hanging off him like leeches. It pissed me off, and we argued. That added fuel to the gossip fire."

But what if Gemma and Kyle weren't around when the next tempting girl threw herself at him? What if *I* wasn't there? *Shit . . . don't go there.*

Naomi clasped my hands and gave them a gentle shake. "I'm not going through with this if he's an asshole."

I half-giggled, half-sighed. "He's an arrogant rockstar. Of course he has his moments. But he's mine. And I love him."

"You're fucking crazy."

"Totally." I patted her arm as I slid off the stool, then hooked my tote over my shoulder. "Let's go get me a baby. Oh . . ." I clicked my fingers. "Before I forget. We might have the paparazzi on our tails. I was followed, but hopefully they've left by now. But . . . if they track us to the clinic, who knows what gossip they'll come up with."

Naomi frowned. "Shit. I wanted to keep this out of the headlines."

"I know. So just stick to the story. You're having IVF. You're not our surrogate." Kate had spoken to Everhide's team, Naomi, and our immediate families. Hopefully, we could keep the surrogacy a secret.

"I don't want any media attention." Naomi's hands trembled as she wiped her brow. She reached for her water bottle on the kitchen counter and had a big drink.

"Nae, are you okay?"

"Yeah." She wiped her mouth with the back of her hand. "It's the vitamins. They make me nauseous." She straightened and pasted on a smile. "But I'm fine. Seriously, I'm good. Let's go get me knocked up again before I change my mind."

"Quick." I slid off the bar stool. "We're off."

Naomi linked her arm with mine, and we headed out the door. "I hope the clinic is on time. I have to be home for a conference call at three."

"What? You're not taking the day off."

"No . . . why would I?"

"Last time this wiped you out. You need to rest."

"I am. I'm working from home. It's not like the embryo is gonna fall out of me."

It did last time.

Giles greeted us in the lobby and ushered us into the car. I kept glancing at Naomi as we worked on our cell phones during the trip to the clinic. She actually seemed relaxed. But my worry for her out-spiked a punk rocker's leather jacket. I worked long hours and rushed all over the world for Everhide and dealt with bullshit gossip. But that was nothing compared to the corporate stress Naomi experienced on Wall Street every day—market ups and downs, crashes and wins, profits and losses. I had to ensure she rested. Relaxed. Remained healthy. She was about to carry the most precious package of all. Baby attempt number two.

This time, it had to work.

For my sanity.

It had to.

Chapter 26

HUNTER

London was covered in a blanket of fall colors, and early Christmas decorations lined the streets. The October skies were dreary and cool. I'd pushed my fatigue aside and hit morning radio and TV shows, lunchtime gigs, and evening broadcasts with Kyle and Gemma. I couldn't recall ever being this tired only three weeks into promo. Most nights, I'd lain awake missing Kara, and hoping that Naomi's IVF implant had worked. We wouldn't know for another couple of days. Performing had been an addictive adrenaline rush. Meeting fans, singing, owning the charts, and cramming as much as possible into every hour of every day was an intoxicating high. But now I'd paid the price.

As our driver navigated through the city traffic, I closed my eyes to steady the haunting drumming inside my head. Had I pushed myself too hard?

No. I refused to believe that.

But my voice had other ideas.

I'd overdone it singing last night. Every time I swallowed, deep inside my ears ached. *Not good.*

I had to be sensible. That never sat well with me. *Should I sing tonight?* The question revved around in my brain like a motorcycle rider gunning a Harley.

With no time to rest, we headed toward the BBC television studios in West London to record *The Graham Norton Show.* I glanced from my watch to my cell phone to every taxi that passed. Kara was due to arrive this evening. I hadn't seen her for almost two weeks. Having her here would ease some of the chaos stampeding through my mind.

Gemma, sitting between Kyle and me, elbowed my arm. "Stop fidgeting. She won't be here for hours."

"I'm not fidgeting." I so was. Turning my cell phone over, I rested it on my thigh. "I was checking our schedule."

"No, you weren't." Kyle chuckled. "Please tell me I was never this bad over Gem?"

"No." I tapped into my energy reserve and put on a fresh smile. "You were worse." I unlocked my cell phone and hit the camera icon. "Quick, let's take a selfie for Insta." I had to do something, anything, to distract me.

Laughing, the three of us leaned together, and I took the snap.

But by the time we reached the studio, just after Hayden, Lexi, and our entourage, the dull ache between my ears had worsened.

Is it just a headache?

As we met with the production crew, Graham, and the show's writers to run through the agenda, questions, and processes, I sipped on a cup of my Throat Coat Tea. But it didn't help. Neither did two Advil.

I stretched and flexed my fingers. A cold sweat broke out on the back of my neck. Before heading onto the set for rehearsal, I pulled Gemma and Kyle aside. "Guys, my throat's playing up. I'm gonna sing, but be prepared to take over if I need to stop."

"If it's bad, don't do it." Kyle hooked his bass over his shoulder. "We'll take vocals tonight. No one will care."

"I care." I hated not singing. This was one of the biggest entertainment TV shows in Britain; I had to give it my best. "I'll go to the doctor tomorrow. I promise. But for tonight, just be prepared to take the bridge." I dug my nails into my palm. I loved hitting the high notes and showing off my vocal range, but I couldn't risk the strain.

I made it through rehearsals, but my blood pressure hadn't lowered. As we hung out in the green room and met the other guests—Emily Carter, some British TV actress I'd never heard of, and Eric Everson, a comedian doing a one-man show in the West End—I barely said a word, determined to rest my voice. Time for the show neared and the exhilaration of performing in front of a live audience meandered and spiraled through my veins in mounting waves. On the monitors displaying the video feeds from the studio, people streamed into the tiered seating, and the camera and production crew prepared the sets.

Damn. I wanted to sing.

Dressed in slim black jeans and a button-down, ready to perform, I excused myself from everyone and headed into the restrooms. I had to run through more vocal warm-up exercises. I'd already done some, but more wouldn't hurt. Acoustics were always better in the bathroom. It made it easier to hear myself and check my tone . . . and walking around helped me relax. I took a deep breath and sang.

Ahh. Ahh. Ahh. A— Eee. Eee. Eee. E— Ohh. Ohh. Ohh. O—

Shit! My heart wanted to cry. Why was this happening now? Why was my voice cracking on the high notes? I was tired but not exhausted. I'd rested. But London had it in for me. I rubbed my Adam's apple, took a sip of tea, and tried the scales again.

Ahh. Ahh. A—A— Eee. Eee. E—E— Ohh. Ohh. O—O—

Shit. It's worse. I checked my cell phone. Still no message from Kara. She'd better be okay.

Ahh. Ahh. Ahh. A— Eee. Eee. Eee. E— Ohh. Ohh. Ohh. O—

Still not right. I filled my lungs, rolled my shoulders, and sang softer.

Ahh. Ahh. Ahh. Ahh. Eee. Eee. Eee. Eee. Ohh. Ohh. Ohh. Ohh.
Ahh. Ahh. Ahh. Ahh. Eee. Eee. Eee. Eee. Ohh. Ohh. Ohh. Ohh.
Ahh. Ahh. Ahh. Ahh. Eee. Eee. Eee. Eee. Ohh. Ohh. Ohh. Ohh.

Yes! Thank fuck!

The door swung open. Kyle stood in the doorway. "You good?"

"I am now. I just needed more warm-up."

"We're on." Kyle jerked his head toward the hallway, but concern swam in his eyes. "You sure you wanna do vocals?"

"Yep. Show me the way, bud." I clapped my hands and followed him out the door. But with every step I took toward the set, the butterflies in my gut turned into circling buzzards. But they'd have to starve. I wasn't going down tonight. Not ever. I'd give nothing less than a perfect performance. I clipped on my transmitter and put on my in-ear monitors. I shook out the ache in my arm and grabbed my guitar off Bryce, our stagehand. *Relax. Focus. Sing softly.*

"You heard from Kara?" Gemma wriggled her guitar into position, then freed her hair from underneath the strap, flicking it over her shoulder.

"Nope. Not yet." I stretched my neck from side to side, but it didn't ease the tension lodged deep inside my nape. The worry of why she hadn't arrived twisted tighter and tighter. "Her plane must be delayed." She was more than an hour late.

Hayden, pacing the floor behind the curtain, didn't ease my stress.

I caught his arm. "Bud, stop. You're making me nervous."

"Me? Make you nervous? I doubt that." Hayden smirked as he twirled his drumsticks around in his fingers. "You can play this song backward in your sleep."

True. Hayden had a point.

"Please, take your positions." Megan, the production manager, with oversized headphones rammed onto her head, waved us toward the set.

"Let's do this." I high-fived my three friends and stepped over to my mic in the darkened stage area.

On the nearby set, boom lights shone down on Graham sitting on his leather swivel chair, talking to the other guests lounging on the bright red sofas. The production crew rolled two cameras into position in front of us. Sound and lighting technicians gave us the green light. The floor manager counted down on his fingers.

The hair on my arms and the back of my neck rose to attention. I loved this moment, when electricity flitted through the air like a firework about to explode. Propping my fingers on my steel strings, I readied to play.

Graham introduced us. "Time for some music. You may have heard of this little band from New York. They've sold over seventy million albums worldwide. Done four world tours. The first single off their up-and-coming album has gone to number-one in eighty-four countries in record time. It is also currently the most-streamed song on Apple Music, YouTube, Amazon and Spotify. To sing their brand-new single, 'Gravitate,' would you please welcome to the stage . . . Everhide."

The audience erupted—arms waved, women shrieked and clapped, guys whistled and hollered. A broad, shit-eating grin charged across my face as we struck and strummed our guitars and Hayden thundered on the drums.

Stepping up to her mic, Gemma sang.

I didn't know what was wrong with me
I'd thought I'd gone totally crazy
Every day, the pull, the drive, the force, set my heart racing
I traveled across the world looking in different places

Everywhere I went, I searched people's faces
I never knew what I was looking for
Then I saw you burning it up on the dance floor

Time stopped
The temperature grew hot
I made my way to you as the music rocked
I had to make you mine
For all time

I gravitate to you like you're my lifeline.

Sliding my fingers over the neck of my guitar, I played hard. Something about the energy in the studio captured me. Was I just excited that Kara would be here soon? Was it the music? The live audience? The cheering? Maybe a combination of everything. With fire charging through my veins, I stepped up to the mic and sang.

I didn't know what was wrong with me
I'd thought I'd gone totally crazy
Every day, the pull, the drive, the force, set my heart racing
I drove around the streets and highways at night.
Every way I turned, the direction felt so right
I didn't know what I'd find underneath the stars
But there you stood beside your broken car

Time stopped
The temperature grew hot
I made my way to you as the music rocked
I had to make you m—
For all time
I gravitate to y—like you're my lifel—.

Kyle shot me a quick glance, ready to take over if I gave him the cue. But I gave him an *I'm-okay* nod. I could do this; I could finish this.

Kyle hit the pre-chorus hook.

I know we just met and it sounds ludicrous
But the way I feel for you makes me all breathless
We're meant to be together, do you feel the same way?
Underneath these disco lights, I want you to be my babe.

In harmony, the three of us hit the chorus.

We can't deny this or fight this
It's like the universe had a plan

And compiled this
Conspired in this
And I'm okay with it
I never needed a map to find you
Align with you
The way you make me feel is worth it.
This force is so strong and I love it.
No matter where you go or what you do
I gravitate, I radiate, toward you.

Kyle sang out the next verse, and then I hit the bridge. Sucking in my diaphragm, controlling my breath, I eased into the high notes.

Baby
I gravitate
I radiate
Toward you

The electric vibe and magic in the air took hold of me. I punched out the lyrics, crescendoing higher and higher.

Toward. Towa—y—

Fuck!
Stabs of pain erupted between my ears. My voice cut out like a knife had sliced my throat. I tried to scale down, but I couldn't make a sound. Wincing, I spun away from the camera. *FUUUUUUCK!*

Clutching onto the neck of my guitar and clenching my jaw, I fought the panic piercing my heart. *No. No. No. NO!*

The air around me prickled. Kyle and Gemma no doubt sensed something was wrong. They would've heard it. Hopefully the audience hadn't noticed anything. Kyle took over the singing. Without missing a beat, we kept performing.

But tears stung the back of my eyes. Shuddering all over, I took a deep breath. *Shit.* Even air hurt.

Swallowing killed, like razor blades were cutting inside my

neck.

I found some composure, turned, and faced the mic. But I didn't sing. I couldn't. Summoning my best, most vibrant smile, I threw a wink at the crowd then jutted my chin at Gemma and Kyle. They needed no other cue to sing out the rest of the song.

At the end of our performance, the audience screamed and cheered. Normally I savored the moment, waved, bowed, and blew kisses, but not tonight. Ripping out my ear monitors, I needed to get off the set. When Graham called us over to join the other guests, I gave one look at Kyle and Gemma and shook my head. Fear darkened Gemma's emerald eyes, but she touched my arm, pasted on her dazzling smile and headed over to Graham with Kyle. I rushed backstage. Sophie and Bec were instantly by my side. The worry radiating off them was nothing compared to the terror tightening around my throat.

I clutched my neck, and a tear escaped my eye. I wanted to speak but was afraid to do so.

Sophie nodded. "We need to get you to the hospital."

I shook my head. "No." *Fuck.* My voice was hoarser than Bob Dylan's.

Sophie tensed her jaw. "Yes. This is serious. Whatever's happened needs to be checked by a professional. At this time of night, it's our only option."

Panic pummeled my ribs. *No. Not the hospital.* My hospital nightmares flashed through my mind—Ryan, Emily, Gemma, Kara, and my arm. Too much loss and too much heartache. *Shit.* But the agonizing ache between my ears flared. I needed to do something. Going to the hospital was just for a checkup, not surgery, right?

Closing my eyes, I reluctantly nodded.

Bec grabbed her purse off the nearby table. "I'll go with him. You stay here and deal with Kyle and Gemma. Mick?" She waved her hand at my bodyguard who sat patiently nearby with Sam and Chester. "Get a car out back now."

"What's happened?" He rushed over.

"It's his throat. Let's pray he hasn't done any serious damage."

Chapter 27

HUNTER

Sitting on the bed in one of the emergency department examination rooms at St Mary's Hospital, I wrung my hands together and twisted my signet ring around my finger. On the way here, I'd texted Kara to meet me at the hospital. She'd landed and was on her way but stuck in traffic. I needed her here to keep me from climbing the walls. Kyle and Gemma couldn't do that. Their concern for my voice would be as heightened as mine.

After an initial examination and waiting around for forty-five minutes, I was beside myself. The apprehension lodged in my neck hadn't subsided. Moments later, a specialist in dark green scrubs, pushing a mobile cart mounted with a monitor, laptop, and an endoscope probe waltzed into the room.

"Good evening." The mid-thirties man halted the cart and held out his hand for me to shake. I obliged, then Bec jumped up from the bedside chair and did the same. "I'm Dr. Freeman, the ENT on duty." His British accent was as rounded and rich as the queen's crown. "You've certainly got the staff in a buzz, Mr. Collins. It's nice to meet you. Shall I look at your throat and see what the problem is?"

I nodded and sat upright, dangling my feet over the side of the bed. I opened my mouth and was given a couple of drops of anesthetic. The ache between my ears pulsed like a distant war drum.

Dr. Freeman stuck the scope down my throat, and the video feed displayed on the monitor. My heart lurched against my ribs at the sight of my bloodshot, raw vocal cords.

"How long have you had nodules?" the doctor asked as he wiggled the scope to the left, right, up, and down.

Bec leaned against the bedframe beside me and answered on my behalf. "He's had them for a few months and has been seeing a vocal therapist and otolaryngologist in New York. What's happened?"

The doctor removed the scope from my mouth and placed it on the cart. "Did they ever advise you to have them removed?"

I nodded, afraid to speak.

"Your vocal cord on the left has ruptured." Dr. Freeman folded his arms and spoke with as much compassion as a dead fish. "It's not life-threatening, but there's significant bleeding in the superficial lamina propria—the layer that is vital to vocal cord vibration. The other nodules are calloused and should be removed."

Ruptured? Bleeding? Calloused? The ache in my ears turned into a high-pitched ringing. My heart grabbed me by the collar and slapped me across the face. *You stupid, stupid idiot!*

The doctor continued. "Due to the discoloration on your cords, I'd say it's happened before. To stop the hemorrhaging, and it from happening again, you'll need surgery. But this doesn't explain the pain. With vocal cord ruptures, you get hoarseness and loss of voice. Has your doctor in New York done any biopsies to make sure the nodules are benign?"

My heart stopped. My vision blurred. My mouth ran dry. *Biopsies? To test for tumors or cancer?* I clutched onto the side of the bed and shook my head. *No, I couldn't have cancer.* Not when I was about to become a father. I was too young. I was healthy. There was no family history. I couldn't have cancer.

I went to speak, then abruptly snapped my mouth closed. Maybe it was too little, too late, but I didn't want to injure my vocal cords further. Instead, I grabbed my cell phone, typed a message into the Notes app, then showed the doctor.

ME: CAN I FLY HOME FIRST?

I didn't want surgery. Not here in London. They'd fucked up my arm. They'd left me with an ugly, disfigured scar running up the length of my forearm. *Damn. Am I pathetic?* I was nearly twenty-seven and hated the thought of an operation.

"The longer you delay this, the greater the risk of permanent damage."

I typed again.

ME: IF SURGERY, HOW SOON CAN I TRAVEL?

"After a week, you should be fine. For recovery, you'll need vocal rest for at least three weeks. No excessive exertion, like hard exercise and intercourse. Then—"

Wait. What? I held up my hand, mouthed. *"No sex?"*

The doctor smirked. "It's not advised for at least three weeks. You need to minimize any strain on your neck and vocal cords. It will take up to six weeks until you're back to normal. With singing demands possibly longer."

Icy chills shot over my skin. My pulse throbbed, no . . . it pounded in my temples. *Shit!* No singing? No sex? Out of action for a month and a half? *I'm in hell.* In December, we had the release of our second single, tour announcements, and events booked. *Fuck*! I didn't want to cancel any of our engagements.

Crap. Crap. Crap.

I clutched my knees and stared at the white, speckled linoleum floor. I hated that this had happened. But I couldn't risk permanent damage. I was terrified. I'd never wanted to put my livelihood in the hands of surgeons. *Again.* This was a fucking nightmare. But I had no other option.

Fighting the bile brewing in my stomach, I nodded at the doctor.

"All righty then, lad." The doctor pressed a buzzer. "I'll get the admission staff to run through the paperwork and book you in, and a nurse to prep you for the operation."

Bec sighed and slapped me on the back. "Another day. Another hospital. I'll call everyone and let them know."

"Thanks," I mouthed and clutched her hand. Then I turned away. I didn't want her to see the fear embedded in my face. Where the fuck was Kara? I needed to see her before I went into surgery . . . in case . . .

Shit! I dragged in a shaky breath and tried to calm my mind. I could perform in front of thousands of people, take on any danger-filled, adrenaline-fueled activity like white-water rafting and black-run snowboarding, but surgery scared the absolute living crap out of me.

***

After being transferred to a pre-op ward and changing into a pale blue hospital robe, I paced the floor. *One. Two. Three. Turn. One. Two. Three. Turn.* Bec sat glued to her cell phone in the corner. Mick waited outside in the hallway. The pre-surgery medication they'd given me to relax clearly hadn't worked.

The door flung open and in rushed Kyle, Gemma, Lexi, and Hayden. Worry was plastered all over their faces. I'd texted them with the details about the rupture and surgery.

"Holy shit. A rupture? Fuck, that doesn't sound good." Kyle clasped my shoulder and gave me a gentle shake, but the quiver in his voice gave away his distress. "But hey, everything will be okay. You've got this."

"Hunt, you'll be fine." The anxiety in Lexi's tone didn't reassure me.

"Absolutely," Hayden nodded, but doubt clouded his eyes.

"Yeah." Gemma threw her arms around me and gave me a big hug. She held me tight for a few long seconds before easing back a step. Any longer and I would've come undone. My singing career was at stake. They knew that. "You'll come out singing better than ever. No more nodules." I hoped so. But then, she grabbed my hands and held them wide. "But fuck. I have to get a photo of you in this gown. It's freaking hilarious."

I sniggered, held up a finger in warning, but it didn't stop her from pulling out her cell phone and taking the shot.

The air around me warmed. I looked toward the door.

It was as if I'd sensed her before she walked in. The door swung open and in rushed Kara. I wrapped my arms around her, nuzzled into her neck, and breathed her in. The scent of her rosy perfume was better than any sedative.

I kissed her, hugged her.

"I'm sorry I'm late. We were delayed in the rain." She cupped my face and stroked my cheek with her braced hand. "How are you doing?"

I half-heartedly nodded, but I was much better now that she was here.

I pointed at everyone else in the room and flicked my finger at the door. I needed five minutes alone with Kara.

After they grumbled and shuffled out of the room, I pulled her into my arms and kissed her hard. As I smoothed my hand over her hair, I rested my forehead against hers. "I'm not supposed to talk—" *Damn*. My voice was as crackly, hoarse, and raspy as an old gramophone.

"Shh. It's okay. You just get better."

"How's your hand?" I swept my thumb across her bandaged wrist as I held it against my chest.

"It's still sore but on the mend."

"How's Nae? And how was your mom's birthday?"

"All good."

"I had to see you before surgery." I whispered as I slid a strand of her long, silky hair through my fingertips. "If all goes well, recovery takes about three weeks. I'm not allowed to talk much. But if something does go wrong . . . and I have no voice, and Nae has our baby . . . you make sure you tell our kid I love them every day."

"Hunt." Tears pooled in her eyes. "Nothing will go wrong."

I wanted to believe her with every ounce of my soul, but my track record wasn't good. I pasted on a brave smile and forced a nod. As I drew her into my embrace, the door flung open and a nurse and an orderly walked in. The nurse, with kind eyes and a sweet smile, looked like Emma Thompson.

"Hi. I'm Gracie. And this is Malcolm. We're here to escort you to the operating room."

"Not the kind of escort I'm used to," I said under my breath. Kara giggled and tickled me in the ribs. I caught her hand and kissed the inside of her wrist. "I love you."

"And I love you." She touched her lips to mine. "You'll be okay. This will make you better. I promise to be here when you wake up."

"Mr. Collins." The nurse patted the bed. "Up here, please."

Shit.

This was it.

"I can walk."

"On the bed, please."

Bossy. I held the rear gap in my gown together and crawled onto the bed. I wriggled around and tried to get comfortable. The warm blanket the nurse placed over my legs helped. *Hmm. Toasty.*

Kara stroked her fingertips across my brow. "This will be over before you know it. You'll be on the road to recovery. Ready for the tour."

"And our baby."

"Most definitely." She kissed me on the lips. *Damn.* I wanted more. "You're in good hands. Off you go. I'll see you on the other side."

Wait. What? The other side of what?

Did she mean when I was dead?

When she was dead?

In heaven? Or hell?

Oh *shit*, wait . . . just after surgery. *Fuck!*

I sank into the pillow. No matter how hard I tried, the tightness, the tension, the tumultuous turning in my head and stomach wouldn't subside. I hoped it was just pre-surgery jitters.

"Righto, Mr. Collins. Off we go." The orderly unplugged the bed and made sure all the cords and remotes were secured. He kicked off the bed brake and wheeled me out the door.

I caught sight of Kyle and Gemma in the hallway. "Wait," I called to the orderly to stop. I waved my friends over and hugged them. "I lo— you gu—s." My voice cracked and cut.

"We love you too." Gemma sniffled against my shoulder.

"See you soon." Kyle patted my shoulder. "Now go."

Kara blew me one more kiss.

I settled back onto the bed. The nurse re-tucked my blankets and the orderly pushed me along the corridor and through a couple of double doors. The bed rattled and clanked as we entered the elevator. I closed my eyes and focused on my breathing to relax as we ascended one floor. But every technique I'd learned evaporated when I entered the operating room. Big, bright lights blazed overhead. Monitors and machines blipped beside the procedure table. More nurses and the doctor, dressed in scrubs, hovered around preparing for my surgery.

Fuuuuck!

My pulse quickened. My palms sweated.

Maybe I should run? Get out now before it was too late?

"Can you shuffle over onto the operating table, please?" Gracie asked.

My heart rate tripled as I slid across and lay down.

"Hi, Hunter." A lady with auburn hair peeking out from her surgical cap gazed at me over her mask. "I'm Sarah, your anesthetist. I need to put an IV in your arm, okay?" She ripped open the packaging. My blood drained from my face. "Are you left- or right-handed?"

"I can do it with either hand." I half-grinned.

Even from behind her mask, I could tell she blushed. "Left or right, Mr. Collins?"

I held up my right.

"Thank you. I'll put this in your left arm."

I winced as she cinched the tourniquet into place and wiped the inside of my arm with a cold swab. "Relax." Sarah pushed my arm onto the mattress. "Anyone would think you didn't like needles."

I hated needles. Hated the scar that curled up my arm. Hated anyone near it.

She smoothed her fingers over my skin and pressed onto my vein. "Here we go. You'll feel a little prick—maybe a sting. One. Two. Three."

Wooziness spun through my head. Nausea flooded my stomach. *Shit!*

Sarah plastered tape over the needle to hold it in place. "All done."

"Hunter?" Gracie hovered above me. "Are you okay?"

"Ah-ha." But I wasn't. Fainting was an option.

"Mr. Collins?" Dr. Freeman loomed overhead. "Are you ready?"

Tears pricked my eyes, but I nodded. I had to get through this. For Kyle and Gemma, for the fans . . .

No . . . for Kara and my baby.

"Okay." Sarah drew liquid into a needle and inserted it into the IV port. "You may feel a cold sensation in your arm. That's just the anesthetic fluid. Close your eyes, take a deep breath, and count back from ten for me."

"Ten . . . nine . . . eigh . . . sev . . ."

Chapter 28

HUNTER

"Welcome back, Mr. Collins."

The nurse's British accent split my head like heavy metal music. I didn't want to open my eyes. My mouth, my throat, and even my cheek muscles ached. My tongue was dry and furry. The low, constant *blip, blip, blip* from a machine reminded me where I was. My pulse scrambled for the door. Fighting against the grogginess, I opened my bleary eyes and sat higher on the bed. I needed my head to clear so I could get out of here.

"Relax, Mr. Collins." The nurse placed her hand on my shoulder. "You're doing fine. You've been transferred from the recovery ward into a private suite."

Clouds fogged my thoughts. I didn't remember being moved. I glanced at the wall clock, and the hands slowly came into focus. 10:34 p.m. I couldn't recall the last one and a half hours either.

"Please remember not to speak." The nurse tucked the blankets around my waist. "I'll let the doctor know you're awake." She handed me the bed remote and hurried out the door.

"Hey handsome." Kara leaned over and brushed her cool fingertips across my brow.

Kara. My head sank into the pillow, and I summoned a dopey smile. Her gentle touch soothed and calmed my heartbeat and settled the queasiness in my stomach.

Wait . . . maybe not the queasiness. *Ugh.*

"You look like shit." Kyle cast me a lopsided grin from the end of the bed.

"Hunt." Gemma rubbed my blanket-covered foot. "Glad you're back. Hayds and Lexi will be here shortly. They're just grabbing some food."

I half-heartedly nodded, but my head was as heavy as a lead bowling ball.

Approaching footsteps pricked my ears. But it wasn't Lexi or Hayden. Dr. Freeman and the nurse entered the room.

"Hello again, Mr. Collins. How're you feeling?" Dr. Freeman peered down at me as he clutched a letter-sized envelope against his chest.

Wincing, I placed my hand on my cramping, churning stomach, then touched my mouth with my fingertips and mimed vomiting.

"That will pass. It's the anesthetic wearing off," the doctor said, but the nurse grabbed me a sick bag and tucked it beside my pillow. Dr. Freeman leaned against the bedframe. "We were successful in removing the nodules and stopped the hemorrhaging. Unfortunately, the large nodule was quite calloused and deep. There were early signs of permanent damage. We've done our best to fix the problems, but you need to be prepared that your voice may not be the same after you've healed."

Damaged? Not the same? No. No. No. No. No!

My breath strangled my throat like a vine around a trellis. I battled to draw breath. Why was that? I waved my hand in the air, gesturing I wanted to write. Kara handed me her cell phone. Waves of wooziness swirled through my head as I typed.

ME: BREATHING DIFFICULT. SWALLOWING HURTS.

The doctor read the screen and nodded. "You may experience some temporary paralysis in your vocal cords, which can affect breathing. And yes, your throat will hurt for a day or two." He handed me the envelope. "Here is a recovery plan and a time for you to come see me at my clinic next week. Hopefully, after that you can return to the States."

My hand shook as I took the envelope and placed it beside me, finally relieved to be on the road to recovery. The nodules were gone. Nothing would hold me back. In six or so weeks, I'd be back on stage.

"I have more rounds to do." The doctor took the clipboard from the nurse and signed some paperwork. "If the nurse is happy with your recovery in an hour or so, you're clear to go. Stay hydrated. Rest. And I'll see you soon."

"I'll take care of him," Kara said. "Thank you, Doctor."

But I closed my eyes and curled onto my side. Take care of me? What could Kara do? I loved that she cared, and was here, but I didn't need a babysitter, a home nurse . . . or temptation. And Kara was all temptation—I couldn't keep my hands off her. The doctor's orders were no exertion, no hard breathing, and no strain for at least three weeks.

That is so fucking long.

And I could take care of myself.

After being cleared to leave, we all headed back to our hotel.

As I stared out the window of the car at the rain, I rubbed my sore throat. I swallowed. *Ow!* Pain ricocheted between my ears. Kara leaned closer and entwined her arm around mine. My fingers twitched, wanting to touch her. *Damn it. No.* Since I couldn't talk, sing, or exert myself, the best thing to do was keep my distance. To be alone. Be by myself.

After missing her, now all I wanted to do was to be away from her.

Healing my voice had to be my priority.

***

The following morning, post-operation grogginess swam through my head. As I sat at the table with my friends and entourage in my hotel penthouse suite, my throat ached. Crawling back into bed and sleeping sounded like a much better alternative than listening to everyone frantically addressing our promotional agenda. I'd secretly wanted Kyle and Gemma to cancel the rest of our appearances, but if I were in their shoes, I knew what I'd want to do. They craved being in front of the fans as much as I did. Well . . . almost. I'd never missed a publicity tour—not once in eight years. It'd kill me not being there, but the show had to go on.

"If it's okay with everyone, I'll stay here and look after Hunt." Kara poured herself a fresh cup of tea from the pot on the table.

What? No. She needed to keep busy. Do her job. Hang out with our friends.

I swiped my cell phone off the table. My fingers flew across the screen as I typed, then showed it to Kara.

> ME: PLEASE GO. FINISH PROMO WITH KYLE AND GEM.

I didn't want to hurt her, but she'd be bored out of her brains staying with me. I didn't need her to sit around worrying about Naomi, our baby, or me.

Kara closed her eyes and winced. Then she looked at me like I'd stomped on her heart. *Shit!* "You don't want me here?"

Sophie and Bec froze with their coffees suspended before their mouths. Kate looked up from writing a press release about my operation to squash the wild rumors hitting the Internet. The gossip ranged from me quitting to me having a mental breakdown. Kyle's hand hovered over the basket full of breakfast pastries. Gemma's eyes widened as she chewed her bagel.

Everybody's gaze jumped from me to Kara and back again.

My hand shook as I typed again. I had Kara's best interests at heart . . . and mine.

> ME: I'LL BE FINE.
> CAN'T RISK TALKING.
> KYLE AND GEM NEED YOU MORE THAN I DO.

"Someone should be with you." Kara curled her hands around her steaming cup of tea and held it against her chest. "That should be me. You're recovering from surgery."

I smirked as I wrote:

> ME: NAH. I HAVE MICK. :-)

I'd love Kara to stay, but my dick didn't understand the post-operative no-exertion rule. Neither did my mouth and tongue. I'd want to do things to her that would make her quiver. Lick every inch of her body and taste her. *Shit!* I had to stop thinking about sex before I got a semi.

"Hunt." Gemma poured herself an orange juice. "Kara can stay. Carla can help us out with wardrobe."

"We survived the last two weeks without you, Kar." Kyle tore off a piece of his croissant and popped it into his mouth. "I'm sure we'll survive one more."

"See?" Kara thrust her hand toward our friends. "They agree. If I stay, it will give me the chance to catch up with some designers and source outfits."

Nope, she could do that during Fashion Week and with our reps back home. I typed madly, then flashed the message to Kyle.

ME: KAR NEEDS TO GO WITH YOU. PLEASE.

Kara's gaze hardened as her eyebrows pinched together. She pushed back her chair and jumped to her feet. "Can I talk to you? Alone?"

Nodding, I rose to my feet. She grabbed me by the hand and dragged me from the dining area into the bedroom. After shutting the door behind me, she spun to face me. "Why don't you want me to stay?"

Madly, I typed:

ME: THEY NEED YOU. YOU'LL BE BORED HERE. NO TALKING. NO SEX.

Irritation flared in her eyes. "We're adults, Hunt. Not animals." *Easy for her to say.*

"What if you hemorrhage, gag, and choke on your blood and can't breathe?"

Shit! Did she have to paint such a gruesome picture? Fuck . . . maybe she should stay. *Wait . . . no.* I shook my head. I'd be fine.

"Someone needs to keep an eye on you, and that needs to be

me. I want to look after you like you did for me after my operation."

My fingers flew across the screen:

> ME: THAT WAS DIFFERENT.

Her hysterectomy had been much more severe. And we'd lost Ryan. Her recovery had been shrouded in our grief. It'd been an awful, emotional time for both of us.

"It's no different. Taking care of each other is what partners do. We'll have fun. I promise. You'll be bored hanging out with Mick."

True. She had a point.

If she stayed, we could sneak out at night to see the city when there was less chance of me being recognized by fans. We could ride the London Eye. See the Christmas lights. Shop. We'd love to do those things. But no . . . I couldn't. I had to rest and recuperate. She wouldn't relax or stop fidgeting. It wouldn't be stress-free for either of us. With Kyle and Gemma, she'd be run off her feet all day and wouldn't have time to think about anything else. Unlike me. I'd worry about everything—her, the baby, Kyle, and Gemma, and my voice. *Crap!*

I typed:

> ME: PLEASE GO.
> FOR YOU. NOT ME.
> KEEP BUSY = LESS WORRY ABOUT NAOMI.

Staring at the screen, her eyes misted. She flattened her hand against my chest and nodded. "That's sweet of you. But I need to make sure you're okay." Mischief crept into her gaze, and her lips slowly curled into a naughty smile. "I could buy a nurse's uniform." She walked her fingers up my chest and tugged on the cords of my hoodie. "Wear it to check your pulse, bathe you, tuck you into bed, and take care of your every need."

Sweet Jeesuz! This was why I didn't want her to stay. Her . . . in a nurse's uniform . . . totally fucking hot. Ignoring the hot rush of blood through my veins, I waggled my finger at her and gave her a warning glare. I'd be an awful patient. I'd struggle to sit still. I'd be on my guitar non-stop. Within hours, she'd be begging me to join Kyle and Gemma.

Her compassion was one thing I loved about her. She'd be the most incredible mom and smother our child in love. But as a grown man, I didn't need to be waited on hand and foot. I loved attention—just not the smothering kind.

> ME: YOU CAN LOOK AFTER ME WHEN WE'RE HOME.
> GO. HAVE FUN.

She lowered her chin and tugged on the bottom of my hoodie. "You really don't want me here?"

I slowly shook my head, hating the sadness welling in her eyes.

She sniffed. "Okay then. How about I come back on Thursday after Edinburgh so we can fly home together?"

> ME: OKAY. DEAL.
> I'LL MISS YOU.

I wrapped my arms around her and held her tight. As her warmth enveloped me, I closed my eyes. Promo would be good for her, and better for my recovery. It was a win-win situation.

I took a step back, kissed her cheek, and then thumbed toward the door. We had to tell everyone she'd be going with them. It was for the best.

As the meeting wrapped up and everyone prepared to leave, I collected the used coffee cups and headed toward the kitchenette. But I overheard Kara talking to Gemma by the sink. I halted at the entrance.

"He doesn't want me to stay," Kara said in a low voice.

"You have to understand." Tenderness trickled through Gemma's tone. "Hunt's always fended for himself. Other than Kyle and me, he's never had anyone truly care for him. He's always been a giver, not a taker. It's hard for him to open up, but he's getting there. Give him these few days to recover and he'll be fine. We need his voice to heal properly. He wants you to come with us *because* he cares about you."

"It goes against every grain in my body not to stay and look after him."

"I know it does. But I promise we'll have fun."

Shit! I leaned against the wall. Gemma knew me better than I knew myself. I was such a jerk. Kara just wanted to take care of me. But it didn't matter. I wouldn't handle her doting on me. Locked in a hotel suite, we'd probably kill each other. We'd just spent two weeks apart; we'd survive another few days.

I'd make up for our time apart when we returned home, after my voice was better. Closer to Christmas, I'd steal her away for a few days of snowboarding. We could stay in a cozy cabin and make love in front of a blazing fire. *Hell yeah.*

Now that was something to look forward to.

That couldn't come soon enough.

***

Four days after the surgery, I sat in front of my laptop, ready to start vocal therapy. I wiped my clammy palms on my jeans. With the exercise videos open, I took a sip of water and licked my lips. My throat wasn't sore anymore, but every time I swallowed, a lump, like something the size of a rice grain, remained lodged inside my neck. My airway was still restricted. Pulling my shoulders back, I filled my lungs, hit play, and made sounds for the first time in days.

First, soft onsets.

Hmm. Hmm. Hm—
Ahh. Ah— Ah—

Shit! My heart stumbled against my ribs. My voice sounded terrible. Hoarse. Scratchy. Broken. That wasn't good. Rubbing my neck, I fought the need to clear my throat. I clenched my fists. Determination kicked in, and I ran through the video. But as each minute passed, hope deflated.

For ten minutes I tried every technique, but there was no improvement in the sound I produced. *Fuck!* With a deep breath, I buried my fear in the far recesses of my mind. Time to rest. To heal. I'd try again tomorrow.

***

Late Thursday evening, a week after my operation, Kara swept into my hotel room. She left her suitcase by the door, wrapped her arms around my shoulders, and kissed me like she'd missed me. Just like I'd missed her. I inhaled her sweet perfume. But as I tightened my arms around her waist, my heart faltered. Had she lost more weight? *Shit!* "Hey, Pearl. It's good to see you."

"Oh wow." She leaned backward. "You're talking."

"I'm trying to." I linked my fingers behind her back. "I'm up to about forty-five minutes to an hour, twice a day."

"That's great. But your voice?" She jerked her chin back and wrinkled her nose. "It doesn't sound right."

"I know." I spoke, low and soft. Every time I'd run through the vocal exercises, my heart had plummeted to the bottom of the River Thames. "It's still early days. Doc said I have to be patient."

But I wasn't.

My follow-up appointment earlier today hadn't gone well. Despite the biopsies being non-cancerous, my left vocal cord was scarred. The paralysis that hadn't disappeared rattled every bone in my body. It was still too soon to tell if the damage was permanent. It'd destroy me if it was. I had to stick to my recovery plan. No diversions.

"You'll get there." She ran her hands up and down my arms. "You better." A saucy, mischievous glint shimmered in her deep blue eyes. "Some girls might go for this hot, sexy rasp in your voice, but me? Nah-ah . . . not doing it for me."

Oh . . . the sass! I tugged her close. "You love it. Turns you on."

"Well, we can't have *that* while you're recovering, so I better find other ways to entertain you."

"Netflix, reading, and sleep are the hot items on my agenda."

"We can also play board games and cards and go shopping."

"Hmm. We'll see." Board games I could skip. "But for now, I have to stop talking and pack for our flight home tomorrow."

"I'll help you."

Once I was on home soil, I'd feel better. I'd go to voice therapy and focus on my recovery. And we'd catch up with Naomi. It had been seventeen days since she'd had the embryo implant. So far, so good. Every day was a new milestone. Every day, I prayed for our baby to survive. And prayed for my voice to come back.

***

I woke a couple of hours after going to bed. Kara wasn't beside me. I caught sight of the digital alarm clock. 1:37 a.m. What was she doing? Still not sleeping?

I headed out into the living room. She sat on the sofa with a pencil and sketchbook in hand. Her hair was twisted up into a big floppy knot on top of her head. I knocked on the doorjamb so I wouldn't startle her.

"Oh, hey," she said softly. "Did I wake you?"

I shook my head. Walking over, I stole a peek at what she was doing. My breath hitched. *Designing?* She hadn't sketched in months—not that I knew of, anyway. I grabbed her cell phone off the coffee table. She lifted her feet so I could sit beside her, then placed them over my thighs. I entered her pin code into her cell and typed on the Notes app.

> ME: WHO'S THAT FOR? GEM?

"It's for no one. It was just in my head."

> ME: YOU MISS DESIGNING?
> WHY NOT GO BACK TO IT?

She read my message. Her eyes clouded over for the briefest of seconds, but within a blink she refocused on her page. She swept long pencil strokes onto her design. "No. I love my job and being invited to fashion shows, private fittings, and having designers begging me to dress you in their outfits. If I went back to a fashion house, that would all disappear."

But there was a distance in her tone that snagged my chest. I speed-typed. Having to write or type everything frustrated the crap out of me. I hated not talking whenever I wanted.

> ME: ARE YOU SURE? WE'D MAKE IT WORK IF YOU DID.

DO IT IF IT'LL MAKE YOU HAPPY.

My chest ached as I typed the last line. I'd done everything in my power to make sure she was. I loved her like crazy. We were having a baby. So why was she fading away in front of my eyes? What was missing? What was wrong? If she wanted to design, there were options. Hell, I'd pay for her to set up her own studio if that was what she wanted.

"I am happy." Tiredness drifted through her words and swallowed the spark in her eyes. "I get to work with my best friends, fly around the world, and be with my hot, sexy boyfriend every day. What's not to love?"

> ME: WHAT ABOUT DOING A FEATURED COLLECTION FOR SOMEONE?
> IVORY MINK?
> YOU LOVE HER WORK.

"No," she whispered, clutching her sketchpad to her chest. "We have the tour coming up. And I'll be a mom soon."

> ME: WHY NOT DO IT ALL?
> DESIGN. DRESS US. BE A MOM.
> HIRE HELP.

"Hunt." She reached forward and touched my arm. "Stop worrying. It's just a drawing."

I wasn't so sure about that. As an artist, I understood the need for a creative outlet. The ability to take an idea and transform it into something new was addictive, a need. A part of your soul. For me, it was taking a tune, a lyric, a riff, and turning it into a song. For her, it would be her concept on the page being made into a gown. Was that it? She missed the full creative process? She seemed so sure that she was content in her current position. Maybe these drawings were just her way to blow off steam and escape the stress.

So, if designing wasn't the problem, what was?

I already knew the answer.

> ME: WHY AREN'T YOU ASLEEP?

ARE YOU WORRIED ABOUT NAE?

Her eyes darkened. "Always. Every minute of every day until our baby is born, I will worry. You just have to accept that. It wouldn't matter if I was with Kyle and Gem, or here with you. I would worry wherever I was."

So would I.

> ME: ME TOO.
> PLS COME TO BED.

We needed to catch a few hours of sleep before our flight home tomorrow afternoon.

She didn't object when I slid my hand up her leg and took the pen and pad from her grasp, or when I lifted her feet onto the floor, took her hand, and led her back to bed. Curled underneath the covers, I held her against my chest, stroked her hair and kissed her head. As her heart beat next to mine, she finally drifted off to sleep. But I lay awake like an owl at night, worrying about my voice, the album, Kara . . . and our baby.

When would my head stop spinning?

Probably not until I could sing. Not until our baby was born. Not until after the tour. I took a deep breath and closed my eyes. I had to take one day at a time, be patient, and everything would fall into place. Right?

I couldn't have been more wrong.

Chapter 29

HUNTER

My plan to recover quickly didn't work. After flying home to New York, my voice didn't improve. Panic had lodged into every cell in my body. I couldn't sleep. I couldn't eat. *Shit!* I'd turned into Kara. I'd seen Vanessa the moment I'd arrived home. It hadn't been a positive appointment, and she'd ordered strict rest and therapy. But after three weeks of intense sessions with Annelise, the hoarseness in my voice hadn't disappeared. I had no singing range, and my breathing hadn't cleared. Annelise couldn't hide the fear in her eyes every time we ran through exercises and my voice cracked and failed to perform.

But I refused to give up.

I couldn't. *Wouldn't.*

I had to work extra hard, be diligent. My vocal cords had to heal.

Failure wasn't an option.

But my voice wasn't the only problem I had to deal with. Kara fussing over me had driven me crazy. There were only so many times I could play Monopoly and cards, or tolerate her braiding my hair, or her constant questioning. *"Are you okay?" "Can I get you anything?" "Let me get that for you."* I could look after myself. I wasn't an invalid. I loved that she cared, but fuck, I needed some space.

So, I drowned myself in work.

Preparations for the launch of the album next month were in full swing. I'd gone to meetings, attended photo shoots, and sat in on interviews, but left the talking to Kyle and Gemma. It'd killed me not contributing. So had not singing. But at least playing had released my frustrations.

"Hunt, you should be at home resting." With her guitar propped across her lap, Gemma tinkered on the strings while we waited for our backup band to arrive at our rehearsal studio in Brooklyn. "Don't overdo it."

"I'm not. I need this." My heart didn't work without music. Just like now, sitting in a circle, the three of us just fed off each other as we slowly strummed through our new songs.

But Kyle killed his bass guitar and rested his arm across the top of it. "We need to talk about the album launch."

I didn't look up from playing. "What about it? We're not delaying the release." We'd worked too damn long and hard to put a pause on the schedule. The album had to go live as planned.

"Okay." He tugged on the neckline of his T-shirt. "But what about the promo? Worst-case scenario, what do you want to do if you can't sing? Do we cancel the live performances?"

I hated the concern in his voice or Gemma's every time we spoke about my voice and our schedule. I stared at the frets on my guitar as I moved my fingers from one chord to the next. I'd get better. I had to believe that. But I also had to be realistic. "If I can't sing, we'll play the *I'm-still-recovering* card. You guys can do the pre-launch interviews at the beginning of December in LA without me. That's only for a few days, and it will give me more time to heal. My voice is just taking longer to mend than expected." I just needed more time. "I meet with Vanessa on the eighth. We'll release the album on December fifteenth as planned."

"So, will you play at the launch?" Hope simmered in Gemma's voice but worry rippled through her eyes.

"That's three and a half weeks away. I wanna sing, so I'm praying for a fucking miracle."

***

No divine intervention occurred. Ten days later, my voice hadn't changed.

I stared into my open refrigerator. As I scanned the shelves loaded with yogurts, fruit, cherry pie, milk, and leftover pasta, nothing sparked my appetite. What I wanted was a drink.

Kyle, Gemma, and Kara would leave for LA tomorrow for pre-launch promotional duties. I was stuck at home for four days alone. Missing out on the fun yet again. *Fuck!*

I slammed the fridge shut and stormed down the hallway toward my home studio. Jamming would help me vent my frustrations. But I overheard Kara in our bedroom talking to Naomi on the phone, so I stopped by the door.

"Yes, Kara. I'm still pregnant!"

I could just hear Naomi, but the wavering tolerance in her tone was crystal clear. Kara called her every day to make sure she hadn't lost the baby. I puffed air through my nose, amazed that Naomi hadn't lost her shit at Kara. I hated to admit it, but I needed Naomi's updates as much as Kara did. Every day Naomi didn't lose the baby was a good day. Not wanting to miss out on the conversation, I slipped into the bedroom. Kara lay on the bed on her stomach. Her cell phone was propped against a cushion in front of her as she talked via video call.

"I'm seven weeks today." Naomi caught sight of me and twinkled her fingers but didn't skip a beat talking to Kara. "The morning sickness is a bitch, but I'm fine by lunchtime."

"I'm sorry you're sick, but otherwise, that's awesome news." Kara's tone failed to resonate with any excitement as she cuddled a pillow to her chest.

I crawled onto the bed beside her and combed my fingers through the long strands of her soft, silky hair cascading down to the small of her back. *So beautiful.*

She curled her hand around my knee and continued to talk to Naomi. "Seven milestones down—thirty-three to go. Weeks, that is. I don't think I'll breathe until you're over twenty-four weeks."

My heart lurched against my ribs. *Twenty-four weeks.* That was when we'd lost Ryan. "Full-term would be even better."

"We'll get there." Naomi rolled back on her office chair. With her cell phone in one hand, she rubbed her stomach with the other. "My suit pants are already tight. I better not end up as big as a whale, and if the size of Hunter's head is anything to go by, I'm not looking forward to this thing coming out of my vagina."

A shudder coiled up my spine. "If it's any consolation, I don't want to see that either."

"Good." Naomi wheeled forward, rested her elbow on the desk, and placed her chin in her hand. "Enough about babies. Hunter, how's your throat?"

Before I could speak, Kara cut in. That wasn't a bad thing. The less I spoke, the better. "The only good thing about it is he can't raise his voice to argue with me." She nudged my leg, and a small smile curled at the corners of her mouth. Then, within a heartbeat, her expression morphed back to being serious. "He's putting on a brave face, but he's worried. His voice hasn't returned to normal as fast as he'd like. He has another checkup next week."

"What are the options if it's not right?" Naomi asked.

My breath shuddered as I stared out the window. The tremor in my chest rattled every bone in my body. "Not sure there are any at this stage."

That was what terrified me.

No options.

***

A week later, at my appointment with Vanessa, the catastrophic news hit like a nuclear bomb.

"I'm sorry, Hunter. The damage is permanent. The scarring is acute."

Vanessa's final diagnosis tore through my heart, ripped my lungs, and shattered my ribs. Keeling over on my chair in her office, I clutched my knees. Her voice echoed through my head in rapid-fire aftershocks.

Damage-is-permanent.   Damage-is-permanent.   Damage-is-permanent.

FUUUUCK!

Seated beside me, Kara ran her hand across my back.

I flinched sideways. I flicked her hand away. I didn't want to be touched. Tears burned like hot coals in my eyes. I wanted to scream and cry and shout, but I fucking couldn't. "That doctor in London butchered me."

Why did surgeons always fuck up? My arm. Kara's body. Now my voice.

Vanessa took a steady breath and straightened her glasses. "Dr. Freeman is a renowned ENT. From the reports and the images he has sent, what's happened is unfortunate."

"Unfortunate? I'm a fucking singer and can't sing." I buried my face in my hands, then wiped the sting from my eyes on my shirtsleeve. "I did everything right."

Tears welled in Kara's eyes, her face was as pale as the white walls. "It'll be okay."

"How? How is this okay?" Every bone in my body ached. I was tired of fighting, following orders, obeying rules, and not singing. "I'm nothing without my voice."

"Yes, you are. We'll get through this." Kara turned to Vanessa. "Is there anything he can do?"

Vanessa folded her hands and placed them on the desk. "There are more surgical options—implants, injections, or vocal fold realignment. They come with more risk. Implants may be rejected by the body. Injections are temporary. Realignment may do more damage. Even if successful, there may not be any improvement in his voice, or . . . it might make it worse. But without any course of action, the damage is permanent. Hunter, your range is seriously compromised."

Damage . . . permanent . . . My singing career . . . *over.*

FUUUUCK!

I couldn't breathe. My heart splintered into a thousand pieces. All my diligence and determination had been for nothing. *Nothing.*

I had to get out of here.

I stormed out of Vanessa's office. Clenching my fists, I paced in front of the elevator as I waited for it to arrive. I wanted to punch a hole in the wall. Rip the tacky abstract artwork off its hinges. Destroy the Christmas tree in the corner and tear every piece of tinsel into shreds until there was nothing left. Air hissed through my clenched teeth. *Why my voice? Why?* I jabbed the elevator button over and over again. I needed to escape. I needed fresh air before I exploded.

"Hunt, please." Kara reached for me, but I held up my hand. "Let's go home and calm down and talk this through."

"Calm down? How the fuck do you expect me to calm down?" I ripped my hand through my hair. "I need . . . I need to see Kyle and Gem."

She stepped in front of me and stopped my pacing. "I know, but can *we* talk about this first?"

"No." The rims of my eyes burned. "I have to go."

"I understand that." She touched my arm. "But you don't need to go over there in this state."

Fire hurtled through my veins. Clenching my hands into fists, I fell back against the wall, and thumped my head on the exposed bricks. "Yes, I have to." My body shook as a tear slid down my cheek. I flicked it off with my hand. "I need to tell them I can't sing. I need . . . them."

Her jaw tensed. "I know, but—"

"Just stop. Please." The pain in my chest crushed my heart. "You don't understand."

"Me?" Hurt swallowed the light from her eyes and turned them to the darkest blue I'd ever seen. "Not understand? Of course I do. I of all people, know what it's like to have my dreams destroyed, crushed and ripped away."

Fuck! I wanted to eat my words. Her body had failed her too. Losing Ryan and her hysterectomy had shattered both our lives. "I know you do, but I need to deal with this, with them."

She took a step back. Her gaze turned to ice. "And not me?"

"Kar." My voice sliced through my teeth. "This isn't about you."

"Yes, it is. Whenever something goes wrong, you push me

away and don't want me around. You always run to them."

"Because they're my fucking life." I waved my hand at her. "And so are you. You're here, aren't you? But before I say something I'll regret, please . . ." I sucked in a breath and softened my tone. "Back off. I need to talk to Kyle and Gem."

Tears welled in her eyes as she nodded. "Fine. Let's go."

The elevator arrived and I rushed inside. Kara stepped in beside me but stood leaning against the far railing with her tote clutched to her chest. *Fuck!!* I hadn't wanted to upset her, but my life had just been shattered. I couldn't think of anything to say that would soothe her, that wouldn't lead to a full-blown argument, so I didn't utter a word for the entire drive.

Trying not to be a total asshole, I took her hand as we headed up to Kyle and Gemma's condo. But I let go of it the moment I walked through the door.

I swerved around the suitcases Kyle and Gemma had left at the bottom of the stairs after returning from LA early this morning, and dashed across the living room to them.

Kyle tossed his tablet onto the sofa beside him as Gemma slid her legs off his thighs and sat upright.

"Bud, what is it?" Kyle asked. "Did you just come from Vanessa's?"

I collapsed onto the adjacent armchair and buried my fingers in my hair. "My voice . . . It's fucked." Tears pricked my eyes. Sobs burned at the back of my throat. "Permanently."

"What?" Kyle gaped and clutched his chest.

The color drained from Gemma's face. She covered her mouth with her hands, and tears slid down her cheeks. "Oh no. It can't be. There has to be something you can do."

"No. There isn't. More surgery is even riskier and unlikely to work. I won't do it. It's not an option." I closed my eyes, horrified that more procedures might make my voice worse instead of better. "My vocal cords are too damaged."

"Oh shit. Come here." Gemma's chin quivered as she waved me over to sit between her and Kyle. The three of us fell into a group hug. "We'll work something out. We stick together, no matter what."

"Always." I clasped their hands and rested them against my thighs. "I need you guys. I couldn't face this without you. What am I going to do?"

Kara cleared her throat. Standing beside the dining table, she folded her arms and hugged herself. "Clearly I'm not part of this love fest. I'll leave you guys alone. I'm gonna go home."

"Kar—" My voice cracked. "Please, just wait."

She sniffled and swiped her damp cheeks with the tips of her fingers. "No. You want to be with them, not me. I'll see you later."

I didn't miss the bite in her tone.

She fled out the door so quickly I barely had time to blink.

Fuck! I'd lost my career today; I couldn't lose her too. I rushed after her. "Kar—"

But it was too late.

She'd already gone.

Chapter 30

KARA

Fog blanketed Manhattan. It rolled up the lane in slow, threatening swirls as I dashed the five hundred yards from Gemma and Kyle's place back to mine. The streetlights shone like hazy halos through the blanket of mist. My heart ached in the frosty early evening weather. The balance between Hunter, his music, and me had blown out of proportion over the past few months. It needed to be restored, but I didn't know how.

Ever since we'd arrived home from London at the end of October, Hunter had been distant. At photo shoots and fittings, he'd mucked around, then taken off with Kyle and Gemma. When I'd come home late from work, he was already in bed. We'd been living separate lives, doing our own things. I didn't want this to be our new normal.

He had every right to be devastated about his voice. I could accept that. But I wanted to be the one he leaned on, not Kyle and Gemma. What I loved about Hunter—his loyalty, his bond with his friends, his concept of family—now just made me feel like an outsider.

As I neared my building, light snow fell and melted against my cheeks. I tugged my beanie low over my ears and tightened my scarf. When Tate, the doorman, saw me approach, he opened the door and dipped his head. "Evening, Miss Knight."

"Evening, Tate."

I'd made it halfway across the lobby when my cell phone rang. *Naomi?*

I swiped the screen and lingered by the potted plant and charcoal velvet armchairs in the far corner to take the call; my cell always cut out in elevators. "Hey Nae—"

I didn't get the chance to finish. Naomi's sobs stopped my heart.

"Nae?"

"Oh, Kar," Naomi blubbered. "I'm so sorry."

"Sorry for what?" Ice prickled my veins. I froze on the spot.

"I'm at the hospital. The baby . . . I lost the baby."

My knees buckled, and I collapsed onto an armchair. I couldn't breathe, couldn't think. My chin trembled. Tears tumbled down my cheeks. "Oh no . . . No. No. No. NO!" Clutching my chest, I whimpered. "Nae, are you okay?"

Eight weeks. Our baby had survived eight weeks.

"Yeah." Naomi's voice, weak and fragile, was barely audible. "Anthony's here. I started spotting at work around three. He brought me to the hospital. I didn't want to worry you until I knew what was going on. But the moment I got here, the cramps grew unbearable. Oh, Kar . . . I'm so sorry."

I covered my eyes with my hand and wept. "I'll come see you." My voice quivered through trembling lips. "I'm on my way."

Hunter. Oh, shit.

How would he handle another blow?

I hung up and clutched my cell phone against the pain spiraling in my chest. My heart cried a torrential river. I had to find the strength to call him. How could I tell him we'd lost our baby?

"Ma'am? Miss Knight?" Tate approached me, holding out a tentative hand. "Are you okay? Shall I call Mr. Collins?"

I dug in my tote for a tissue and wiped my eyes. "No. I've got this."

Tate helped me to my feet and called the elevator. In a cloudy haze, I stepped inside and pressed the button for the top floor. As

I entered the hallway of the penthouse, an eerie silence hung like death in the dim light. No lights lit the living room. No TV blared. The flowers in the vase on the hall console table were all dead.

Like my heart. Like Ryan. Like our baby.

This vicious cycle had to end.

Nausea pooled in my stomach. My knees wobbled with every step I took. As I sank onto the sofa, my heart collapsed. My vision blurred. With trembling hands, I dialed Hunter.

He didn't answer.

I tried again. Same thing.

What the fuck?

I rang Gemma's number.

"Hey, Kar—"

"Put him on the phone, now." I struggled to speak through my tears.

"Shit." Gemma's voice was faint, as if she'd covered the speaker. "She's really upset, Hunt. Just talk to her."

"Fine . . . hey." He said, his tone a little frosty. "I'll be home soon."

"It's Nae." My chin trembled. "You have to come home. Now. She's in the hospital. She's lost the baby."

"What?" His voice sliced my heart into two.

"Please. Come home. We have to go see her."

"I'm on my way . . . I'm already out the door."

Five minutes later, he dashed from the elevator and flicked on the lights. "Kara?"

The frantic tone in his voice tore at my soul. Shaking all over, I stood, staring out the balcony window. I slowly turned to face him. He rushed toward me and flung his arms around me. I was too weak, too exhausted, too emotional. My knees gave way, and we crumbled to the floor. My tears soaked into his hoodie. "Na-Naomi lo-lost our baby."

As he held me against his chest, his heartbeat pounded against my ear. "No. No. This can't be happening. Not again."

Naomi was supposed to be perfect. Supposed to be the perfect candidate to carry our baby. My body was fucked up—not Naomi's.

This wasn't supposed to happen.

"Why can't we get a break, Kar. Why?" His voice rasped like a steel file across concrete.

"I can't handle this." I rocked in his embrace as I clutched my hands against my chest. "This pain. This worry. This heartache."

"I know." He kissed the top of my head. "Is Nae okay?"

"She's exhausted."

"Let's go see her."

He went to help me stand, but I couldn't move. My body had turned numb. "All I wanted was to be a mom, but it's not working. It's not meant to be. It's put too much strain on Nae's body. I can't put her through this again. I won't."

"Then we'll find someone else."

"No." I closed my eyes and shook my head. "It's stressing us out. I'm done."

"Babe, don't give up." He rested on his knees in front of me, stroking my hair away from my face. "We'll find a way."

All my pent-up frustrations from the past few days, weeks, months, constricted my veins. "You never wanted a baby in the first place."

"That's not true." He caressed the back of my head. "I wanted to wait, not *not* have kids. Things changed and that was okay. I want a family with you. We'll try again. We have two more embryos. If they fail, we'll find a donor. If that fails, we can adopt. I'm not giving up, and neither should you."

"Why not? You've given up on your voice."

"Kar, my voice is fucked. But I won't give up on music. I can't. It's in my blood."

"You could have more surgery," I snapped. "Yes, it's risky. Yes, it's scary. Yes, it may not work. But what if it does?" I splayed my hands across my abdomen. "If I could have an operation to fix my body so I could carry our child, I wouldn't hesitate. You still have options. I have none."

He closed his eyes and lowered his chin. "I hate that you can't have a baby. But we'll find a way that works."

Hurt squeezed my heart. "If my sister can't carry our child, how can I rely on some stranger to do it? It's too stressful. I don't sleep. I don't eat. Worrying about having a baby consumes me."

He wiped the pad of his thumb across my damp cheek. "All I do is worry about you."

"No, you don't." My voice sliced through my teeth. "All you care about is music."

"That's not true." His voice, laced with hurt, sadness, and a dash of anger, grated in his throat. "Today I had to see Kyle and Gem because my damaged voice affects our future. Music is them. Everything else is you." He cupped my neck and softened his tone. "Don't you see that? I do everything possible to make you a part of what I do. If there's a problem, we'll fix it. Please don't blow things out of proportion."

"Me?" I jerked my head back. Had I? My head hurt from crying. I couldn't think straight.

"Can we talk about this later?" His hands dropped to his knees. His shoulders slumped. "We just lost our baby."

The anguish in his tone crushed my heart. "And I'm heartbroken. I'm broken again."

"So am I." He drew me into a hug, kissed my head, and held me tight, so, so tight. "But we'll make it through this together. Always."

***

After hours at the hospital, Hunter and I returned home in a daze. Naomi had been released but ordered to have a few days of bedrest. I sank onto the sofa next to Hunter. But after a couple of JDs and barely a word exchanged, we went to bed. He held me close, but his arms held little comfort. I'd felt numb after losing Ryan, but this . . . losing another baby . . . had formed a new abyss that swallowed my heart. Exhaustion had seeped into my bones and sapped every ounce of my energy.

What would I do now if I couldn't be a mom?

Early the next morning, I packed a carry-on suitcase and trundled it toward the elevator. I left it by the hallway console table and walked into the living room. Hunter sat at the dining table, staring into his coffee. No steam rose from the cup. Had it gone cold?

He was up early. It was only seven-thirty.

"Morning," I said softly as I walked into the kitchen to make a cup of tea.

"Hey." He wiped his hand over his face and rubbed the back of his neck. "Sleep okay?"

"No. You?"

"Nope."

After making my tea, I sat at the table and curled my hands around the hot cup. "Um . . . I'm going to spend a few days with Nae."

"What?" He pushed his cup out of the way. "Why?"

"She's just had a miscarriage. *I* need to be there. To make sure she's okay."

"But Anthony's there. So is Erika. Go see her, but please . . . come home."

I shook my head. Tears threatened to fall. Just like he needed Kyle and Gemma, I needed Naomi. And she needed me. "No."

"Yes." He clutched my hand. "Let's go away for a few days. Like we did when we lost Ryan. Just be together."

"Not this time."

"Why not?"

My hand splayed across my chest. "Because I'm lost. Our baby is gone. And every time I look at you and think about what could have been, it hurts."

"Don't you think it's not the same for me?" A vein throbbed in his temples. "Yes, this sucks. Yes, this hurts. But we'll get through it. I don't want to give up."

"We have to, Hunt. We're not meant to have a baby." I stood, scraping my chair backward. "I don't want to fight. You have your album launch preparations. I need time to accept I won't be a mom. We need to get over another loss. But so we don't break each other in the process, a few days apart will do us some good."

"No." He leaped to his feet, darted around the table, and caught my arms. "Don't do this. I need you. Please stay."

I closed my eyes and swayed. I'd wanted to hear him say he needed me for so long. But grief consumed me. The walls caved in around me. I had to fight my way out of the darkness that lurked in the depths of my mind. Losing another child had devastated me but losing him would be worse. "It's just for a few days."

I stepped out of his hold, turned, and headed for the hallway.

"Kar, wait." He dashed after me and blocked my path.

It took all my strength to remain upright, for my knees not to buckle, and not to fall into his arms. "Hunt, I love you." I reached around him and hit the elevator call button. "But I've gotta go."

Panic flashed in his eyes. "Kara. No."

"Hunter. Yes."

The elevator doors opened. I grabbed my tote and carry-on and stepped inside the car.

"Fuc— N—!" His strained voice cracked. Spreading his arms, he held the doors open. His panicked, bloodshot eyes punctured my heart. "Don't go. Not like this. Let's talk this out."

Steeling my stance, I shook my head. "I'm done talking." The elevator alarm beeped. The doors shut slowly.

"I love you," he said.

Stubbornness nailed my UGG boots to the floor. "And I love you. That's why I have to go."

His shoulders drooped. He stepped backward, hit the wall, and let the doors close.

I heard his heart break through the steel.

The elevator descended and I burst into tears.

I had no baby. No dreams to chase.

Somehow, I had to find my way back to the light.

I just hoped Hunter would wait for me.

I hoped our love was strong enough to survive.

Chapter 31

KARA

I sat on the sofa at Naomi's and stared out the window across Central Park. Fatigue had threaded into my limbs one slow stitch at a time and pressed down on my shoulders. It was only ten a.m. but I wanted to go back to bed. My head throbbed from too much crying. My heart ached from walking out on Hunter this morning.

But until I dealt with the loss and came to terms with never being a mom, I needed time apart.

Anthony came into the kitchen, grabbed a couple of apples from the fruit bowl and bottles of water from the fridge, then stuffed them into his daughter's bright pink backpack.

"Hey, Kar." Tiredness after the long night at the hospital lingered in his voice. "I'm going to take Dakota to the park, then come back and do some work. Are you going to be okay here? Nae's still resting."

"Yeah." I rubbed my runny nose. "Thanks for letting me stay."

"You're welcome." He smiled but it didn't touch his eyes. "Stay as long as you need to."

I should be preparing Everhide's outfits for the album launch next week. But instead I curled into a ball on the sofa and drew the throw up to my chin. I had most of their clothes organized. They'd be fine in anything, anyway.

Dakota ran out of her bedroom dressed in a bright yellow T-shirt with a unicorn on the front and blue denim shorts. "Daddy, I'm ready."

Anthony rubbed the top of her head. "Hmm. I'm not sure if that's good for the park today. It's about to snow. How about I come and help pick out something to wear that's more appropriate for the cold?"

"But it's Wednesday."

"And it's chilly outside." He tapped her printed T-shirt. "Let's save this pretty unicorn for a sunny day."

"Okay." Dakota grabbed Anthony's hand and hauled him toward her bedroom.

Visions of Hunter being sweet to our child flashed through my mind, but I flicked them away like a fly. That dream had to die.

A few minutes later, Dakota reappeared with Anthony. This time she wore woolen leggings and a sweater. Anthony grabbed Dakota's backpack and shuffled her out of the condo. I stared at the closed door and clutched the blanket against my chest. Fresh tears welled in my eyes. I'd never get the opportunity to take my baby to a park for fun playdates.

I rubbed my wet eyelashes. Bed called to me. As I walked down the hallway, I passed Naomi's room. The door was slightly ajar.

"Kar?" Naomi called out.

I pushed the door open a fraction and peered inside. Naomi lay curled on her side, stretched out in the middle of the bed with a woolly blanket draped over her waist.

"Hey?" I leaned against the doorjamb and wrapped my long cardigan around my waist. "How are you feeling?"

"Better." Naomi's voice was weak and frail. "I still have cramps, but the meds and heat pack are helping."

A dull ache exploded in my abdomen. I remembered that sensation all too well. The cramps. The pain. The blood.

But my sister still had her lady parts. I didn't. "Okay. Get some more rest."

I turned to leave, but Naomi called me back. "Kar, come here." She patted the bed.

Scuffing my UGG boots against the carpet, I crossed the floor on autopilot and sat on the edge of the bed next to her.

She placed her hand on my knee and gave it a gentle rub. "I'm sorry. I truly am."

"You've said that a gazillion times already. It's not your fault. It was my dud eggs. I'm sure of it."

She threw me a faint smile. "Could've been Hunter's sperm?" But then her chin quivered, and her eyes clouded over. "Or maybe there's something wrong with me."

"No. Never." I covered her hand with mine and squeezed it. "It's just not meant to be."

"Kar," Naomi sniffled and whispered. "Don't give up."

"Yeah, I have to. I know how much it hurts. Your body has been through enough hell. No more."

"But Dakota needs a cousin. This was just an awful, heartbreaking miscarriage. I'll be fine. The doctor said we can try again in a couple of months."

Tears pooled in my eyes. "The likelihood of it working isn't good, and you're moving to London."

"I'm the vice president. I make my own rules—not our father. We'll move when I'm ready, when you have a baby in your arms. Kar, I know how much you want a child. There are two embryos waiting for a chance at life. Your babies. This is worth the risk."

I lowered my chin and stared at one of the tiny white embroidered flowers on Naomi's quilt cover. "I can't lose another child."

"I pray that doesn't happen." Hope hovered in Naomi's tone. "But if it does, you have me, and Hunter, Gemma, Lexi, Kyle, Hayden, Anthony, and a bunch of other friends and family to support you. We'll be there to pick up the pieces, like always."

"No. The anxiety is killing me. Look at me." I pointed to my bony arm, then jabbed my fingers against my ribs. It had taken me too long to admit I wasn't well. I hadn't wanted to see it. I'd denied it. I hated Hunter had noticed.

"Because you take on too much." She jabbed my leg. "Slow down. Take care of yourself."

"Ha." I tilted my head back and gazed at the ceiling. "We'll be on tour next year. There's no slowing down."

"You don't have to be Superwoman. Ask for help."

Hmph. Bec and Kate had said the same thing to me in Sydney. Margo, Everhide's former stylist, had hired an assistant. Maybe I could too.

Ugh! I didn't want to think about work.

Naomi took my hand again and clutched it. "Hunter worries about you. He loves you."

"Hunter loves himself." And me. And his friends. And his family. It was what I loved about him. But how could he love me when I wasn't well? Where would I find the strength to get healthy again?

And what was the point when everything I wanted was out of my reach?

"Yeah, he does. I don't think I know a successful male . . . or female . . . who doesn't have some air of cocky arrogance about themselves. But it's what's underneath that counts. You both want to be independent, to be the stronger one, the better one, when if you just stopped, you'd see you're perfect together."

"He's not perfect," I mumbled. "Far from it."

"No one is. We're all flawed and fucked up somehow."

"True."

"Don't be harsh on him." Naomi dialed down her tone. "After what you said last night, I'd say his life is more fucked up than yours at present. He's lost his voice. He's lost a baby. You just walked out on him. I'd say he's way ahead of you on the fucked-up factor."

"We're both a mess, aren't we?" I grabbed a tissue from the box on Naomi's nightstand and wiped the tip of my nose.

"You can't run away when things hurt, or go wrong, or rip your heart apart." Concern flooded Naomi's eyes. "You stand beside each other and fight the battles together."

"That's just it." My hands flopped into my lap. "Everything's a battle. I'm tired of fighting. For him. A baby. My sanity."

"It's a battle because you're scared. And that's okay. But don't let your fears destroy something amazing. I've seen the way you look at each other, act around one another and stand up for each other. Finding someone like that is rare. You love each other so much."

"It's not enough."

"By God, Kara, then what is?" Exasperation furled in Naomi's voice.

A tear rolled down my cheek. "I'm so afraid. Afraid of not being enough for him. Afraid of relying on him more and more. I'm afraid he'll break my heart like Conrad did."

"Oh, sweetie." She held her arms wide. I lay down and curled into her embrace. "Yeah, Conrad did. But never forget what he did to you. He used you, was threatened by your talent, and didn't stand by you when you couldn't get pregnant. He was a weak little man. I hope Jasmine eats him alive. Hunter pulled you out of your heartache and away from our father's clutches. I've never seen you shine like you do with Hunter. Your eyes light up when he is in the same room. Your smile is so bright and gorgeous. You belong in that world of music and fashion. You own what you do, keep pushing the boundaries and breaking the rules. That's who you are and always have been. That's what Hunter loves about you . . . That's what I love about you."

"Really?" I sniffed and clutched my hands against my chest. "I'm sorry. I'm just not in a good place right now. Hunt and I have had a rough few days . . . no, weeks, if not months. Once I get some sleep, clear my head, I hope things become clearer." I sat upright and slid off the bed. "You get some more rest. I'll see you soon."

As I curled into a ball on my bed in the guest room, the past few days throbbed deep in my skull—doctors, babies, lost paths . . . Hunter. Squeezing my eyes closed, I willed the pain in my chest to stop.

Nothing worked.

With each shaky breath, heavy emptiness engulfed my heart. How could I go home to Hunter when he reminded me of everything I'd lost? Drowning myself in work wouldn't help; it had already run me into the ground. Nothing would ever fulfill me like being a mom would. If I couldn't find something, anything, that would allow me to exist in Hunter's presence without falling apart, did we have a future together?

Without a purpose, love wouldn't be enough.

Chapter 32

HUNTER

Kara had been gone two nights. As I sat on the floor in my living room, the whiskey glass dangled between my fingertips. I leaned back and thumped my head against the floor-to-ceiling window. *Thud. Thud. Thud.* I'd lost my voice, my baby, and Kara wasn't home. *Fuck!* Through the haze in my sleep-deprived brain, I couldn't comprehend the new pain and emptiness that had consumed me. My friends had been over, been here for me, but it wasn't the same. Without Kara, for the first time in my life, I felt . . . lonely.

Fuck!

I closed my eyes. What was she doing? Was she still crying? Hurting? Grieving over our loss like I was? We'd talked, but it'd been short. She'd said she needed more time.

Time for what?

It was time to come home.

As I downed another shot of whiskey, I let the burn soothe my throat. My voice was ruined, so I may as well enjoy my JD.

Gray clouds cast a dull gloom into my penthouse and darkened the hardwood floors, making their sheen look less than lackluster. I poured another JD, took a sip, and stared at the baby furniture catalogs Kara had left sitting on the coffee table. The cover image of an infant curled up in a crib, cuddling a teddy bear blanket ripped the hole in my heart wider. *Fuck.* My eyes stung. I clutched my sweatshirt and rubbed my chest. I'd looked forward to hearing our baby's voice filling the hallway, to seeing toys scattered across the floor, to holding my child in my arms, to seeing Kara happy. To being a family. But once again, the chance had been torn away from us. Why, when we both wanted a child, did it have to be so hard? I'd done everything right this time—I'd gone to the agency with Kara to sign the agreement and to the IVF clinic for Naomi's first implant. I'd made sure I didn't make the same mistakes I'd made when Kara was pregnant with Ryan. But she'd still stressed, still worried. The baby had still failed.

Maybe Kara was right. We weren't meant to have a child.

Or had she changed her mind and wanted to try again?

I wouldn't fucking know because she wasn't here.

I placed my glass on the floor, took a swig straight from the bottle, and picked up my acoustic guitar. Resting it on my lap, I played one of my favorite songs off our new album. But instead of the vibrant beat, I slowed it down. Slipping my fingers over the steel strings, I played the chords lower, so they echoed the emptiness resonating in my chest. *Dum . . . dada . . . dum. Dada . . . dum.*

Fighting the burn in my muscles, my heart, my eyes, I spoke the lyrics.

> *I just want to call, come and pick you up*
> *Take you for a drive, and never stop*
> *Watch the city lights, shine on your hair*
> *Laugh and sing, like we have no cares*
> *I wanna see you smile, beneath the stars*
> *Feel your touch here, against my heart*
> *Want to breathe you in, have you next to me*
> *Be all that you need, your everything*

My breath shuddered; my soul crumbled. I let all my pain, heartache, grief, and loneliness flow through my fingertips. This wasn't just about losing our baby; it was about Kara. Why wasn't she here?

I struck the strings harder and wrung the neck of my guitar. As I hammered out the notes, I raked in a sharp breath through clenched teeth and attempted to sing.

You—ve go—ten un—neath my s—in.

FUCK! My voice rasped like a rusty pipe. The sword drove deeper into my chest, twisted, turned, and scraped against my bones. I reverted to talking.

You've gotten underneath my skin
Like a tattoo, a permanent markin'
Oh, baby, it's true, can you not see?
It just might be love that has blinded me
I can't recall the moment I fell
But I do know you're my everything

Concentrating, I tried harder to hold a note.

Your l—ve, g—ves me str—ngth
Your t—ch, g—ves m—

Argh! I dropped my guitar on the floor and buried my head into my hands.

No voice. No baby. No Kara.

What the fuck!

The elevator pinged. Hope spiked through my veins. *Kara?* But it disappeared in a puff of smoke when Kyle and Gemma walked into the living room.

Gemma tossed her woolen coat onto the sofa, rushed over and fell to her knees beside me. She wrapped her arms around my shoulders and gave me a warm hug. "Guess it's wrong to ask how you're doing if you're drinking JD at ten in the morning. Where's Kar?"

"Still not home."

"What?" Kyle dumped his leather jacket on top of Gemma's coat and stretched out on the rug in front of me. Concern loomed in his eyes.

I struggled to inhale; every breath seared my lungs. "I don't know what's wrong, why she won't come home. We lost our baby, and she'd sooner be with her sister than with me."

"Bud." Kyle rubbed the back of his neck. "She's devastated. She'll come around, and it won't be long before you put this loss behind you and try again."

"She doesssn't want to," I slurred and swayed. Yeah, I'd drunk a quarter of a bottle of JD for breakfast. "The stress fucked her up. Did I fuck her up? I've been sitting here trying to work out what I did wrong. Am I missing something?"

Kyle poured a shot of whiskey into my glass and knocked it down. "Yeah, have you ever considered she might need her sister like the three of us need each other?"

Shit. I hadn't thought of that. *Dickhead!*

Gemma curled her arm around mine and rested her head against my shoulder. "After talking to her last night, I still can't get much sense out of her. She can't see the way forward yet."

Neither can I.

"Shouldn't we be doing that together?" I clenched my hands in frustration. "Be there for each other? I should just go over there and bring her home." My voice slashed through my teeth as I tried to get to my feet.

But Gemma grabbed my shirt and pulled me back onto the floor. "Don't." Gemma's tone held an amber warning. "She's not ready. I know you're hurting, too, but you have to be patient."

I was sick of being patient. I'd done that for my voice, and look what had happened? It was fucked too. "Why? It's killing me."

"This is her way of dealing with things." Gemma rubbed my arm. "After Ryan died, she ran away with you to the beach house. When she fell for you on tour, she fled home from Rio. Now, after Naomi's miscarriage, she's run to her sister. Sometimes people need space to clear their heads."

"Don't I know it," Kyle mumbled under his breath as he picked at the rug pile.

I tilted my head back against the glass. Kyle and Gemma had

done the same thing after her kidnapping. He'd taken off to the beach house. It'd nearly torn them apart. But if anything, it had made them stronger. I didn't hold the same hope for Kara and me. Time had never been our friend. "This sucks."

"Yep." Gemma slapped my thigh. "But you're one of the strongest people I know, and one of the most caring. You take on so much and do everything you can for those you love, regardless of how big the burden—from your autism foundation, to our Everhide family, to Kara. You put on a smile, crack a joke, move mountains, and shine light into everyone's hearts. But sometimes *you* forget to be loved and let others take care of you."

I puffed air through my nose. "Gem, I think we all know I've had a ton of loving in my time."

Kyle flicked my shin. "She's not talking about sleeping with a gazillion girls and having millions of fans, dipshit."

"He's right." Gemma nudged her elbow into my ribs. "Kara just wants to look after everyone, especially you. It's in her nature. But she's struggled over the past few months dealing with gossip, your surgery, and the time you spend with us. She worries about you and is concerned you don't want her around."

A knife speared my heart. I'd been open and honest with Kara. How had I not seen she still had issues? I'd thought she understood and accepted my music and work commitments and thought we'd cleared the air about the gossip. But the over-caring when we'd returned home from overseas had done my head in. I just wasn't used to it. But that didn't mean I didn't want her around. Far from it. "That's not true. You know me better than that."

"We do." Gemma jutted her chin toward Kyle, then jabbed her finger against my thigh. "But she doesn't. We have over fourteen years of history; she's barely had two with you. Seven, if you take it from the start of my friendship with her."

I pinched my eyebrows together. "How do you know all this crap?"

Gemma exaggerated her blink and raised one shoulder. "Girls talk."

"Why doesn't she tell me this stuff?"

"She's afraid of losing you." Gemma softened her tone. "She loves you so much, but she's afraid she's not good enough for you, and is afraid of being hurt. If you love her as much as I think you do, you've gotta put her first. We'll always be here for you, no matter what. But if you want a future with her, a family, she has to be number one."

"No." An ache rippled through my chest. "Music comes first."

"No, man, it doesn't." Kyle's tone was backloaded with sincerity. He shook his head, but his styled, swept-back bangs didn't move. "Love does. Kara, then us, then music. That order."

Did I love Kara that much? *Shit . . . yes. No. Yes. Maybe.* The JD fumes fogged my thoughts. "No girl is worth this shit."

"Yeah, they are when you find the right one." Kyle's eyes glinted as he looked at Gemma.

Her cheeks blushed. "Absolutely." She picked up my guitar and played a soothing melody.

The love radiating between Kyle and Gemma struck deep inside my heart. Their connection had grown so strong, so intense, it blew my mind. From meeting in school, to their love of music, to surviving broken hearts and hardships, to experiencing every up and down together, their love had become an uncanny, profound life force. That was what I wanted with Kara. No . . . had with Kara. *Didn't I?*

"That's just it." I stared at the whiskey bottle. "I thought—" *Shit!* Was Kara the one? *Fuuuuck.* I was way too drunk to go down that path right now.

"Thought what?" Intrigue glinted in Gemma's eyes as she strummed the strings.

"Nothing." I grabbed the whiskey and took another swig.

"Dude." Kyle slapped my ankle. "I know what your problem is. You haven't been drunk in months. Drunk Hunter gets emotional and real. You need to get wasted . . . or in this case . . . stay wasted . . . and talk to Kara. Stop pushing each other away when you need each other the most."

"She walked out on me." Right now, I'd settle for her coming home. "I don't know how to stop hurting or how to make this better." How could I prove to her I loved her and needed her? We'd been through so much together. I wanted a baby with her. Wasn't that commitment enough when she didn't want to get married?

Gemma placed my guitar on the floor. She took my hand in hers and jabbed it against my thigh. "Be there for her when she's ready. Kar wants what most people want." Gemma counted out on her free hand. "Love and security. Trust and faithfulness. Marriage. Family. A career. To be accepted. Supported. To be happy."

"That's a long fucking list." I smirked. But none of it scared me.

"Yeah, but you've made her question every dream and path she's ever wanted to take because you take her out of her comfort zone."

I rubbed my eyes and swayed. It was hard to make sense of anything with the quantity of JD intoxicating my brain. "Is that a good thing?"

"Yes. You've opened her eyes. She's not naïve anymore. She's met your family and had to accept there is a risk involved in having your child. And she's had to face her insecurities. It's been a big change for her, moving from the Upper East Side-Hamptons lifestyle into our world. Instead of gracing the socialite pages, she's on the cover of gossip magazines. Instead of hanging out at country clubs, she's backstage at concerts. She's never had to deal with millions of girls throwing themselves at her man. When she was with Conrad, they were social equals. In our sphere, you will always outshine her. You forget she struggles with those things on a daily basis."

Yeah, she didn't like the fans. I wouldn't give up the meet and greets, but I'd toned my behavior down after Sydney. There'd been no more kissing, not even on the cheek. And as for the never-ending gossip? I'd gladly forgo that. Her insecurities? My God, she shouldn't have any. She was so smart and talented and so stunning it hurt just looking at her sometimes. I told her she was gorgeous all the time. But as for outshining her? I'm not sure I could do anything about that. "What's your point, Gem?"

"She's still adjusting to this new life with you. Kara has *always* known what she's wanted. She loves her job. But for as long as we've known her, she's always wanted a baby. So her taking time out isn't *just* about dealing with losing another child—it's about your future together too."

I slid an inch sideways against the slippery window, then pulled myself upright. Dizziness swam through my skull. "What are you talking about?"

"She said she didn't want to try for another baby—no more surrogacy and IVF procedures." Gemma stilled her strings. "So, have you thought that through? Are you prepared to love her no matter what? If there's no baby, can *you* live with the possibility of never having children? . . . Or if it's yes to a baby, you have to find the strength to do whatever it takes to make it happen. Every time you try, every time it fails, you need to be there for her. Be her shoulder to cry on. Love her unconditionally. And in return, she'll do the same for you. I think she's terrified that you won't want to be with her after this loss and, if you do, she has to deal with her insecurities."

My mind throbbed and pulsed. There were too many things to think about. I hadn't thought things through. My heart shuddered and constricted into a tiny ball. After unleashing my desire to have children, I didn't know if I wanted a future without them. As for Kara and her insecurities, I didn't know what more I could do. "Maybe we're just too different and not meant to be together."

Kyle shook his head and scratched his stubble. "No . . . that's what makes you work. Relationships are hard. You have to work together, not against each other. Adjust, grow, move on."

"Nope." I dragged my hand down my face. "I'm done. It's draining. I'm tired. Exhausted."

"But you're not a quitter." Gemma jabbed her finger into my bicep.

Ow! I rubbed my arm and then slumped my shoulders. "Maybe this time, I am."

"Now that . . . is bullshit," Kyle said, getting to his feet. "You're just drunk, upset, and you need a distraction. So grab that guitar and the JD, and let's hit the music room. We need to work out what to do with that voice of yours. We have to make a decision about the tour, so let's move. My ass is dead from sitting on the floor."

"You don't have an ass," I sniggered.

"Oh yeah, he does." Gemma threw Kyle a saucy smile before turning to me and offering her hand to help me up. "Stop your moping. Let's play some music."

"Fuck." I wobbled to my feet. I swiped my guitar off the floor and the JD, then straightened my back. "What the fuck do I have to do to get rid of the two of you?"

"Nothing." A smug smile curled across Kyle's mouth as he caught my arm to steady me. "You'll never get rid of us. Ever."

"Good." I swayed and staggered down the hall.

But as I sat at the piano and tried to rearrange a song to work with my shot voice, my heart shrank with each key. My vocal cords wouldn't vibrate. I couldn't form a note. It crushed me from the inside out, pulverized my bones to powder.

How could we tour when I was like this?

Fuuuck!

We couldn't.

I wanted Kara. I wanted her arms around me, her soothing touch, and her tender kisses. But she wasn't here. Home wasn't the same without her in it.

My eyes stung like a thousand bee stings. My heart tore apart. If she no longer wanted to have another baby, and I was no longer the rockstar I used to be, and I couldn't give her more of my heart than I had already given, maybe I wasn't the right man for her.

I'd tried. I wanted to be.

But all I'd done was fail.

Chapter 33

KARA

I flicked my fingernails together, back and forth, back and forth. Nausea and nerves pooled in my stomach as I waited for Gemma and Lexi at a café in Brooklyn for lunch. They were about to grill me on open flames and try to roast some sense into me. They'd want me to put losing another baby behind me . . . and in the not too distant future, try again. I was sure of it. But I was adamant about not going through the surrogacy and IVF process again. Not now. Not ever again. It had been too stressful and heartbreaking. My health had suffered, mentally and physically. My sister had been through enough. Hunter had enough of his own concerns. He didn't need anymore. I hadn't been home in four days. I'd needed time to accept my new fate. I prayed that the tumultuous past few months hadn't broken what Hunter and I had. But I had to prepare for the worst.

A black SUV pulled up outside the café. Chester, Gemma's bodyguard, jumped out of the front passenger seat and opened the rear door.

Gemma and Lexi stepped onto the sidewalk. Gemma pulled her beanie down low, then drew her long woolen coat across her chest. Lexi's blonde spiral curls caught in the breeze as she pulled her scarf tight. Lowering their heads, they dashed into the café and joined me.

The laidback venue with its dark wooden furniture and exposed brick wall with sepia-toned photographs of the Brooklyn Bridge wasn't busy for a Sunday. It wasn't the summer tourist season. There were only four other tables occupied with a mix of middle-aged men and women lost in conversation and drinks. Gemma shouldn't be swamped by any fans here.

I was baffled as to why she'd chosen to meet at this tiny, *out-of-the-way* café. It wasn't near Everhide's rehearsal space, or home, or where Lexi used to hang out. But the delicious aromas wafting from the kitchen had me sold.

After quick hugs hello, the girls sat opposite me. Chester dipped his chin in greeting, then took a seat nearby at the bar.

"How are you doing?" Lexi clutched my hand across the table. "It's good you're back in the land of the living."

"Almost." I feigned a smile. Lexi had visited me at Naomi's place on Wednesday afternoon after she'd lost the baby. But I'd been too much of a mess to talk sense or think straight. Now, my mind was clear. I fidgeted with a napkin and glanced at Gemma. "How's Hunt?"

"You could ask him yourself."

I didn't miss the snark in her tone. But then Gemma sighed and pulled off her beanie and tossed it on the chair beside her. "To be honest, he's a fucking mess." She picked up the menu and scanned the list. "He mopes around all day. Drinks. Gets angry at rehearsals. He's in a constant state of depression. But you know that."

Yeah. I'd talked to him a couple of times to let him know I was alive, but we hadn't talked about anything else.

Gemma peered over the top of the menu. "When are you going home?"

"Soon." Tonight? Tomorrow night? I had no plans. I was terrified of worst-case scenarios.

"He's really hurting, Kar." Lexi grabbed the jug of water on the end of the table and poured three glasses. "He misses you."

Our conversation was interrupted by a waitress in skinny

black jeans and a neat white blouse with an apron tied around her waist. Without making eye contact, she waved her pen over her notepad. "What would you like to order?"

I blinked. I should've met the girls at the wine bar near Naomi's place, not a café near the bridge. Much better service would've been guaranteed. But I let it slide. "I'll have the warm chicken salad." I'd read the menu while I'd waited for the girls.

Lexi made popping, smacking sounds with her lips as she skimmed the list of food. "I'll have a beef burger with fries and a cola, please."

"And … for … me …" Gemma's eyes darted over the laminated page. "I'll have a large pasta carbonara, loaded fries, and a garlic bread." She collected the menus and handed them to the waitress. "Thank you. And see that guy at the bar in the black jacket?" She pointed at Chester. "Add whatever he wants to my bill, please?"

The waitress smirked. She still hadn't lifted her eyes, so she hadn't recognized Gemma. "Trying to get lucky, are you? In this joint?"

"Yep." Nonchalance swung in Gemma's tone. "He's freaking *so* hot! Gotta take my chances."

Lexi and I giggled as the lady headed over to Chester. He threw them a questioning look. His eyes glinted with humor as the waitress took his order.

Poor Chester. The shit he had to put up with.

I turned back to the girls and leaned toward Gemma. "My God, how much food did you order? You won't finish all that."

"Wanna bet?" She threw me a challenging grin. "The guys and I started fitness training and nutrition this week. It's time to jump on the treadmill, and amp up our stamina for more promo and the tour."

"But the tour isn't for seven months." My brow furrowed as I sipped my water. With no baby due, the tour could start in July as originally planned.

Gemma sighed and sank an inch in her chair. "We have album promo until Christmas, then awards season and other appearances and events until the end of March. Then we hit rehearsals for the tour. I need to get fit. I need energy to burn." Normally, Gemma would be a bundle of excitement, but she lacked her usual spark. That wasn't Gemma. Something wasn't right.

"You should see Hayden." Lexi nudged her elbow against Gemma's arm. "He'll eat three massive pizzas by himself. It's insane. Maybe I should take up drumming. He never puts on weight. I look at a pizza slice and I gain ten pounds."

I felt her pain. I'd been like that until recently. I folded my arms across my nonexistent stomach. My bony ribs and protruding hips dug into my forearms. I'd always wanted to be skinny. Now I was, I didn't like it. I missed my curves and hated that my boobs had shrunk. They'd been my best asset. Caught up in my head, I'd been too blind to see what had been happening to my body . . . but not anymore. I needed to get better, and the only way to do that was to lower my stress levels.

"Kar, talking about the months ahead . . ." Gemma flattened her palms on the dark wooden tabletop. "I need to ask a favor."

Shit. Here it comes. I drew in a deep breath and braced myself, ready to take on board whatever the girls dished me.

"We know you're going through a lot right now, and we understand that." The beautiful emerald shine in Gemma's eyes faded to black. "But we need your help. Hunt doesn't want to come on the album promo and wants to cancel the tour. I need you to change his mind."

"He *what*?" My heart cracked like an egg and dribbled onto the floor. He lived for touring.

Gemma put on a brave face, but tears welled in her eyes. "We've worked on modifying the songs, but he still can't sing. Kyle and I suggested he play up to the crowd with guitar solos and take on all the onstage talking. We even suggested using backing tracks—but none of us wanted to do that because we never lip-sync; we always sing live—but he doesn't want to do anything. Nothing's getting through to him."

I closed my eyes and fought back the sting.

"He's so broken by what happened to his vocal cords." Gemma's voice wobbled. "Losing the baby and you leaving has crushed him."

My chest constricted. I hated hurting him. He was one of the most resilient people I knew, and I'd cut him deep. Would he ever forgive me? "I needed time."

"We get that." Gemma's tone sharpened. "But this is urgent. We can't and won't tour without him."

I closed my eyes. "What do you want me to do about it?"

"Convince him to say yes." Lexi leaned back on her chair. "He won't listen to us. He's lost hope and needs to find his way forward. He can't do that until the two of you sort out your shit."

I fidgeted with my napkin on my lap. "Have you convinced him to have the surgery?"

"Surgery?" Gemma grimaced and shook her head. "What surgery? He said another procedure wouldn't work. His cords are too damaged."

I jerked my chin back. "No, another procedure is risky and dangerous, but there is a chance his vocal cords could be fixed. He's petrified that the surgeons will fuck up again and make things worse. He's terrified of operations, of hospitals, and thinks that nothing but bad things will happen to him when there."

Gemma's gaze fell to the tabletop. Her brow furrowed. "*Shit!* I never knew that."

Hmph. That surprised me. Kyle, Gemma, and Hunter knew everything about each other. *But not this?* My head spun so much I nearly fell off my chair. *Wow.* Maybe I shared something truly unique with Hunter. I knew more about his darkest fears and concerns than Gemma and Kyle did.

"So, his voice could be fixed?" Hope swung in Gemma's voice. When I nodded, Gemma snapped. "Then fuck." She slapped her hands on the table. "You have to change his mind."

"How?" My voice wavered. "He's more stubborn than a mule."

Gemma leaned forward and pleaded. "Go. Home."

My heart crumbled like dried flower petals. "What if I break him further?"

"What? How?" Lexi's tone softened. "Kar, what's going on?"

I closed my eyes and took a breath to find my strength. "I don't want to try for another baby. I don't want one anymore. And if he does, we might not have a future together."

"You? Not want a baby?" Lexi stared at me for a second, then threw her head back and laughed. A big, loud cackle that filled the restaurant.

I wriggled on my chair and smoothed my hands over my dress pants. I gazed around the place, hoping Lexi's outburst hadn't disturbed the other diners. No one stopped eating or glanced in our direction.

Lexi grabbed a breadstick from the jar next to the water and snapped it in half. "What drugs are you on, girl? You can't switch off that shit. You've always wanted a baby."

Tears loomed at the back of my eyes, but there was no way I'd come undone. I wouldn't cry over this issue anymore. I lifted my chin, remaining defiant. "Well, now I don't."

Lexi's face blanched. "Oh shit . . . you're serious? Well, fuck . . . Now I feel like shit. I'm so sorry."

My bones sagged like a cowl. "I can't go through the process again. It kills me every time. I can't face any more heartache, or shattered dreams, or go through more loss and disappointment."

Gemma's jaw set with steel. Emerald shards flashed in her eyes. "Bullcrap. What you've been through is awful. Yeah, it hurts, yeah, it sucks, yeah, it breaks your heart . . . I know. I've been through it all . . . not the baby thing . . . but failures, and heartbreaks, and shit that has scared me to death. But I got through it because I have people who love and care about me. So do you. Hunt fucking loves you. He wants to have a baby with you. He's committed to that. To you. Don't throw away your dreams just because you've had a few setbacks. Don't give up because you're afraid to fail and afraid of being hurt. Learn from what's happened and take the leap again. Keep fighting for what you want. I promise we'll be there for you. And so will Hunt."

Gemma's words tumbled around inside my head as the waitress interrupted us. She placed a huge tray on the table and handed out the meals. "Enjoy." She deadpanned as she picked up the tray and waddled off.

I wouldn't let Gemma get to me. I took a steady breath, rolled my cutlery out of the napkin and cut into a piece of chicken. "It doesn't matter. I don't want a baby anymore. Dreams die."

"No, they don't." Gemma shook her head, picked up a fry and dipped it in the ooey, gooey cheese. "They sometimes just need adjustments, tweaks, and changes." She jabbed the fry at me. "But you're the only one who can do that."

As Gemma and Lexi devoured their fries, I nibbled on a piece of chicken and pushed the lettuce leaves around the plate. My appetite had gone.

Glancing out the window, my heart lurched. A young couple with two young children walked down the street toward the park. To ward off the cold, they were dressed up in puffer jackets, beanies, and scarves. The dad carried his daughter on his shoulders. The boy swung and skipped between his parents, holding onto their hands.

"Be honest, Kar." Lexi sipped her soda and pointed toward the family. "You still want that."

I closed my eyes. Hunter's smile, his laugh, and images of him hugging and rocking our baby in his arms filled my head. The way he looked at me with love and adoration flooded my chest with warmth. *Fuck!*

"You love him, don't you?" Lexi stabbed her fork into the pile of fries and stuffed them in her mouth.

"Yes." I couldn't deny that even if I tried. "Of course I do."

Lexi covered her mouth with her fingertips and spoke over her mouthful of food. "Then stop lying to yourself."

The tears I'd been holding back finally came unstuck. They pooled on the rims of my eyes before one escaped and meandered down my cheek. My heart cried. I wanted a baby. More than anything. Biological or not. I wanted a family so badly. "Fuck, I hate you girls." I dabbed my eyes with the edge of the napkin. "Just when I think I've got my shit together, you blow it all apart."

Lexi shrugged. "Because we know you."

"What am I going to do about Hunt?" I dabbed my eyes with the napkin. "I've been awful to him. Haven't I?"

"Yep." Gemma bobbed her head as she twirled pasta around her fork. "You can sort the baby thing out when you're ready. And I know you struggle with all that comes with being Hunt's girlfriend, but you shouldn't worry about our fans or what the media says. You should own being with him. Flaunt it. Rock it, like he does. Tell him off when he's being a dick. And always remember, Kyle and I are like flies hovering around him. We're *Big Brother,* watching his every move. He can't set a foot wrong because if he did, we'd kill him before you or anyone else got the chance."

Yeah. They'd always have my back. So would Lexi and Hayden. I rounded my shoulders. "Do you think he'll forgive me?"

"I'm sure once you talk, you'll work things out." Gemma dug into her pasta. She sucked up a strand of fettuccine and swallowed it down. "But . . . there is one way to prove to him how serious you are about being together."

"How?" I was all ears.

"Put it in ink." Gemma smiled over another mouthful of pasta.

I wrinkled my nose. "You want me to sign something? Like what?" I'd already signed so many legal agreements. What else would Everhide's lawyers want me to sign?

"Not paper." Gemma's eyes glinted with mischief. "I mean . . . *ink.*"

She pointed a short way down the street.

A yellow shop sign caught my eye. My mouth fell open. "A tattoo. Are you serious? I'm not getting a tattoo."

"We are!" Lexi clapped. "That's why we wanted to meet here. We had no idea what to get the guys for Christmas, so we're getting their names in ink."

I broke out in a cold sweat. I didn't want to be branded. *Did I? No.* I loved Hunter's tattoos, but I didn't want one myself.

Gemma covered her inner left bicep with her hand. "I'm getting '*Kyle*' inked right here."

Gemma had several tattoos, but if that gesture was anything to go by, the new one would be the biggest.

"I want it to be a heart monitor line with his name in the middle and treble clefs on each end. He's my lifeline, makes my heart beat, and we live and breathe music. It'll be perfect. He has my name inked on a tulip on his chest, so this will make us even. It will bind us together forever."

"I'm nervous as hell." Lexi fidgeted and swooped a stray curl behind her ear. "It's my first tattoo. I'm getting '*Hayden*' inked on my wrist. Like the '*GKH*' initials Gem has on hers. Only smaller, so I can cover it up with a big watch or bracelet."

"It'll hurt," Gemma warned her. "Getting the one on my wrist was the most painful."

"You didn't tell me that." The blood drained from Lexi's face.

"It's not unbearable." Gemma shrugged her shoulder. "When you're getting inked, you've just got to zone out and think about something else. That's why Kar has to come—so she can distract us."

"I can do that." Why had my palms turned clammy? "But I don't want ink." My parents would really disown me if I got a tattoo.

Wait . . . they basically had anyway.

"Okay." Gemma licked her fingertips after polishing off a dozen more fries. "That's fine. No pressure."

"None." I fumbled with the pearl pendant on my necklace. "No ink."

Absolutely.

No. Ink.

***

As Lexi and Gemma got inked by two men covered from head to toe in tattoos, I sat on a chair between the two beds. But the whir of the tattoo gun drilled into my head. Each stroke the tattoo artist made hit my heart. Ink was true commitment—a show of love, dedication and forever. Marriage could end. Divorce was too common. Ink was permanent. There was no erasing it . . . aside from laser removal . . . but it was a true forever. *That* was what I wanted with Hunter.

We were bound to each other after everything we'd been through.

He was my forever.
I wanted him to be permanent.
There was only one thing to do.
Then, it was time to go home.

Chapter 34

KARA

The elevator pinged and the doors opened into the penthouse. Butterflies turned and twirled in my stomach like pirouetting ballerinas. I had no idea how Hunter would react to me being home. I'd hurt him. I deserved whatever he dished out to me. But I wouldn't run away from my fears or lie to myself anymore. I'd dug myself into this mess; I had to live with the consequences.

I stepped into the hallway, dropped my purse and my carry-on suitcase by the console table, and headed toward the living room. I expected the place to be littered with takeout dishes and empty bottles, but it was completely tidy.

There was no sign of Hunter, though.

After tossing my coat and scarf onto the sofa, I checked the office, the bedrooms, and then opened the door to the music studio. *He's here.* He sat at the computer, staring at the monitor covered in music software as if lost in troubled thoughts. My heart sank to the pit of my stomach. Dark circles surrounded his eyes, like he hadn't slept in days. He hadn't shaved. His shoulders slumped as if they were too heavy to hold up. He hadn't even noticed me in the doorway.

I knocked softly. "Hunt?"

"Kar." He wheeled his chair back from the desk and hit the

wall. He leaped to his feet, took three massive strides toward me and wrapped his arms around me. He reeked of whiskey and cologne—so *him*. I held him close, tight, and ignored the ache in my ribs.

He pulled back and cupped my face. His bloodshot eyes raked over me. "You're home."

"Yeah," I whispered and clutched his forearms. "I hope so."

"I've missed you." He pressed his forehead against mine and stroked my hair. But then, he shuffled back a foot. The air around me prickled. Anguish hooded his eyes. "Wait . . . hope so?" The color drained from his cheeks. His hands fell to his sides. "What's that supposed to mean?"

I wrung my hands together. "I'm sorry I've been so messed up. I hate that I've hurt you." I glanced at the half-full bottle of JD and tumbler on the desk. It was six in the evening. How much had he drunk today? "But I'm here. Ready to talk when you are. Maybe when you're sober."

"I'm sober enough." He wiped his hand down one scruffy, stubbled cheek, then the other. "So talk."

"Can we sit?" I waved toward the old blue sofa on the far side of the room by the guitar rack.

"I'd prefer to stand." He walked backward until he connected with the desk. Resting his butt on the surface, he folded his arms.

Shit! He had every right to retreat. But if we were to move forward and have a future together, we needed to be on the same path. I filled my lungs, then exhaled slowly to make sure my head was clear. *Okay. I've got this.* I stepped in front of the piano and spun on my heels to face him. Standing six feet away felt like a mile.

"I'm sorry I haven't handled the loss of our baby well. I was upset. Worried about Nae. Devastated that my dream had been taken away from me . . . from us . . . again. It broke me, and I couldn't see my way through the darkness."

"Sorry really doesn't cut it." The edge in his husky voice cut deep into my chest and scored my heart. "We lost our baby, and you walked out. You haven't been home for days. How do you think that makes me feel?"

"Heartbroken and hurt. Because I feel the same way."

"You should've been here." He jabbed his finger toward the floor, then flicked it toward the door. "Not run off to your sister's. When times are tough, you don't run. Not ever. I've gone through hell over the past few months with my voice. Not once did I push you away."

I closed my eyes and shook my head. "You did. In Sydney, you wanted to be with the fans, not me. In London, you didn't want me to stay. Since being home, you've spent every second possible with Kyle and Gemma and drowned yourself in work. I read those things as a sign you didn't want me around anymore."

"I had to recover and do my job." He spoke as if every word caused him pain. "Yes, there were some days I needed space because every day my heart broke when my voice didn't get better. Every day I struggled through vocal therapy. No matter what I did, nothing made any improvement. But regardless of how much I was dying on the inside, I came home to you every night. You being here got me through everything."

Tears pooled in my eyes. "You were so distant sometimes. I thought we were growing apart."

He beat his hand against his heart and fisted a handful of his hoodie. "I was fucked up. My life was shattered. How could you think I wanted nothing to do with you after a few rough weeks? Not every bad day or fight means I want to break up with you." His shoulders sagged. "Why didn't you talk to me?"

My chin trembled. My breath burned my lungs. "I was afraid of losing you. Afraid for our baby. Afraid of another failed relationship."

"And so am I." He clutched onto the edge of the desk and lowered his chin. "I've never had one this long before. I've done everything to make you happy, tried to do things right, but whatever I did never seemed to be enough. *I* wasn't enough." He waved his hand up and down at me. "You're fading away before my eyes, and it scares me. Is this because of me? The baby? Do you expect me to be perfect when I'm not?"

The helplessness hooding his eyes crushed my ribs.

I grabbed onto the edge of the piano to steady myself, to stop my knees from shaking. "I've never expected perfection. I was naïve to think I had that with Conrad, and look what happened—he left me for another woman. He gave up when things got too hard." I placed my hand on my stomach to keep the unease at bay. "I don't want that to happen to us. I didn't go into this relationship blind. I knew your past, your heartache, who you were, and yes, I've struggled with some things, especially the gossip and the fans. It doesn't make me love you less—it makes me cautious."

He trudged toward the sofa and sank onto the padded arm. Shaking his head, he rubbed the back of his neck. "The gossip and fans are always going to be around. I took your concerns on board and have toned things down. What else can I do to get you to trust me?"

"You don't have to do anything." I took another small step toward him. "Because I do trust you. With all my heart. It's taken time and another gut-wrenching loss to realize that. You've trusted me by telling me about your childhood and showing me where you grew up. You stood up to my father when we decided to find a surrogate. You made plans for our baby in your tour schedule. You made sure I was okay after the Camilla incident. You came running when Nae miscarried. Anytime I've had a smidgen of doubt, you've stepped up and exceeded my expectations. You've done everything for *us*. You are more than enough. You are my everything."

He turned his head, grimaced and pursed his lips. When he looked back at me, tears had pooled in his eyes. "I've wanted to hear you say that for so freaking long."

"I know." I wrapped my arms around myself, hit my tender ribs too hard and winced.

He shot to his feet and took a small step toward me. "Are you okay?"

"Yes, I'm fine." Here I was trying to be honest, and what did I do? Lie! *Ugh!*

But I loved that he cared. So much. I straightened, gathered my thoughts and refocused. "Hunt, I don't want any more problems between us. I'm ashamed to admit I got jealous of the time you spent with Kyle and Gem, and how you ran to them after the doctor gave you the devastating news about your vocal cords." I slowly closed the gap between us and placed my hand on his chest. "I lost sight of us and our balance."

He caught my upper arms. Fierce passion burned in his gaze. "Gem and Kyle are a huge part of my life. They always will be. But they're not my whole life." He softened his tone. "You give me more than music. You *inspire* my music. Every song I write is about you. You've given me something that Kyle and Gem never have . . . a home and the want to have a family of my own. You lost sight of the balance because you worry about everyone else but not yourself, and you're not doing what you love."

Tears hovered on the rims of my eyes. "I wanted to be a mom, but it keeps failing."

"I know. It's been hard, and shitty, but we'll get through it. But what about designing?"

What?

I'd been drawing to take my mind off worrying about the baby, but the spark had grown brighter and brighter. I'd tried to hide it, suppress it, but the need to design wouldn't die.

He rubbed my arms. "Every night, you sit up drawing, denying it's not what you want to do. It's in your soul, like music is in mine. Let it shine. We'll make it work. I'll pay for you to set up your own fashion house. You can run your own fashion empire."

My chin quivered. "But I want to go on the tour and work with you."

"Then do both. Build a team you can trust. Do a collection with someone, like I suggested. Work with Ivory Mink. Use her enterprise to make it happen. *Fuck,* I'll buy her out or invest in the business if you want me to."

I didn't need his money. I had enough of my own. But my heart galloped. He made everything sound so simple, so exciting. Maybe I had to stop making things hard and take the easy route for a change. "And you just want to click your fingers and make that happen?"

He puffed air through his nose. "For you, yes. I'd do anything for you."

I took his hands in mine and held them in front of me. "Did you mean what you said about us being a family?"

He let out a slow breath, then nodded. "You've always been part of our Everhide family and always will be. But regarding us…" He closed his eyes. He raised my hands and kissed my fingertips like he needed a second to regain his composure. "I want a baby with you. I want one day … somewhere down the track … to get married. But if you don't want a baby anymore, now or at any time in the future, I don't know how I feel about that. I still want to have kids."

A sob escaped me. "Oh, Hunt." I released his hand and touched his cheek with my trembling fingertips. "I still want a baby. I tried to talk myself out of it and convince myself to let go of my dreams, but I can't."

Confusion clouded his eyes. "But … I thought … you didn't want to try again."

"More heartache and loss terrifies me. But I can't give up. I want to be a mom. We have incredible friends and family to support us if it fails. I want to keep trying."

He nodded and sniffled. "Kar, I want that too. But first … you need to get better. I don't want to see you stressed out again. You've fretted over Naomi, you've lost too much weight, and you keep looking at those pictures of Ryan. I worry about you all the freaking time. I feel so helpless. You just have to ask, and I'll do anything to help you."

My heart ached that he'd seen what I couldn't. "Just be here for me. I'll go to more therapy, take meds, and do whatever it takes to get well. But the next time, or however many more times it takes for us to have a baby, we're more prepared for whatever happens."

"Yeah, we are."

Daydreams filled my head as I clutched and squeezed his hands. "I can't wait to see you with our baby in your arms, see you teach them music, and when they're older, I want to see them at your concerts"—I covered my ears with my hands—"with huge noise-canceling headphones on, watching all the flashing lights and going, 'That's my daddy singing up there.'" I hooked my fingers into his belt and tugged him closer. "We have two embryos left . . . Let's try for a baby again soon."

"I'd like that." But the glimmer of light snuffed out in his eyes. His shoulders sank two inches as he stepped out of my hold. "But I won't be singing."

My heart collapsed, but fire flared in my veins. "Yes. You will. You, of all people, are not a quitter. I tried to convince myself to give up on a baby out of fear, failure, and hurting those involved. But I can't switch off who I am. You can't either. I'm not giving up on a family, so you can't give up on your voice." I jabbed my finger against his chest. "You need to go back to the doctor, have that surgery, and get your vocal cords fixed."

"There's no point. They're fucked."

"Yes, they are. But you have a chance to get better." I tugged hard on his hoodie cords. "I know you're scared. But I promise to be by your side every step of the way. I will love you no matter what happens. Even if you come out mute."

"Mute?" He dragged his fingers down his face. "What the fuck? Do you have to put more horrific thoughts into my head? I'm not going under the knife again."

I wouldn't buy it. "Yes. You. Are." I flattened my palm against his chest. "You need to do this. Because right now, you don't have closure. You have a carrot dangling in front of you—the chance to be fixed. So take it. If it doesn't work, you'll be no worse off than you are now. If it fails, you try something else. You keep going and going until you've tried every experimental, trial, crazy-assed medical procedure out there. Only then can you pursue other avenues of just playing, producing or writing. Even then, you never give up . . . because what if this surgery, or the next one, or the one after that works?"

"It won't."

I threw my hands up and spun away from him. I threaded my fingers into my hair, clutched a handful, and crushed my knuckles against my scalp. "You can be so infuriating sometimes."

"I know. I've perfected that."

"No, you're afraid." What could I do to convince him to have surgery? Gemma's words rang in my ears. *'Don't give up . . . Keep fighting for what you want.'* My hands fell to my side. "But together we'll get through anything. We're going to have a baby together. And we're going to get through your surgery together. To show you how serious I am about you, about us, and our future together, I got this." I lifted my knit top and showed him the skin beneath my bra line. Covered in plastic film, my flesh pulled as I bent sideways. *Ow!*

"Holy shit." He rushed over and cupped my side. His hand, big and warm, fanned across my skin. "You got ink? My name?"

Just *Hunter.* In cursive. With a heart at the end.

"Yeah. Peer pressure from Gem and Lexi." I lowered my top.

He shook the daze out of his eyes. "You're crazier than I am."

"No . . . as crazy as you are. Crazy about you."

One corner of his mouth quirked into a smile, but within a heartbeat, it disappeared. He took a deep breath, caressed the sides of my face, and his beautiful blue eyes locked onto mine. "So, you want to try again? For a baby?"

"Yes." My voice was barely audible. "In a few months."

"You think I should have surgery?"

"Yes. As soon as possible."

"I'm scare—" His voice cracked and wavered. "Scared of losing more than I already have."

"You won't." I brushed my fingertips down his stubbly cheek. "You can't. The people who love you aren't going anywhere. You'll always have me. Whether you can sing or not, I will always love you."

Pain rippled across his face.

The reality of him not singing again was too real at present. But I had faith. "Let's keep trying for a baby and keep trying to fix your voice until there are absolutely no options left."

"Only if you promise to do some things." He took my hands in his and shuffled back a step. Silver shards quivered in his eyes.

"Promise me you'll never walk out on me again." He gave my hands a little shake. "That hurt the most. That you wouldn't let me be there for you. I know I did the same thing to you. And I'm sorry. I won't ever do that again. No matter how crappy things get, we stick by each other. Got it?"

"Yes."

"If we need time out, that's okay. But we promise to always talk things through."

"Always."

"You tell me off, pull me into line, smack me in the head if I do something you don't like or don't listen."

"Okay."

"And we never give up on our dreams."

"Never."

"And one more thing . . ." His gaze fell to my chest, then jumped back to my face. His eyes shimmered with a new devilish glint. "You getting inked is *the* hottest, fucking sexiest thing ever." His shoulders relaxed; his tone softened. "Kar, I love you. I can't turn it off. I don't want to."

"Me neither. I love you."

He drew me into his arms and kissed me. Slow and sweet, warm and tender. With a flick of his tongue, he deepened our kiss and tugged me hard against his chest.

"Ow!" I winced. "Too tight. My ribs are sore." *Damn ink.* "I got tattooed there because you like my boobs." And I could cover it up with clothing.

"I love your tits." He ran his hands up my sides and cupped my breasts. He swiped his thumbs across my nipples, hardening them beneath his gentle touch. "They are perfect."

Hooking my hands behind his neck, I threaded my fingers into his hair and drew his lips to mine. The taste of whiskey on his tongue intoxicated my senses and erased the tension from my muscles. *Damn*, I loved his kisses. I loved *him*.

His hands slid onto my hips. Holding me firmly, he guided me back across the room until my spine connected with the wall. "Is there anything else we need to talk about?"

I tugged and pulled at his hoodie and sweatshirt, ripped them over his head, and tossed them on the floor. "I don't think so. But if there is, it can wait. We have a lot of making up to do."

"Fuck yeah."

Chapter 35

KARA

With one quick yank, Hunter removed my knit top and threw it on the chair. With one quick flick behind my back, he undid my bra and dropped it on the floor. With one deep kiss, he stole my breath and injected fire into my heart. The flame I held for him had never died. It could never be extinguished. We needed each other like oxygen to keep burning bright.

He trailed hungry kisses down the length of my neck and made his way to my breasts. He circled and flicked his tongue over one hardened nipple, then the other. Each delectable lick shot sparks through my veins. His hot breath sent goosebumps skipping across my skin. Moaning, I collapsed against the wall. Dizziness swam through my head. *Damn*, I missed his mouth.

A smile quirked and curled at the corner of his lips. Yeah, he knew the effect he had on me.

He splayed his fingers beneath the edge of my covered tattoo and ran his thumb over the bottom of the clear film. "Is it hurting?"

"It's okay." I combed strands of his hair off his face and tucked them behind his ear. "It hurt getting it done. The needle, the wiping, the jabbing. But once it was over, it wasn't bad. Now it's like a bad sunburn."

He straightened and smirked. "When have you ever been

sunburned?"

"Once." I winced, remembering my sore, red skin during vacation in Florida. "When I was twelve. Never again."

"Wait until your tattoo oozes and peels."

"What?" *Yuck!*

He jutted his chin toward the tattooed swirls covering his shoulder. "This one was the worst. I thought I had some disease."

"With you? It's highly possible."

His eyes twinkled. "Damn, I love your sass." He kissed, bit, and sucked on my lower lip. "I'm gonna get your name inked too. What do you reckon? Big bold letters across my chest?" He swiped his palm across his pecs. "Or on my arm? My neck? Or like you, on my heart, since it's yours."

My insides melted into a puddle of liquid honey on the studio floor. *So sweet.* I cupped his cheek. "I'd like that, but you don't have to."

"I like ink."

"I like *your* ink." I traced my fingertip over the swirls on his shoulder.

"I'd *like* to get into your pants now." His hands trailed down my stomach, yanked the clasp of my dress pants open, and lowered the zip. "Is that okay?"

My knees weakened, and my insides clenched in anticipation. My heartbeat thudded faster as I nodded.

With a wicked grin, he dipped his hands inside my pants and rubbed his palm over my silky panties. He drove his finger against the soft fabric, pressed, and teased my clit.

His mouth hovered an inch from my lips. "You've been gone for too long. I'm gonna have to reacquaint myself with every inch of your body. Your neck." He kissed the bare skin beneath my earlobe. "Your shoulders." He nipped a line toward the top of my arm. Then, he drifted down and flicked his tongue over my nipples again. "And definitely these."

My eyes fluttered closed. His vocal cords may have been damaged, but *by God*, the new rasp in his voice sent the most exquisite shudders through every nerve in my body, especially between my legs.

Sliding his hand into my panties, he continued his seductive torture. As he kissed his way back to my mouth, he drove a finger into my pussy, slow and deep. In and out. In and out.

The breath shot from my lungs. Thank God the wall kept me upright. Hovering near my ear, he lowered his voice. "I'm gonna re-explore every damn inch of you, Kar." He drove his finger deep into me. "Here for starters. Got that?"

I licked my lips, trying to find some moisture so I could talk. "Yeah. But let's start with just fucking."

Grabbing his belt, I undid his jeans and wriggled them toward his ankles. Urgency took hold. He yanked them off, along with his boxer briefs and socks. I slipped off my boots, dress pants, and panties. But rather than toss them aside, I dropped my clothes at his feet and fell onto my knees. I glanced up at him and threw him a devilish grin.

"Ka—?" His voice cracked.

"Yes, Hunter?"

He didn't move.

Yeah, he wasn't going anywhere.

I raked my fingers up his long legs, through the fine hairs, and circled his muscular thighs. Every inch of his flesh quivered and tensed. His perfectly man-groomed groin and rock-hard erection loomed before me. I caressed his cock with one hand and cupped his balls in the other. Then, I took him into my mouth.

"Jeesuz!" His head lolled back. His knees buckled.

With languid flicks, I teased my tongue across the tip, licking, circling, and sucking. His musky scent intoxicated me. Savoring the salty taste on my tongue, I took him deeper into my mouth and stroked him harder.

He groaned, low and gravelly. He tangled his fingers in my hair and cradled the back of my head. His hips pulsed in time with my rhythm. As he thrust his gorgeous cock into my mouth, my want for him flared. Bobbing my head, I took him deeper, harder. Deeper. Harder.

His thighs tensed.

A raw, guttural moan escaped him. "*Mmm.*"

But then, he ripped his groin away from me.

"Kar?" he panted. His chest heaved. "I love this. I do. But I want to be inside you." He offered me his hand and helped me stand.

Once I found my feet, he caught my hips and pressed my back against the wall. With his naked body flush against mine, he cupped my face and brushed his lips across my mouth. "You're mine, Pearl." The possessiveness in his tone claimed my heart and hummed through my veins. "You're so beautiful."

Before I could say anything, he kissed me. Wrapping my arms around his shoulders, I melted against his body. Every time he flicked his tongue against mine, tingles charged across my skin. His roaming fingers were as magical as his lips. He massaged and teased my nipples. He stroked between my legs. He explored my flesh. Each touch ignited a fire in my belly and hot need in my core. I slid my hand between us, took hold of his cock and guided it toward my pussy. "In. Now."

Smiling over our kisses, he rocked his hips against mine. With a gentle thrust, he entered me. Sparks shot up my spine, coiled down to my toes and pooled at the base of my neck.

As he drove deeper into me, his eyes darkened. "Feel this, Kar? This connection? I've never had this with anyone but you. This is our bond. Exclusively yours. You okay with that?"

My heart filled my chest. Tears welled in my eyes. I'd always have to share him with music and fans . . . but this . . . his love . . . was mine. "Yes. I am."

I clutched the back of his head and kissed him. I loved him with all my soul.

With blazing kisses, smoldering touches and fiery thrusts, our bodies became one. United, we took each other over the edge. Electric jolts. Fiery sparks. Hot rushes.

Quakes and quivers coursed between us.

Over scorching kisses, sexy smiles, and sensual touches, we shuddered.

Here, with him, is where I belong.

Lying on the music room sofa in the aftermath of bone-melting lovemaking, I lay against his chest. Gliding my hand over his smooth skin, I pressed my lips against his warm flesh. No doubt we'd have many more life hurdles to overcome and more challenges ahead. We'd survived the loss of our first child and two failed IVF attempts. We'd been dealt some soul-crushing career blows and health scares. But if I'd learned one thing over the past few months, it was that our love and trust in each other had grown and it was strong enough to survive anything.

I'd ensure Hunter had surgery, even if I had to drag him there myself. I'd sort out my health issues, eat better, and have more therapy. I should've never cut back on my sessions. And most of all, I'd put our baby plans back on the agenda.

I pressed my hand over my tattoo, grinned and bit my lip.

I can't believe I got inked.

I love it.

I lifted my head and met Hunter's gaze. The warm glint in his azure eyes made my heartbeat soar. "I love you."

"That's good." The corners of his lips curled into a smile. "Because I love you."

He tugged me forward and pressed his mouth to mine.

Together, we'd put our dreams back on track.

Chapter 36

HUNTER

The new year hit. Time for new plans. Ones that could affect my band's up-and-coming promotions and the tour. My gut refused to settle. I wasn't looking forward to telling everyone the latest news about my vocal cords. As I waited in my management team's office, I fidgeted with my cell phone, flipping it around in my hands. Kara sat beside me sorting through the photos from the shoot for the cover of the next single.

Having her here for support was the only thing that kept me calm.

Over the past few weeks, we'd reset our balance. She'd cheered me on as I'd played beside Kyle and Gemma at every album launch event. Not singing had burned holes in my heart, but the influx of love and well wishes from fans had kept my spirit alive. Our album, *Kiss This*, hitting number-one had helped.

For Christmas and New Year's, we'd avoided the stress of visiting relatives and had gone to the mountains with our four friends . . . our true family who'd seen us through everything. We snowboarded, ate too much and drank too much . . . especially on the day after Christmas, to celebrate my twenty-seventh birthday. Kara was healthier, happier, and held more color and plumpness in her cheeks. Therapy had helped her. I couldn't thank her shrink enough for bringing her back to the light.

As I sat beside her, my gaze dropped to her ribs. My name inked on her flesh beneath her sweater had erased my doubts about her love for me. I'd always thought I wasn't good enough for her—not smart enough, or classy enough—but her tattoo had proven me wrong.

I was hers. She was mine.

My new ink, her name running down my left side, verified that too.

I grabbed her hand, drew it toward my mouth, and kissed the inside of her wrist.

An impish smile curled across her pink-glossed lips. "What was that for?"

"I just love you. That okay?"

"Yeah."

The door swung open. My band's management team piled into the room. Behind them, Gemma dragged Kyle in by the hand—those two were rarely unattached. Kate dropped a stack of folders onto the table. Sophie carried a tray of coffees. Bec sank onto a chair as she skimmed through her cell phone. No doubt there were a million emails to address since this was our first day back at work after a two-week break.

"Good to see y'all." While everyone took a seat, Sophie handed out the coffees, and a tea for Kara. "Better make yourselves comfortable. We have a ton of planning to get through."

No kidding.

I pulled my chair closer to the table. "Before we start, I'm gonna throw a curveball." I rubbed the tip of my chin. I still couldn't believe I'd agreed to do this. "I'm booked in for vocal surgery next Thursday in Boston." I'd met Vanessa this morning. The operation was all systems go.

"Awesome!" Gemma play-punched my arm, then half-hugged me. "You need this."

I'd talked to my friends about the procedure while we were away. Kara was right. I couldn't face the tour without trying to fix my voice. Gemma would be stoked I hadn't chickened out. Not yet anyway. I had reservations. Things could still go wrong.

"That's great." Strain hovered in Sophie's tone as she rubbed her brow.

More surgery meant more pressure in planning the tour. Every day, the rumor mill on gossip sites escalated with concerns over my voice. The thing was, at this point in time, the stories about me never singing again were true.

"What are you having done?" Bec stopped typing on her cell phone and tossed it on the table.

"Vocal fold realignment." I wrung my hands together. Sweat broke out on the back of my neck. Just thinking about what I'd have done freaked me out. Having to be awake under local anesthetic so Vanessa could manipulate the vocal cords and tune my voice while in the operating room seemed horrific. "But hopefully after this, I won't need an implant or future injections."

Kara placed her hand on my thigh and gave it a rub. Her touch was all the calming reassurance I needed.

"My recovery will be like last time," I continued. "No talking for the first few days, then a gradual increase over the following two to three weeks. It will be at least six to eight weeks after the surgery before I know if I can sing."

Kate unfolded and laid out a tabloid-sized printout of a two-year planner; it took up a quarter of the desk.

I stared at the color-coded dots and squares, black and red lines, and different colored pen marks that filled the page. *Wow!* That was our schedule for the next year and a half. It felt like a lifetime ago since we'd done a plan like this for our last tour. I just followed what Kate, Sophie, and Bec put into our agenda on an app.

Kate grabbed a red pen from her pile, pulled the cap off with her teeth, and hovered over the calendar. "So that puts you out of action for the next single promotion. That's when we planned to announce the tour. We've already delayed it once. What do you three want to do now?"

Kyle drummed his fingers against the edge of the table. "Whether Hunt can sing or not, we'll still tour. We've got him on board."

I smirked. It had taken a bottle of JD to do that. But I was in. All in.

"But . . ." Gemma fidgeted with her coffee cup. "We need to delay the announcement until Hunt has a hint of where his voice is at. We don't want tickets to go on sale without being honest with the fans. If he can't sing, we have to let them know beforehand."

"I agree." Sophie scanned Kate's agenda as concern darkened her eyes. "We're cutting it super fine, but we'll make it work. This tour is all booked, so for now, we'll keep the meetings, rehearsal schedule, and creative projects as is."

"Sounds good." I rubbed my hands together. Seeing the plan in front of me stoked my fire and reinvigorated my soul. "Tour number five, here we come."

"So, it's not all doom and gloom?" Bec arched her thin eyebrow.

"No. It's not." A smile inched across my lips. I clutched Kara's hand in my lap. "There's one more thing. Kar and I are going for baby attempt number three." We'd had dinner with Naomi and Anthony over the weekend. They were set. "We're timing it so the baby will be due after the tour. But during the last leg here in the U.S., we'll want to fly home a few times to see Nae."

"Nae's agreed to try again?" Gemma sat two inches taller. Her eyes shone bright.

"Yeah." Kara's voice was soft, but excitement flitted through her tone. "We have two embryos left; we're going for it."

"Oh wow." Gemma leaped to her feet, dashed behind me, and hugged Kara over the back of the chair. "I'm so happy for you." She then wrapped her arms around my shoulders. "You too. You've got this."

"Yep." I rubbed the back of her hand. Kara and I were determined to keep trying for a baby, and downright committed. We wanted a child. I grinned and puffed air through my nose. Bring on being a daddy. And get my surgery over and done with.

***

Damn, these drugs are good. Stronger than last time.

When I'd arrived with my friends in Boston and checked in to the Massachusetts General Hospital for vocal cords surgery at lunchtime, my anxiety had had me breaking out in feverish sweats. I didn't want to be awake during the procedure. I didn't want to see, or hear, or feel the torture they were about to inflict on my throat. Vanessa had authorized a nurse to give me some medication to help me relax. I didn't think anything would've worked.

Wrong!

As I lay on the bed in my hospital room, the drugs clouded my mind and tried to lure me into a false sense of security. I wouldn't let them win. I clutched Kara's hand. Every time my eyelids grew heavy, I pinged them open. I didn't want to relax. What if I fell asleep and never woke up? What if I came out of surgery worse off? What if . . .

"Hunt, you're hurting my hand." Kara winced and tapped my arm.

Shit. I lessened my grip.

She gazed down at me, stroking my brow, my cheek, my hair. "Babe, stop stressing. You'll be okay."

"Yee—ah. I'm cool." I so wasn't. I was shitting myself. But as long as Kara was here, I'd be fine. As long as I came out of surgery with a voice, I'd survive. If I couldn't sing again, Kyle and Gem would support me. We'd find a way forward, no matter what. I'd almost cut off one of my limbs before, and that hadn't stopped me from playing music. This wouldn't beat me either.

Kara would kick my ass if I ever faltered again.

I dragged her hand to my lips. My arm weighed a ton . . . *stupid drugs.* "I loooove you, Pearl."

She giggled. "You've told me that twenty times in the past ten minutes."

"I soooorry. But it's truuuue." How lucky was I to find someone who drove me completely crazy, who I cared for, loved unconditionally, and who lately . . . had meant more to me than music?

The door swung open, and in walked the nurse and the orderly.

"Okay, Mr. Collins." Beth, the evil nurse who had given me the pills twenty minutes ago, raised the safety rail on the side of my bed. "Are you ready to head to the operating room?"

"No." I squeezed Kara's hand. "Have I told you hhhhow much I hate hospitals?"

"Yes. On countless occasions." She kissed my forehead, then my lips. "You're in good hands. I'll be here when you come back."

I went to sit upright, and hug Kara, but my head spun like a caster wheel. *Damn, what did they give me? It's the shit. Am I floating?*

"Please stay down, Mr. Collins." The nurse draped a warm blanket over me and tucked it tight across my chest.

So niiice.

I sank into the pillow as the heat enveloped me. *That's better . . . wait. No.* I twisted my hips to roll off the bed, but the blanket had turned into a straitjacket. I couldn't move. *I don't want to do this. I've changed my mind.*

Kara touched my shoulder. "Hunt, you're okay. I love you."

Her voice soothed my troubled mind. I reached up to caress her cheek, but I had little control of my hand. Rather than a tender touch, it was more like a sloppy swipe. "I loooove you. And drugs." I waggled my floppy finger. "You should say no to drugs. But whatever this shit is they've given me, it's fuuuucking awesome."

"Okay," Kara giggled again. "You have to go. I'll be here waiting."

As a cloudy haze took over me, I smiled. She was so gorgeous. So beautiful. *My Pearl.* My eyelids grew heavier and heavier. "Promise me . . . you'll marry me . . . when this is over."

"Wait? What?" Kar's voice hovered somewhere above me.

The world spun before my eyes. *Nope . . .* it was the orderly pushing the bed toward the door.

"Hunter?"

Kara?

"I wouldn't take anything he says right now too seriously." The nurse chuckled beside me. "He's under the influence of some pretty strong meds."

"Hunter?"

Kara's voice grew more distant by the second.

I was definitely floating this time. Lights and colors swirled above me. White, red, blue, green.

Shit!

Here goes nothing.

***

Laughter?

Laughter pummeled my ears and rattled around inside my head like ball bearings. *Kyle? Gemma? Kara?* What was going on?

I forced my heavy eyelids open. Back in my private hospital room, three sets of eyes bore down on me. I winced and furrowed my brow. *Remember. No talking.*

Gemma wiped her wet eyes with her palm. Kyle clutched his stomach. Kara splayed her hand across her chest.

Kyle slapped my thigh. "Oh dude. You're with us? Man, we need to give you anesthetic and drugs more often. The shit you've been spinning has been hilarious. You told the orderly he was hot. You asked the nurse for more drugs. And you proposed to everyone in the entire ward before you fell asleep. So far, everyone, including the male nurse, has accepted your offer."

Oh shit. Propose?

Oh crap.

Did I ask Kara?

I pouted, hopefully conveying I was sorry.

If I was ever ready to propose, it would be a grand affair, not some lame-ass, *hey-how-about-it* moment. And I'd want to remember it.

Kara leaned forward and kissed my cheek. "I'm glad you're awake. No one has taken you seriously. You were very cute, though."

Cute was not the word I wanted to be described as. Well . . . not right now anyway.

"Are you feeling okay?" Gemma clasped my hand.

I smiled a sleepy smile and gave her a thumbs up. But yeah . . . my breathing was better than after my last surgery. That was already a win.

This whole no talking thing sucked.

But I was on the countdown.

Three days, no talking. Fourteen days of gradually increasing the use of my voice and a truckload of vocal therapy. Whether I could sing again or not, I had the best friends in the world. Kyle and Gemma, Lexi and Hayden . . . and Kara. I didn't need drugs to know that. And as for Kara? I planned on never letting her go. Not ever.

***

The first three days at home after surgery nearly killed me. I didn't know if there had been an improvement in my voice, if it was the same, or if it was worse. On day four, I used my voice for the first time. My hands shook; my heart chewed its fingernails. Sitting in front of my laptop, I filled my lungs and ran through a set of soft onsets for five minutes.

There was less rasp.

My breathing was good.

But then my voice cracked and cut out.

I clenched my fist and stretched my neck from side to side. *It's okay.* Rest. Be patient. My throat was already much better than last time.

After two weeks of careful, meticulous, and gruelingly painful vocal therapy that pushed my patience to the limits, and under Annelise's guidance in her office, I attempted to sing.

Hmm. Hmm. Hmm.
Nng. Nng. Nng.

A wave of overwhelming shudders washed over. My heart barreled through my chest as I scaled up the notes again.

Hmm. Hmm. Hmm.

Nng. Nng. Nng.

Fuck yeah!

I flung my arms around Annelise and hugged her tight. "I held notes."

"Don't get too excited." She stepped back. The tiniest spark of hope twinkled in her eyes. "We have a long way to go."

My voice was nowhere near great, but... I could hold a fucking note. I wanted to shout and sing and cheer from every rooftop in Manhattan. But it was still early days, and I had to be careful.

Week after week, my voice improved and grew stronger. Note after note, I sang, but with reserve.

Six weeks after surgery, I stood in Annelise's office. After an hour of warm-ups and exercises, she hovered her fingers over her piano keys. "Okay. We'll start low and scale up. You ready?"

Nerves rippled and quaked through my gut. But I was ready. Ready to push my voice and test my vocal range.

I filled my lungs to capacity.

As she played, I ran up the scales. I started low, deep and slow, then crescendoed higher and higher. Up and up. My heart boomed in my ears. Holding my hand against my diaphragm, I drove my voice higher than I'd ever thought possible. Higher and higher and higher, then ... I collapsed. I sank onto my knees. Tears rolled down my cheeks. I sobbed and wiped the dampness from my eyes. "Holy shit."

"Hunter?" Annelise rushed to my side and placed her hand on my shoulder. "What happened? Your voice sounded perfect."

"That's just it. It's back." Excitement charged through my veins and roared in my chest. "I can fucking sing. I. Can. Really. Fucking. Sing." I leaped to my feet, hugged Annelise, and spun her around before I placed her back on the floor. "You're a genius."

"Thank you." Annelise realigned her jacket. "But it's all your hard work and commitment." She leaned slightly forward and raised her eyebrows. Her eyes shone as bright as a laser beam. "Did you hear something else?"

I couldn't stop grinning. I placed my hands on my chest, then touched my throat. "My range? It's more than before. Higher."

"Yes. You've gone up an extra note, maybe two."

"Holy fuck." I tilted my head back and thanked the heavens. "This is amazing. Lise, how can I ever thank you?"

"No need. I'm just doing my job."

"So, now what?"

"We keep at it. We need to strengthen your voice, work on those breathing techniques and ensure you don't ever damage your voice again."

Too fucking right.

"You can't go overboard." She pointed at me. "But I think it's safe to say, you'll be set for the tour."

Fuck yes!

***

I rushed home. The second the elevator doors pinged open, I charged into the living room. Kara stood hovering over the table, sifting through printouts of outfits Kyle, Gemma and I had tried on at a fitting. She dropped the picture in her hands. Her concern morphed into a huge smile as she caught my energy. I picked her up and kissed her hard. So hard. "It's back. I can fucking sing. More range than before."

"Ahhhh!" She shrieked and hugged me. "That's amazing."

"Hell yeah. And I have you to thank for it. This would've never happened if it wasn't for you. I owe you my life."

"Have you been to see Kyle and Gem?"

"Not yet. I had to tell you first." I caressed her cheek and met her gaze. "I've gotten my priorities right, Pearl. You come first."

She kissed me so hard my heart soared through the roof.

Chapter 37

HUNTER

After months of promotion, rehearsals, meetings, stage-set design and construction approvals, photo shoots, recording video for our onstage projections, selecting outfits, and locking in set lists, my friends and I hit our fifth world tour.

For the next eleven months, we'd take our *Kiss This* tour to thirty-two countries and perform one hundred and ten shows. Nearly every city had sold out on the day we'd released tickets. More shows had been added in select cities like London, Tokyo, Melbourne, and Rio de Janeiro.

Opening night in Toronto on July 6th had come around fast. Backstage at the Rogers Centre, I paced the floor between two racks of clothing. I ran through vocal warm-ups as Kara finished dressing Gemma in her leather pants and vest top, and Carla styled Kyle's hair. No point in the latter; his hair would be a sweaty mess within twenty minutes.

My heartbeat pummeled my ribs. I placed my hands on my diaphragm and continued my trills.

Kara came over and caught my arm. "Hey." She straightened the collar on my black Prada shirt and undid another top button, so it hung open down to the center of my chest. "You look and sound amazing. You've rehearsed, trained, and are ready. Your voice will be fine. Kyle and Gem have your back."

"Yeah. It's just first-night nerves." And worry about my voice. And praying everything went according to the plan. And hoping the fans would love the show.

"You?" She wrinkled her nose. "Nervous about singing in front of fifty thousand fans? Nah!" She kissed my cheek. "Within five minutes of being on that stage, you'll be on fire. Now go break a leg."

I formed a circle with Kyle and Gemma and drew Kara into it as well. We hugged and held each other tight.

"Thank you." I splayed my hand over the warmth swelling in my heart. "Words can't describe how much the three of you mean to me. For months, I doubted whether we'd be here. But I'm back. We're stronger than ever. We have an incredible team who have helped us bring this show to life. We have each other. Always. We're gonna rock the shit out of this tour. Let's go."

"Woohoo!" Gemma hollered, raising her arm in the air. Her glittery eyeshadow sparkled in the lights.

"Yeah!" Kyle slapped my shoulder.

I kissed Kara one last time before Sophie dragged me out the door with Kyle and Gemma in tow. We joined the rest of our crew and backup band behind the stage. Nervous whispers hovered through the air as everyone shuffled into position.

I gave Hayden a big pat on the back. It may have been my first tour after my vocal cords surgery, but it was Hayden's first big tour ever. "Bud, you ready?"

"I've only thrown up twice." Hayden grinned and wiped his sweaty brow on his T-shirt sleeve. "So, I'm good."

At the signal from Olsen—our tour manager—Hayden took off with the band and headed onto the stage.

Taking slow, steady breaths, I led Gemma and Kyle underneath the maze of scaffolding to the steps that led up onto the center of the stage in front of the drum kit.

I grabbed their hands and whispered, "I love you guys."

With excitement buzzing between us, we gave each other one last big hug.

We stuffed in our in-ear monitors and turned on our transmitters.

We checked our mics.

Kyle gave Bryce—our lead stagehand—the nod. Bryce murmured into his headset.

The crowd warm-up music ended.

It was showtime.

Three. Two. One.

The lights in the auditorium dimmed. The audience erupted, shrieked, and hollered. I smiled and tilted my head back and fought the sting in my eyes. I was one lucky man to be here. I'd never take my voice for granted again.

Hayden's hard drumbeat filled my in-ear monitors. Beams of light swung across the stage. The fog machine hissed to life. The band kicked into playing the introduction to our first song.

Gemma took my hand and Kyle's and mouthed, "Let's rock."

Go!

The three of us charged up the stairs and ran onto the stage, straight into singing "Dance With Me," the party song from our new album.

> *I've got the moves just right*
> *Gonna hold you good and tight*
> *Burn up the floor with you all night*
> *We can do it fast or slow*
> *This club is gonna blow*
> *So come on and dance with me*
> *Dance with me*
> *Dance with me*

As I sang, wriggled, and shook my hips and ass, the fans danced, and screamed and cried so loud I thought half the front row in the VIP section would pass out. I blew them a kiss and took off to the other side of the stage to swap positions with Kyle while Gemma owned the center. Perfect choreography. Perfect timing. Waving and pumping our fists, we hyped up the crowd. Electric energy coiled through my veins and fueled the fire in my heart.

The fans had come in droves to see us play. I wanted to put to rest any doubts they, or any gossipy reporter, may have had about my voice.

At the end of our first set, while Gemma and Kyle grabbed their guitars from the stagehands, I strode down the catwalk to the small stage at the front. As I clipped my mic onto the stand, the auditorium lights brightened.

I pulled out one of my in-ear monitors.

The crowd erupted and cheered. "Arrrrgh!" They screamed. "Hunter. We love you." "Woohoo." "Yeah!"

My heartbeat quickened. I grinned, wide and full. Their energy reverberated through to my bones. *So fucking cool!*

"Good evening, Toronto," I hollered into my mic.

The sea of concertgoers waved their banners. Their LED bands glowed on their wrists. Their cameras flashed. Cries, wails and shrieks filled the air.

Awesome.

"I'd just like to thank y'all for coming tonight." I placed my hand over my chest. "From the bottom of my heart, I personally want to thank each and every one of you for the love and support I've received over the past several months. As you know, I had vocal cords surgery. So now you've heard me sing a couple of songs with Kyle and Gem . . ." Talking to the crowd, I pointed to myself and wrinkled my nose. "Do you think I sounded all right?"

"YES!" They screamed and screeched.

I placed my hands on my hips as my mouth hovered near the mic. "Are you sure?"

"YEEES!" The yells came louder.

"How about we do a test?" I held up one finger. "How's this? . . . Okay. Here goes."

I widened my stance, relaxed my shoulders, and licked my lips. As I held my hands wide, I filled my lungs to capacity. Then, I sang, scaling up the notes, reaching higher and higher.

Whoa. Whoa. Whoa. Yeah. Yeah. Yeeeeah. Yeah!

My voice boomed through every amp and speaker in the venue. The entire audience cheered, clapped and hollered. They waved their arms and whistled.

My heart boomed like a beatbox. "All right, then." I could hardly hear myself talk over their cries. "If you think I sound okay, would you like me to head back there . . ." I jerked my thumb toward Kyle, Gemma and the band. "And sing a few more songs?"

"*YES!*" they cried.

With an ear-splitting grin, I ran back along the catwalk, grabbed my guitar from Bryce and jumped into playing another hit.

Magic.

Yep, this was where I belonged . . . in front of a packed auditorium, surrounded by the people I loved—Kyle and Gemma singing by my side, Hayden on the drums, Lexi taking photos, and my girlfriend, Kara, waiting in the wings.

The stage was home, but it was nothing like the home I shared with Kara.

As Gemma ripped out the chorus, I closed my eyes and let the music embed itself deep into my soul. Each muscle, cell, and fiber in my body absorbed each note. I glanced offstage. Kara stood next to Sophie and Bec, singing along to our song. Sparks skipped across my skin. I was here because of her. She'd made me face my fears, made me a better person, and made me be the man she deserved. Thank God I could sing again. But even more so, I thanked God for bringing her into my life.

My heart swelled, beating in time with the drums. We may have permanent ink on our skin, but now, it was time to take a step toward putting permanent ink on paper.

Chapter 38

KARA

I tilted my head back, held my hands above my head, and hollered at the Parisian night sky. "Woohoo! Yeah!"

"Kar, hold on." Hunter gunned the motorcycle down Rue de Rivoli, faster and faster. Three months into the tour, we had a rare night off in Paris. The adrenaline from the speed, the wind in my hair, and the thrill of sneaking around the gorgeous city, trying not to be recognized, had my heart pounding and my head spinning.

It was a night to celebrate.

Naomi had called earlier. She'd just had an IVF implant. Baby attempt number three was underway. Hunter had insisted on taking me out to mark the occasion. Hiring motorcycles, doubling me on the back, while Giles and Mick tailed close behind, had not been what I had in mind though. But cruising from our hotel, out through the charming district of Montmartre with its cafes and nightclubs, up past the white-domed Sacre Coeur Basilica, and then back toward the Seine River had changed my opinion. With the roar of the engine, and my body pressed against Hunter's, this was a spectacular way to see the city.

Wrapping my arms around his waist, I rested my chin on his shoulder. The leather of his jacket was cool and soft against my skin. *Perfect!*

Hunter eased the throttle and turned onto the Place du Carrousel. As we passed the Louvre, people enjoying the gorgeous October evening lingered in the square, taking photos in front of the illuminated glass pyramid and surrounding majestic buildings. If Hunter and I wanted to do that, we'd need an entire army to keep the fans away. Gone were the days of walking down the street without being recognized. But I wouldn't give up what I had with Hunter for anything. It made moments like this more magical.

Turning onto Quai des Tuileries, the quay that led along the Seine, we whizzed past the glorious gardens where the brightly lit Ferris wheel dominated the skyline. We sped around the Place de la Concorde, then headed up the Avenue des Champs-Élysées. As Hunter approached the busy congestion at the Arc de Triomphe, I tightened my grip and held on for dear life.

He lifted his helmet visor and spoke back over his shoulder. "You okay?"

The multiple lanes of traffic spiraling around the monument made my eyes blur. "Yes." My voice squeaked. There wasn't an ounce of confidence in it. "Please don't kill me."

He placed his hand over mine. "I won't. I promise. Just hold on. Lean into the corners. Breathe."

He circled and navigated his way through the lanes. I laughed when he missed the exit, having to make his way around twice. As we headed along another beautiful tree-lined avenue, I tried to get my bearings. Unable to see the Eiffel Tower above the height of the quaint Renaissance buildings, I had no idea where we were heading. If it wasn't for Hunter following Google Maps on his cell phone clipped into the holder in front of him, I was sure he'd have no idea where we were either.

I just glimpsed the Eiffel Tower ahead on the other side of the river when Hunter slowed to a crawl. He turned onto a side street, pulled into a parking space behind a curved building surrounded by a high wrought-iron fence, and killed the engine. Mick and Giles stopped beside us.

Hunter tapped my thigh to hop off. As I found my feet, my legs wobbled. Hunter unclipped and removed his helmet, then shook out his long hair.

Him. Leather jacket. Motorbike . . . So hot!

"That was insane." His fingers trembled as he helped me take off my helmet, his voice high with excitement. "I've been to Paris eight times and have always wanted to ride like that through the city."

I combed my fingers through my flattened locks to give them back their bounce. "Other than a few hair-raising turns, I have to agree. That was wicked."

"And you questioned my ability to ride," he teased. "Shame on you." He placed my helmet on the bike next to his and unzipped his jacket. "Just because I haven't done it for years didn't mean a thing."

"You're full of it." I play-punched his arm. "You were nervous at the start." A few takeoffs were jerky, and he'd missed a gear change or two.

He threw me a sly smile and tapped my butt. "I'll never admit anything."

Mick stepped onto the sidewalk. The shimmer in his eyes was brighter than normal. "That was very cool, guys. But we'd better get you inside."

"Where are we?" I unzipped my leather jacket and looked around the street for a landmark but saw none. Even the Eiffel Tower was blocked from view. "Where are we going?"

"In here." Giles waved toward a huge limestone arched gateway at the back of the building.

Before I took a step, Hunter placed his hands on my upper arms. His azure eyes glinted in the streetlights. Vibrant energy radiated from him. "We've just done something I've always wanted to do—now I want to do something for you."

For me?

I had no time to ask questions. Hunter took my hand, and we followed Mick and Giles to the gates. They were locked. But the three of them didn't look deterred.

I read the glass-framed sign on the wall. My heart skipped a stitch. My hands shot over my mouth, then fell to my chest. "Palais

Galliera? We're at the Galliera?"

I'd always wanted to come here, to the museum that was dedicated to centuries of fashion, exhibiting some of France's finest designers and collections.

"But it's closed." I pointed to the opening times. "It shut at nine." It was now ten.

Hunter half-grinned, tilted his head to the side, and shook it. "Kar, do you forget who I am?"

"But . . ."

Across the curved cobblestone courtyard, the door to the museum opened and a young lady about my age, dressed in a tight pencil skirt and Chanel blouse, stepped outside and headed toward us. Her hips swaggered with exaggerated confidence, and her pout was enhanced with too much filler, but still, she radiated suave French sophistication.

I folded my arms and raised a questioning eyebrow at Hunter.

He threw me a dazzling smile, slipped his hand beneath the back of my jacket, and held me close. "She's an old friend who works here in item restoration." Humor hovered in his voice. "I asked her for a favor. And no, we haven't slept together."

I nudged my hip against his side. "Is this the way you're going to introduce every woman you know?"

"You gave me *the look*." He chuckled, then his tone turned serious. "Do you need me to tell you?"

I curled my arm around his elbow. "No." There were no swirling pots of jealousy boiling inside my stomach. I trusted him and had faith in our love. I no longer stood in front of the women he knew, wondering if they'd slept together. It wasted too much time and energy. "Whoever you've been with, as long as they're in the past and stay there, it's cool. You're mine now. And I'd like to keep it that way for a very long time."

"Good." His smile touched his eyes. "I'll hold you to that."

The lady swiped her access card through the reader beside the gate and let us in.

"Hunter." Her French accent flowed with finesse. She kissed him on one cheek, then the other. "It's been so long."

"Natalie. Yes, it has." He placed his hand on the small of my back. "I'd like you to meet Kara."

Natalie held out her hand for me to shake. Natalie's hand may have been tiny and delicate, but her grip was firm, all businesslike. "Nice to meet you, Kara. Hunter tells me you used to work at Conrad's. That must've been exciting. I love his designs. But working for Everhide, having access to fashion from all over the world, must be exhilarating too. How are you handling the tour with this scoundrel?"

I slipped my arm back around Hunter's waist. "It's busy, tiring, but fun."

Hunter waved his finger between Natalie and himself. "We went to high school together for two years. Her family came to the States for her dad's work. Nat was way into science, so we didn't hang out often. We've kept in touch . . . occasionally . . . rarely. I stretched the point of knowing her very thin."

"Your promised social posts and four VIP tickets to your show tomorrow night will be sufficient payment." She clicked her long fingers at him. "Hand them over."

Hunter dug inside his leather jacket and slapped the passes into Natalie's palm. "You drive a hard bargain."

"I know. What are *friends* for?" She turned on her heels and headed toward the entrance. "Let's go. I don't want to be here all night."

My hand fell into Hunter's and our fingers entwined. I glanced down; I could've sworn I detected a shake in his grip. Was he as excited about seeing exhibition halls full of fashion finery as I was? *Maybe.*

I dragged him across the courtyard, up the couple of steps, and into the building. Shivers darted across my skin as I gaped at the high mosaic ceilings and scanned the mannequins in glass display cabinets draped in exquisite gowns.

Natalie crossed the lobby, turned and waved like an old-school usher toward the entrance hall. "I hope you enjoy the collections we have on display. Take your time. You have the place to yourselves. I'll babysit your security team over there in the office." She pointed to the door on the other side of the lobby. "Have fun. We'll see you soon."

Walking along the curved corridor, my heart fluttered toward my throat. Precious attire, accessories, and shoes sparkled under ambient spotlights. Making my way down the line of costumes, I admired the delicate materials and attention to detail. My fingers twitched, itching to touch the soft, silky threads used in the embroidered flowers on the jackets, and the smooth ridge of each hand-sewn bead and sequin on the French lace, and the fine needlework on the handmade couture gowns.

"Do you know how many hours it would have taken to do this work by hand?" I pointed at the studs on a pair of men's leather pants in the contemporary department.

Hunter leaned in to examine the garment. "I wouldn't have the patience to do something like that. But it looks cool. I'd definitely wear something like that on stage." He grabbed my hand, twirled me around like a ballerina, then hugged me from behind. As we shuffled forward, he pointed at the pair of bright orange quilted pants on the next mannequin. "I'd never wear something like that, though. I'm not sure if they'd look good on anybody."

"Oh, I don't know about that." I giggled. "I could see you, Kyle, and Gem performing in them."

"We could start a new trend. Let's see what our fans think." He pulled out his phone, took a selfie with the pants in the background, and posted it to Instagram.

"Anything you wear becomes a must-have item," I mused.

"It's tough." He stuffed his cell phone back into his jacket pocket. "But someone has to do it."

I groaned, grabbed his hand, and moved on through the collection.

At the end of the hall, we headed downstairs to the Salles Gabrielle Chanel hall, the museum's basement that had been renovated into exhibition rooms. The long corridor adorned with Chanel attire, stole my breath.

"This is incredible." I strolled along the row and read the labels. "Look at this evening gown. That pleating in the silk is so hard to do." I had talent, but not that much. No . . . wait. Yes, I did. I'd done something very similar to that at Conrad's. *Shit.*

I didn't want my skills to go to waste.

I'd love to design again.

But I didn't want to stop working for Everhide. I loved it too much.

Maybe Hunter was right, though. Maybe doing a collection with someone like Ivory Mink could be explored. No . . . had to happen. *Damn you, Hunter.* Was this why he'd brought me here?

He didn't make a sound. I peered over my shoulder. He stood a few yards away, staring at me.

"What?" Heat flushed my cheeks.

With his hands tucked in his pockets, he shuffled toward me. "I love seeing you light up."

The hair on my arms tingled. "This place is inspiring. It's amazing."

He cupped the side of my head and brushed his lips against mine. "No. You are."

"Of all the things you've done for me, this is one of the best."

"I'll see if I can top it . . . one day." His lips quivered and quirked as if he were trying not to smile. His eyes sparkled like the rhinestones and crystal embellishments on the gowns behind him.

"Is this why you brought me here? To convince me to design?"

"Actually . . . no. But are you thinking about it?"

"Yeah." I tugged on the lapels of his jacket. "I like the idea of doing a limited collection so I can stay working for you. I'd love to work with Ivory Mink if she'll have me."

"You're an influencer and a talented designer. She'd be crazy not to." His gaze softened and he jerked his chin toward the end of the room. "But we'd better keep moving or we'll never get out of here."

We headed up to the main gallery. But as we passed the huge arched windows that looked across the gardens toward the Seine, something on the floor caught my eye. It was a red rose petal. Then, I saw another, and another. My pulse quickened. The trail grew heavier and led toward the stairs that led out to the gardens.

"Hunt?" I tugged on the back of his jacket. "What is . . . what are they?"

Oh wow!

He shrugged his shoulder and held out his hooked arm. "We'd better investigate."

"Investigate?" *What is going on?*

Butterfly wings quivered in my stomach as we scaled the stairs, and he opened the door. I stepped outside, and my breath hitched. My eyes widened. My mouth gaped. My heart raced. Along the ground, candles in silver lanterns lined a pathway of thick rose petals that led to the fountain in the center of the garden. An elaborate setup of scattered blankets, cushions, more candles, and champagne on ice lay in front of the small pond.

My knees buckled. Luckily, I held onto Hunter's arm otherwise I would've crumbled to the ground. Tears welled in my eyes. *Oh my, was this . . .? Would he?*

My feet wouldn't move. I wanted to take in the most beautiful setting I'd ever seen. The flickering candles. The gardens. The top of the Eiffel Tower peaked over the buildings across the road. Rose petals filled the air with their sweet scent. I was here . . . with Hunter.

Hunter excelled in romance, but this was up there as one of the most magical things he'd ever done. A private garden fenced off from outsiders—just the two of us . . . and no doubt, security lurking in the shadows.

He placed his hand on mine. There was no denying his shake this time. "Come on. Let's have a picnic."

The clear October night was cool with just a hint of breeze. In a trance, I walked with him down the stairs, across the path of flower petals, and over to the fountain. "This is beautiful. How? When? Did you arrange this?"

"It was my idea, but let's just say, Bec has earned her keep again."

She certainly had.

Hunter turned to me and held my hands between us. In his

black leather jacket, dark denim jeans, and biker boots, and with the lights from the museum haloing around him, I lost the ability to breathe. He was breathtaking. *Mine.*

A divot formed between his eyebrows as if a million thoughts raced through his mind. Lowering his gaze, he cleared his throat. Then he lifted his chin. His stunning azure eyes shimmered in the candlelight, but nerves flickered in their depths.

My heart dared not beat in case I missed a millisecond.

He blew out a deep breath and rolled his shoulders. "Kar—" His voice snagged. With a grimace, he cleared his throat and tried again. "Kara. There are days you drive me crazy and have me in a constant spin, then there are days I'm overwhelmed by how much I love you. But there is never a day I don't want to spend with you.

"We may have come from opposite sides of the track, but we will defy anyone who stands in the way of the life we want to build together.

"Last tour, we grew close when you were pregnant with Ryan. We fell in love after we lost him. Now, on this tour, I want to ensure you're mine forever." Tears glistened in his eyes. "I can't wait to have a family with you. But one thing has always burned in the back of my brain." He swallowed hard, then licked his lips. "I was brought up to believe in some traditions—that one day I'd meet a girl, fall in love, get married, and have a family. We haven't done everything in order and haven't always followed the rules, but I'd like to do one thing right. So before we have our baby, whether it's this one that works or the next or the next . . ." He dug into his jeans pocket, got down on one knee, and held my quivering hand in his. My free hand shot over my mouth. A tear threatened to fall. He gazed at me with so much love in his eyes and held up a huge, sparkling diamond. "Kara Knight, will you do me the deepest honor and marry me?"

My heart cartwheeled and danced and pirouetted across the lawn. Shivers skipped across my skin. Had I heard him correctly? *YES!* I nodded, blinking tears from my eyes. "Yes. Yes, I will marry you." There was no hesitation. I loved him with all my heart.

He slipped the ring on my finger and leaped to his feet. He

flung his arms around me and kissed me, hard and deep and so full of tenderness my head spun. Surrounded by the warm glow of candlelight, the sweet scent of his cologne, and my undying love for him, I kissed him back. Swirling tongues, hot breaths, beating hearts—we were together.

Three years ago, he wasn't my idea of marriage material. Now there was no one else I'd ever want but him. He was more of a gentleman than three-quarters of the guys I'd ever known. Hunter truly owned my heart.

Taking half a step back, I held out my hand and gazed at my stunning emerald-cut diamond. It dazzled, refracting the light from the pathway lamps and the candles flickering around us. "Oh, Hunt, this is the most gorgeous ring I've ever seen." After accessorizing every outfit for Gemma and myself to attend awards shows and events, I knew my jewelry. This had to be at least ten carats. *Holy. Freaking. Wow!*

He took my hand and brushed his thumb over my fingers in soothing strokes, but it did little to calm my buzz. He raised my wrist and swiveled the diamond left and right. "You always wear rings of this shape when you borrow items from jewelers. I had Leonard's source one of the best diamonds they could find and make this for you."

"Wait?" I jerked my chin back. "Leonard's?" Everhide's favorite jeweler in New York. "Have you had this with you since we began the tour?"

"No." He kissed my fingertips. "I had it couriered to our hotel at the beginning of the week. I've been planning this since the first night of the tour. That night, being back on stage, singing, was all thanks to you. We've talked about our future together, we have our love declared in ink, but I want to put it on paper too. I want to say 'I do' in front of friends, family, and the heavens and let the world know I'm yours."

"I'd like that too. I'm still shaking all over." I flattened my other hand against my stomach to stop the swirling butterflies, but nothing worked. I was as hyper as a kid overloaded on candy. I pointed to the ice bucket. "Can we have some champagne?"

"Hell yeah." He helped me onto the blanket. "I definitely need a drink after that." He settled in front of me, so close my knees rested on top of his. He grabbed the bottle and popped the cork off the Krug, his favorite champagne. "My nerves were rattling. Did you hear them?"

"I knew something was up. I thought you were just nervous about the Palais." I held the flutes as he poured. "But the second I saw the rose petals, I had my suspicions."

"You could've just said *yes* then and not made me do the whole speech thing."

"Absolutely not." I giggled. "I wanted you down on bended knee." We clinked glasses and took a sip. With my heart still soaring in the heavens, I curled my hand around his thigh. "This night has been perfect. The ride. The museum. This gorgeous setup. I'm surprised you didn't do something outlandish like dragging me on stage to propose."

"Are you disappointed?" He put the bottle back on ice.

"No. Not at all." Absolutely not.

He entwined our fingers. "Good. I know you struggle with the fans and reporters, and you'd prefer this over a million onlookers. This moment was for you, Kar, so I could show you how much I love and care about you. So I could get down on one knee. And . . ." His eyes glinted as he took a swig of his champagne. "So I wouldn't be humiliated if you said no."

"Me? Say no? No chance." I caressed his cheek, then touched his chest. "I'll admit it's taken time to erase my doubts, but you've won me over completely." I pulled my cell phone out of my jacket pocket and took a photo of us with our cheeks pressed together and my ring sparkling as I held my flute. "This is our moment. And it was magical. Thank you." I wrinkled my nose. "Do the others know?"

"Yeah, sorry." He winced. "Kyle busted me talking to Bec two days ago. Everyone's back at the hotel waiting for us to celebrate."

"Well, they can wait." I leaned in and kissed his lips. "We have a picnic to enjoy. And I want to keep you to myself for a bit longer."

He caught the tip of my chin between his fingertips.

"Hmm . . . I'd love to stay here with you all night underneath the stars, but I don't think Nat would like that. She was a trooper to let me do this. Security will be itching to get us out of here." He glanced at his watch. "We have to head off in about half an hour, so let's eat. In the basket, there should be some dessert."

I slapped his arm. "Are you still trying to fatten me up?" Digging into the basket, I pulled out a patisserie box and opened the lid. My mouth watered at the assortment of miniature delicacies— chocolate éclairs, pink macarons, petite cupcakes and strawberry mille-feuille. *Yum.*

"No." Hunter swiped an éclair out of the box and offered me a bite, then took a mouthful for himself. "But I love that your curves are coming back. I've missed them."

Yeah, I had too. I scooped up a cupcake and sank my teeth into the light, fluffy treat. *Mmm. So good!*

"Oh, and one more thing." He leaned forward and hovered his éclair before my lips, tempting me to take another decadent bite. I'd prefer to lick the vanilla cream off his body. "I meant what I said about being married before we have a baby. So, assuming this one stays on track, we have to tie the knot before July."

I took a nip of the éclair, but vertigo blurred my vision. "In nine months?" I swallowed the mouthful whole. "How can I organize a wedding while we're away on tour?"

He devoured the rest of the pastry and licked his fingertips. "We have an incredible team that can help. I want you to have your dream wedding. Anything you want, I'll make it happen." He stared toward my ring and smiled. "I'd love a big, outrageous wedding. I want everyone on the planet who sees our photos to go '*Wow! That was freaking spectacular!*' But ultimately, I'll marry you anytime, anywhere. Small or big, with as many friends and family as you want."

My mind still spun. I took a breath to find some calm among the clouds he'd catapulted me into. There was none; no quiet at all. But if he could organize tonight in a number of weeks, I could organize a wedding within several months, right? I'd been planning for this day since I was six. Half the details I'd wanted for my big day were pinned to my boards on Pinterest. I could do this. "You're serious?"

"Yes."

I downed half my champagne and let the sweet bubbles pop on my tongue. A checklist flashed through my mind. *Dress. Venue. Cake. Rehearsal dinner. Bridesmaid dresses. Shoes. Suits for the guys. Invitation designs. Flowers. Colors. Themes. Guest list. Bachelor parties. Wedding night. Honeymoon.* I rubbed the tension mounting in my temples. Where would I find a venue in New York in such a short timeframe? So much to do. So little time.

But . . . achievable.

I'd marry Hunter on a river barge if I couldn't find a place within the city.

"Okay. Let's do it." My heartbeat drummed loud and fast, but somehow, I maintained my composure. "In New York. In June. And yes, Hunt . . . it will be big."

He leaned over and kissed me. "I wouldn't expect anything less from my fiancée."

Fiancée!

For years, all I'd wanted to do was get married and have babies. Now, my dreams were coming true. "I like the sound of that . . . fiancé." I glanced at my beautiful ring. I couldn't contain it anymore. I flung my arms around him and hollered. "ARRRGGGHHHH! I LOVE YOU . . . THIS IS AMAZING! WE'RE GETTING MARRIED!"

"I love you so much, Pearl."

I sat back on my haunches and wiped my eyes. "Can I text everyone? I'm so excited. I don't want to wait until we're back at the hotel."

"How about . . . if you're up for it . . . post it to our social feeds. I want the world to know we're engaged. That I'm yours."

He didn't have to ask me twice.

I snatched up my cell phone and attached the image I'd just taken of us and my ring to my post. I typed a quick message and hit *Send.* "Done." *Wow . . . So surreal.* "Are you ready for the Internet to go into meltdown?"

"Always. But what did you say?" He reached for my phone and read the post.

Underneath the photo I'd typed:

I SAID YES!

Chapter 39

KARA

The drone of the tour bus's engine normally lulled me to sleep, but not tonight. My head was like a web browser with twenty tabs open, running and processing multiple tasks all at once. I still needed to secure a wedding venue, finalize Everhide's outfits for the Grammys, buy Christmas presents and something for Hunter's twenty-eighth birthday, and repair the zipper on Gemma's vest that lay on the table at the front of the bus. But my body ached with exhaustion.

Hunter had always said that around the halfway mark of the tour was the hardest. Fatigue kicked in, travel grew tiresome—new day, new city, everything on repeat—and there were still months of the same ahead.

He'd been spot on.

This was month six out of eleven. Five days out from Christmas.

Hunter never seemed to have trouble sleeping. The minute we were on the bus or a plane, or in a hotel, or he had spare time backstage after soundcheck, he'd crash.

I'd kill for my bed, shower, and closet full of clothes. The thrill of living out of a few suitcases had died weeks ago.

I wriggled my head against the hard pillow and closed my eyes. *Nope . . . I'm wide awake.*

Hunter stirred and rolled over to face me. But he didn't open his eyes. "You need to sleep," he whispered. "We have a big couple of days coming up."

After the show tonight in Edinburgh, everyone had clambered onto the tour buses and had hit the road for the long haul back to London for the last three concerts of the European leg. Then we were off to Japan over Christmas and the New Year, then onto Asia and South America before hitting home soil in March for the last few months of the tour.

"I'm okay. I didn't mean to wake you." I could just make out his features—his long, straight eyebrows, the arch of his cheekbone, the curve of his lips—in the soft hue emanating from the blue LED strip lights that ran along the aisle outside our bedroom door.

His brow furrowed. "You stressing?"

"No. My to-do list is a mile long, but no, I'm not stressed." Not yet anyway. I hadn't heard from Naomi in four days, but no news about the baby was good news, right?

"Well then, you need to stop thinking about *stuff* and sleep." A lazy smile slid across his lips. "I have the perfect remedy."

He rolled on top of me and edged between my legs. He tugged off my panties and went downtown. All mouth, hot licks, and fiery swirls across my clit. Every flick of his tongue sent sparks coursing through my veins, spiraled tingles up my spine, and had me clutching at the bed linen for more and more and more. I wasn't sure if this would put me to sleep, though. My legs quaked. My muscles screamed. As he dug his fingers into my thighs and swiped and circled his tongue over my sensitive spot, I exploded. Before I could catch my breath, he buried himself inside me. He didn't relent until I'd orgasmed again, and he'd found his release.

Wow!

Totally spent, sated, and satisfied, I curled into his embrace. Heat still blazed in my cheeks and curled through my belly as he drew the quilt over us. A huge smile was stapled onto his face as he closed his eyes. "Sleep time."

"Okay." I kissed his shoulder and neck. I'd try to get some rest.

In moments like this, I was grateful we had our own bus,

just like Kyle and Gemma. We weren't crammed into one of the fourteen-berth coaches like the rest of the band and crew. Being engaged to the boss had its perks. We could make as much noise as we liked, sprawl out on the big bed, and didn't have people listening outside our bedroom door.

As my heart beat next to Hunter's and our breathing synced, his body heat enveloped me like a cozy cashmere pashmina. The stiff starch in my bones had totally dissolved.

"I love you, Pearl," he whispered and kissed the top of my head.

Smiling, my eyelids finally grew too heavy to keep open.

***

The ringtone of Beyoncé's "Run the World (Girls)" and my cell phone vibrating in time with the bootylicious tune startled me from my sleep. *Naomi.*

I shook the sleep from my head. My heart hammered as I grabbed the phone off the nightstand and swiped the screen. "Nae?" I whispered. "Is everything okay?"

"Yes. Oh, shit. Did I mix up the time zones again? What time is it?"

"Um." I glanced at my cell phone; the bright light singed my eyeballs. I'd scored a couple of hours of sleep. "Nearly four in the morning." *Ten at night in New York.* "We're ahead, Nae, not behind."

"Oh, crap. I'm so sorry? Where are you?"

"On the bus," I muttered. "Somewhere between Edinburgh and London."

"How are you handling the travel?"

"Nae. Stop. You're killing me. What's happened? Is everything okay?" I braced myself for the worst. Was Naomi trying to soften the blow? Had she lost the baby?

Hunter rolled toward me and draped his arm across my waist. "Is that Nae?" He kissed my bare shoulder and nuzzled in close. But it wasn't a relaxed cuddle, like earlier. He was as anxious as I was for any updates.

I hit the call onto speaker.

"Heeey Hunt." Naomi's voice twanged as if she were sorry for waking him. "I've seen you guys on the news. You must be happy with the tour."

"Yeah. It's awesome," Hunter mumbled half-asleep. "Now get to the fucking point."

"Okay. Okay. I just wanted to know how you're doing." Naomi's soothing tone escalated my nerves rather than lower them, especially at this hour. "I'm just making conversation."

"Nae!" we said together.

"All right. All right."

My stomach cinched. I clutched my cell phone and held my breath. *Please be okay. Please be okay.*

"I went to the doctor today for my checkup. I had a blood test, did a pee test and had a scan. But . . ."

Oh no!

I squeezed my eyes shut. The rattle and hum of the bus and the thuds of the tires on the road turned into a loud ringing in my ears. Naomi's voice was nothing but a fuzzy murmur inside my head. *Found . . . wrong . . . oh well.*

"It's okay." My chest ached as I sniffled. "Don't worry about it. We'll try again. We have one more embryo to go."

"Kar." Hunter slapped my thigh and sat upright. "Nae's still pregnant."

"Wait. What?" The clouds in my head vaporized.

"Yes, deafo," Naomi reiterated. "I said the doctor found nothing wrong. I'm still pregnant. All is well. I'm twelve weeks today. Officially, unquestionably pregnant. A picture of the scan in on your email."

Oh shit. I'd misheard. My heart ricocheted off the walls. "Pregnant. You're still pregnant! Argh!"

I opened my email and the image. The black and white blur filled the screen. I could just make out the kidney shape of our baby. *Our baby!*

"Yes." Naomi's voice remained cool and level. "The heart is beating. It's a good size. I'm feeling great, even after the long day at the office. We're all systems go. I have one Hun-Kar bun in the oven."

"Argh," I screamed again and flung my arms around Hunter's neck. Tears of joy fell down my cheeks. "We're pregnant."

"Fuck, yeah." Hunter grabbed his cell phone and dialed Kyle. "I have to tell the others."

"What the fuck?" Kyle sounded as sleepy as a sloth. "This better be an emergency."

"Nae's officially pregnant." Hunter's voice hummed with excitement.

"Holy shit!" Gemma's voice shrieked through the speaker. "Stop the bus. Stop the fucking bus. Pull over somewhere."

Naomi's laughter erupted through my cell phone. "Sounds like you won't be sleeping. Go. Have fun. I'll keep you posted."

A few minutes later, on the outskirts of Leeds, several of the tour buses pulled into a service stop. After dressing in warm clothes and pulling on our UGG boots, we headed out of the bus. The moment we stepped onto the asphalt in the parking lot, Gemma shrieked and ran toward us.

"Congratulations." Gemma threw her arms around me, then Hunter. "This is incredible. We need to celebrate."

"I'm already on it." Hayden walked around the corner of the bus with a couple of champagne bottles in his hands. Lexi, who still looked half-asleep, carried half a dozen glasses in a salad bowl beside him. Everhide's entourage trailed behind them.

"Guys, it's still early days." I wrapped my woolen coat around my waist. It was freezing outside. I wanted to be excited, but history had made me cautious. "We've got a long way to go."

Lexi hugged me, then rubbed my arm. "Make the most of every milestone, babe."

Hunter slid his arm around my waist and kissed my cheek. "I think they're just looking for an excuse to have a drink."

"Too fucking right." Bec's breath misted in the pre-dawn chilly air as she grabbed a bottle off Hayden and popped the cork.

As the band and crew gathered around the buses to congratulate us, and the champagne flowed, my heart filled my chest. I had the best family in the world. *This* was my family. And soon, it would expand a little more. *Hopefully*.

I turned to Hunter and gave him a quick kiss. Pressing my forehead against his, I lowered my voice so only he could hear. "This one's gotta work, right?"

He wrapped his arms around me and rested his chin on my shoulder. "I hope so, Pearl. I can do many things, but I can't control fate. Believe me, I wish I could."

Naomi had months to go. Each day, each week, I'd pray our child grows stronger, healthier, bigger. But something about this baby felt different. There was this warmth, this glow, this positive energy swarming through my veins, and homing in on my abdomen.

Could I feel Naomi's pregnancy?

Did I have couvade syndrome? Sympathy pains?

I closed my eyes, hugged Hunter tighter, and said a silent prayer.

Dear Fate, stop being a fucking bitch and give us a baby ... please?

Chapter 40

HUNTER

The tour hit home soil in early March, a week before the Grammys. I stepped off the plane and savored the glorious rays of spring Californian sunshine on my face, so welcoming after the sticky summer heat and humidity in South America. With a couple of days off and rest before some award season events and our shows, I doubted I'd get much downtime. Now we were back in the States, wedding plans would hit full throttle. Baby plans would escalate. With the tour the priority, I worried about time.

Was there enough time to plan the wedding?

Would I have enough time to live it up with my friends and Kara before life changed forever?

At what point in time would our baby be okay?

Soon. In another couple of weeks, we'd be out of the risk-of-loss zone.

I was counting.

We high-tailed it from the airport to Kyle and Gemma's house in Pacific Palisades. It had become our home away from home. We chilled all afternoon and crashed just after midnight.

The following morning, I savored lazing in bed. Kara was already up, so I spread out across the mattress. This time two years ago, I'd never expected to be engaged or have a kid on the way. I'd just wanted to enjoy life and perform. Now, I still did those things, but everything had become more vivid and intense. Each day, I cherished every second of singing. My voice was better than ever. I had a deeper appreciation for my friendship with Kyle and Gemma; they'd stuck by me through thick and thin. And after soaring through many uplifting highs and wading through some harrowing times with Kara, I'd fallen more in love with her. I couldn't wait to marry her, to have a family, and to have a life together.

If we could just agree on the wedding details and her parents would come around, everything would be less stressful. But I'd learned nothing was easy.

I'd promised Kara her dream wedding. That was until I'd seen her Pinterest boards. There was no freaking way the day would turn into a frilly princess fiasco.

With time off before my band's next concert, I had to sit down with Kara and finalize some plans. We both hated compromises, but decisions had to be made.

After shaving and showering, I headed downstairs. But when I heard Kara talking, I stopped halfway down the steps. She sat on the sofa with her back to me. Her cell phone was on speaker.

"Mom." Kara leaned forward and rubbed her brow. "For the hundredth time, why does Dad hate Hunt so much? We're getting married."

"You know he's always thought you could do better. That you'd find someone with a more stable career, and come from a more suitable and respectable family." Carol's pretentious tone suggested she shared the same opinion as Walter. "Your father worries about you. He's afraid that Hunter will slip back into his drug-taking and wild ways."

Really? You're a dick, Walter. I shouldn't be eavesdropping, but I sank onto the step and listened.

"If he did, I'd kill him before Daddy ever got the chance." The fire in Kara's voice always flared hot and angry when she spoke to her parents. "Hunt has had a more worldly and open-minded upbringing than I ever did. So what if his family never had money. They're good people. Hunt's career is stable. He may have come from nothing, but he worked damn hard and has become successful. If he never worked another day in his life, he'd be fine. You could learn a thing or two from Hunt. He's kind and loving and respectful. He's super talented and amazing. I'm glad I met him and my friends. They make *me* a better person."

I rested my head against the glass balustrade and my heart ached. I loved how Kara thought so highly of me, but it hurt that her parents hadn't changed. For Kara's sake, not mine.

"I'm not getting into this argument again. I can't change your father's opinion," Carol said.

"No. You just go along with it. So pop another pill and have another drink, right, Mom?"

"Kara," her mother snapped.

"Whatever." She flopped back onto the sofa. "Is Daddy even coming to the wedding? Is he gonna walk me down the aisle? We're having it at The Ocean Blue Resort. It should be right up his alley. The wedding of the season in the Hamptons."

"He's adamant about not paying for it." Carol's voice remained cold and heartless, but I detected a touch of sadness. "So, I doubt he'll want to be a part of it."

"If he's going to be an ass, I don't want him there." Kara sniffled and wiped her eyes. I hated that every conversation with her parents ended in tears. "What about you? Are you coming?"

"Of course, dear." Carol's tone softened. "I'm in this for my grandchild."

I wasn't sure I wanted Carol at our wedding, or around our child, if she didn't respect our union. At least my parents were happy for us. They'd had their reservations, but, like always, they'd never stop me from being with someone I loved, and they adored Kara.

"Okay, Mom." Kara grabbed a tissue from the box on the coffee table. "I've gotta go. I have a wedding to plan. I'll talk to you later."

She hung up and dropped her cell phone into her lap.

I jumped to my feet and headed over to her. I sank onto the sofa beside her and wrapped my arm around her shoulders. "You okay?"

"Did you hear?"

"Some of it."

"I'm sorry."

I pulled back. "Why are you sorry? It's not your fault your parents don't like me. I feel bad for you. I know how much they mean to you. But I don't like that they upset you every time you talk to them." I rested my head against hers. "You're strong, beautiful, and don't need anyone telling you otherwise. You don't have to put up with being treated like that. It's your call, your decision, but maybe it's best if your dad doesn't come to the wedding."

Her chin quivered. "But he's my dad."

"I know. But I don't want him ruining your day." I kissed her temple and rubbed her arm. "I promise we're going to have a fabulous wedding day with friends and family who love us, and we're going to have an amazing life together." I brushed a teardrop off her cheek. "So, no more tears."

She lowered her chin and fidgeted with her engagement ring. "Let me think about Dad, okay? We don't have to send out the invitations yet."

"All right."

"Thank you."

I knew one way to make her feel better. I nudged my knee against hers. "Are you up for more wedding planning?"

Her gorgeous smile returned. "Always."

"I'll make a coffee, and grab you a cup of tea, and we'll go through some things."

"I'm ready when you are."

For the next hour, I sat beside her, and we sorted out suits, selected a cake, ran through menus for our rehearsal dinner and reception, picked out the wedding invitations for our black-tie affair, and finalized our wedding party—Kyle and Gemma, Hayden and Lexi. Kara had wanted her sister to be a bridesmaid, but Naomi had tentatively declined. If Naomi was still pregnant, she'd be close to thirty-eight weeks. She'd said she'd be *"too fat and too uncomfortable"* to stand on her feet all day.

I was happy either way.

But one thing Kara and I couldn't agree on was the table decorations.

I stretched my neck from side to side and stared at the photographs Kara had printed out. There were too many options, and none of them appealed to me.

The glass doors to the outside deck slid open, and Kyle and Gemma came in from their walk in the canyon.

"Hey," Kyle hollered as he headed toward the kitchen. "Can I get you guys anything?"

"No, thank you." Kara shook her head.

"Hunt, you want a beer?" Kyle opened the refrigerator.

"Nah, I'm good." I didn't look up from the images of pink roses in tall vases and blingy crystal candelabras. Maybe I should have a drink to help me make some decisions. But I didn't drink much anymore. I was too conscious of looking after my vocal cords.

"Watcha doing?" Gemma slid her butt, followed by her legs, over the back of the sofa, and plonked down beside me.

"Wedding stuff."

"Ugh, count me out." She went to stand, but I grabbed the back of her exercise T-shirt and pulled her down. "I hated planning my wedding. There's no way I'm helping with yours."

Kyle handed Gemma a beer and then slapped my shoulder as he walked behind me. "Don't overthink things." He sat on the sofa adjacent to Gemma. "Go with your gut. That's how Gem and I selected most of our wedding stuff."

"You two freakishly liked the same things. Kara and I don't." I sifted through the images again.

"That's because you're both stubborn."

"We are not." Kara straightened. Then, she giggled and relaxed her shoulders. "Okay, maybe just a little."

Gemma took a swig of her beer, placed it on the coffee table, and grabbed the pile of centerpiece images from my hand. "Okay. You want some help. Here it is. I'll make it easy for you because I know both of you." She glanced at the pictures. "This is just fucking ugly, so it's a no." She tossed an image of a big black vase with red flowers onto the coffee table. "This is a no; Hunt, you don't like daisies. These two are out; Kara, you won't want tulips or peonies; you'll want something different from what Kyle and I had at our wedding, or what Lexi and Hayden had at theirs. I could be wrong, but I doubt it. And this one is out because the flowers are all pink, and I hate pink."

I chuckled. I liked her process of elimination. "Gem, this is supposed to be our wedding, not yours."

"I know. But do you want me there?"

"Hell yeah." I nudged my shoulder against hers. "I wanted you to be in my groom's party, but no, you wanted to be a bridesmaid instead."

Her eyes glinted as she picked up her beer. "What can I say? I'm loved by many, and more popular and more in demand than you."

"Never." I shook my head. "But you're just awesome, and I love you to pieces."

"Don't forget it." She downed a mouthful of beer, but it didn't hide her cheeky smile.

"But what about—" Kara reached for the discarded picture of peonies on the table.

"No buts." I caught her hand and snatched the three remaining table decoration images out of Gemma's grasp. "Let's make this quick and simple. I'll go with my gut, all right?" I scanned and shuffled through the printouts. "This one goes—it's too big and tall. I hate going to functions where you can't see the people on the other side of the table because of the damn centerpiece. And not these. Too blingy." I tossed the crystal candelabras and some weird-looking glittery blue orchids on the *discard* pile. One image remained in my hand: a low-set, round bowl of hydrangeas, white roses, and viney-ivy-looking stuff. Not too pretty or prissy. "Guess this is it."

Kara took the picture, and a huge smile spread across her face. "I love it. Perfect."

"See? It's easy." Gemma smacked Hunter's thigh. "Glad we could help . . . can we go now?" Gemma attempted to stand.

Yet again, I stopped her by tugging on her T-shirt. "No. I need your help with something else . . . the honeymoon."

Kyle choked on a mouthful of beer. "Dude, have you got wedding night performance jitters?"

"Me?" My voice jumped two octaves. "What the fuck? God, no." *Bedroom performance issues?* That wasn't even a thing. "We need to find somewhere to stay. Kar wants a place within two hours of home in case the baby comes early . . . if we make it that far."

Our baby was five months along; surely nothing would go wrong. But that was what we'd thought about Ryan. We didn't want to go through a loss like that again.

"Do you want the beach, the mountains, or lakes?" Gemma curled her feet underneath her butt. "You wanna stay in a resort, a cabin, or rent a house?"

"We're open to anything," Kara curled her arm around mine. "But we'd really like somewhere private to avoid the paparazzi."

I slumped back on the sofa. "I wanted to give Kar the perfect honeymoon, where we'd fly off to some tropical island surrounded by white sandy beaches and stay in a gorgeous villa. Where we'd have the whole place to ourselves."

"What?" Kyle interrupted. "Like Gem and I did for ours?"

"Shut up . . . but yeah." Excitement simmered low in my stomach. "But we can't go far because of Nae and the baby." I quirked a smile at Kara. "I really didn't think this whole *let's-get-married-before-we-have-a-baby* thing through, did I?"

I wished we had more time. More time to plan the wedding and more time for a proper honeymoon.

But . . . we didn't. Having a baby would be worth it.

"We'll find somewhere." Kara nudged against me. "We're going to have a wonderful day and an amazing honeymoon wherever we go."

But sadness returned to her eyes. Was it the ever-present worry about our baby? *Yes.* Was it over her parents? *Probably.*

I tensed and curled my hands. I had to do something about Walter and Carol.

Once and for all.

After we finished our wedding plans and the girls headed out to pick up Gemma's dress for the Grammys, I headed outside by the pool. My fingers trembled as I found the right phone number and made the call. I closed my eyes and tilted my head back. I could do this. I had to do this.

"Hello."

My pulse throbbed in my temples. "Walter. It's Hunter Collins."

"What do you want? I have a meeting in ten minutes."

"I only need five."

"What have you done to my daughter now?"

"Nothing." My jaw tensed. My hand tightened around my cell phone, and I let out a breath to stay calm and focused. "But you have, sir. You have broken her heart and continue to do so. I love your daughter. We're getting married and having a child. You can't get rid of me. Kar is an incredible woman, and if you took a moment to see her for who she truly is instead of trying to mold her into your puppet, you'd see that too. She's devastated that you despise me for whatever pathetic, shallow reason you have. I can live with the fact that we may never get along. But, for once in your life, can you think about her? For some insane reason, she loves you and wants you to be part of her life."

"Don't tell me what to do." Walter's surly tone slithered through the speaker.

"Yes, Walter, I will." My voice was full of tenacity and confidence, but my insides shook like a wind chime in a hurricane. I didn't want this to backfire. "For Kara's sake, if you love her, shove whatever grievances you have against me where the sun doesn't shine. She is my world, and I'll do anything to make her happy. We want you to be part of our child's life, our life, but if you continue down this path, you will lose Kar. That's not of my doing but of your own."

"Listen, you arrogant, son-of-a—"

"No," I cut in. "I've said all I wanted to say. The ball is in your court."

I hung up. The breath shot out of my lungs.

Fuck!

I ripped my hand through my hair and stared at the bottom of the pool. Would Walter come around? Or had I just made things worse between Kara and her father? *Crap.*

Would they sink or swim?

I guessed time would tell.

Chapter 41

KARA

I stepped off the plane in New York with Hunter, then security ushered us through the airport. We had three days off from the tour and had a ton of wedding items to tick off on our quick visit agenda. But there was one place I wanted to go first more than anywhere else. *Naomi's.*

Naomi was twenty-five weeks pregnant.

My stomach fluttered, anxious to see my sister and the progress of our baby, and nervous to ask a huge favor . . . from Anthony.

My father still hadn't come around. He wanted nothing to do with the wedding. So be it. After years of hoping he'd accept who I was, my career, and the man I loved, I'd finally taken my friends' advice. I wouldn't waste my energy on him anymore. It left a hole in my heart the size of the moon, but that would heal in time.

As our driver headed into the city, Hunter squeezed my hand. "Hey, you okay?"

"Yeah."

"It's always good to be home, even if it's only for a few days." He drew in a deep breath as if absorbing the city's energy as we crossed the river and the skyline of Manhattan filled the view.

"I know what you mean." I'd been away for eight and a half

months. It'd felt like a lifetime.

"You ready to see our baby bump?" His eyes glinted as he raised a questioning eyebrow.

Me? Ready?

My hands shook and sweated. My heart thudded against my ribs. My toes curled inside my suede Chloe boots. The nerves wouldn't stop flipping inside my stomach. I was more than ready. "Yes. I am."

At Naomi's, Erika opened the door for us. Her cheery smile was warm and welcoming as always. "Good afternoon, Miss Knight. Mr. Collins. So nice to see you again."

"Thanks, Erika." I placed my tote on the console table.

As I turned to head down the hallway, Dakota charged toward me and shrieked.

"Auntie Kara. I missed you." Dakota wrapped her arms around my legs and clung to me like a leech.

"Hello, monkey." I kissed the top of her head. "How are you? Where's your mom?"

"On the sofa, resting. The doctor said she needs bed rest, so she shouldn't be on the sofa, right? She should be in bed?"

My thudding heartbeat morphed into panicked patters. *What? Bed rest? What was going on?*

Hunter's eyes reflected my concern. Naomi had said she was fine, that the baby was fine. I tried to peel Dakota from my legs, but I couldn't release her clasp.

Hunter came to the rescue. He splayed his hands around Dakota's waist, tickled her, swooped her up in the air, and hung her upside down over his shoulder.

"Uncle Hunter." She giggled and twisted. "Put me down."

"Never." Heading down the hallway, he tickled her again, and she squealed even louder.

My heart melted. He'd be an amazing dad.

But . . . *Naomi.*

I rushed after Hunter into the living room. Naomi sat outstretched on the sofa with a tartan blanket draped over her waist.

"Oh my God." Naomi flapped her hands, waving me forward. "You're home. You made it." But after hugging her and I stepped back, Naomi wrinkled her nose and grimaced. Her gaze darted to Hunter, then back to me. "You two look like utter crap."

"But we're doing well." I may look tired, but I hadn't felt this good, this healthy in months. Hunter, even on a bad day, looked like a god. He'd thinned in the face a touch—that happened when he performed for two grueling hours on stage every night—but he was still a ball of bouncing energy. "The tour is tiring, but it's nothing to worry about."

Hunter placed Dakota on her feet, and she raced to Erika, grabbed her hand, and dragged her toward her room. "Come on, Erika. Let's go find my Gemma doll so she can sing with the real Hunter."

Hunter chuckled, shook his head, and stuffed his hands in his pockets. "Oh, dear Lord, what am I in for?"

"Nothing." Naomi swiped the air. "I told Erika to keep her busy."

"Thanks." He threw Naomi a warm smile. "It's good to see you."

I sat beside Naomi. "We couldn't get here fast enough." I scanned my sister and oh, my . . . our baby bump. "What about you? How are you? Look at you." I held out my trembling hand toward Naomi's round stomach. "May I?"

"Sure can." Naomi lowered the blanket. Her belly bulged beneath her pale blue maternity top. "It's your baby."

I placed my palms on Naomi's tummy, and warmth shot up my arms and exploded in my chest. It wrapped around my heart and hugged me tight. *Oh wow.* My breath shuddered, and a sob escaped me. "Hi little one. You're so big." I had never gotten this large with Ryan. I'd never gotten this far through term.

"May I?" Hunter took a tentative step forward.

"No." Naomi whipped her head toward Hunter and glared. He froze. His face blanched. "Ha!" Naomi's eyes twinkled, and she laughed. "I'm just fucking with you. Of course you can. You may touch my tummy. Nowhere else. Got it?"

"Geez, Nae, you're worse than Kar. You do my head in." He fell to his knees beside me and placed his hand on Naomi's stomach. "But this is worth it."

I clutched my hand over his. "Hunt, that's our baby."

"It certainly is." Tears welled in his eyes.

"I'm twenty-five weeks." Naomi straightened the pillow behind her back. "We're more than halfway."

"What's this about needing bed rest?" I couldn't keep the shake out of my voice. "Dakota said in the hall . . . the doctor . . . is there something you're not telling us?"

"I've told you everything." Naomi's tone remained calm and reassuring. "There's nothing wrong with the baby." She circled her finger at me. "So you can wipe that look off your face."

The blood had drained from my face when Dakota had told me the news.

"I have bad sciatica pain and an aching lower back." Naomi wriggled and pulled herself up straighter. "The baby is in the large percentile. It's big and strong and healthy. The doctor suggested bed rest to ease the pressure on my pelvis."

I let out the breath I'd been holding. "Our baby is healthy? You're fine?"

"Yes."

I caught and squeezed Naomi's hand. "I nearly died thinking the worst."

"I know." Naomi's eyebrows shot skyward. "I could tell."

Hunter flattened his hand against his chest. "Don't scare us, Nae. We're on edge every fucking day."

"I'd tell you if something was wrong. Right now, both of us are great. Oh . . ." Her eyes widened and she clutched her stomach. "Oh, quick. The baby just kicked." Naomi lifted her shirt, grabbed my hand and Hunter's, and placed our palms on the lower right side of her tummy. "Feel that."

Nope. There was nothing.

No movement at all.

Would I feel the baby move beneath Naomi's skin? I closed my eyes and held my breath. Then *kick*. Little protruding mounds and fluttering pulses rolled in waves across Naomi's tummy beneath my fingertips. *Up. Down. Push. Kick.* I pursed my lips. My vision blurred with tears. Overcome with emotion, I uttered, "Oh my goodness. Our baby."

"Wow. That is so weird." Hunter's eyes roamed Naomi's stomach as it bulged, receded, then bulged again. "It's like in *Alien*, isn't it? Like something will explode out of there at any second."

"I hope not." Naomi glanced down at her tummy; a motherly glow was rosy on her cheeks. "That's a foot."

"So cool," Hunter flattened his hand on her belly to feel the kicks.

"Did you find out the gender?" My heart fluttered as the baby butted against my hand.

"No." Naomi shook her head. "I haven't. I did what I was told."

"Thank you. We want it to be a surprise." I rubbed Hunter's back, leaned over, and kissed his cheek.

"As long as it's healthy, we don't care." Hunter gawked at Naomi's stomach, mesmerized by the movements.

"I think the baby recognizes your voice, Hunter. I've been playing your music every night through the headphones like Kara wanted."

"Really?" Hunter sat back on his haunches. "That's awesome."

The front door opened, and Anthony walked in. "Hey, Kara. Hunter. Nice to see you." He strode over and kissed Naomi on the top of her head. "Nae's taking good care of your little one."

"Thank you." I stood and hugged Anthony. He'd been incredibly supportive of Naomi being our surrogate. A rare good-hearted man indeed.

Hunter jumped to his feet and shook Anthony's hand. "Hey man, it's great to see you."

"Can I get y'all a drink?" Anthony headed to the kitchen and opened the wine fridge. "It's been a long day. I'm having a wine. Want one?"

"Sure," I said.

"I'll pass," Hunter grumbled. "Gotta watch my voice."

As we sat around on the sofa catching up on news about the tour, work, and Naomi's decision to delay the move to London indefinitely, the conversation rolled into the wedding. This was another reason why we'd visited and had waited for Anthony to come home.

"Is everything on track?" Naomi asked.

"Yes." I put my empty wine glass on the coffee table. Wedding talk always sent a buzz through my veins, even after all the dramas with my parents and their lack of participation and enthusiasm. "We have an amazing wedding planner. We're meeting her at the venue tomorrow. In the afternoon, we're cake-tasting and selecting our wedding rings. Then, the next day, I'm being measured at Ivory Mink's and finalizing the design and fabric for my dress." I clapped, then clutched Hunter's hand. "It's so exciting."

I'd also discussed designing a limited collection for Ivory Mink. Ivory had been ecstatic during our initial conversations and wanted to continue discussions after the wedding. *Designing. Husband. Baby.* Would everything fall into place?

"Hunt, what are you doing while Kara's busy?" Anthony raised a questioning eyebrow.

He leaned back and crossed his ankles. "Sleeping . . . and trying to sort out the honeymoon. It's hard to find something that's private and near home. We'd prefer somewhere outside the city. It has to be secure from the paparazzi. And it has to have a wow factor."

"Those are tough criteria," Naomi said, then took a sip of her peppermint tea.

"You'll find something." I patted and ran my hand up and down Hunter's thigh. "I have faith in you."

The honeymoon was one of the loose ends in our wedding plans. I didn't like unfinished tasks; they made me restless. While my anxiety was well under control, it would be even better if we'd secured somewhere to stay.

And I'd be even more at ease once I'd resolved another outstanding issue.

I drew my shoulders back and turned to Anthony, sitting beside Naomi. "Anthony, can I ask you a huge favor?"

"Shoot." He waved his wine glass at me.

I took a deep breath. "Would you walk me down the aisle?"

Anthony's face split into a wide smile. "Yes. Absolutely. I'd be honored."

"Whoa, Kar?" Stunned, Naomi shook her head. "You want Anthony to do that?"

I lifted my chin a fraction. "Yes. Daddy won't. He doesn't want anything to do with the wedding."

"He *what*?" Naomi sat upright, holding her belly.

I had set my resolve in place. I wouldn't let my father ruin my wedding. "When I asked him, he refused. So, I'd love Anthony to give me away instead."

"Oh, sweetie." Anthony came over, sat beside me, and gave me a big hug. "I'd love to walk you down the aisle. Walter's just an old fool." He jutted his chin at Hunter. "If it's any consolation, I wasn't in his good books for a long time either. He thought I was just like my baby sister."

I gaped. How had I not known this? When Anthony and Naomi had dated and had gotten engaged, I'd been at college. I wasn't close to my sister back then. Our lives had been totally separate. "But Alicia's a mega movie star."

"Yes, but she was fucked up on cocaine and alcohol for years. She made Lindsay Lohan look like an amateur." Gray clouds fogged Anthony's eyes, but he forced a smile and they evaporated. "Now she's clean, shacked up with some rich Italian businessman, and doing well. Your dad's just a super-judgmental buffoon. He stereotypes everyone and thinks they're incapable of change. Just like him, really. He'll come around one day. He warmed to me."

Maybe my father would. But I wouldn't sit around waiting for it to happen.

Hunter leaned forward and rested his elbows on his knees. "Anthony, thanks for saying yes. This means the world to Kar."

"As I said, I'd be honored."

I gave Anthony another hug. "Thank you."

"Come on, babe." Hunter clasped my knee. "It's late. We'd better head home."

"Yeah. It's been a long day." I rose to my feet. The weariness from flying in from Seattle, and the fatigue from touring and visiting Naomi had taken their toll. Every cell in my body wanted sleep. I eased over to Naomi, bent forward and hugged my sister. "You take care of yourself and our baby."

"That's the plan." Naomi straightened the blanket over her tummy and legs.

"Um . . . Hunter?" Anthony jumped to his feet and pointed toward the office. "Can I see you for a sec?"

Hunter's brow furrowed. "Yeah. Sure."

Apprehension spiked through my veins and swirled through my gut as the two men disappeared into the office. *Oh no.* What was Anthony talking to Hunter about? My dad? The wedding? Naomi? Oh no . . . the baby? Was Naomi keeping something from us? Had all these niceties been part of the plan to keep my anxiety under control?

"What's that about?" I sank onto the sofa beside Naomi's hip and searched her face for an answer, but it was as blank as a plain piece of paper.

Naomi peered over her shoulder toward the office. "I honestly don't know."

I clasped Naomi's hand. "Is it about the baby?"

"No. I told you. The baby is fine." She sighed. "Kar, I know you're worried. But I've got this."

I nodded, but it wasn't a confident one. My doubts and concerns always hovered just beneath the surface.

Naomi rubbed my arm. "Enjoy your couple of days at home and come see me before you go."

"Will do."

Five minutes later, Hunter and Anthony came out of the office. I rose to my feet and stepped toward them. "Is everything okay?"

A bright smile slid across Hunter's face. "Yeah. It's awesome."

"Well?" I jammed my hand onto my hip. Did I have to beat the information out of him? "What?"

"The honeymoon. It's sorted. Anthony offered us the use of his sister's house in Bridgehampton. It's not far from where we're getting married. He rang Alicia in Italy to confirm it's okay. He showed me pictures. It's on the beach and has a lake out the back. It's huge, bright, modern, and has a pool." Excitement elevated his voice as he ran through the list. "It's on a couple of acres, so we won't have neighbors peeking over the fence. It has security. A deck—"

"Okay. Okay." Light filled my chest as I clasped his upper arms. "It sounds wonderful. You're fussier than I am about where we stay."

"Wanna see?" He jerked his head toward the office.

"Yeah."

As Anthony showed me the pictures of his sister's house on his laptop, the tension in my brow eased. The place was gorgeous. A beautiful beachfront property in the Hamptons. "It's perfect."

Another item could be ticked off our wedding to-do list. I'd mark off a few more things over the next forty-eight hours.

I couldn't deny there were some planning stresses, but I'd handle them. Thanks to Hunter, my friends, and Everhide's team, the wedding planning had been relatively easy. I didn't have to do everything on my own. Not everything had to be a battle to prove I was strong and independent.

Our wedding day would be incredible, a celebration with those who loved us. I didn't care if it rained, or if there were gale-force winds, or if decorations flew away. As long as Hunter turned up, nothing else mattered.

After seeing Naomi and how healthily she glowed, my worries about our child eased a fraction too. I'd be on edge until I held my baby in my arms—that was a given. But every day, that dream was one step closer to becoming a reality.

I followed the guys out of the office. I kissed Anthony goodbye, and Naomi waddled over to join us.

"See you two soon. Have fun." Naomi kissed Hunter on the cheek, then hugged me again.

I couldn't help myself; I rubbed Naomi's belly. I missed being pregnant. I remembered what it felt like to have the baby kick, roll, and flutter inside me. Having Naomi as our surrogate was surreal and mind-blowingly perfect. It had brought us even closer together. Naomi and Anthony had become friends with Hunter.

We were family.

In ten weeks, I'd be Mrs. Hunter Collins.

In fourteen weeks, I'd be a mom.

Finish the tour. Get married. Have a baby.

That was the plan.

It hurt that my father would miss out. But that was his choice. Not mine.

This was my life. I'd live it to the fullest. I was in love and had to follow my heart.

Nothing and no one would stop me from marrying Hunter.

I was so close to having everything I'd ever wanted.

So close.

So, so close.

Chapter 42

HUNTER

Standing center stage at Madison Square Garden, I wrapped my sweaty arms around Kyle's and Gemma's shoulders. The three of us stank of damp leather, deodorant, and perspiration. Tears of weariness, relief, pride, and exhilaration welled in my eyes. We'd done it. We'd sung the last song on our fifth world tour. Confetti-filled pyrotechnics had exploded into the air. The glitter foil rained on us, caught in our wet hair, and the audience hollered for more. I savored the moment. My heart cheered and sank as I held Kyle and Gemma extra tight. Our hard work had paid off. The tour had been a huge success. We wouldn't be back on the road again for another couple of years. But life would never be the same. In two weeks, I'd marry Kara. In six weeks, our baby was due. But one thing that would never change would be the bond I had with Kyle and Gemma. What a journey we'd been on, and I hoped we'd continue on this path forever.

With one last wave and air kiss to the shrieking crowd, I rushed off stage after my friends and into the massive gathering of crew. People cheered and hollered, hugged and cried around me, but there was only one person I wanted to see. *Kara.*

She charged forward, weaving past Olsen and Sophie, and threw her arms around my neck. She kissed me long and hard.

My sweat-drenched T-shirt clung to every inch of my upper body, and my leather pants were glued to my legs. Strands of damp hair stuck to my face, and heat poured from every pore of my body, but Kara didn't seem to care.

"That was incredible." She laughed as I spun her around and placed her back on her feet.

"Such a rush." My heart still thundered after the show. My voice had survived. I'd sung better than ever before. "I love finishing the tour in front of our home crowd."

Kyle shoved a champagne bottle at me and another one at Kara. Gemma waved her bottle above her head. "Woohoo! Let's party!"

Hayden veered toward us, shaking another bottle of Bollinger.

"We've finished!" He popped the cork. Champagne sprayed over Kyle, Gemma and me. Kara copped a dousing too. As Gemma put up her hand to protect her face, Kara shrieked, and Kyle tilted his head back and laughed. I opened my mouth and relished the shower of champagne on my tongue.

"Yeah!" I flicked my hair from side to side and tousled my fingers through the loose, wet strands. The cold Bollinger was an icy heaven on my hot skin—sticky, but good. Within seconds, two more bottles from Sophie and Adam, our backup guitarist, were popped, and spurted over us. Lexi, standing next to Hayden, captured the whole thing on camera.

With a grin as wide as the stage, I wiped the droplets from my face with my hand and cleared my eyes. Yep, just another Everhide party. I grabbed Kara and licked the champagne off her cheek.

"Ew!" She giggled, flinched, and turned away. "Gross."

Locking my arms around her waist, I held her so she couldn't escape. "That's not what you usually say when I lick you."

"You usually don't lick my face."

True. She had a point.

"Folks," Sophie yelled over the crowd, her voice as loud as a megaphone. "Let's move this into the dressing room so the road crew can dismantle and roll out."

I took a swig of my champagne and glanced around the

gathering of people. This was it. Eleven months of traveling together had come to an end.

The six of us—Kara, Gemma, Kyle, Lexi, Hayden and me—linked our arms around each other's waists or shoulders and headed toward the corridor. But at the back of the stage, we stopped and looked up. The towering height of the scaffolding that held our projection screens, lighting, and speakers would be nothing but a pile of poles, equipment trunks, and trusses soon. I leaned sideways and kissed Gemma on the temple. "We did it, didn't we?"

"Yeah." She rested her head against my arm. "I'm gonna miss it. Performing every night. The crowds. The magic."

"We always do," Kyle said from beside her. "This is home."

"We'll be back." I tugged Kara on my other side closer and kissed her on the cheek.

"You bet," she said.

Lexi grabbed Bec as she walked past and shoved her camera into Bec's hands. Bec snapped several photos of the six of us huddled together.

I glanced at my friends. I'd never forget this tour. I'd kept my promise. We'd lived it up and had the time of our lives. There were ultimate highs—playing to our largest crowd at Wembley Stadium, my proposal in Paris, Kara saying "*yes*," and spending every day with the people I called family. There were also some lows—when my arm ached too much from playing, Gemma sprained her ankle falling down the stage steps in Cleveland, and Kara had gotten a stomach bug in Shanghai . . . That hadn't been fun.

"Touring with you has been a dream come true." Hayden broke our huddle, grabbed my bottle of champagne, and took a mouthful. "I won't miss the tour buses though."

"Nope. Never do. But we keep coming back for more." I slapped his shoulder. "Let's get this party rolling."

I took Kara's hand and we followed everyone into the dressing room. It was already swarming with our entourage and crew members drinking.

Kyle, Gemma, Hayden and I slipped out to our private dressing room for quick showers. After changing into fresh clothes, we returned to the party. For hours, I mingled and drank and said heart-tugging farewells to crew I may never see again. Taking a breather, I flopped onto the sofa, squishing between Kyle and Gemma. Laughing, they groaned and inched apart for me to fit. We clinked our cups of JD together, took a sip, and relaxed our heads back against the sofa.

"I can't believe the tour is over." The reality hadn't hit me yet. It usually took a day or two for it to sink in.

"Wanna start working on the next album?" Kyle swiveled his head toward me. An element of seriousness hovered in his tone. "We came up with some great material while we were away."

"We did." I chuckled. We hadn't even been off stage for two hours and the next album was already brewing inside our heads. It had to wait, though. "But we might have to take a small break. Just a small one. 'Cause I'm gonna be busy for the next few months." My heart rocked to a wicked beat as I gazed at Kara on the other side of the room. She stood talking to Bec, Sophie, and their partners. Her eyes sparkled like the huge rock on her finger. "Can you believe I'm marrying her in two weeks?"

"Yeah, I can." Gemma rested her head against my shoulder.

I draped my arm behind her and ruffled her hair. "I'm sorry you guys can't take off on vacation until after the wedding."

"Don't be." Kyle rubbed his tired eyes. Weariness seeped into his voice. "We wouldn't miss your wedding for the world, and we're more than happy to just hang out at the beach house for the next couple of weeks. I don't want to see the inside of a plane, bus, or hotel for months."

"So true." I raised my cup, downed a mouthful of JD, and let the sweet burn soothe every ache in my neck, my arms, and my chest. Fatigue slowly crept through every inch of my body. My head spun after just a few drinks now that I didn't drink much. My vocal cords were too precious. And so was Kara.

Kara smiled and twinkled her fingers at me but continued to talk to Bec. I couldn't help but smile back. Everything about her filled my heart with warmth.

Gemma swiveled her head toward me and nudged her elbow against my side. "I love seeing you happy." She patted and rubbed my thigh. "Can you believe how much life has changed in the past few years? Last tour, Kyle and I got engaged. Then, we got married. Lexi and Hayden joined us, and they got hitched. Now, it's your turn. I can't wait. I love that you love my bestie."

"Yeah. It's fucking awesome." I unhooked my arm from behind Gemma and sank deeper into the sofa. "Life will certainly be different when Kar and I have a baby, but the three of us will never change."

"Yeah, we will." Gemma curled her legs up and rested her knees against my thighs. "But for the better. The three of us have become six. Six is about to become seven. Our Everhide family is growing, evolving, and getting stronger. Because *we*"—she swayed and slurred as she waved her cup of JD between the three of us—"love the absolute fuck out of each other. Music and the shit we've gone through will bind us together forever. We've stuck by one another through every up and down. We've learned to live our lives to the fullest and have gotten rid of the crap that held us back. And because of that . . . our future will be amazing."

Kyle stretched out his legs, crossed his ankles, and scanned the room. "Who would've thought that three hopeless teenagers from New Jersey would turn out to be this living, breathing, incredible band? Man, we've made it. We've fucking made it."

Sitting with my friends, with my body buzzing from the end-of-tour celebrations and too much alcohol, I glanced at everyone partying. Life had turned out to be pretty fucking incredible. A new chapter was about to begin. But this . . . the music . . . my love for Kyle and Gemma. . . would never die. "Promise me we'll be doing this in our graves."

"Hell yeah." Gemma downed the last mouthful of her drink and slammed the cup down on her thigh. "In this life and every one after it."

I glanced at my watch. "It's four in the morning. You think we should call it a night?"

"Yes, please!" Kyle groaned. "I need my wife. My bed. And a

decent sleep."

Gemma shot her arms up into the air. "Baby, take me to bed and show me the way to heaven."

I laughed and staggered to my feet. "You guys are freaking awesome. Grab your stuff and I'll see if I can drag Kara away from Bec." They'd grown closer during the wedding preparations. That was cool. "I'll meet you over there in five so we can head home."

"On it." Kyle stood, held out his hand, and hauled Gemma to her feet. She collapsed against his chest and laughed.

Yep, everyone had drunk too much. Everyone had earned the celebration. The tour had been phenomenal.

I snuck up behind Kara, slid my hands around her waist, and nuzzled into her neck. *Hmm.* She always smelled of roses. "You ready to go home, party animal?"

She melted against my chest and reached up to touch my cheek. "Yeah."

"Can I steal my girl, Bec?"

"Are you wrapping this party up so I can kick everyone out? So I can go home and sleep for two weeks?" Bec swayed on her feet. The sickly scent of champagne on her breath nearly knocked me out.

"Yeah. It's a wrap." I nodded.

"Yes!" Bec pumped her fist, slammed her cup down on the table, then waved toward the partying crew. "Would you like to do the honors, or shall I?"

"I will." I grabbed a nearby chair and stood on top of it. I whistled everyone to attention, then clapped my hands. "Everyone." The conversations died. The music was shut off. Kyle and Gemma came to stand beside me. "This has been the most incredible tour. We've loved all the laughs, the pranks, and have appreciated your hard work. Thank you for putting up with our shit for the past eleven months. We visited many amazing cities and played in front of fantastic crowds across the globe. But sadly, and thank God, finally, it has come to an end. So with hand on heart, Kyle, Gem, Kara and I thank you. We bid you goodnight, farewell, and we hope to see you on our next tour. Love to you all. Be kind. Stay safe. We're out of here."

The crowd cheered, clapped, and whistled as I waved and blew kisses to the room. I jumped off the chair and draped my arm around Kara's shoulders.

Lexi and Hayden rushed over to say goodnight.

"Love you, guys." Lexi flung her arms around Kara and me. "We'll catch up in a couple of days, ready to nail this wedding. Hayds and I are heading back to Adam's in Brooklyn to continue the celebrations."

"Party isn't over until the sun comes up." Hayden hugged me goodbye.

"Dude, I think it nearly is." I chuckled and slapped him on the back. "I loved having you on the tour, man. It was the best."

Hayden stepped back, drumming his fingers in the air. "You're stuck with me now."

"We wouldn't have it any other way." Kyle said his farewells.

"I'll get security to take us out." Gemma headed toward the door where they lingered.

I drew Kara in close and rested my forehead against hers. "So, my Pearl. Did you have fun?"

"Yes." She slipped her hands into the back pockets of my jeans.

"Are you ready to come home with me?"

She tugged my hips forward and erased the gap between us. "Hmm. Yes."

As I ran my hands down her back, I brushed my lips against her soft sweet mouth, then smiled against her lips. "Are you ready to marry me, Miss Knight?"

The biggest smile slid across her gorgeous face. Her eyes sparkled in the soft light. "Yes, Mr. Collins. I can't wait to be a bride. To be Mrs. Collins. To be a mom. To be yours."

The next two weeks would be crazy as we finalized our plans. Excitement rippled through my veins. Gemma was right. Things had changed for the better. I had more than music to live for—I had Kara and my baby to love and protect for the rest of my days.

I couldn't wait.

"Then let's get out of here. I can't wait to marry you either."

Chapter 43

KARA

As I stepped into my wedding gown, my knees wobbled and my hands trembled. I shimmied my dress over my hips and covered my chest. Gemma and Lexi zipped me in.

I pressed my hand against my stomach and took a slow breath to calm the butterflies that dipped and dived like seagulls in a feeding frenzy. It didn't help. Too much excitement hummed through my veins. As Gemma did up all the tiny buttons at the back of my ivory silk gown, I ran my fingertips over the dazzling waistline. Sheer French lace embroidered with dainty pearls, sequins, and tiny rhinestones covered the entire dress. The strapless bodice fit snugly against my breasts. The gorgeous skirt fell straight to the floor at the front and flared to a two-yard train at the back. It weighed a ton but felt like a cloud swirling around my ankles.

I designed this. My *wedding dress.* Holy shit! *I'm about to get married.*

I ignored Lincoln, the photographer, darting around in front of us, jumping on top of chairs and the bed, and dashing around the bedroom suite taking photographs of me and my friends.

"Oh, Kar." Lexi hitched up the skirt of her champagne-colored bridesmaid dress and bent down to straighten the front of my gown. "This dress is beautiful."

"You look stunning, Kar." Naomi wriggled on a padded velvet chair by the mirror and rubbed her hands over her very, *very* pregnant belly.

"Thank you." I flapped my hands in front of my face, not wanting to cry before my wedding. My makeup had taken too long to do to risk ruining it before the ceremony.

Naomi picked up my veil and played with it, threading the soft tulle through her fingers. "And I'm *very* glad I opted out of bridesmaid duties. I feel like a bloated whale, and there is no way I'd pull off one of those bridesmaid dresses. The thigh-high split would show off my cankles. The cowled neckline would make Dolly Parton's boobs look small compared to mine. And I can't wear fitted waistlines. I need everything to be loose, stretchy, and flowy."

"You look amazing." I swooned at my sister, dressed in an Ivory Mink ruby-colored wrap dress with a flowing skirt. Perfect for handling the summer heat. "Thank you for being here. You had to be part of my day."

Naomi pressed her palm against her belly again. "I hope I make it through the day and don't burst."

That would make for an interesting wedding day. "No bursting until after the ceremony." I pouted, waggling my finger at Naomi. "Hunt wants to tie the knot before the baby comes."

"It's a bit out of my control, but I'm fine," Naomi reassured me. "There are no weird pains. No more than usual, anyway."

Gemma did up the last button on my dress and tapped my ass. "All done, Kar. But fuck me, Hunt's not gonna like undoing those little shits later tonight."

"I've gotta make him work for it." I threw her a playful wink.

Gemma grabbed our champagne flutes off the dresser and handed me one. "Why didn't you design something that could be ripped off in a second?"

"Because the buttons are sexy and flattering." I clinked my flute against hers.

"Yep. But so is a plain zip." Gemma took a swig of her drink.

"Hunt will get her out of it. I have no doubts." Lexi's eyes glinted as she jumped to her feet and dashed toward the bed. "But it's time for presents. Something old, something new, and all that jazz." She dug into her overnight bag. "First, something blue." She handed me a long, thin silver box.

I opened it and pulled out a lacy blue garter. "Oh, nice. Thank you." I tossed the box on the bed, lifted my skirt, and eased the elastic into place. Hunter could take that off with his teeth later.

"Something old." Naomi dived into her purse, pulled out a velvet case, and gave it to me. "These were Great Grandma's. If you don't like them, you don't have to wear them."

Inside the case, on a pillow of white satin, lay a single-strand choker of pearls and diamonds with matching drop earrings. I touched my throat. "They're beautiful." Absolutely perfect, and not much different from the jewelry I'd planned to wear.

After I'd clipped the pearls on, Gemma handed me a velvet pouch. "And something new."

Wait. Slow down. I wanted to cherish every moment and every second of this day. I'd dreamed about my wedding for so many years. Now that it was here, it was zipping by too fast.

With shaking hands, I tipped a diamond tennis bracelet into my palm. *Oh wow!* I had the most incredible friends a girl could ever hope for.

"And finally . . ." Lexi glided over to the velvet box on the dresser, opened the lid, and pulled out a diamond and pearl tiara. "Something borrowed. Thanks to Leonard's jewelers. I don't want to know how much this thing actually costs."

"Neither do I," I said and bobbed down. Lexi placed the tiara on my head like Carla had shown her two days ago when we'd had a practice run of our hairdos.

Naomi waddled over and clipped my veil into place above my bun. Gemma helped fan it out behind me. Adorned in my full wedding gown, sparkling shoes, and accessories, I couldn't hold back my tears. *I'm a bride.*

Gemma gave me a hug and handed me a tissue. "Don't ruin your makeup."

After dabbing my eyes, the four of us posed around the room for a ton of photos. But when I glanced at the clock, my nerves jumped fifteen notches. Ten minutes until showtime. "I think I'm going to be sick."

"No, you're not." Gemma downed the rest of her champagne. "Remember to have fun. You're the bride. This day is all about you . . . and somewhat Hunt's. This is your day to shine. Own it."

Yeah. I will.

There was a knock at the door. "Kara, it's your father. Can I come in?"

Fuck! "What is he doing here?" What did he want? He hadn't wanted to come. Mom must have dragged him along. I didn't want him to ruin my wedding day.

"Do you want me to get him to leave?" Naomi took a step toward the door. A subtle, wicked glint flashed in her eyes. "Your bodyguard is outside. I could get Giles to throw Daddy out of the venue."

God, I loved my sister, but I hoped Giles's services wouldn't be necessary.

"Please?" my father pleaded. "For five minutes?"

Shit!

I glanced at the girls. They'd have my back. "Fine."

Dad opened the door and stepped inside. He smoothed his hands down the lapels of his black dinner jacket, then held his palms wide. His usual stony gaze softened. "Wow, Kara. You look beautiful."

I straightened. I stood an inch taller than him in my high heels. "What do you want? I thought you weren't coming."

He took a cautious step toward me. "Can I talk to you in private?"

"No." I lifted my chin and held onto Gemma's and Lexi's hands. Naomi flanked Lexi's side. We were a united front. "Whatever you have to say, you can say in front of my friends."

Irritation flashed in his eyes, but he nodded. "Fine." He tugged and wriggled his bow tie. "So . . . you're really going through with this? Are you sure about marrying Hunter?"

"Um . . . yeah. I wouldn't be here otherwise."

"No, that's not what I meant." He grimaced. The crinkles at the corners of his eyes deepened. "Isn't that what every father asks their daughter before she weds?"

"No. Most fathers accept and respect the man their daughter loves." I held my ground. "I'm marrying Hunt whether you like it or not. If this is your last feeble attempt to get me to change my mind, you're wasting your time. Please leave."

"No. I'm sorry." He steepled his fingers and touched his fingertips against his lips. "This hasn't come out right." His hands fell to his sides. "Hunter wasn't who I envisioned you falling in love with. I loathed him when you got pregnant, and he initially wanted nothing to do with you." My father splayed his hand over his chest. "My heart hurt for you so much when you lost Ryan. I wanted to protect you. Wanted you to leave that music crowd you'd fallen in with so I could keep you safe. But you defied me. The two of you grew closer. I was convinced you dated him to upset me. That rebellious, strong streak you've always had made you dig in your heels. I wanted to drag you out of his home when you moved in together. I was afraid of losing my little girl forever."

My blood simmered through my veins. "Geez, Dad, if this is supposed to be a feel-good pep talk, it's not working." My girls shuffled closer to me and tightened their hold on my shaking hands.

He swept his palm over his thinning salt-and-pepper hair, then brushed it against his groomed beard. "I thought you'd break up within a few months. That you'd come to your senses. But it was me who had to do that." He took another small step forward. "When you announced you wanted a baby, I panicked. The surrogacy process frightened me. I didn't want you to suffer more hurt, more loss. Seeing my girls go through that tore my heart in two." He glanced at Naomi, then returned his gaze to me. His eyes welled with tears.

My breath shuddered. My bodice suddenly felt too tight. What was my father's point?

Dad's voice thickened. "But through all of this, for nearly three years, Hunter has been there for you. I haven't. You've always been so strong and independent. What I thought were phases you'd grow out of were your passions. He's encouraged them and given you the life you've always wanted and deserved. You're happy. I see that now." He sniffled and pressed his palm against his chest again. "I stand before you with my hand on my heart and apologize. I'm truly sorry for being so hard on you. I'm proud of what you've achieved and even prouder that you have found an honorable and decent man who loves you. I was wrong about him, and I wish you every happiness in your future together."

I flung my arms around Dad's neck and sobbed. "Oh my God. Do you mean that?"

"Yes." Dad held me tight and stroked my veil. "You fled the nest a long time ago. I was the one who couldn't let go. What I thought was best for you wasn't your path. You've found someone who adores you and wants a family with you. You go marry your rockstar, okay? I love you."

I closed my eyes. Tears zigzagged down my cheeks. My heart pounded so hard against my ribs I struggled to draw in air. *Wow.* "I love you, Daddy." I stepped back, and Naomi handed me several tissues. She had tears in her eyes too. "Have you talked to Hunt? Given him your blessing?"

"No." Dad shook his head. "I will. I promise. Maybe after the service . . . if I'm allowed to come."

I dabbed the tears from my face. *Shit.* I needed Carla to fix my makeup. "I'd like that. Very much."

Dad straightened his jacket. "Do you think Anthony would mind if I stepped in to walk my daughter down the aisle and give her away?"

"I'm sure he won't." I quickly glanced at Naomi for confirmation.

She blew her nose and nodded. "He'll be fine. He loves you."

As I turned back to my father, the hope and heartfelt sorrow embedded in every wrinkle on his face wrapped around my heart. I didn't think he and Hunter would be out playing golf together anytime soon, but this was an incredible step toward making amends.

"You ready?" Dad buttoned up his jacket and straightened his lapel buttonhole rose.

Naomi clambered to her feet. "Let me grab Carla to freshen Kara's makeup first, then we can start. We're running late."

Five minutes after a touch-up, I was set. So were my girls.

I filled my lungs with a huge breath, held my bouquet of cream roses firmly in front of my waist, and stared at the door. I had to walk out of here, along the hall, and down the path to the pavilion. The sun was shining. The gentle ocean waves crashed in the distance. The guests would be seated. My dad was here. Hunter was waiting.

Two helicopters hovered somewhere above. It was no doubt the paparazzi trying to capture a photo of the wedding. Let them. I didn't care. This was my day.

I exhaled, nice and slowly. *This is it.*

Dad held out his hooked elbow. "Shall we?"

I took his arm. "Yes."

The day I'd dreamed of since I was six was here.

It was time.

Time to get married.

Chapter 44

HUNTER

Standing at the front of the wedding tent at The Ocean Resort, I glanced at my watch. Kara was ten minutes late. She was never late. I tugged on my collar and stretched my neck from side to side. My damn bow tie was too tight. Despite the air conditioning, it was hot. Sweat pooled beneath my hair and soaked the back of my button-down shirt. *Why did I choose to wear a tuxedo in June?*

Kyle and Hayden chuckled.

"Shut up." I smirked as I glanced at my groomsmen standing beside him. "Is it hot in here? Or is it just me?"

Grinning, Kyle stepped in front of me and straightened my pocket square. "It's not hot. She'll be here. It's a tradition for the bride to be late."

I scanned the congregation of two hundred gathered family and friends in their black-tie finery. Mom, Dad, and Jenny occupied the front row on the left. Kara's family was on the right. Everyone giggled and chatted with the surrounding guests. No one looked like they were overheated or uncomfortable.

Just me. Great.

My gaze jumped to the rear entrance of the event tent, where Kara should appear. There were no signs of any movement. "She's not coming, is she?"

"Dude." Hayden tugged on the cuffs of his dinner jacket. "Nothing, not even an outbreak of war, would keep her away."

"You'd better be right." I clasped my hands behind my back, rolled the tension out of my shoulders and put my mask of cool composure back in place.

Grinning, Kyle fell in beside me. "Chill. It's fine."

I was okay for just a few seconds. Then Anthony and Naomi entered the tent. Kara's sister waddled in, holding her baby bump, leaning on Anthony's arm. *Oh wow!* That was my baby in there. But . . . *oh shit! Anthony?* My pulse skyrocketed. He was supposed to walk Kara down the aisle. Something was wrong.

I held my breath as they headed toward the front. Even Kyle and Hayden had stopped ribbing me. But rather than come up to us, they just smiled, nodded and took seats in the front row next to Carol.

What was going on?

The wedding planner rushed into the tent and gave me, the videographer, and Flint, who was playing for us, the thumbs up. *Oh, thank God.* I let out the breath I'd been holding. My nerves evaporated. *Let's get this show on the road.*

Flint's acoustic guitar filled the air, strumming out a sloweddown romantic cover of Bruno Mars's "Marry You."

Yeah. Our wedding would be fun.

"See." Kyle slapped me on the back. "Told you she'd be here."

In walked Lexi, then Gemma.

Wow!

Tears loomed at the back of my eyes. I wanted to memorize every detail of this day, even how gorgeous the girls looked. With bouquets of cream-colored flowers clutched in their hands, and wearing beautiful flowing dresses, they headed toward the front.

Nope. I'm not gonna cry.

But then Kara stepped through the entrance.

On her dad's arm.

Well, fuck me!

As if in slow motion, she floated behind the back row of people toward the aisle.

My hand shot over my chest. My heart thudded hard against my palm. She was the most beautiful bride I'd ever seen. *How did I get so lucky?*

When she reached the aisle, our eyes met. I had to remember to breathe. Her gorgeous red-lipped smile and sparkling eyes shimmered behind her veil. Her stunning lacy dress highlighted her perfect curves. Her glittery tiara was fit for a princess. No . . . *my Pearl.* As she headed toward me, passing underneath the strands of ivy and twinkle lights, warmth charged through my veins, coiled around my heart and squeezed it tight. Dragging in a deep breath, I blinked the tears away.

"You okay, dude?" Kyle whispered, nudging his elbow against my arm.

Too overwhelmed, I just nodded.

When Kara reached the front, I stepped forward to take her hand.

Walter placed it in mine. "You have my blessing. Take good care of my little girl."

"Yes, sir." I nodded. *Well, holy shit.* Crazier things had happened.

I threw a questioning glance at Kara. Her soft smile and happy tears were all I needed to confirm that everything was okay.

Dizziness spun through my head. My heart beat too fast. My love for Kara filled my soul. *Fuck this waiting shit.* I scooped back her veil and kissed her, savoring the taste of her sweet lips and soft touch. "I fucking love you, Pearl," I whispered. "You look incredible."

Tears glistened in her eyes as she cupped my face. "I love you, too. But you're supposed to wait to kiss me."

The congregation laughed, ohhed and ahhed.

Grinning, I brushed my lips against hers again. "I couldn't." Now I understood why Kyle had done the same thing to Gemma on his wedding day. "You're too beautiful."

"Huh-hum." Regina, our officiant, cleared her throat. "Shall we get started?"

"Yeah." I stepped back, unable to erase the smile on my face. With Kara's hand in mine, we headed toward Regina. "Make it quick, so I can kiss her again."

Regina proceeded with her welcoming introduction and segued into our official nuptials. "I believe you've written your own vows. Are you ready, Hunter?"

"Yeah." *I am.*

Kara handed her bouquet to Gemma, then turned to face me. Her beautiful dark-blue eyes glistened in the afternoon sunlight streaming through the tent windows. I took her trembling hands in mine. My heart overflowed with love. I'd found my perfect match. Everything about us worked, and we shared a wicked sense of humor. We'd even agreed on injecting fun into our vows.

I licked my lips and grinned. "Kara, you were *not* the woman of my dreams." She smiled and shook her head. I kept my voice light, but I backloaded it with some sexy, arrogant attitude. "I honestly never had one in mind. Everyone knew I had no intention of *ever* settling down."

The guys from our backup band, sitting in the third row, chuckled, but I remained focused on Kara.

I swiped my thumb over the back of her hand and softened my tone. "But by some twist of fate, now you've become my dream and so much more. One night, almost three years ago, we were put on a path we could've never anticipated. Since that day, you have gotten under my skin and completely stolen my heart. I fell in love with your strong will, your tender soul, and your true sincerity. Your courage, confidence, and compassion continue to inspire me *and* light a fire under my ass. Your talent and passion are exhilarating. Your kindness and caring, incomparable. Every day I learn something new about you and fall in love with you more and more. After one hell of a bumpy road . . . we're here. I can't wait to start our family. I can't wait to spend the rest of my life with you. I promise, with all my heart and soul, to love you forever and always."

Kara blinked and brushed a tear from her cheek.

"Miss Knight." Regina dipped her chin at Kara. "When you're ready."

She nodded and placed her shaky, clammy hand back in mine.

Oh, she's nervous.

"Hunter, you were *soooo* not the man of my dreams." With a big smile, she packed on the drama with a roll of her eyes, then turned her head toward the audience and shook it.

Laughter rippled across the congregation.

Okay . . . she didn't have to go overboard. But I loved that she had.

"You were the dream man for the majority of women on this planet, but never mine." Her eyes shimmered as she gave my hands a small shake. "But everything changed. Fate had other plans. Now you're not only my dream man, but you've made all my dreams come true. I fell in love with your heart and all the layers that lie beneath your charming charisma and ridiculous good looks . . . but I won't deny they are a huge bonus. Your loyalty, devotion, and profound love for those around you is breathtaking. Your love of music and your success is admirable. Your heart in helping others is golden. Despite the circumstances that brought us together, and our past loss, I will be forever grateful that it has united us and that I'm now on this journey with you. I look forward to our future together. To our baby and becoming a family. I love you with all my heart, forever and always."

My eyes stung, and I sniffled. *Yep*, I was an emotional wreck. My heart pounded with so much love I thought it would burst through my chest. I leaned in and kissed her. "You're amazing, you know that?"

"So are you," she whispered over my kisses. "Can we get married now?"

"Yeah."

We exchanged golden wedding bands, were announced *husband and wife*, and had another epic kiss. After we put signatures on paper witnessed by Kyle and Gemma, the officiant led Kara and me back to the front of the congregation.

"Ladies and gentlemen," Regina waved us forward. "I present to you, Mr. and Mrs. Collins."

The brilliant smile and happy tears lighting Kara's face stole my heart all over again. Everyone in the tent rose to their feet and cheered.

"Woohoo."

"Yeah!"

"All right!"

As I held Kara's hand, I led her down the aisle. A giddy high swirled through my head.

We're married.

Totally. Freaking. Amazing.

Outside on the lawn, I picked up Kara and spun her around. "We did it."

"Argh!" She crushed her arms around my neck. "I love you. So much."

Our friends swarmed around us. They were quick to congratulate us before the sea of people trickling out from the tent followed suit. Through the throng of guests, Walter and Carol appeared. My arm tensed around Kara's waist.

Walter thrust out his hand for me to shake. "I owe you a huge thank you and an even bigger apology." As I shook his hand, Walter held his chin high, and his tone remained blunt. "Thank you for your brutal honesty during your phone call."

"What call?" Kara tugged on my jacket.

"I'll tell you later," I whispered back.

Walter slipped his hands into the pockets of his suit pants. "And I do apologize for being hard on you. I wanted what I thought was best for Kara. You were right; I didn't see what she wanted. Clearly, that is you. I hope you are happy together. I can't ask for more than that. So, congratulations . . . And just know, I will kill you if you hurt her."

Kara gaped at her father. Walter didn't sugarcoat the small step toward being nice to me, but . . . it was a step. For Kara.

"I don't intend to, sir. Thank you." In true style, I widened my arms and went to hug Walter, but he put up his hand.

"Don't push it, son. We'll take this slowly. Be civil. Deal?"

"We can do that." I gave Carol a hug, though. She didn't seem to mind.

"Congratulations," she said. I smelled scotch on her breath

already. The reception would be fun.

"Any chance of you ever getting a haircut?" Walter waved his finger toward my long hair brushing my shoulders.

"No, sir."

"Hmph. I'll work on that." Walter shook his head, his tone dead serious. "Now, go. Enjoy yourselves. We need a drink."

Kara hugged and kissed her parents, then they disappeared into the crowd.

"I didn't see that one coming." I drew Kara into my arms.

"Neither did I." She placed her hand on my chest and tapped it. "Your charm finally broke him down."

"No." I kissed her forehead. "It was the thought of losing you."

As the guests mingled around the pool and the drinks flowed, my friends, Kara, and I were whisked away by the photographer. We had photos down on the beach and on the boardwalk with the setting sun providing a magnificent backdrop.

By the time we headed into the ballroom for the reception, my cheeks ached from too much smiling. Every time I glanced at my wife, she glowed more and more. After dinner and speeches, the cake cutting, garter removal, and bouquet toss, all the guests returned to their seats for dessert.

It was my turn to step up to the mic.

I'd originally wanted a big, bold, and outrageous wedding, but tonight, the simple and sophisticated celebration with two hundred of our closest friends and family had been perfect. It had been elegant and romantic. But there was always room to top it. After more praise for my beautiful wife and a final toast, I threw her a wicked grin. "Kar, I love you. But it wouldn't be an Everhide wedding if we didn't sing."

Kara blushed, nodded and touched the pearls at her throat. The twinkle in her eye and cheeky smile told me she hadn't expected anything less.

I pointed to my friends sitting at the bridal table. "So, if I could call upon my two trusty partners-in-crime . . ." Kyle and Gemma stood and headed toward me. Hayden and Lexi shuffled over to sit beside Kara. "I'm gonna play a little song for you."

I joined Gemma and Kyle over by Flint's band, where three stools and one mic were set up in front of the drum kit. Flint and his boys graciously bowed and stepped aside to give us the floor.

We grabbed our acoustic guitars off the rack, hooked the straps over our heads, and took a seat. I adjusted the mic and shuffled closer to the stand. The chandeliers in the room dimmed, so the twinkle lights dominated the ceiling. A lone spotlight shone on me and my friends.

"Okay." I cleared my throat as I dragged my pick down my guitar strings. "This song is a little different. Kar, this is our story. This one is just for you."

I tapped my guitar three times and played the slow tune in sync with Kyle and Gemma.

My eyes locked onto my gorgeous wife. I licked my lips and sang in a low, husky voice.

> *Dark night . . . warm lips*
> *Secrets . . . we kept*
> *One kiss . . . three times*
> *I'll never . . . forget*
> *You in . . . my bed*
> *I hit . . . rewind*
> *Replay . . . that night*
> *Feels like . . . yesterday*
> *Was the . . . first time*
> *I fell a little bit*
> *In love with you*

I glanced around the room. Everyone was held captive. But it was Kara, with tears in her eyes, who had me struggling to sing the next verse.

> *Rain clouds . . . your tears*
> *Touches . . . we needed*
> *One kiss . . . and we cried*
> *We held . . . on so tight*
> *All night . . . 'til light*

I hit . . . rewind
Replay . . . that night
Feels like . . . yesterday
Was the . . . first time
I fell a little bit more
In love with you

City lights . . . your place
My heart . . . on the line
One kiss . . . you were mine
I'll never . . . forget
The look . . . in your eyes
I hit . . . rewind
Replay . . . that night
Feels like . . . yesterday
Was the . . . first time
I fell completely
In love with you

Tonight . . . your dress
Gold rings . . . on our hands
One kiss . . . sealed lives
Two hearts . . . unite
Forever . . . starts tonight
New memories . . . to rewind
To replay . . . in my mind
Together . . . as one
Each day . . . from now on
I get to fall . . . more and more
In love with you
Each day . . . from now on
I get to fall . . . more and more
In love with you

Kara glided to her feet and rushed over to me. I jumped up, handed Kyle my guitar, and met my wife halfway across the dance floor. She flung her arms around my shoulders and kissed me.

Tears dampened her cheeks. "That was so beautiful. It's our

story."

"Yeah." I wiped her tears away with the pad of my thumb. "And I look forward to many more. May our stories go on and on, forever."

Kyle and Gemma broke into playing Andy Grammer's "I Am Yours."

Taking hold of Kara's hand and waist, I waltzed and twirled her around the dance floor in our first dance as husband and wife.

As the song concluded, Adam, our emcee for the evening, slapped his hand against his chest and spoke into the mic. "Hunter, man? Ah-mazing. Feeling the love, bro. Feeling the love. But . . ." He upped the excitement in his voice and addressed the room. "Now, with the formalities out of the way, I declare it's time to par-tay. Would you all please join the newlyweds on the dance floor? It's time to get your groove on!"

Flint and his band, The Flintlocks, broke into playing P!NK's "Let's Get The Party Started."

I swirled Kara around. She threw her head back and laughed. *Pure magic.*

Dancing led to more drinking and a bonfire on the dunes. But like Cinderella, the clock struck midnight, and the ball had to end. We were having such a good time; I didn't want to leave. But then . . . yes, I did. I couldn't wait to be alone with my new wife.

As Kara and I made our way down the line of people gathered on the dance floor for our final farewells, I reached Mom, Dad, and Jenny. I gave them a big hug. "Thanks for everything. Love you." It had been nice to see them over the past few days.

Continuing down the line, I laughed and cheered as I shook hands, slapped shoulders, kissed and hugged relatives and friends. Near the exit, I stopped in front of my four besties. My heart filled my chest. What did you say to the people who meant the world to you? I group-hugged Lexi and Hayden. "You're awesome. I love you so freaking much."

"Get going, you big softy." Lexi dabbed tears from her eyes and play-punched me in the arm.

"Have fun, man." Hayden patted my shoulder. "Love ya."

I slid sideways to Gemma. I wrapped my arms around her and lifted her up. "Gem, I love you and thank you. For everything." I placed her on her feet, then caught her arms. "We're gonna rock the world with our music until the end of time. But this feels fucking surreal. Like this is the end of an era."

"Yeah." She hugged me tight, resting her head against my chest. "But it's the start of a new one. And it's gonna be great. Love you, goofball. Always."

I slipped out of Gemma's hold and walked over to Kyle. I hugged him tight. "Thank you. For being my best man. For being my best friend. For always being there for me. For everything. We're brothers for life. Love you, bud."

"Always. We'll rock on forever. Love you, too." Kyle stepped back. His eyes were as wet as mine. "You better go. Your wife is waiting."

I turned and kissed Kara before I swung her around, and we ended up on opposite sides of the gathered group. I said quick farewells to her parents, Anthony and then Naomi. I kissed her on the cheek, then placed my hands on her belly. I bent down and spoke to my baby. "Thank you for not coming today. But we look forward to seeing you real soon."

Kara caught my hand and dragged me backward. "I'd like to steal you away now, husband."

"I'm all yours, wife."

Our friends and family followed us through the foyer and out to our waiting car. Mick opened the rear passenger door of my brand-new black turbo Porsche Cayenne. It was a sad day when I'd parted with my beloved Ford GT supercar, but I couldn't fit a baby seat or stroller in it. This new one was perfect.

I helped Kara into the car and made sure her beautiful dress was clear of the door before I slid in beside her. After a final wave goodbye, Mick shut the door for us and Giles, playing driver, headed off.

I swiveled to face Kara. Her smile was radiant and glorious. "Are you ready to start your life with me, Mrs. Collins?"

"You've been my life for a while now, but yes. Bring it on."

Pulling her into my arms, I kissed her. Long and hard, sweet and slow. *Easy, tiger.* I had to get to the house before I got too carried away. Luckily, it was only five minutes down the road.

Chapter 45

KARA

I squealed. My heart soared as Hunter scooped me up in his arms and carried me over the threshold into our honeymoon house. But he didn't place me on the floor. He headed straight for the staircase.

"Hunt, put me down. You'll kill yourself carrying me up the steps."

"Never. You're tall, but light."

In the master bedroom, my mouth fell open. A sprinkle of red rose petals covered the polished timber floors and king-sized bed. White candles with battery-operated lights flickered on the drawers and nightstands.

"Oh wow. Who did this?" I asked as he set me on my feet.

"Sam." Hunter's eyes twinkled in the ambient light. "Our head of security secretly loves us. I made him do it when he dropped off our luggage earlier. He's a softie at heart."

"It's beautiful. Very romantic."

The high-pitched bedroom ceiling, the bay window that looked out over the dunes toward the ocean, and the pale, earthy-toned furniture was rich in Hamptons chicness.

"That was the plan." In soft strokes, he swept his fingertips up my arms, then down my cheek. "Today has been incredible, Kar. I hope it was everything you dreamed of."

"That and more." I slipped my hands underneath his jacket and snaked them around his back. "The venue was spectacular. My dad walked me down the aisle. Naomi didn't go into labor. You and the guys looked handsome. My girls were amazing. Everyone seemed to have a great time. And your song was beautiful."

He touched his forehead to mine. "And you, my gorgeous wife, stole the show. This dress . . ." He glided his fingertips down the center of my chest, splayed his hand over my stomach and then hugged my hips. "Is exquisite. Just like you."

Warmth crept into my cheeks. "Thank you."

"But . . . I'd very much like to get you out of it."

"And I feel the same about you and your suit." I peeled the jacket from his shoulders and tossed it onto the velvet armchair in the corner of the room. After removing his bow tie, I undid the buttons on his dress shirt. One. Two. Three. As his shirt fell open, I leaned forward and kissed his exposed bare chest. Then, I popped open another button and kissed downward. Lower and lower I went. I dipped my tongue into his bellybutton and nipped his flesh. He chuckled and flinched as I made my way back up to his lips. I tugged his shirt out of his pants and slid it off his shoulders.

"Hmm." His eyes darkened; the flickering candles caught the smoldering shards of silver in their depths. "I don't think I'll ever tire of you kissing and undressing me." He swept loose strands of my hair behind my ear. "And vice versa. Is there a trick to removing this tiara and veil or do I just rip them out?"

"How about I take it off and the pins out of my hair, and you start on the buttons on my dress?"

I turned to face the mirror above the dresser, pulled off my tiara and veil, and placed them on top of it. Hunter stood behind me and kissed from the tip of my bare shoulder to my neck, then up the side of my throat, and nuzzled into my ear. "I just want to devour you. Make love to you . . . *my wife.*"

My knees weakened. "Then help me get out of this thing."

I smiled as he trailed his fingers down my back; goosebumps danced in their wake. He fumbled with the top tiny silk button and popped the elastic off. One down, nineteen to go.

Eighteen . . . seventeen . . .

"Wow." I pulled out several bobby pins from my hair and dropped them beside my tiara. "Gem thought you'd have trouble with those."

"I have many talents. Remember that."

Sixteen . . . fifteen . . . pop . . . pop . . .

Slow. Sexy. Seductive.

Shit. I'd better hurry with my hair.

With each button he undid, flutters skipped through my stomach. The warmth of his body wrapped around me and raised my temperature. Dizziness swam through my head. I ripped out the last pins from my hair, combed my fingers through the braided bun, and let the strands fall forward over my shoulder in gentle waves.

Hunter buried his nose in my hair and chuckled. "You smell like the ocean, the bonfire, hairspray, and shampoo."

"Do you wanna take a shower first?"

"Nope. You?"

"Later."

After undoing the last button on my gown, he brushed his fingertips over my bare shoulder blades. He found the hidden zipper at the top of my gown and slowly eased it downward. His gaze locked onto mine in the mirror. A tiny smile curled at the corner of his mouth as the dress opened, inch by inch by inch.

My husband was a master at tantalizing.

I spun to face him. Gliding my hands up his toned, bare chest, every muscle, every ridge, every groove I touched sent tingles charging through my fingertips. As I clutched onto his shoulders, he lowered the zipper on my dress the last couple of inches. A devilish glint shimmered in his eyes. He let go of my dress, and it fell to the floor in a pool of embellished lace and silk. His gaze followed the gown, then raked slowly up my body.

"Wow." His fingers quivered on my waistline. "You've worn some amazing lingerie, but this is instant boner stuff."

He got a hard-on anytime I was naked or wore lingerie, but

still, my nipples hardened as he scanned my La Perla white lacy strapless bra, tiny matching thong, suspender belt, and stockings.

I reached for his suit pants, undid the clasp, and lowered the zipper. His rock-hard cock strained beneath his boxer briefs. "We better not waste it."

"I agree." He teased his lips across my mouth and unclasped my bra. It joined my dress on the floor.

Over kisses and soft playful laughs, we discarded the rest of our clothing—shoes, socks, panties, stockings, and boxer briefs. They all littered the floor. After ripping the bedcovers aside, Hunter wrapped his arms around my naked body and eased me backward toward the bed. My knees connected with the edge. With my chest flush with his, our hearts beat in time. Every touch of his hands on my skin and brush of his lips against my mouth ignited a fire in my veins. I'd never get enough of him. We were made for each other.

He caressed my breasts and dragged his thumbs over my nipples. He tweaked them gently, softly, provocatively, sending them into rock-hard peaks. My eyes fluttered closed, and I arched into his touch. "I love it when you do that."

"I prefer this." He dipped his head, flicked his tongue over the bud, and drew it into his mouth. As he nipped, licked and sucked, shivers danced across my skin.

Oh yeah, that's good too.

I drew him down onto the mattress, and we shuffled up toward the pillows. Hovering over me, he ran the tip of his nose along the edge of mine. His wavy hair curtained our faces as his hot breath teased my skin like a soft feather. "So, Mrs. Collins, I guess there's only one thing left to do."

I tucked his hair behind his ears and cupped his cheek. "What would that be?"

"Consummate the marriage."

"Hell yeah." I slid my hands around his broad shoulders and drew him in to kiss. As our lips parted and tongues touched, a moan rumbled deep in his throat. Every inch of my flesh sparked to life as his hands roamed over my legs, my breasts, my face.

Each kiss was like a blazing fire that grew hotter and hotter. The frenzied burn was a fine line between pleasure and pain.

He meandered down my body, nipping, licking, and kissing my skin, and headed between my legs. The rush of his warm breath teased my groin as he edged closer and closer to my sweet spot. The spot where I wanted his mouth, his tongue, his kisses. I clutched at my pillow. The anticipation was pure, delicious torture.

As he rubbed his thumb in slow, sensual circles against my needy clit, he gazed up at me and arched one cocky eyebrow. "Want me to stop?"

I wriggled my hips to find more friction against his touch. "No."

"I like it when you want me."

"I always want you." Our sex drives had never been a problem. His ability to render me crazed with want was another matter.

He eased two fingers into my pussy. Slowly, tenderly, gently. As he drove them in and out, hunger flared in his gaze. He went deeper. Harder. Faster. "Fuck, I love touching you. It turns me on so fucking much."

My heart rate doubled as my hips pulsed against his hand. My insides wound tighter and tighter. I wanted to savor making love to him, but I wanted to explode right then and there. "If you don't make me come, I'll file for an annulment right now."

"You can't. I won't let you." He kissed across my sensitive groin, heading lower and lower. "I'm never letting you go."

His mouth claimed me.

My breath shot from my lungs. Goosebumps coiled up my spine. Delicate swirls and licks of his tongue roamed my clit, ran along my slit and dipped into my pussy. I clawed at the bed sheets and arched my back. Yep, I'd never get enough of this. As I widened my knees, my hips pulsed in time with his rhythm. Threading my fingers through his hair, I moaned. My body was his for the taking. But just when I was about to burst, he stopped.

What? No.

A devilish grin curled across his lips. The darkness invading his eyes quickened my pulse and dialed up my hungry need for him. He zigzagged a path of tender kisses up my stomach and returned to my mouth. "I promise to make love to you all night, but right now, I need to be inside you. Is that okay?"

"Oh, yeah." I clutched the back of his head and pulled his lips to mine.

He lowered onto me and guided his hard cock into my depths. One thrust, two thrusts, three thrusts. My heart pounded, and stars swirled before my eyes as our bodies connected. His hot kisses seared my lips. His sensual touches ignited my flesh. His deep drives heated my core. But I wanted more. I pushed against his chest, flipped him down onto the bed, and straddled his hips. As I eased his cock back into my pussy, my core clenched around him.

Having him beneath me made me feel sexy and powerful. I was *his*.

He may have learned to become a brilliant lover from his countless encounters in the past, but no one had gotten to know *his* body like I had. The only spot he was ticklish was beneath his lower right rib. He loved *his* nipples being licked; the left one was more sensitive than the right. And when I dangled my bare boobs in front of his face, he'd smirk, and a cute dimple would form on his right cheek.

I leaned forward. He ogled my tits, cupped and massaged them, then, there it was—the little divot appeared. *So cool.* Rocking my hips, my slow, languid movements turned into hard, hot drives. I rode him, driving his cock deeper into my pussy. His eyes snapped shut. Every vein in his neck bulged, and every muscle in his jaw tensed. His fingers dug into my thighs.

Our breaths panted.

"Kar." He sat half upright, curled his hand around my neck and kissed me hard. All tongue and tiny nips on my lower lip, then deep assaults into my mouth. Every kiss sent jolts of electricity zipping through my veins. "Roll over."

"But . . ."

I was close. He was close.

Before I could argue, he twisted sideways, and I tumbled onto my back. "What was that for?"

"Because . . ." He edged between my legs and slid inside me again. With rhythmic pulses, he penetrated me hard and deep, driving toward that spot that sent me over the edge. "I want to come with you."

He wouldn't get any argument from me. I looped my arms under his and clutched his back. I melted and moved in time with his body. My hands slipped on his hot skin, and my fingernails sliced across his shoulder blades. "Oh. Sorry."

"Mmm." He flinched, then grinned over our kisses. "You can mark me as yours, Pearl." He rocked and drove into me harder. "We've done ink and paper—may as well do blood too."

"Let's skip blood." I wrinkled my nose as he kissed my cheek.

"Okay, Mrs. Collins."

I smiled as I kissed him. Loving him physically had always been easy. Loving him with my heart had taken time. But now that the barriers were gone, I'd love him forever.

Sweat slicked our skin as we touched, tasted, and teased each other's bodies. The tension inside me coiled tighter and tighter as we rocked and pulsed and kissed. But then he groaned and thrust into me hard and deep. As the drive of my hips met his, we took each other over the edge.

Over sensual kisses, we smiled, shivered, and shuddered. Sparks jolted and coursed through my veins and settled in my chest.

"I love you." Caressing his head, I threaded my fingers through his hair. My pulse strummed in time with his heartbeat. "And I love that you love me like a rockstar."

His low laugh, full of sexy rasp, made my insides flutter. "Good thing I am one."

"Absolutely."

He stole my breath with a kiss so powerful and so intense, my mind spun. It was so tender, my heart exploded with love. We'd come from different worlds and had united in one where we could be true to ourselves. A world ruled by love, passion, and music, fashion, trust, support, and devotion. He'd become my world. And I was his.

We would have an incredible life together.
One filled with love and family.
Everything I'd ever wanted.
There was only one piece of the puzzle to go.

Chapter 46

KARA

I lazed against Hunter's bare chest. Lying naked and wrapped in a twist of white sheets, I couldn't wipe the dreamy smile off my face. Half of the pillows and the quilt had fallen off the bed during our latest round of lovemaking. Hunter did things to my body I'm sure they should be illegal. No, it should be part of sex education. What he did with his cock and tongue was pure, pleasurable heaven.

The sun's rays streamed in through the huge bedroom windows that looked across the pool, sand dunes, and the ocean in the distance. The warm mid-June sunshine had tried to entice us outside, but we'd hardly left the house. Day five of our honeymoon had been just like the previous few. Lots of lovemaking throughout the house—in bed, in the ensuite spa, on the sofa, on the floor, in the shower, in the kitchen, and, oh my, on the dining room table.

It was just after lunch, but I hadn't had my fill of Hunter yet.

He lay with one arm hooked behind his head. His hair fanned across the pillow in a tousled mess as a lazy smile curled at the corners of his mouth. His other arm draped behind me as he drew tiny circles on my back with his fingers.

How long did he need to rest before we could make love again? It had been twenty minutes. I'd recovered. I hoped he had too.

There's only one way to find out.

I dipped my hand beneath the sheet hanging over his hips. I combed my fingernails through his fine hair, then cupped and stroked his warm cock.

He chuckled, rolled toward me, and buried his face in the small of my neck. "You ready for more?"

I flinched at his tickles and giggled as he rained kisses over my skin and nibbled on my earlobe. "Have I worn you out?"

"Never." He tugged the sheet clear and sailed his hand over my hip and down my leg.

But just as things heated up, my cell phone rang on the nightstand. I furrowed my brow. It wasn't a personalized ringtone, so I ignored it, and let it go to voicemail. But it rang again . . . and again.

"Ugh . . . let me see who it is." I tapped him on the shoulder and grabbed my cell phone. There was no caller ID—just a cell phone number lit the screen. I hoped it wasn't a reporter. I swiped the screen to answer the call and put the cell to my ear. "Hello. This is Mrs. Collins."

Hunter's gorgeous smile touched his eyes, then he dipped his head and licked my boob.

"Hello, Mrs. Collins."

My heart jumpstarted. *Holy shit!*

"This is Erika." *Naomi's housekeeper.* I pushed Hunter aside, sat upright and put the call on speaker.

"Is Nae okay? Is everything okay?" My pulse zipped through my veins and rushed into my head. Anxious excitement lit Hunter's face as he leaned closer.

"Yes." Erika's voice shook. "Naomi's water just broke. Contractions have started. Anthony has taken her to the hospital and asked me to call you. Would you like to meet them there?"

My hand shot over my mouth. Tears pricked my eyes. Our baby was coming. Two and a half weeks early. "Oh my God, yes. Yes. YES! We're on our way. Thank you."

I tossed my cell phone aside and flung my arms around Hunter's neck. His heart beat as erratically as mine. My whole body shook and shivered. "Our baby. It's time to get our baby."

"I can't wait." Holding me tight, he cupped the back of my head. The reality of what was about to happen crashed into me. He gave me one last big hug, then helped me to stand. "Let's go."

We scurried around the room finding clothes to put on. My fingers trembled as I did up the buttons of my blouse and slipped on a long, flowing skirt. "Oh shit. We have to pack. We haven't cleaned. Oh, Hunt, we have to go."

As I grabbed my suitcase and ripped the clothes from the closet, he caught my arms. "Kar."

I couldn't tell who shook more—me or him.

"We'll have time." He rubbed my arms. "You grab the stuff from the bathroom. I'll grab everything from downstairs."

Within half an hour, we'd packed and were in the car, heading for the city. Hunter clasped my knee, his palm clammy and hot. "You ready?"

"Yeah." I nodded. My head circled with a dizzy high. "I've waited so long for this."

"Me too. Let's go meet our baby."

***

As I clutched Naomi's hand, my stomach cinched and lurched and contracted like I felt every push and cramp and stab of pain Naomi endured. On the other side of the bed, Hunter held onto Naomi's other hand, but the color had drained from his face. Was he about to pass out? He could, but there was no way I'd miss a moment of this experience.

After eight hours of grueling labor, Naomi screamed. "Hunter, I hate your fucking big head." Sweat beaded on her brow and dampened the strands of hair dangling around her reddened face. "I want this thing out of me."

"That's it, Naomi. I can see the head." Dr. Arnold hovered behind the sheet blocking Hunter and me from the view between Naomi's legs. "You've got this. One more push."

Naomi screamed again. "AAAARRRGGGHH!"

Tears streamed down her face. She panted and gasped. Her

chest heaved with each breath. With a weary sob and smile, she collapsed against the pillow and released the death grip she'd had on my hand.

I held my breath.

The doctor lifted the baby into the air, and the most wonderful cry filled the room. I clutched Hunter's hand tight behind Naomi's head. *So tight.*

"It's a girl." The doctor held our baby to face us.

The cutest little round face screamed and wailed. Covered in goo and blood and gunk, she was the most beautiful thing I'd ever seen. My heart cartwheeled around the room. My vision blurred with happy tears. "Hunt, we have a daughter."

"Fuck. We're in so much trouble." Water welled in his eyes. He leaned over the back of the bed and kissed me on the lips, then kissed Naomi's forehead.

"Naomi?" Dr. Arnold asked. "Is it okay if Kara or Hunter cuts the cord?"

"Yeah." Her voice was an exhausted whisper. "Of course."

We rushed over to the examination table and did the token cut together.

"Oh my God, she's beautiful," Hunter said as we hovered near our baby. She wriggled and wailed on the table, kicking and stretching her tiny legs, and waving her tiny arms about as the doctor weighed, measured, and checked her over. "She's already got my lungs."

Clutching a handful of Hunter's T-shirt at the base of his back, every muscle in my arms burned. I desperately wanted to hold our baby. I wanted to touch the soft brown patch of hair on her head, feel her warm skin, kiss her, breathe her in, but with surrogacy, there were processes to follow—*checkups . . . Naomi . . . handover.* Hunter must have sensed my anguish and hooked his arm around me. "She's here. It won't be long now."

"She's perfectly healthy." Dr. Arnold swaddled our baby, then placed her onto Naomi's chest.

Sniffling and sobbing, Naomi held our daughter in her arms. "I did it, Kar. She's amazing, right?"

"Yes." I kissed the top of Naomi's head. "You did good."

"We can never thank you enough for this." Hunter kissed Naomi's cheek. "You've given Kar and me our baby."

"So . . ." Naomi gazed down at our daughter and smiled. "Have you decided on a name?"

"Yeah," I whispered and cupped my daughter's head. The tiny hairs were as soft as silk. "Meet Ashleigh. Ashleigh Mae."

"Ashleigh." A tear trickled down Naomi's cheek as she brushed her fingertip over our daughter's forehead. "That's so beautiful. Hi, Ashleigh. Thank you for being a good baby."

Hunter rubbed Naomi's shoulder. "She's amazing."

After the doctors had finished attending to Naomi, it was time for Hunter and me to take our daughter into the room next door to bond with her. I shook all over. I had to let Naomi have her parting moment. Naomi had carried Ashleigh for nine months. I understood it would be hard to part ways.

The nurse came up to Naomi and placed her hand on Naomi's shoulder. "It's time."

This is it.

My head spun with giddiness. My heart fluttered with too much eagerness.

Naomi nodded. Another tear slid across her temple and disappeared into her hairline. "Yep." She blinked and wiped her eyes with the back of her hand. "I'm good."

She looked far from it. She looked like she'd run one hundred miles through a downpour of rain. I was in awe of what she'd done for us.

"Okay, little one." Naomi kissed Ashleigh on the head. "It's been an awesome ride, but it's time for you to go with your mommy and daddy now. You be a good girl. And I'll see you real soon."

Naomi lifted Ashleigh off her chest and handed her to me. My hands trembled so much I was afraid I'd drop my daughter. Tears zigzagged down my face as I cradled Ashleigh against my chest. She was so light. So tiny—barely the length of my arm. Her little cry was music to my ears. She was so beautiful. No . . . she was *perfect.*

Hunter stepped in beside me. He swept his hand over Ashleigh's head, then kissed her. "Hey princess."

I gazed at my husband and my daughter. Tears clouded my vision. My chin trembled. I was too emotional, unable to speak.

"Please, follow me." One of the other nurses in pale pink scrubs headed toward the exit. "Once we've cleared the room, Mr. Astor can come in and be with his wife."

Glancing at Naomi, I projected as much love as possible toward her. "Thank you. I love you."

"Love you too. Now go be with your baby."

Hunter placed his hand on my lower back. As I held Ashleigh in my arms, we followed the nurse out of the delivery room and into a bonding room down the hall. The small room was decorated with baby prints on the wall, a double bed, and a pale green sofa.

"If you'd like . . ." The nurse fluffed a pillow on the bed. "Lie down here with your baby, unbutton the top of your blouse, and place her against your chest so she can get used to your smell, your voice, your touch."

"Okay." I'd wanted to do this ever since I'd laid eyes on Ashleigh. "Here, Hunt. You hold her while I get ready."

I handed Hunter our daughter. Tears pooled in his eyes. I'd never seen him look so terrified, so in awe, so in love, and happy all at once. He cradled Ashleigh's head and cupped her tiny body in his big hands. "Wow. She's ours."

I kicked off my shoes, undid my top, and climbed onto the bed. I held out my arms, and Hunter placed Ashleigh into them. "Kar, this is so surreal. I can't believe she's here. She's so tiny. So . . . perfect."

"You should join your wife, Mr. Collins," the nurse said. "Lie together. You both need to bond with your daughter. I'll give you a few moments alone. I'll be back with a bottle, and we'll try to feed her."

"Thank you." My gaze never left Ashleigh.

Hunter kicked off his shoes and crawled onto the bed beside me. He kissed my temple, then Ashleigh on the head. "I'm exhausted, but she's so worth it."

"Yeah." I swept my fingertip down Ashleigh's cheek and traced the fine line of her jaw. "We have a baby. A daughter."

This was everything I'd ever wanted and had ever dreamed about.

I have a husband. A baby girl. A family.

This was and would always be my reason for living.

Epilogue

HUNTER

Stretched out on the fluffy floor rug in my living room, I stared down at my daughter lying on her baby mat beside me. She was one month old today. I'd never known love like this existed. Every time I inhaled, I thought my heart would explode. This love I had for Kara and my daughter was a gazillion times better than anything the millions of my fans could ever give me, and more profound than the bond I shared with Kyle and Gemma. This was truly deep, intense, and unconditional.

Ashleigh's eyes fluttered closed. Milky drool dripped from the corner of her mouth, and her head lolled to one side. Her tiny pink lips parted as she breathed. She had an *I'm-totally-blissed-out-and-drunk* look on her round face after having her bottle of warm milk. I should have burped her, but I loved watching her sleep. I loved her sweet scent filling the air. There was nothing like that newborn baby smell of milk, talc powder, and fresh diapers.

Over the past several weeks, my penthouse had been transformed into a baby haven. Bottles of Jack Daniel's had been replaced with baby formula and a sterilizer. The largest spare room had been set up as the nursery. Throws on the sofa had been replaced with baby blankets and burping towels. Life had changed. And I wouldn't have it any other way.

"We've cleaned up," Kyle hollered from the kitchen. "Leftovers are in the fridge."

I gave him the thumbs up, then placed my finger over my mouth, shushing him. I didn't want Ashleigh to wake.

Our friends had been amazing. Kyle and Gemma had made dinner for us and had brought several dishes to put in the freezer. Lexi and Hayden had sorted through the hundreds of gifts we'd received for our wedding and the birth of our daughter. They'd all kept me up-to-date with our music agenda. Thanks to the lack of sleep, my brain had turned to mush. Luckily, we only had a few events to attend over the summer—nothing major. After the tour, the wedding, and Ashleigh's arrival, we'd all agreed we needed a decent break.

"Sorry." Kyle winced and lowered his voice. "I'm not used to babies."

Neither was I. I'd been thrown in at the deep end, but I loved it.

Gemma slinked toward me. "We're gonna go," she whispered. "Kar's taking too long in the shower."

"She might've fallen asleep in there." I needed some shuteye, too, before baby-feeding duty tonight.

Lexi and Hayden gathered their belongings.

"Get some rest, Hunt." Lexi waved and dragged Hayden toward the elevator. "We'll see you soon."

I went to stand, but Gemma held up her hand. "Don't get up. You both look content and comfortable."

"Thanks." I propped my head on my hand. "Love you."

"Yeah." Her gaze softened. "Love you too, goofball."

Kyle came up behind Gemma and snaked his arms around her waist. "And I love you." He kissed her cheek. "Hunt, we'll leave you to it. We'd better get out of here. I don't want Gem to get any funny ideas about wanting a baby."

"Me?" She screwed up her nose. "No chance. Not ever. I like kids. I don't ever want one."

A sadness flickered in Kyle's dark eyes, but within a heartbeat, it was gone. I smirked. Poor Kyle. He'd have a hell of a time ever convincing Gemma to have a child. Music was her life, but she'd be the best aunt to Ashleigh.

"Night, Hunt." Kyle took Gemma's hand and tugged her toward the hallway. "We'll see you here tomorrow for rehearsal at eleven. Vegas is in two weeks."

Shit. Awards show. I'd forgotten about it. "Sure. I'll be here." Yep, I wasn't going anywhere.

I had music, incredible friends, a baby, and a beautiful wife.

Five minutes after my friends had left, Kara came into the living room. Wearing a cotton tank top and pajama shorts, she combed her fingers through the long hair that cascaded forward over her shoulder. She smiled and joined me on the floor, lying with our gorgeous daughter sleeping between us.

"She drink all her milk?" Kara whispered.

"Yeah. She's a guzzler." I held up the empty bottle. "Everyone left five minutes ago."

"Oh, sorry I took so long."

"I'm sure they'll forgive you."

Ashleigh stirred and wriggled. I placed my hand on her tummy to settle her. Her little heartbeat fluttered beneath my touch. Her belly gurgled, and she let out an unladylike baby belch. After licking her lips, she relaxed and continued to sleep. She didn't even open an eye. I stroked her tiny hand. Her little fingers curled around my index finger. She gently squeezed and released it before her whole arm went limp.

"She's an angel." Adoration overflowed in Kara's eyes as she gazed at Ashleigh. "You're so good with her."

"I'm learning everything from you. She has the best mom in the world."

Ashleigh's brow furrowed. She lifted her legs and farted.

Kara's giggle was as quiet as a mouse. "Oh no . . . she's just like her daddy."

"Hey." I caught Kara's hand and kissed the inside of her wrist. "No . . . just like her mommy. Beautiful. Just absolutely beautiful."

I leaned over Ashleigh and kissed Kara's lips. My wife, the mother of my child, my true love. Her kiss was soft and sweet, her touch, tender and warm.

"I love you." I cupped her cheek and stroked my thumb over her lips. "I love our daughter. I love our little family. This, what we have here, is everything. Don't ever forget that."

"Never. I love you, too."

As I kissed her again, my heart filled my chest. Music was one thing—but this was everything. It had been a treacherous road to get here, one full of heartache, loss, and tumultuous challenges, but we'd made it through . . . together. We'd found love. My family had given me a new purpose. I would love and protect them for all time. From this point on, every rhyme I wrote, every rhythm I played, every raw beat of my heart would now and always be for my amazing wife, Kara, and my gorgeous daughter, Ashleigh.

. . . and Everhide would rock on forever!

***

Thank you for reading **REWIND – The Price of Fate.**

Hunter and Kara finally got the happily ever after they deserved. Yay!

But wait! There is one last story in the Everhide series. If you have been on the journey with Kyle and Gemma, Hunter and Kara, and Lexi and Hayden, join them as they navigate their way through life altering decisions. Be prepared for an epic and emotional conclusion. Continue the series with Book 6 : **RETUNED – The Price of Time**.

A vacation. An unforgettable accident. Lives are changed forever.

AVAILABLE ON AMAZON and KINDLE UNLIMITED

P.S. If you enjoyed **REWIND – The Price of Fate**, would you kindly take a moment and leave a quick product review. They are music for an author's soul.

Thank you,
Tania Joyce

BEFORE YOU GO.

Would you like a BONUS EBOOK for FREE?

Find out how my world of rockstars began with the Everhide Rockstar Romance series.

ROCKED – The Price of Dreams is the origin story to my bestselling Everhide Series. Find out how the band met in high school, experience their heartbreak and hardships, and follow their journey to stardom. It is the pre-romance to the adult relationships that develop, evolve, and change throughout the six books. (Three standalones, three follow-ons—all happily ever afters, no cliffhangers).

This series will have you falling in love, shedding tears, and laughing out loud.

Read the prequel, **ROCKED – The Price of DREAMS,** for **FREE** when you subscribe to my newsletter. I only send emails about once a month, so your inbox won't be inundated with my news. Please subscribe here: https://taniajoyce.com/subscribe.

NEWSLETTER

For information about my new releases, events, and special
offers, please subscribe to my monthly newsletter.
Join at: https://taniajoyce.com/subscribe
REMEMBER: You get a BONUS BOOK if you join.

***

FOLLOW TANIA JOYCE

You can follow and find Tania Joyce on the following social media
platforms.

Amazon: https://amazon.com/author/taniajoyce
BookBub: https://www.bookbub.com/authors/tania-joyce
Facebook: https://www.facebook.com/taniajoycebooks
Goodreads: https://www.goodreads.com/taniajoyce
Instagram: https://www.instagram.com/taniajoycebooks/
Pinterest: https://www.pinterest.com/taniajoycebooks
TikTok: https://www.tiktok.com/@taniajoyce
Web: http://taniajoyce.com

ABOUT TANIA JOYCE

Tania Joyce is an author of rockstar, contemporary and new adult romance novels. Her stories thread romance, drama and passion into beautiful locations ranging from the dazzling lights and glitter of New York to the rural countryside of the Hunter Valley.

She's widely traveled, has a diverse background in the corporate world and has a love for sparkles, shoes and shiraz.

Tania draws on her real-life experiences and combines them with her very vivid imagination to form the foundation of her novels. She likes to write about strong-minded, career-oriented heroes and heroines that go through drama-filled hell, have steamy encounters and risk everything as they endeavor to find their happy-ever-after.

Tania shuffles the hours in her day between part-time work, family life and writing. One day she hopes to find balance!

She loves to hear from her readers.

Visit: www.taniajoyce.com
or email her at: tania@taniajoyce.com

***

MORE BY TANIA JOYCE

Visit Tania Joyce on Amazon.Com

* 9 7 8 1 9 2 3 6 5 3 1 1 5 *